# TWO TRUTHS AND ONE THIEF

### DEIRDRE RIORDAN HALL

Copyright © 2022 by Deirdre Riordan Hall

All rights reserved.

No part of this book may be reproduced in any form or by any electronic or mechanical means, including information storage and retrieval systems, without written permission from the author, except for the use of brief quotations in a book review.

This is a work of fiction. Names, characters, businesses, places, events, and incidents are either the products of the author's imagination or used in a fictitious manner. Any resemblance to actual persons, living or dead, or actual events is purely coincidental.

*Dedicated to my family*
♥

# Chapter 1

IT'S BEEN TWO MONTHS SINCE I ESCAPED FROM DARTMONT...AGAIN. Two weeks since I disappeared myself. Two days since I last saw my twin, Vicky, who's letting me lie low at her place in Boston.

Two minutes since I decided I need new underwear.

When I need something, I take it. This works well with pretty much everything except for pineapples and people. Prickly and unwieldy, respectively.

The other day I surveyed the store, the Clothing Cloud—pretty low-key. No cameras or pasty loss prevention specialists loitering in the blind spots.

Back again, I approach the saleslady with chunky highlights—very soccer-mom-ish. I offer a perfunctory smile. Her name tag says *Regina*.

"I'd like to try these on," I say, wearing a face that my sister would call the picture of innocence even though she knows better.

I hold up two bras, one black and one beige because I'm sensible like that. Under the arm of my coat, I conceal the fistful of underwear and a couple of other bras, including one with pink polka dots, because maybe I'm not so sensible. If Regina notices them and tells me I can't bring other merchandise into the dressing room, I'll act polite and dumb and then move on to Plan B. What that is, I'm not sure because Plan A has never failed.

"How many?" Regina asks. Her eyes flash with recognition like we're acquainted or like she's seen a ghost. People often tell me I look familiar. It's probably my dark hair—which I share with seventy-five percent of the world's population. Also, what my sister calls our non-specific ethnicity makes us blend in well—a craft I learned from the best.

Regina's expression returns to neutral. The last thing I want is a lengthy conversation about a friend's cousin or a summer camp student that looks exactly like me, during which she memorizes my features.

"Just two," I respond.

*As if. This'll be a cinch.*

Once in the dressing room, I try on the bras like an ordinary girl out shopping on a weekday morning. I make sure they fit nicely and gaze at my reflection, glimpsing my twin sister's features reflected in mine. A sigh escapes—not because I don't like what I see. The problem is there are two of me. Rather, of us. I'm a twin and for my whole life, I've gotten the message that one was enough.

In other words, our parents favor Caroline—our older sister and the recently graduated Dartmont celebrity. Everyone is quick to remind me that Caroline is perfect in every way: academically, athletically, was on the student senate, and was involved in several clubs.

Everyone except my twin, Victoria. As far as I'm concerned, my twin and I are the perfect pair.

I'm not ordinary. My life isn't normal. As the heiresses to the Goldfeather popcorn fortune and daughters of the famous Kenyan supermodel Istar, neither Caroline, Victoria, nor I are what anyone would call normal.

But sometimes I want to be, which is a secret I'll never tell. I have a lot of those.

It's like the Goldfeather sisters are on a spectrum of naughty and nice. Let's just say Santa Claus actually left coal for Vicky once. Caroline got everything she wanted on her wish list and then some. I was smack in the middle. Then everything changed.

However, if only I weren't the spare bad sister—a wry, internal laugh tips my head back slightly—maybe things would be different.

But there's no time for thinking or doubt or hesitation. I double the bras up under my shirt. My pulse quickens as if neon light runs through my veins and out the ends of my fingertips. This moment of purpose, the quickening of success, the sly thrill charges me with meaning. I ignore the thick knot in my stomach as I put the other bras on the hangers, stuff the panties in my bag, and stride out of the dressing room.

"How'd you do?" Regina asks.

She studies me from behind a pair of outrageously round glasses sorely in need of updating with something more sophisticated, especially considering she works in an upscale women's boutique.

It's my job to notice details.

I shrug. "Wrong size."

"You should've called for me. I would have brought a different one." A smear of fuchsia lipstick stains Regina's two front teeth. "How about I measure you? You know, most women wear ill-fitting brassieres. That's a fact. You can ask Oprah."

I gauged myself in the changing room and didn't take a suspiciously long time, but the red flags and sirens in my mind tell me to get out of the store. Now.

Regina is engaging me and although appearing friendly and agreeable is part of my role, it's time to disappear into the crowd bustling along the sidewalk outside. It's what I do.

The bells on the door jingle. Perfect, another shopper—a man. I'll count on him to fluster the meddlesome lady. She nods at him. In greeting or acknowledgment, I'm suddenly not sure. Time to flee.

"Uh, no thanks," I reply as I make my escape. Stepping into the flow of pedestrians, the crisp autumn air beckons like freedom.

A hand grips my shoulder.

"Miss, please step back inside." The middle-aged man who I thought graciously and unwittingly abetted my escape, wears khakis and a navy blue shirt—the male counterpart to the saleslady. I should have known. He escorts me back inside.

I resent the cheerful jingle of the bells on the door. Nothing was stopping me from walking out with a couple of new bras and underwear except for my own stupidity. I underestimated Regina. She must have been watching me carefully from the moment I walked into the Clothing Cloud.

She hawks over the cash register, looking ghastly like one of the stone tragedy masks at the theater on the Emerson campus.

The pudgy and balding security detail directs me to a dim stockroom—putting the alleged shoplifter with all the untagged merchandise. *Real genius, guys.*

Regina's voice rises exponentially while the man remains hushed. The door jingles again. I stuff the underwear in a box. Sweating, I take the bras off from under my shirt. I stash them too. Now no one can accuse me of stealing unless Clothing Cloud has cameras. Doubtful, I checked. Despite my experience in the shoplifting profession, an elastic band stretches tight in my stomach. I bargain with my fingers to stop trembling.

I scan the room. There's a door, but these old Boston buildings are as maze-like as the streets, which usually works to my advantage. However, an easy escape is unlikely.

*Penny, you have nothing to hide.* My sister's voice plays in my head like a steel reel, unbendable and ceaseless.

I have nothing to hide. The anticipation of my twin's rare, but crushing, expression of disappointment finds its way out of the corners of memory. Guilt claps heavily against my chest. I don't want to let her down.

The man pokes his head around the door. The light from the front of the shop follows him into the dusty space. I have the inappropriately hilarious thought that he's the comedy mask to the saleslady's tragedy. Laugh lines curl around his eyes and mouth like punctuation marks. I stop my lips at a smile, not daring to let out a laugh.

"Do you mind coming with me?" he asks in a thick Boston accent.

I want to shout, *Of course, I mind!* and then shove my way out the door, but I wear the mask of innocence and comply. The front of the shop is empty. Maybe the saleslady went to lunch. The man takes a seat behind the register and gestures for me to sit on a stool opposite him.

"I'm not very good at this. Regina is more the bad cop, you know," he says, wincing slightly.

I want to tell him that, *No, I don't know and don't care*, but get the sense that he's not going to call the actual cops, and right now that's all I care about.

"I have to ask you to empty the contents of your bag?" It's less a demand and more of a question.

My twin, Vicky, has three ironclad rules in the game of theft.

*Rule number two: never admit to anything.* Be polite, and accommodating even, but don't give yourself away, ever.

Without a word, I carefully unzip my designer crossbody shoulder bag. Out falls my MAC lip-gloss, my Prada reading glasses—that was a creative lift—and a pair of socks I don't recognize. I must have had cold feet one day, grabbed them, and then forgotten. There's a wallet with a fake ID, a few bills—just for show—note cards, and a water bottle. Then, out slides a pair of black lacy undies.

The dreaded knots pull taut inside my stomach. A churning sensation follows. In my haste in the back room, I must have missed them.

Good Cop pinches the underwear uncomfortably between his forefinger and thumb. The price tag hangs guiltily from the waistline. From behind the lace, he shakes his head, almost imperceptibly, as though he doesn't want to believe I've done wrong.

I want nothing more than to shield my embarrassment. I was almost out the door.

*Penny, you're innocent. Don't tell. Not guilty.* Vicky's voice insists in the privacy of my head.

"Miss, did you take these?" Good Cop bobs his head self-consciously toward the undergarment.

Vicky races across my inner vision with her eyes narrowed. I rehearse every possible denial.

I'm intensely aware of Good Cop's discomfort and my challenge to preserve my innocence. But an unnamed, deep-rooted, stubborn sense prevents the word *no* from passing the gate of my lips even as the truth tightens in my belly. I tilt my chin toward my chest in defeat.

Good Cop presses his lips together in a frown and exhales a sigh of regret.

The door jingles. Great. A witness.

## Chapter 2

THE UNDERWEAR FALLS TO THE COUNTER, CURVED LIKE A QUESTION mark. Good Cop's cheeks match the pink ribbons for breast cancer awareness on display next to the register. The smell of coffee and a toasted onion bagel overpowers the powdery and perfumey scent of the shop.

"Gotcha lunch, Dad," says a low voice from behind me.

I freeze at the word *gotcha*. As in, caught ya, caught ya red-handed.

"Oh, uh, thanks, Julian." Good Cop reaches behind me for the bag.

I slowly turn around, unable to resist the lure of the smell of a warm cup of coffee and a toasted bagel. Close-cropped hair that hasn't settled on brown or strawberry blonde moves neatly toward the center of Julian's forehead, almost, but not quite, forming a widow's peak. He presses his fingers into his shoulder as if rubbing a sore spot. I instantly want to camouflage into the foliage green-gray of his hoodie. He scuffs his boots on the floor. His lips and eyes meet in amusement when he looks up like he did the courtesy of sparing us a moment to reclaim our respective dignities.

"So, Dad, what are you doing?" He eyes the underwear as if entertained.

*No, please. No. Please don't expose me.*

Good Cop/Dad turns back to me. His lips are still a thin line. This time, he exhales softly through his nose.

Julian saunters over as if to survey the items I spilled onto the counter when Good Cop told me to empty my bag. I sweep my things back inside, all except the underwear. Now, in a messy fold, they sit there, alone, black against the scratched white countertop, mocking and mortifying me.

"Mom is going to be mad you're not wearing your name tag." Julian leaves his empty coffee cup next to the underwear and disappears to the room behind the sales counter. He may have chuckled. A bathroom fan hums to life.

Good Cop's shoulders drop a notch and he opens a drawer, retrieves a nametag, and pins it to his blue shirt. Phil. "I'm Phil Freese." He clears his throat. "Your name, please?"

"Penny Goldfeather." Reflexively, I clamp my hand over my mouth. I should have at least used Jenny, Kathy, or Marlo. None of those will match the ID in my bag, though. Most of the time, I hardly know who I am.

Vicky's voice whispers, *Penny, never tell anyone your real name. Keep it like a secret.*

I'm officially off my game today.

"Well, Penny," he clears his throat, "You know that shoplifting is a crime. It's against the law. This is my wife's shop." He crosses his arms in front of his chest and gazes at the ceiling as if in memory. "Used to be a sporting goods store." He grunts. "Things change. Anyway, it's not my job to lecture you or anything. I think you know that stealing is wrong, right?"

I don't let myself think about this. Not today, not ever.

"Listen, I don't want to get you in trouble with the police." His eyebrows lift. "To that end, you're lucky Regina had an appointment today, and I had to mind the store." His shoulders sag as if defeated by the racks of blouses and shelves stocked with denim. "Tell me, why aren't you in school?"

A hand dryer hums from behind the bathroom door and then it opens.

"Why isn't he in school?" I ask, thumbing Julian, who is unaware I threw him under the bus. The curve of his eyebrows matches his dad's. The former, arch with amusement. The latter, salted and hinting at the memory of delight.

"It's parents' weekend, so we get Monday off. As you can see, my parents are—" Julian gestures.

The bagel sandwich and steaming coffee tease me. Prepared foods are harder to take, especially when made with the honest effort to earn a dollar. Julian catches me gazing at the meal like a hungry orphan. I snap my eyes back to my hands.

"Where do you go to school?" Phil asks.

I fled last spring just before Caroline's graduation. Then when school resumed last month, I made myself scarce.

Phil leans in, awaiting my answer.

I gesture vaguely over my shoulder.

"Kid, there are a lot of schools out there. Where are you registered?" There's something about Good Cop that draws the answer to my lips. That makes me want to spill my secrets. Tell the truth.

I mumble, "Dartmont," hoping he's not familiar with the elite New Hampshire prep school.

Both pairs of eyebrows lift in surprise. "That's where I go," Julian offers. "I've never seen you there."

My stomach tumbles as I glance over my shoulder toward the door. Is this a setup? Vicky has never warned me about the con artist getting scammed. There must be a name for it. *Rob, Wreck & Ruin* or *Thief's Folly*? Is that what's happening?

"Big school." My voice catches in my throat.

I'm torn between creating a diversion then running and apologizing to these guys for being so far from normal that if I could find the words to explain, they might not believe me anyway.

"Hey, Julian, would you please grab those boxes that came in from Bella Fashion, I think that was the name of it. Colorful scarves. They're in the back behind the rack of sale items. Your mother wants me to update the stock." Both Phil and Julian may have just rolled their eyes. Clothing Cloud doesn't seem like their choice business venture.

When Julian is out of earshot, Phil goes on. "I believe in second chances. I won't call the police if you agree to go to school."

I don't answer. I can't.

"And agree not to steal again," he adds.

Still, I don't say a word.

"These the ones?" Julian asks, poking his head out from the back, blissfully unaware of Phil's ultimatum. I hope Julian is naïve enough to think I'm looking for a job, and the underwear thing was me demonstrating my extensive knowledge of women's intimates.

Phil nods. "Thanks. Set them over here. Julian is heading back to Dartmont soon. He has a special arrangement to keep a car on campus. You can go together," he says as if we're about to get on a rollercoaster or embark on a grand adventure.

Pins and needs travel through my limbs, making me feel wobbly and like I can't trust myself. I let him decide for me, at least for now.

"Okay?" Phil asks, still waiting for my answer.

This time I nod. Ready to make my getaway, I turn to the glass door, toward something like freedom. Phil slurps coffee through the plastic opening of the cup's lid. The paper bag crinkles. If I had to order a last meal, it would be a bagel and coffee. Hoping he's preoccupied now, I pull the door open.

"Oh, wait, uh, do you want to pay for these?" Phil asks, gesturing to the underwear.

I turn around, drop a twenty-dollar bill on the counter, and hastily exit. Julian follows at my heels, quickly catching up.

I welcome the brisk early October day. The air fills in the crevices that crimped and shrunk as I held my breath for the last half hour, worried I was going to have to call Vicky from a police station.

"Laundry day?" Julian asks, ripping me from my thoughts.

"Huh?"

"The underwear?"

I pull them out of my bag and shove them in his hand. There is no way I can tell him that I'm a thief. No, it isn't laundry day, unless you're Vicky and then I suppose every day is laundry day if using the secondary definition of *launder*.

I force in a breath of the cold air.

Julian looks at the underwear, obnoxiously amused. "You met my mother, Regina. That's her shop. Let's say you got lucky."

My stomach plummets with shame because he knows what I was doing. I part my lips to deny it, but his eyes, suggesting both honesty and mischief, pull me out of my orbit. Julian scrambles my system to silence.

He adds, "My dad is way cooler interview material. He'd be happy to swap his days filling in for her with you. He works the second shift doing community outreach for crime prevention."

I choke. What? Does his father work in law enforcement?

"He's not a cop—more like social services. He works with delinquents."

I sputter as I swallow back disbelief. "I guess you're my lucky charm."

The chill air pinches my cheeks red. Unsure where the ridiculous words—that would have sounded flirtatious had they come from Caroline's lips—about him being my lucky charm came from, I avoid looking past the sleeves of his hoodie. There are a few cuts along the knuckles of his right hand. I'm known for many things, but flirting isn't one of them and if that was flirting, I have some remedial work to do, apparently along with my pilfering skills, and possibly every subject in twelfth grade.

Julian walks as if he's on edge like there's a chasm to one side, but if he's steady, he'll find his way right out of the city. "So are you from here?"

"Sort of."

"You can't really be sort of from here," he says.

"I'm staying with my sister." If Julian is a Dartmont student, I find it hard to believe he's never heard of, no less seen, Victoria Goldfeather. She's notorious.

"Staying with her for the weekend?"

"No, it's more of a long-term situation."

"So you're skipping school?" he asks as if he'd join me if it were a dare.

I don't answer.

"Is that why I don't see you at Dartmont?"

"I'm mostly homeschooled."

"You can't be mostly homeschooled. Either you go to public school or private or not. There's no in between."

"If you lived my life for a day, you'd see that there's a lot of gray area." I pick up my pace, eager to leave Julian and today behind. However, a steady stream of cars, buses, and cabs cut me off at the next crossing. I dart left, but a wall of pedestrians blocks my way.

"Listen, I know you want to run to wherever you don't go to school, but you have to admit we're supposed to be back by eleven for check-in." He shrugs like following the rules isn't typically part of his repertoire, but if he has to go then I do too. "Just saying, karma or dharma or something."

He doesn't even know why he's right, but he is. His dad let me off easy. If Julian lets it slip that I bolted, I might find myself in a pair of handcuffs.

But Vicky. I avoid the foreboding battle drums that play in the background, challenging me to make a choice.

At last, I turn my gaze up to meet Julian's expressive brows. There isn't enough milk chocolate in his eyes for them to be brown, but they're not green either. Hazel maybe? And his lips—they're full and one is slightly bigger than the other.

I inhale and then look down at my hands. "Lead the way, lucky charm," I say and if I weren't me, I'd have giggled like a girl who just met a cute boy.

## Chapter 3

VICKY ISN'T WRONG ABOUT HOW MIND-NUMBING SCHOOL CAN BE, BUT she isn't right either. Gray area. Shadows. Disappearing myself again would come in handy right now. So would knowing what the flip first-degree inequalities and polynomial expressions are. Math sucks.

Wearing the Dartmont Required Attire, consisting of a plaid skirt, maroon jacket, white polo T-shirt, and knee socks with a maroon stripe around the top, my bare legs stick to the wooden chair when I shift, eager to beat everyone to the door when the chapel bells ring.

At first glance, Dartmont is perfection in the form of east coast prep school charm with its classical architecture, including stone and brick buildings stretching skyward toward academic heights. One of the buildings facing the quad is what's called collegiate gothic. Let it be known: there are spires and towers aplenty.

Caroline was in her element, parading around campus like she owned the place. No, that title goes to the lost heiress, Jane Swift. I don't begrudge boarding school like Vicky. Quite honestly, I've never minded it here. No nanny. No nagging. No problem.

Vicky hated it. I'd never tell her this, but without the potential of Mum and Dad as her audience, she had to rework her attempts to vie for their attention. Usually, it came in the form of outrageous acts of rebellion. Her behavior at Dartmont wasn't that different, except there was an administration and they have rules...until Mum and Dad disenrolled her.

Thankfully, I'm mostly immune to the *lengthily Dartmont Book of Rules and Regulation for*

*Responsible Stewardship and Accountability* because of the Goldfeather Family Endowment. It's huge, comparable to the gross domestic product of a small country.

During passing period, I walk under the rows and rows of maple trees with their leaves hinting at the first blush of fall. The air is crisp and despite what happened at the Clothing Cloud, relief at not being in the city breezes through me.

It's like I'm split in two. A twin torn between my sister and myself. Between life on the wealthy private school campus and the gritty streets of Boston.

I avoid the stares and murmurs as students speculate which half of the "Goldfeather Girls" I am. If Caroline left her mark as the Golden Girl. Vicky was the Wild Card. Emphasis on *wild*. I'm always just in the wings. The extra in the play.

Whispers of cheating, spying, pranks, and much worse, meet my ears. Tate Kennedy and Becca Brown speculate about why Allie Dennis was found tied hiding in the boat house wearing a gorilla suit. Two other girls from volleyball talk about how Robbie Benson was last seen conscious with Vicky and then was discovered tied to the school gate, unconscious. Then there was the burned yearbooks incident.

When I enter the Beaux history building with its columns across the front, Howard Waddleston catches up to me. "Hey, Victoria."

I should've dodged behind one of the columns when I had the chance. Instead, I stop and my shoulders lift and lower on an exhale.

His naturally pink cheeks go darker as he realizes he's not about to get a juicy lead on the return of the infamous Goldfeather sister. "Not Vicky. Penny."

"Oh. My mistake. You're identical. But yay. You're back. Should I stop, you know...?" he hints at our arrangement.

"For now, I guess. What do I owe you?"

He waggles his eyebrows. "How about a barter?"

Unless he wants a pair of underwear from the Clothing Cloud... "I know you're going to ask me about something my sister allegedly did, so go on."

Howard opens his mouth to ask, but with my arms crossed in front of my chest, I cut across him to keep control of the situation. "If you're wondering if the issue of the Walrus Weekly covered in blood had anything to do with her, the answer is no." Probably not, but I'll always deny it. There's no telling what Vicky did.

"Did Vicky actually break into Dean Cortez's house off campus and steal his cat?"

I almost laugh but force my lips into a flat line that Vicky would appreciate. "Why don't you ask your aunt, Dean Hammond?"

Caroline was an integral part in exposing how Howard's family was involved in a scandal of their own. For all Dartmont's pomp and circumstance, there is an equal amount of deceit and corruption.

"Is the cat okay?" he asks.

"My sister would never hurt an animal. Not even Dean Cortez's beloved Snowbell."

Howard's lip curls like he just got a hit of some hot gossip. As the wizard behind the Dartmont Dart, our online social media slash news source, he deals in hearsay and hope that the leads he gets rake in a lot of likes and engagement.

"Then she did take Snowbell?"

"No comment." I turn on my heel and stride down the hall, already knowing I said too much.

Whenever my Vicky's name is associated with a misdeed, there is always an alibi and never a direct witness. I don't know the truth, but I will protect her. My sister is a thief and a liar, but not a killer and she'd never hurt a cat, dog, child, or anyone who didn't deserve it.

Probably.

IT'S FINALLY LAST PERIOD. US History. I hope there isn't going to be a quiz or a test. I haven't opened a school-issued history textbook since late sophomore year. I had a nasty case of cabin fever that winter and went to visit Vicky for what I dubbed *Snow* Days even though by the time she got back from Italy, it was spring. That's also when I learned the fine art of the *Hot Cocoa Con*.

Per our arrangement, Howard hacks into the school's database and *unclicks* enough absent boxes to keep my name off the truancy list so the admin doesn't call my parents. It's not because they'd get upset. Rather, it's their lack of caring that I try to avoid.

Everything is always *Caroline, Caroline, Caroline*. She's the golden girl and I'm more like the feather, forgotten. Vicky is just always in trouble.

Professor Sharpe, standing motionless at the front of the classroom, sounds like she has sand in her mouth as she drones on about Truman's Fair Deal program. I got a bum deal having to sit here for the next forty-five minutes. Then again, it's my fault for not assessing Regina's hawkeyed vision more accurately. At least I'm not in juvenile detention. My parents would probably leave me there.

"To help you prepare for the mid-term, I'm going to pair you up with study buddies," the teacher says.

The girl to my right snickers. "Seriously, study buddies? What is this, third grade?" she asks above a whisper.

Sharpe, hearing the comment, offers a lean smile. "If that's the way you feel about it, Miss Turner, you may work on your own."

Miss Turner shrugs. I try to think of something banal to say so I can work on my own too, but we're already counting off numbers to partner up. Then again, I don't intend to come back on test day, so why should I care?

"Thirteen," I mumble when it's my turn.

All at once, everyone scrambles around the room to find the other person with their number. I stay put.

"See, karma," a deep and familiar male voice says.

I glance up to see Julian, standing a few steps away.

I'm not sure that's how karma works. Maybe he means fate or

destiny. I can never remember the difference. I keep my head out of the clouds of existentialism.

"I'm number thirteen too." Wearing the boys' version of the Dartmont uniform his button-down shirt untucked against the dress code, his eyes spark.

In the twenty-four hours since we met, I haven't been able to forget his hazel-brown eyes.

"More like a lucky charm," I say but am not sure he hears me as Sharpe explains how she wants us to work together over the next weeks, giving careful instructions for how to record our progress.

"If more people learn to work cooperatively, the mistakes of the past are less likely to be repeated," she says sagely.

In Julian's presence, my attention falls back to the minutes leading up to being caught at the Clothing Cloud, wondering what I did wrong, and assessing Regina—wanting to be sure not to ever repeat the mistakes in my recent past. There had been another customer in the shop, loitering by the shoe section. Maybe she ratted me out. Whatever. As long as Vicky doesn't find out. I look down at my hands, and then beyond to the patch of sunlight on the floor. My vision settles on a pair of scuffed brown boots and legs filling in his slightly wrinkled slacks. Julian's upper lip peeks ever so slightly over his bottom one. The saturating light catches tiny scars on his face along with a scattering of freckles.

"Don't dally. Move along. Pair up and get to work reviewing the handout." The professor grates on with a sharp eye in my direction.

"Study buddies? Yeah, whatever." I get to my feet since there isn't a vacant desk next to me for Julian to sit in.

"I imagine you're pretty far behind," he says, implying my prolonged absence.

"In history? Yeah, you could say that." I don't mention the world-class education I've received, that I can speak Russian, Chinese, and Italian, or that my knowledge of art history grows by the day—over the years, I took Vicky's place and doubled up on our private tutoring lessons.

Pride gives way to dread as it spirals through me. I failed. Stealing underwear. Maybe I should stick to Dartmont, go to college, and become an accountant or something. Make Mum and Dad proud. Oh yeah, I hate math.

Julian reviews the instructions Professor Sharpe passed out. In a low voice he says, "Sharpe might be loaded with creative ideas and unrivaled humor," his eyebrows drift toward sarcasm, "but she's serious business. She failed a dude last year for not doing this same assignment correctly. He and his partner never got together. They just plagiarized. They were put on student probation." Then he adds, "Maybe she's psychic."

Maybe he's teasing. I close my eyes for a moment. He can't know what happened at Clothing Cloud.

*Penny, it's a secret. We're a secret.* My twin's voice is never far from my thoughts. Twintuition isn't real, but we share a special connection.

The bells ring, startling me.

"You're wearing murder face." Julian probably noticed I was in my own zone—what Caroline calls my "Resting Witch Face."

She'd originally used a stronger version of that expression for Vicky, but not to be left out, I whined, so she declared that I have a resting witch face. One level down from an RBF. When Mum asked what that meant, Caroline explained that it's when someone looks like a mean girl without trying.

"See you tomorrow, Penny," Julian says.

"No, you won't," I mutter because I'm not going to be here. He doesn't hear me over the rustling of students stuffing their backpacks, the zip of vests, and the scratch of chairs against worn linoleum. I have no intention of returning.

As I leave the cacophony of the end of the day behind me, the noise falls away except for one word in Julian's voice. *Penny.* The way he spoke my name, the soft *P*, the flurry of the *N*s then the long *E* sound at the end that he capped off as if not wanting to temp himself. He made my name seem like he tasted something sweet, something delicious.

Penelope Ava Goldfeather is my real name. Everyone calls me

Penny because Caroline did. Ask any number of people in Boston, they'd give different names: Rachel, Teresa, Jessy.

Except Good Cop and Julian. I told them who I am.

*Penny, Penny, Penny.* The recent memory of Julian's voice speaking my name telegraphs something I've never felt before. It's like snow dusts the inside of my head and then a single flake melts on my tongue. I try to deny that intention and desire are two very different things. I don't plan to see him tomorrow, but today I don't seem to be in the habit of sticking to the few rules I ought to follow.

I rush down the granite steps of the history building, considering making up for my failings earlier. I could use a new notebook and some pens—back-to-school "shopping" in the student center.

When Vicky and I were younger, we'd tug our nanny by the hand, rushing up and down the aisles in the stores. We'd fill our cart with pencil cases and binders, shiny new supplies. Caroline would inevitably go out with Mum and return with new shoes and a few outfits for casual Friday at our day school. Last year, Vicky and I did our own version of back-to-school shopping. She called it a free for all. We took whatever we wanted.

I do my best not to think about how it would be much easier to pull out our parents' credit card and charge it to them. Sure, it would tick them off but isn't that the point? Then again, they cut her off completely.

The knot in my stomach clinches, pulling me in two different directions as I debate whether to go through with Phil's conditions or head back to Boston.

As my shoes crunch in the leaves dotting the sidewalk, I shake the burning what-is-wrong-with-me question from my mind.

Vicky is the one who convinced me to leave Dartmont not long ago. Live with her. Be free. Sounds good on paper.

Since sophomore year after she got back from Italy, I've sporadically shown up when I'm bored or want to feel normal for a day or month. No way would admin kick me out. One, I haven't broken any rules except for not attending classes. Thankfully, my student record doesn't reveal my truancy. Two, Daddy Goldfeather makes the single largest donation to the school. Now that Caroline graduated, they don't want to lose that.

Learning about dead presidents and failed administrations isn't going to aid and abet my future. I make my decision and turn toward the long lane that leads to the school's gates.

## Chapter 4

My long shadow contrasts with the rusty sunshine spilling onto the sidewalk. I'm suddenly ten feet tall. I wonder about Peter Pan and freedom and what shadows do when the sky is dark.

A figure marches up beside me. Our shadows momentarily overlap. I suddenly have two heads and broad shoulders. I look over, expecting the person to walk past me.

When they don't, something rattles inside my chest and I press my palm to it. "Where'd you come from?"

Julian's expression suggests mischief like he's a wild thing. "My dorm is over there—Prince Dallywimple," Julian says as if we've been walking and talking all along.

He may as well be saying *Penny, Penny, Penny...remember the agreement?* I halt.

"I didn't know anyone actually lived in that dorm. Most of the guys live in Dader."

"It's where they send the overflow. I was going to be a day student." He shifts from foot to foot. "Last summer my parents decided it would be better if I board here."

"By *decided*, do you mean forced?"

He snorts softly through his nose in assent.

Perhaps we're cut from the same cloth...not something I'm going to say out loud considering the incident at Clothing Cloud.

"Which is your dorm? Wait. Let me guess, Margaret Ellicott?"

"No, my sister Caroline lived there. I'm in Moore."

"With about two thousand students here, it's interesting that we didn't know each other before now. Although the more I think about it, maybe you were in my freshman year English class."

"You sure it wasn't Vicky?"

Our eyes meet and Julian holds my gaze for longer than I've ever let someone look at me. "Your eyes are different. Distinct. They're brown and streaked with gold."

And hers are gray. So he has seen us...or one of us.

Julian breaks the silence lengthening across the broad moor. "Do you need help with homework or anything?"

"Probably not," I blurt.

"I'll see you tomorrow then," he says again. Yet he doesn't continue down the sidewalk toward Prince.

If this were a city street, traffic would creep past on the cobblestones, imprinted with history. Instead, it's like something else is being recorded as the sun dips lower. We both stand there as if daring ourselves to outlast its light.

I wonder if Vicky is home. If she's questioning where I am. My mind races with ways to explain to her why I'll be unavailable Monday through Friday between the hours of seven and four. I'm a thief and a liar, but not to her. I don't imagine Julian's dad would really go through the trouble of telling the cops if I don't show up at Dartmont tomorrow. But if Regina catches wind, I might be done for. Bad Cop and all that.

"Yeah, tomorrow. I guess so," I say, this time unable to resist the pull of what my life could be like if I were normal.

The truth is a gummy thing and sticks to the gray area of my life as I take my time going to Moore Dormitory.

The heady scent of oleander slinks toward me before I open the door to my single. I shouldn't be surprised to find Vicky sitting on the floor, running through a set of architectural plans. She drapes the vellum in half and flicks her long dark blonde hair over one shoulder when I set my bag down. "Where've you been?" she asks casually.

The answer isn't, *If admin sees you after you were barred from the campus, you're in trouble*, so I don't utter it.

I shrug and don't take the opportunity to make this into a confessional with obvious answers:

- Caught stealing
- In class
- Fantasizing about a boy

I wish a great cloud of eraser dust could obscure the transcript of the last couple of days.

Apparently, Vicky is a lot like Regina and can see through obfuscation. Our mother is hands-off, focusing her attention on Caroline. Vicky and I have always been here for each other though. We have to be. Plus, I don't know of any other twin thief duos. We're an original act.

I toss my bag onto the floor and then scrounge through my desk drawer for something to eat before moving to the mini-fridge. Nothing appetizing.

"Figured I'd find you here," Vicky says.

"Figured I should show up for class. Don't want to arouse suspicion."

Her eyes slit as she surveys me. Too late for that. I sense she's onto me.

"You hardly belong here, Penny. Want to leave?" Her expression is pure mischief.

It's hard to say no. An hour later, we're back at her apartment in Boston. She studies the architectural plans again.

I scrounge through her fridge where I find a couple of bottles of a sports drink—probably left over from one of Flavio's visits. He's a few years older than us and the only person Vicky has ever allowed to come over. That tells me one thing. She trusts him. In fact, he's been around a lot lately. I'm guessing they're working on a job.

There is also leftover spaghetti and sauce. The rare times Vicky cooks, she favors Italian cuisine that is only successful half the time—meaning there are often pungent experiments that do nothing to appetize me. I think of the toasted bagel and coffee from yesterday. My mind lands on Julian. Then being caught. Then Julian again.

When I sit down with a box of stale crackers, she raises her eyebrows and the dark pools of her eyes devour me like a supernova. *She knows.* There are only a few rules that mark my life and in one afternoon, I broke them all.

*Rule number two: never admit to anything.*

*Rule number one: never get caught*—especially when your twin is a professional thief.

I'm screwed. I could really use a Plan C right now.

I fold myself into the nest of the papasan chair we lifted from a store just outside the city last summer. Carrying it on the train was harder than actually taking it from the sidewalk display out front.

But Vicky says that's part of the fun—the challenge.

"You shouldn't bother with Dartmont. It puts you too much on the radar," Vicky says.

I try not to squirm under her scrutiny.

She goes on. "Or with a boy. We've talked about that. Better not to get involved. Keep things simple, Penny. We don't need unnecessary complications in our lives."

I stuff a cracker in my mouth to cut my guilty smile. We've run through how to withstand interrogations, but I'm starting to doubt I have the knack. A small voice inside claims a boy isn't an unnecessary complication. But what would I know? This is unchartered territory.

Her voice startles me. "Or you were caught. Empty your booster bag," she commands.

The air is suddenly still as if Vicky sucked all the energy from the room and used it to propel her words at me full force. I stagger.

I flash to Julian's dad, the underwear on the counter, and the humiliation. Nonetheless, I retrieve my bag. It's specially lined with foil to act as an electromagnetic shield when taking stuff from stores with sensors. I'm thankful she's never seen the socks—at least it looks like I made myself useful recently. Then the pair of black undies tumble out. There couldn't have been two. Phil was very thorough. Julian must have stuffed them back in my bag when he caught up to me on the sidewalk. My cheeks burn and not only because I didn't notice his sleight of hand.

"Cute," she comments. "History notes?" she asks, flipping past coded details about my observations taken at different stores and establishments with various levels of security. Her lips turn down in disappointment when she reaches the page from my last period—actual history class.

As nearly identical twins, Vicky and I share the same dark blonde hair, medium skin, and an athletic build. We're alike in all ways but two. Her eyes are gray. Mine are blue. I'm like a muted version of her, a shadow, and with far less skill. Also, I'm not naturally predisposed to breaking every rule on principle alone.

I don't always mind school, classes, and what most people consider normal, traditional. But if I veer away from Vicky, there's no telling where she'll end up.

Then her eyes and lips narrow, crocodile-like. "You should have *bought* me a pair, too."

Our currency doesn't involve real dollar bills or credit cards. Vicky is subversive and fiercely independent, with a deep disdain for ordinary commerce after being disinherited from the famed Goldfeather popcorn fortune. Then again, if I'm honest about the timeline, her life of thievery started long before that. Mum and Dad disowning her only accelerated her quest to take everything she can.

I don't know how she pieced yesterday's ordeal together. Her approval means more than our parents because it's not the kind of win Caroline so easily achieves.

I've never failed my twin. Despite this singular disaster, and the covert criticism, I want to prove to her that I do have what it takes. That all this practice of nicking things when surrounded by a store full of people will make working in larger settings, with cameras and intense security, a piece of cake. She's preparing me. I'm her prodigy, and I've let her down.

"We all get caught once." She grips my shoulder and leans in close. "Only once."

"You?" The room brightens. Vicky? Caught? Maybe my superstar twin is human.

Her lips turn into a sly grin and she straightens. "No, not me, everyone else. Don't ever let it happen again, Penny."

I'm mortified, distracted, with a stupid pair of underwear, and lingering thoughts over a boy. I'm hopeless.

"What are you working on?" I ask, trying to change the subject.

Her brisk motion overturns the folded vellum. I glimpse the blue lines of building plans. "Reviewing the specs for the Institute of Fine Art." Her gaze barely hides a dark spark of excitement.

"Does that mean the Cuore d'Oro...?" I ask, referring to the golden heart encrusted with gems and pearls—her big score. She's coveted the precursor to the Faberge Egg collection for as long as I can remember.

"It's part of a traveling exhibit. How about some meatballs and then we'll go and get me a new hard drive." She snatches the box of crackers from my hands.

After we eat, I change into a puffer vest, lace-up boots, and pull a knit hat over my hair, sure that the warmth of the day has been lost. It's time to prove myself, again. The fire from the spicy meatballs fuels me as I set out to face Vicky's challenge and redeem yesterday's loss.

We board the train to take us to the electronics store she selected. I'm sure it's the one on Boylston with the new security system. I pat my booster bag, making sure I have my magnetized spider wrap key, even though I packed it less than an hour ago. It wouldn't be beyond Vicky to slip it out of my bag and leave me to do this old school. Fortunately, I thought of that and have a backup. I'm determined to be on my game.

On our way, Vicky reviews how the metal security sensors in the spider wraps will sound an alarm if I try to take it out of the store, even if visible metal detecting towers don't line the exit. Of course, I know how this all works. Apparently, I need an embarrassing refresher since I botched a simple grab-and-go yesterday.

I know the spider wrap key blind and run-through scenarios Vicky might set me up with. We used to do drills all the time, but lately, she's trusted me on my own. My skilled hands have practiced using the key in the dark. I refuse to fail. I load myself with gigabytes of confidence.

The brightly lit store radiates possibility against the night as I sweep inside, consulting an employee about a new laptop. I ask enthusiastic questions about music-recording programs as if I'm a Berklee student. He excuses himself to ask a more well-versed associate to help while I take the opportunity to stash the hard drive Vicky wants on the shelf beneath the computer display.

When a different guy comes back, we both lean in, huddled around the screen's glow. He launches into how the data-this and the memory-that is ideal for the recording program I mentioned. I'm only listening for the soft click of the spider wrap releasing on the hard drive box as my hands work discreetly out of sight. I ask a few more questions as I hide the metal wrapping and slide the hard drive into my bag. I try to dull the glitter of triumph as my lips tease toward a smile.

*Vicky, I got this.*

"Thanks so much," I tell the employee.

Vicky appears wearing glasses, a wig cut like a bob, and offers a subtle nod of approval.

"I'll have to give my father all the details. My birthday is next week. He asked me what I wanted so this is the perfect gift." I proffer a smile.

One of the things I said is a total lie—our father would have his assistant do the shopping if we were to be so lucky. I doubt the other slightly since Caroline was the kid who'd get a birthday magic show, bounce house, and even a merry-go-round one year.

The ease with which the hapless sales clerks believe stories like these is laughable.

"What's your name? I'll make sure you get the commission." Vicky winks at the salesman. Her hands, the left one wearing a rock of an engagement ring and coordinating wedding band as part of her get-up, are cleverly out of sight. I wonder what she took.

I saunter out of the store. My pulse races and I have to push back against a toothy, boastful grin. Jolts of adrenaline and triumph sprint from my fingertips to my toes.

"I taught you well," Vicky whispers as we board the train.

I let myself glow in the applause of her words even as an internal rope, growing ever tighter, nooses my insides.

## Chapter 5

Pleased with myself, I crawl into bed, pulling the stuffed-animal-soft blanket I nicked last time Vicky pretended to be a pregnant young mom at the bed and bath store. I played the role of a doting friend, stuffing everything in the baby carriage.

I replay successfully swiping the hard drive for her as she clacks away on her computer in the other room, no doubt going over schematics for the next heist—the Cuore d'Oro. I pause at the smile of approval she gave me. Then my mind drifts to guilt and then my failure, back through the corridors of Dartmont, and then settles on Julian when his shadow merged with mine.

The final rule in our world beeps like an alarm in my thoughts.

*Rule number three: never get involved.*

It bookends the others:

*Rule number two: never admit to anything.*

*Rule number one: never get*

This includes avoiding romantic entanglements with cute boys. Vicky calls it fraternizing with the enemy. She'd definitely veto Julian.

His hazel eyes and playful lips dance through my mind. Something about the cool city air yesterday and the angle of the sun this afternoon and the stupid idea of *normal* magnetizes me. On the topic of rule number three, Vicky says love is a dangerous thing. Then again, she's also trained me not to avoid risk.

※

A HISSING VOICE rises and then falls, pulling me from a dream. I lay still and listen.

"I told you, not yet." Even from the other room, I feel the ice in Vicky's voice.

There's a pause and when someone doesn't answer, I realize that she must be on the phone.

"Why? Because...not ready." A door opens and closes, muffling her for a moment. I lose track of what she says as urgency sends turbulence through her otherwise cool tone.

I only hear one side of the conversation, but as it continues, I imagine they're talking about the golden heart job that Vicky has been planning for ages and has finally arrived on our doorstep at the Institute of Fine Art.

"We can't—" Then, "But—" As a rule, people don't interrupt Vicky because she drives conversations. However, it's as though she can't get a word in edge-wise. "I just need more time."

She's quiet for a while, and I wonder if she hung up on the person —that's totally something she'd do. My twin is fierce and takes names as she shoves her enemies out of the way.

Then she speaks again and this time her tone thaws as she pleads, "Just give me a little more time." Pause. "I can't." Long pause. "I know, but—" Longer pause. "The answer is no." What feels like infinite silence passes as I try to calculate what it could all mean. "You remember what I said. Freedom or death." Then as though interrupting the caller, she adds, "My wings will never be clipped."

Absolute silence. Yet the air stirs with so many possible meanings. Was she talking to someone about me? When I hear a sniffle from the other room, my instincts leave me uncertain.

My thoughts thick like syrup, I drift in and out of sleep. Vicky has taught me to notice everything, working from the corners inward. To observe where wires lead, to quickly find blind spots, and to listen for the squeak of approaching footsteps. She's shown me how to conceal items, move stealthily, and scout hiding places. Being observant and surveying my surroundings is what I do. I notice details. What she hasn't explained is what to do with the long image of a boy and the freckles from summer spilling from the bridge of his nose and fading.

Usually, I'm able to quickly process and dismiss irrelevant information and move on. But the tilt of his head when he said my name and the way he leisurely leaned against my desk, suggested life could be simpler, more straightforward. The question in his eyes—that I'm not sure how to answer—sticks in my mind until a thin shaft of light slices through my room. I sense Vicky standing in the doorway, checking on me, and I tell myself that she's making sure no one will ever steal me away from her.

Her proximity reminds me of something else I don't know—the meaning of the conversation I wasn't meant to overhear.

I WAKE up to the sun burning through the morning haze, she's already gone, as usual. Vicky takes up the space my own mother doesn't. Mum distanced herself from me when I was still little. For her, I think one child was enough—not that Caroline was a handful. No, that was Vicky and me. Caroline, our older sister, has always been perfect.

All the same, sometimes part of me wanted a mom who'd drive a mini-van, bake cookies, and give me more than the crumbs of her attention. Too late for that, but when I didn't so much as get a morsel, I turned my attention to my larger-than-life twin.

I once overheard Dad say that I was an anchor to Victoria's kite-like tendencies.

To me, she's less like a kite and more like a cloud. A very glamorous one when she wants to be especially with the pair of Chopard drop earrings with diamond encrusted anchors on them and the matching tennis bracelet she frequently wears. Wonder where she got them?

But she's not here, and I shouldn't be either.

I launch out of bed, rush to the shower, and prepare for a day at Dartmont. Vicky's quiet disappointment and challenge the day before were enough, there's no need to drag the police into our lives. I don't imagine hawkeyed Regina approving of Phil's lenient sentence, so I hastily dress, not wanting to give him a single reason to think of me ever again.

At least this is what I tell myself. It has nothing to do with his son.

Not. A. Thing.

I'll be back later and Vicky won't miss me. She's not in her room —festooned with thousands of paper cranes, hanging from the ceiling. From the disarray on the kitchen table, and early morning departure, I'm guessing she's scouting the IFA—the Cuore d'Oro job probably— the one she's been obsessing over since she came back from Italy, the golden heart we're going to pinch together. The late-night conversation echoes dully as though tugging me toward the confusion of dreams. What was the call about?

## Chapter 6

To get to Dartmont, I charge an Uber to my parents. It's not the first time. Yet I miss first period. I slump through the next couple, eager to show Julian that I followed through with my end of the agreement in case his dad asks if I was here today. He's not in my morning classes so far.

I'm considering skipping out, at least until history, when Julian slides into the desk beside me at the back of the English classroom. He nods at me with the smallest smile on his lips as if despite himself.

I steal a glance at him. Nothing hides behind Julian's eyes, but he keeps his hands tucked in his pockets.

A new teacher replaced the famed Professor Groff. Based on what I'd heard, I was actually curious about his class. Too bad he's dead.

She wears a yellow shirt, black Capri pants, and sculpted her black hair into a beehive. She writes the word *Poetry* on the dry-erase board at the front of the classroom. Her voluminous updo points to a poster board with the name *Enni Honig* set against a puzzle-piece-shaped map of Germany and little cutouts of bumblebees. She's modern and retro and scary in an I-don't-think-she's-capable-of-smiling kind of way. She must be a few years out of college—mid-twenties?

With a faint accent she says, "Last month, I told you was National

Honey Month and as you know, I am a beekeeper. It's October now, the farmer's markets are winding down, the weather is cooling off, and the particular industriousness of autumn is in the air. We gather on the cusp of change before the snap of winter and the outer world retreats to slumber." She passes out sheets of paper. "In keeping with our theme of recognizing national months, we will now move on to our poetry unit."

A hipster trying, but failing, to grow a mustache raises his skinny arm.

"Yes, Whitley?" Ms. Honig asks.

"National Poetry month is in April, as you said, it's October."

"Correct. How astute of you to know which month it is. Perhaps you can hone this skill and be more diligent about when assignments are due." Honig silences the sniggering with a sharp glare. "As far as I'm concerned every month, every day, is worthy of poetry," she says dismissively as if personally insulted someone consigned poetry to just one month.

She stops in front of my desk, appraising me. "Thank you for joining us, Penny. We've missed you." She buzzes to the front of the room.

I didn't realize anyone noticed me, in class or absent. I don't recall her during my pop-in back in September. Maybe there was a sub while she was busy keeping her bees.

"Your assignment is simple. From now until mid-term you will eat, sleep, and breathe poetry. You will work independently and in pairs, you will recite in front of the class, and you will research and write. Poetry, for the next weeks, will be your life." There is no sweetness in her words as she strides up and down the aisles as if she's challenging us to criticize verse, rhyme, and simile just so she can refute our flimsy claims. She is like a drill sergeant aiming to make us stronger via stilted lines of gooey and obscure emotion by the time she's done with us.

Vicky advised me against trusting people with bleeding heart passion. I'm so not on board the poetry train.

I glance down at the syllabus that's reached me and pass the spare copy to Julian. There are three projects highlighted in bold font *Reading, Writing, Reciting*. I scan the detailed outlines for each, concluding with the requirement to recite poetry to the class instead of a midterm exam.

"I imagine you all have questions about the four letters, E-X-A-M, that befoul everyone's lives. For this unit, instead of a written test, you will perform an oral recitation." As if anticipating objections, she says, "I'm the teacher. I have that authority. And no, there are no exceptions. If you suddenly find yourself unable to speak, I will put you in contact with someone skilled in instructing Sign Language." She moves her fingers briskly as if demonstrating that she is that person. Maybe she signs to her bees, urging them to collect more pollen. But her voice is not syrupy and her eyes harden as if she's determined to convert us all to poets.

"We start now. As most of you know, we do not raise our hands to answer in this class." She looks sharply at Whitley. "I call on you as I see fit. Penny, give us your first thoughts on poetry. Go."

I stutter, caught off guard. If she asked me if I'd failed and then succeeded in stealing hundreds of dollars worth of items the other day, I would have an easier time explaining. In my world, words mean nothing. Doing is everything. I sense eyes on me, Julian's in particular.

Honig closes in, leaning over my desk. In a sudden rush of defiance, sentences spill from my lips. "I've never understood the purpose of poetry. It seems strangled, misappropriated from prose to do the dirty work of making the reader push the lines apart and figure out what's between them."

Her eyebrows practically tuck into her beehive. "Unique take. Yes, sometimes poetry is more about what's unsaid than what's printed—" She continues blabbing about her beloved poetry.

I already hate this lesson. There's enough ambiguity in my life as it is. I get to my feet.

"Leaving us so soon, Penny?" Honig asks, interrupting herself.

She stands behind Julian leaving me no choice but to look at them both head-on. His honest eyes. Her demand.

I wonder what telepathy would be like. Maybe I should ask Mrs.

Sharpe from history, though that might be a different skill set than being psychic. Maybe Julian is thinking about the evolution of bipeds, the noxious smell coming from the hallway, or about a girl with a few freckles like his. I don't even want to know what buzzes around in Enni Honig's head. I imagine honeycomb-like recesses filled with incongruent lines of poesy.

"I, uh, have to use the ladies' room." I excuse myself down the hall with no idea where the door with the little figure wearing a skirt is. My footsteps squeak. I feel as if Julian is following me, but it could be that he's taken up residence in my head, inhabiting my thoughts like he might a chair or like all those people who occupied the steps of the New York Stock Market building last year. Vicky had considered we join them and set up a tent. Then thought better of it when police reports flooded in. If there's anything she hates more than money, it's authority.

Actually, I take that back. She hates a guy named Sandro the most, but that's another story.

I crash through the girls' bathroom door and splash water on my face. It's like Julian plunked down in my head and decided to stick around. Pre-Julian my thoughts were my own:

- Contemplations about the next store I was going to fleece
- The possibility of officially working with Vicky before long
- Adding the golden heart to our collection.
- Or taking a trip—I could stand to get out of here.

There are plenty of jobs in Europe and a lot of stamps in Vicky's various passports that I'd someday like in my own. Instead, I wonder what Julian's house looks like. And his dorm room, and what hides behind his eyes—they look more hazel than brown today. I gaze into the mirror as if it will reveal this strange and sudden shift to a new interest in a boy whose name begins with the letter *J*.

I'm back in my seat just before the bells signal the end of English.

As everyone gathers up their stuff, Julian reads from our homework sheet. "Ms. Honig said we have until next week to, 'find a poem that captures our hearts and then write one in which we pour our hearts onto the page.'"

"Great," I mutter. My heart is a dark, unknown thing. Nothing about it belongs on a clean white piece of paper.

"Then we have to read them both aloud to our partner."

A wobbly breath escapes as he looks at me. "Let me guess, we're partners, again." I don't mean to punctuate my words with contempt. It's as if I'm having an inner rebellion with myself, east and west vying for sovereign rights to the Nation of Penny.

He nods and then with the ghost of a smile, says, "And Shakespeare. Lots of Shakespeare. See you in history."

I slip my notebook into my bag, wondering why he seems slightly down today and what karma or dharma or fate has to do with all this. Seriously, partners again? Penance? Payment? Am I to find a lesson in words and history? Doubtful.

"Penny," Ms. Honig calls when I reach the door. "All original work, you know that right?"

My brow furrows. "Of course."

I can't possibly have a record that I don't know about. Vicky keeps track of things like FBI watch lists and felonious report profiles. I hadn't even thought of plagiarizing, but an idea blooms as I tick down the minutes of history class.

## Chapter 7

It's Friday morning, which means I only have to endure school for about six hours until time is my own for the weekend unless I decide not to go back to Dartmont on Monday. Maybe by then, Phil will have forgotten all about our little snafu at the Clothing Cloud.

I glance at my bag, still sitting by the door where I left it yesterday. It contains a tedious amount of homework that I neglected to do last night.

My phone blares with a ring, startling me. Because I'm more of the loner type than my sister, Caroline the socialite, the thing rarely makes a peep.

"Hey, Penny," Vicky says.

In the background, a loud squawk sounds over her voice. "Hello, Bird." I leave the endearing letter *Y* off the name of Birdy, Vicky's beloved white-crested cockatoo with a tuft of golden feathers. He screeches whenever she says my name or when I enter the room as if I'm an intruder and must be jealous that we're on the phone.

Six months ago, she brought the bird home, saying he was a rescue. At the time, I was jealous of all the attention she gave him, but she explained he'd been abused and couldn't help his brash behavior—

dumping his food all over the floor, flapping and screaming wildly, and glaring at me like he might peck my eyes out.

She says, "My Birdy, Birdy, Birdy-boy."

He coos in response.

I grab a cup of yogurt I stole from the Refectory out of my mini fridge, peel the foil top off, and take a bite.

Vicky abruptly says, "Does the name *Montague* mean anything to you?"

"Uh, no."

"Regina Montague?" she clarifies.

The yogurt is suddenly thick in my throat. Regina?

Vicky describes the owner of the Clothing Cloud, but I maintain innocence even as I imagine her leveling me with her dark-eyed stare. "Penny, if you should suddenly recall encountering her, know that she's conniving, vicious—stay away from her and anyone related to her."

I stutter out something that sounds like agreement. In the pockets of my mind, I hide the possibility she means Julian's mother.

"Also, why did you go back to Dartmont?" Disdain peppers her voice. Before I can answer, she adds, "Remember what I said."

I do remember—every word from her covert conversation the other night. If I ask what it meant, I'll trip over her silence—her refusal to reply.

"I'll be back in time for our birthday. Eighteen and—" There's a contemplative pause. Vicky falters. She always speaks deliberately except during the phone conversation I overheard the other night and now.

My breath is shallow as I wait for her to finish.

"Never mind." She hangs up.

I push back against the feeling of loneliness that creeps in as I exit my room at the sound of the chapel bells.

Girls chatter in the halls. They wear gossip and prying questions on their glossed lips when I pass. I recognize a few of them. Tegan teased me for not being able to shoot the basketball into the hoop during our freshman-year sports evaluation. Now I can get a grappling hook on the side of a building, no problem. I also earned my black belt in not one, but two martial arts disciplines.

Jordyn looks me up and down as if I'm the one suggesting I have something to prove. I don't—at least not here. She flicks her hair at me as she turns to talk to her hulking boyfriend.

I cruise past Neda, Maria, and Kristina. They cluster around a locker, giggling and speaking in rapid-fire Spanish—probably so none of Señora Henderson's students can understand them.

During freshman year, before Caroline graduated, she told me to smile more. Said to lose the resting witch face. Vicky is the queen of the RBF as well as the resting I'm done with you face, the I don't care face, and the eye roll face.

The girls like Tegan and Jordyn return my expression. I can't help my perma-scowl, how my eyes verge toward calculating, that poetry is my nemesis, or that right now, I hate this place.

Ms. Honig hastens by me in the hall, implying that I'd better hurry up. I take my time before vanishing into Forensic Science.

I manage to survive the periods before English. Like yesterday, Julian slides into his seat after me. His eyes reflect the cloudy weather. I wonder what he sees.

"Hey," he says quietly.

I nod in his direction as Honig, wearing a yellow blazer, proselytizes about the merits of poetry throughout time, quickly zooming us to the present with how we may interpret our own innate yearning for verse.

*Blah, blah, blah.*

She passes out wrinkled and smudged sheets of paper that appear to have been recycled through multiple iterations of this lesson. "Send them back. It doesn't matter which one you get. We'll rotate through. Some of these pieces are classics that you may recognize. Others are likely less familiar. I also snuck in some of my favorites. Today we're going to read these poems aloud. No pressure. Casual. Let the lines flow naturally. Listen for cadence, rhyme schemes, and syllables. For now, it isn't about the words themselves, but what they sound like."

I roll my eyes, turn to Julian, and launch into a short poem by

Langston Hughes. I wonder what he hears in the lilt of my voice. I wonder if the words mean anything more than the vowels and consonants. He doesn't look at me, but instead at the Times New Roman font on the page in front of him as if he's already memorized my face and my lips. Then I notice the soft bruise on his hand as he clutches the paper tightly.

"Switch," Honig orders after a couple of minutes.

"Mine is by Esperio Camusso." As he reads, Julian's voice sounds like a beginning. It's the sun lifting itself over the horizon, a fresh notebook with empty pages, and clean sheets promising a good night's sleep. He stretches out the word *stars* like a promise. But his expression, a study in grayscale, doesn't reflect this brilliance. A shadow crosses his face when he says, "I will love you during the darkness, through it. After."

He looks up. Our eyes float softly together. For a moment, I'm transported elsewhere.

Then his eyes break from mine and he looks over my shoulder. A bulging man dressed in a brown suit asks, "Ms. Honig, is Penny Goldfeather in class today?"

My stomach swings nervously for a moment, but there's no way he's a detective here to question me. He has academia practically written in the creases of his maroon tie.

It's also impossible for Ms. Honig to know about my deal with Julian's dad, but it's like something, or someone, conspires to keep me rooted to Dartmont. Or to be arrested. Either way.

"Ah, yes, Dean Porter. As a matter of fact, she's right here. A pleasure to have in class."

Apparently, even English teachers fluent in Sign Language and German sound the same as everyone else when they're speaking with sarcasm.

"She has a call at Ambrose," he says to Ms. Honig by way of explanation that someone reached out to me via the administration building.

The fine hairs on the back of my neck lift and a chill works its way across my skin.

I do a better job brushing off the increasing sense that I should be freaking out than I did in the stockroom at the Clothing Cloud. I concentrate on the waves of my breath, inhale-exhale, as Vicky taught me, in the event I ever get nervous and choke.

I'm certain Phil decided to turn me in, thanks to hawkeyed Regina. I don't even give Julian the courtesy of a glare. He probably already knows the score. I stomp out of the classroom, leaving the stupid love notes and soliloquies behind. Ms. Honig can keep them.

I follow the dean down the hall of Arundel—the English building. Muffled lectures seep through the closed classroom doors. An errant piece of paper breezes as I walk by, catching my draft, and then fluttering to the floor.

Inhale, exhale.

Dean Porter is silent, but I know I'm about to get an earful. The dim corridor gives way to the brightly lit lawn stretching toward the flagpole and then the Ambrose Administration building beyond. There's no sign of the law, but I imagine myself responding with a mouthful of sass at whoever commands that I go to the precinct.

He gestures to the empty secretary's desk—Mrs. Dugas. She must be at lunch. A bowl of candy corn invites me to take a handful. A black phone with dozens of buttons blinks. "Line three," he says and then vanishes into an adjacent office.

Despite my tough front, my pulse stalls and my throat thickens as I prepare to face whatever is coming.

## Chapter 8

As I pick up the receiver of the phone in Ambrose, a million possibilities ping through my mind until a familiar, accented voice narrows it down. The caller says, "Hey, Jude."

I instantly know something must be wrong beyond my blunder. Earth tilting off its axis wrong. Flavio is the only friend slash cohort of my twin's who has been to the apartment and was the single reason she convinced herself the Brandywine job wasn't worth it.

I let these thoughts cram out the other ones that tell me I should worry. I dig out the memory of Vicky when she said in an offhanded way what to do if Flavio ever tried to reach me. It was a casual conversation, hypothetical, like what to do if I spill tomato sauce on a white shirt.

Blot. Water. Dish soap.

"Hey, Paul." This is the code to confirm that it's me, Penny.

Last spring, the song "Hey Jude" by the Beatles came on the radio. I started to sing along. Vicky quickly turned it off, squelching my enthusiasm. When I asked why, she said it was her favorite song, which didn't make sense. She gently pinched my chin and lifted my face toward hers. *"It's safer not to have favorites."* When I hear it now, I wonder what made her hate it so much that she refused to listen to it.

One name floats into my head and remains there *Sandro*.

Flavio goes on to say, "We have a change of plans for the weekend, heading up to the cabin. So look after yourself, okay?" Flavio says. The underlying nervousness sounds strange coming out of his mouth, in his accent. His lips are more comfortable with words like *risk*, *voluptuous*, and *persimmon*.

We're both quiet. The words *silent* and *listen* share the same letters.

Going to the cabin means either Vicky has been forced into hiding or arrested. The shock of something happening to her forces the breath out of me so quickly I doubt I'll ever be able to inhale again.

"Okay?" he asks again.

I know better than to ask questions such as, *Do you mean a rustic log cabin by a lake, a cellblock, or another country?* There is no way to answer whether I'm okay. Whatever has happened is not okay.

A door across the office opens. Dean Porter peeks his head out. "Okay?"

*No, no, no.*

All I can manage is a strangled groan, not unlike the sound Bird makes when Vicky leaves.

The dean looks at me expectantly. "Everything alright, Penny?"

I stare into space, noting the printed vines edged with gold creeping down the wallpaper on the wall across from me. Vicky would want me to keep calm. She'd want me to carry on. I dip my head in the dean's direction and dart out of the office.

I need open air. I need space. I need to know what happened to Vicky.

The cloudy afternoon light gleams too brightly against my distress. I feel blind for a moment, but there is no escaping the truth even of that which I cannot see. Vicky is either in jail or somewhere far away.

I pound down the granite steps. The ashen sidewalk matches the sky. Then I remember I left my bag back in Ms. Honig's class. Also, there's the agreement with Julian's dad.

There is no keeping calm. I streak across the quad as the bells ring and students pour from the classrooms. I press my way through the heaving mass of people, all utterly unaware of the crisis that asphyxiates me.

Keep calm. Inhale.

Exhale. Carry on.

Yeah right. Both notions are ridiculous. However, I convince myself that this will be okay. It'll be all right. There's probably a reasonable explanation. Vicky is tough. She knows what she's doing. She's sly and capable. Conniving and vicious if she needs to be, reminding me of her question about Regina Montague.

Inhale, exhale. Keep calm.

The simplest thing to do and the most reasonable thing to do would be to go immediately to the nearest police station and inquire about her whereabouts slash arrest or file a missing person's report. But we're not normal people. If I did that, and this is all a mistake, she'd...I don't really know. Kick me out of her life?

Going to the authorities is forbidden. Bottom line. We've done too many wrongs. I immediately strike it from the list of options.

I must carry on.

I slip into Ms. Honig's empty classroom. My bag is not at my desk, nor is it at hers. I retrace my steps back to Ambrose, wondering what separates me from the moments before Flavio called when I walked this same path, and now.

Fear. Uncertainty.

Inhale. Exhale.

Mrs. Dugas fills the chair I occupied minutes ago. Her white hair almost brushes her shoulders. Her glasses pinch her nose. "Everything alright, dear?"

I rearrange my expression. "I forgot my bag in Ms. Honig's class. It's not there."

"The lost and found is outside the Refectory entrance. I imagine you'll find it in there. If not, come back and we'll track it down." She adjusts her glasses. "You sure you're okay?"

"Thanks," I say, afraid to answer the question.

## Chapter 9

Looking for my bag, I enter the Refectory. It's not there so I grab a bottle of water, scanning the room for Julian. When I land on him, his eyes meet mine. He peels himself out from a tightly packed table and fist bumps someone. I wonder about his battered hands. Tegan tugs on the edge of his shirt, but he doesn't seem to notice.

He reaches me in twenty-three steps. It's the only thing I can focus on to keep from imploding.

"Hey, how's—? You okay?" Concern creases his features.

I must really look a hundred degrees from okay. "My bag?"

"It's in my dorm," he says, walking back the way I came.

The door to the Refectory closes behind us, sealing out the clatter of lunch. The quad is uncomfortably quiet. I follow Julian, acutely aware of our footsteps, the brush of his pants, and the bob of his head as he moves as if the earth isn't shaking under my feet.

When we reach the entrance to Prince Dormitory, I follow him inside. We remain by the entrance. I expect him to rush upstairs and grab my bag. Instead, he leans his head against the doorframe as if his thoughts are heavy. Maybe he forgot his key. I can open almost any lock without one, but right now, my fingers tremble.

No longer in motion, the tremors and aftershocks of my world, slowly exploding somewhere beyond the walls of Dartmont catch up with me. I stare helplessly at my hands, willing them to steady and trying to ignore the fact that a boy and I are alone in the hall and he's gazing at me intently and I can't tear my eyes from the curve of his lips.

"I know you're not going to tell me what happened, but I know something did." He lifts his hand, looks from it to mine for a flash, and tucks it in his pocket. If someone took a thermal image of the two of us right now, it'd be molten. But aside from this sudden blindside of girly feelings, I feel the need to—I don't know what. Go? Where? What do I do?

"My bag?"

"Right, your bag." He takes the steps two at a time and returns less than sixty seconds later.

His hands brush mine as I take the strap. A fizzy rush charges through my fingers and up my arm. At that moment, I want him to hold my hand, the strength of our grasp ensuring that I'll keep calm, no matter what. I want his lips on mine in the lonely hallway. I want to erase all the days leading to today and find myself in a real, actual cabin somewhere far away, just the two of us. The excitement rising up from the idea suggests that my life could indeed carry on, instead of the mess it's been becoming for the last seventeen, almost eighteen, years. Or if anyone asks, three, going on four days.

"Thank you," I say, unsure if I mean for the bag, the fleeting fantasy, or both. The words linger between us along with the trail of imaginary light from when he reached out his hand and our fingers touched.

The look he gives me suggests he knows I've gone off course, that the wind tore my sail, and that I've lost my navigational tools. But it also suggests that he understands or cares or knows where to find a solid lighthouse to guide me home.

Despite this, there's no way to explain this to anyone, anywhere, ever. There is no room for fantasy or a boy in my life.

*Rule number three.*

My immediate world is infinitesimal. It consists of Vicky and me with our parents and Caroline on the periphery—did I push them there or did they find their own way?

I have no one to talk to without the worst act of betrayal. The screaming inside my head gets louder and louder as the minutes pass from when I received the call in Ambrose. My worry deepens. I try to recollect the last time I saw Flavio in person. It was a couple of weeks ago. He and Vicky conspired over coffee at the kitchen table early one morning. Tired, they slouched, leaning heavily on their elbows like they'd been up all night. I don't even know where to find him.

"Are you, uh...?" Julian pulls my attention back. The words to finish the sentence are *okay*, or *alright*, or *good*, but I am none of those things.

"No." I shake my head and desperately want all my fears and worries to spill out, freeing my mind from the possibilities that take shape. "It's complicated." I close my eyes, again wondering how my life became so thorny.

His eyes try to pour into me the words that I'm not yet ready to hear. Assurance. Trust. Understanding.

The bells ring. "History?" he says, asking if he'll see me there or as if that's actually the source of this trouble.

First, we have an assembly—the vivid memory of my sister up on the stage with a group of potential criminals defending their innocence and exposing the admin tries to take shape. Instead, I alternate between dread and worry during the inspired presentation about online safety. They bullet point risks, warning signs, and the importance of reporting incidents.

It's hard to focus because right now, my life is ten shades of dismal. I can hardly see my way toward the first *O* in good.

I slink into history early, take my seat, and survey the classroom while Mrs. Sharpe corrects papers. I consider my plan for the history exam. Her desk is on the right by the windows, but we're two floors up so no threat of observation from passersby. The door cut with a small rectangular window is opposite her desk. If someone happened by, they might notice. Hmm. The desk itself is old and wooden, likely the keys to the iron locks are long gone. A leather bag leans up against the sturdy oak leg. *Aha.* It looks like it would hold an answer sheet.

Me, study? Pfft. Vicky says there are different shades of smart.

Sharpe looks up at me. "Can I help you?" she asks in her scratchy voice.

I clear my throat, once again, totally off my game. Fear for what's happened to Vicky paralyzes me.

"She was waiting for me. We're study buddies," Julian says, sauntering into the room and wearing a reckless, confident smirk.

I give Mrs. Sharpe a self-satisfied smile, irritated she interfered with my casing her classroom.

Julian leans in and whispers, "She's a hawk."

He can't know what I was thinking about or the nickname I gave his mother—Hawkeye—but I buckle down and pay attention as Mrs. Sharpe lectures on Truman's presidency. Maybe cheating isn't an option.

Somehow, Caroline got by without doing that. At least, I think so.

After the final bell, the reality of my situation catches up with me as I step back into the cloudy day. I work through the bustling crowd, analyzing the call from Flavio. Maybe it was a joke or they wanted to teach me a lesson even after I redeemed myself by successfully nabbing the hard drive. Then again, Flavio's sense of humor isn't cruel. His laughter is dry and witty. He takes his work seriously and wouldn't make that call unless…unless it was a test. I contemplate how Vicky would be disappointed that I'd gotten sloppy and would want to prepare me to handle tense situations.

Then I recall her on the phone—everything about it suggested business as usual. Then again after her late-night conversation, I realize Vicky's life is wider and more mysterious than I've ever admitted.

I try to wrap my mind around scenarios as I walk mechanically toward my dorm.

Questioning Flavio's honesty isn't an option. Vicky trusts him. Granted he was in her inner circle, maybe he'd gotten in trouble and was saving face, turning her in, bargaining with the police.

Fact: thieves are liars. If anyone ever asks if we've taken something, we'll deny it. I'm the exception except I'm still a liar.

I hang my head. The shame of the moment in that fusty clothing store rushes back to me. I admitted it. I broke the cardinal rule and the guilt compounds with the possibility that all these stupid feelings I've had since Flavio's call, might be related to my confession. Maybe I got us all in trouble.

Written somewhere in the cells and molecules of my genetic make-up, I know that stealing is wrong and that my life, as I know it, is a million miles past right. Phil and Regina, Julian, and Ms. Honig and Mrs. Sharpe know it, intrinsically. Does Vicky? Do all those people see the conflict that I've mostly successfully suppressed as if it's written on my skin in invisible ink? Did I inherit this singular moral from Mum and Dad even though I've fought to be nothing like them? Or is someone trying to get me off this dissolute path?

What do I do? What would my twin do?

## Chapter 10

EITHER TO QUELL THE WORRY AND THOUGHTS I'VE BEEN STRUGGLING with or maybe in defiance of them, I get an Uber back to Boston and hop the Green Line to the Institute of Fine Art just before it closes.

I circle the Cuore d'Oro—the golden heart covered in sparkling bling. I admire the meticulous placement of the gems and the shine of the gold. This is Vicky's prize, her big score, and I will help her get it no matter what it takes.

I scout the area. The one-sided conversation I overheard between Vicky and someone late at night echoes in my thoughts.

Was she talking about me? I am ready. I am capable. Why would she think otherwise? And who was she talking to? She works with other thieves, but I've never heard her let anyone try to convince her of something. Usually, she starts the conversation with the word *no* and goes from there. I draw a breath to get my head back in the game.

The cameras are where I expect them to be. I study the lines of sight and angles. I observe the shadows and surfaces. The shades of wood and alabaster. I pace a loop around the heart one more time, determined. Then doubt creeps in. Why would she think I'm not ready? Why did she need more time? Why wait? A speaker, announcing the museum's closing, startles me.

Perhaps she has her reasons. When she gets back, I'll ask her about the call. I'll find out because whatever pull this heart has on Vicky, the desire to prove to my twin that I have what it takes is just as strong. I don't want to let her down.

As I make my way back to her apartment, I find myself standing in front of a department store between the Financial District and Chinatown. I go in. The girl with the red bob (a wig), cashmere sweater (the softest thing I've ever did steal), and leopard print flats (less comfortable than I remember) smiles in my reflection. I hardly recognize myself, and I'm glad. Right now, I don't want to know my name or that my favorite food is gelato even though Vicky instructed me not to have favorites—and that the insistent pulsing rhythm I've felt over the last days whenever I see or think about Julian is my heart.

The girl in the mirror laughs at this notion.

I'm good at hiding. With few exceptions, I rarely wear the same thing twice. My skill in the art of appropriating goods helps with this and is one of the purposes behind it. My twin says this is practice for taking what really matters.

As I browse the items on display, I note the camera on the south wall and the potential obstruction a tall rack of jeans poses. The salesperson lingers by the register, glancing into the glow of her cell phone whenever she has the chance. Some people steal clothes, food, or electronics, others cars and valuables, and still others, time and hearts. I push thoughts of my twin away. She's always advised me to keep calm, to have distance between my mind and my emotions.

I'm doing what I know. I square my shoulders against the uncomfortable tightening in my stomach. It's time to be awesome.

As my light fingers do what they do best, a feeling of peace washes through me like a rising tide. The thunder in my mind quiets. The music in this section is loud enough to mute the dull pop when I disengage the security tag. I feel like dancing to last summer's hit song filtering through the junior's section. The jacket I grab goes nicely with my outfit. It's the same unique shade of gray-green as the hoodie Julian wore the day we met. I slide it on, concealed by a row of mannequins. I anticipate the hit of ecstasy when I walk through the doors and into the night.

However, before leaving, I slip a few pairs of underwear into the pocket of the coat, certain that this time I'll get away. The blood in my veins charges like a high voltage current, the prim smile on my face holds behind it a gloating grin, and the sureness in my step dares anyone to stop me.

I am electric.

The walk from the train toward Fleet is long enough that the rush fades and my thoughts and worries crowd back in. My insides twine and knot. The coat keeps me warm, but at the same time, I want to take it off. It's itchy and the fit isn't quite right after all.

My stomach growls. I imagine Vicky, waiting for me, a warm meal of spaghetti, meatballs, and garlic bread as she eagerly inquires about my day. In this fantasy, she'll go on to say she got tickets for Les Miserable at the theater on the Emerson Campus—we went there a few times: Robin Hood, Esperanza Rising, and multiple Shakespeare productions, including Romeo and Juliet. I realize now she was probably working—scoping out the scene or observing a person intrinsic to one of her schemes. I was studying how to inhabit a role too. Back in fantasyland, she'll suggest we have friends over. We could do a spa and other slumber party activities. The vision slips into the lonely night as Mum's face takes her place. Vicky is my twin and a thief, neither inclined nor interested in playing the maternal role. Then again, neither is my actual mom. But a friend? A sister? Sometimes I'm not so sure.

I slouch against the brick wall outside a pizza place, the smell of fresh dough and garlic enticing me to linger. I try to recall the last thing Vicky said. Wrapping my arms around my chest, I search for a hug and her scent, sweet and perfumed like oleander. I let go and sigh. Another fantasy.

Vicky is not a typical twin. I'm not a regular girl. Despite her interest, bordering on obsession, with Italian food (and jewels) she doesn't do the typical set-the-table and let's have dinner together thing. I often find her up, in the middle of the night, the stove and oven cranking as she transcribes recipes from the internet onto index cards as if passed onto her from a doting grandmother. I've never had friends over to watch movies all night nor have I had a boyfriend.

To my knowledge, neither has she. Then again, there's Sandro.

That's Life *B*. As for Life *A*, in my parents' mansion in Newton, my companion was the nanny while Mum accompanied Caroline to ballet performances and dressage. Vicky was content to misbehave.

Dad was always on some business trip or other. I guess managing a popcorn empire is time-consuming. I hardly know my family at all.

Unable to help myself, and knowing the apartment will still be empty when I return, I step into the crowded pizza parlor. Employees call orders hurly-burly. They wear matching sauce-stained aprons. Dough sails in the air. Slices on thin, grease-soaked paper plates pass overhead, challenging gravity. I get in line and wait. The loop of hungry people, organized by a flimsy nylon cord, creeps forward to the sign that says *Place Orders Here*. I usually don't pinch things so close to home, but my stomach rumbles insistently. Judging by the chaos in the shop, after I get my slice, it'll be easy enough to walk off without getting in the *Drinks/Pay Here* line.

A cheese pie comes out of the oven, bubbly and golden. My mouth waters. Through the crowd, a single eyebrow, bordering familiar hazel eyes, lifts. My heart flutters. A group I vaguely recognize from Dartmont surrounds Julian. Three of them engage in a debate about the promise of a hockey player. Tegan, the empress of the mean girl crew, edges toward Julian. He edges toward me.

Under his gaze, I don't know what to say. *Like my new coat, it matches your hoodie. Even when I'm not thinking about you, I suddenly can't stop thinking about you.* I think I need to see a doctor—have my head and heart checked.

Before he sees me smile, a gruff pizza slinger asks to take his order. The line continues to snake forward and my stomach gurgles again. Maybe I've entered some kind of alternate world where I'm not a young thief, my twin isn't missing, and I live a normal life with friends and pizza nights and not so much fear. I replace the scratching image of Vicky sitting in a cold cell with her in front of a fire in a secluded cabin somewhere in the sticks.

## Two Truths and One Thief

Julian reappears holding two pieces of pizza in one hand and a skateboard in the other. My breath catches at the sight of my reflection in a map of Italy painted on a mirror. The girl wears a red wig. My jaw falls open. I forgot I was incognito.

"Got you a slice," he says, passing one to me. A cut slices his lip and his front tooth is chipped, missing the edge, but I know better than to ask questions.

He lifts the nylon cord so I can pass under it and then walks toward the door. I follow. With each step, I try to come up with a plausible excuse for my getup. *I'm an understudy in a play, totally normal to go in full costume. I'm trying a new look—thief. I'm completely lost and thought looking like someone else would bring me back to myself.*

It's relatively quiet on the street. The smells of cheese, turning leaves, and the city after sunset intermingles.

"What about your friends?" I ask.

He shrugs. "I'll catch up with them later. We came down here for a hockey thing."

"Won't they wonder where you went?"

"No worries. I'll text."

"How did you recognize me?" I tug at the wig.

He interrupts. "Can I ask a question?"

"You just did," I counter.

"Ha ha. When did you go red?"

I shake my head.

"Wig and..." I muster up a rare sort of courage, not because I'm embarrassed, but because I've recently learned that I'm not a good liar, at least when it comes to males with the last name Freese, but then I shrink. "You're better off not asking why."

"What are you hiding from?" His expression slides between teasing and seriousness.

The truth, the lies, the confusion. The question of where Vicky is. Who I am. My own fears. My shining brilliance. I tug the wig off and brush my fingers through my dark hair. I offer a smile.

"I like your regular hair. It reminds me of a horse I used to know."

I cock an eyebrow. I may have an extremely limited understanding of how flirting works, but I'm pretty sure being compared to a horse doesn't count as smooth. Then again, I'm no ace flirt.

"Her name was Felicity and when she ran, the wind blew her mane back like pure freedom." He rubs his forearm and exhales.

"Oh." I take a bite of pizza. "Do you ride horses?"

"When I was a kid with my sister."

"Does she go to Dartmont?" I ask.

"No." The word floats with the kind of finality that suggests his sister might be gone. My mind flashes to Vicky.

"I better go," I say.

"I'll walk you home or I can give you a ride back to Dartmont. Everyone else took a school van, but I rode down by myself."

"You don't have to."

"I want to," he answers.

## Chapter 11

Too soon, we're at my sister's door. Our pizza is gone. I fuss with the paper plate, nervously tearing little pieces of the edge into fringe. My mouth is dry.

"Thirsty?" I ask, not knowing if, along with sparkling water and coffee, I'll find the FBI upstairs in the kitchen.

"Yeah, actually," he answers.

Again, I'm acutely aware of Julian's presence as I take each step to the third floor—all thirty-nine, including the landings. Up until last year, Vicky lived in a posh building in Back Bay, left for several months, and then when she got back, she moved here. The other place must've been too high profile or something.

I pause outside the door, listening. The neighbor's television is a couple of decibels too high and cars toot outside. The floor creaks under our feet. My line of vision comes level with Julian's chest. His shoulders are square and strong. He has a nice nose, too, like a Renaissance sculptor formed it from marble and intended for there to be a scratch on the bridge. He hovers next to me like he might spring or bolt, or both. I slide my key in the lock, wondering if we'll explode like in the movies. Or maybe that's the sound of my pulse, tripping like a live wire.

The apartment is empty. Bird chirps when I flip on the light. I poke around, but everything is exactly where I left it. All at once, it's abundantly clear that I've brought a boy into Vicky's lair. But it's my home too—at least I thought so since I have a room here that's my own and not styled like a Parisian flat. Mum had her interior designer redo my suite in Newton without asking when I turned sixteen. She also threw out most of my stuff.

Tonight, being alone doesn't seem like the best idea. I stand frozen for a moment, shocked by how our footprints and not a magic carpet or a wish or a fairy godmother brought us both here, together. This is real. I part my lips to say so, but then remember we're thirsty.

I open the fridge. Take-out containers. Leftovers. Old orange juice. A bottle of flat sparkling water. Two bottles of something with neon writing. Must be Flavio's.

I open a new bottle of sparkling water and then move us through the kitchen and past the dining table, afraid to find traces of Vicky there. When we enter the living room, Bird squawks. I roll my eyes. The enormous television where, I realize, Flavio has watched almost every soccer game leading up to the World Cup, is dark, like one of Vicky's plots.

"Peck your eyes out," Bird caws. "Peck your eyes out."

Julian's head jerks toward the perch. "Did that bird—?"

I nod.

"Should I be worried? Is it like the doubly warped version of a dad on the porch with a shotgun?"

Is that what this is? But I laugh away my rosy cheeks. "No. The most my dad would do is throw popcorn at you. That's Birdy. I call him Bird. He's a cockatoo. Cuckoo-mah-roo-coo," I say, making a silly face at the made-up word.

"Peck your eyes out," Bird repeats, sidestepping along his perch.

"That's wacky."

"Vicky taught him to say, 'I'll peck your eyes out' to anyone that comes into the room." Bird repeats it.

Julian squishes his eyes and lips in an expression that I interpret as adorable even though he probably means that it's twisted.

"It makes for a good parlor trick and for scaring off guys."

I worry he's been scared away. Then he takes off his coat, sits down, and sips his water slowly. "So who's Vicky?" he asks in a way that invites me to tell him about her—not because he doesn't know who she is. Everyone at Dartmont has heard of her.

Bird calls loudly while I juxtapose the boy in the blue sweatshirt—with a tiny dimple in his chin, and lips that form words that charge something inside me that has only ever come alive from pages in fiction, actors on the screen, and glimpses snatched in crowded rooms—against my bizarre life.

Good question. Who is Vicky?

"I don't know," I whisper, but Bird is so loud Julian doesn't hear. "Unless you know some freaky bird wizardry, the only way to quiet him is to leave the room," I say more loudly. I don't mention Vicky is the one with the magic touch. I sprinkle some food in Bird's feeder. "She'll be back," I whisper. "I hope."

I lead the way through the apartment past all the electronics. Modern mixes with antique vases and giant woodcarvings that are probably from Brazil. Question marks fill the vacant spaces on the walls, along the floor, and in front of what I thought I knew about my sister.

Julian's phone vibrates and he pauses to check it outside the linen closet door. I lean against the wall, letting the cool plaster support me. My gaze catches on the old box on top of Vicky's dresser across the hall. It was the only thing she was allowed to take when our parents disinherited her.

What else don't I know about my twin? It suddenly feels like I hardly know her, like she's slipping away, and if I reach out to grab for her, I'll lose my footing. But isn't that what we do for family? Risk everything for the bonds of love? And if not, what else do we risk for? If I fall, is there someone there to reach for me, to love me? She's the only person who understands me.

I want to scour the apartment for clues, to find out where she is. Should I be breaking her out of jail or stealing her away in the night, so we can hide out together? Scrounging up some cash to pay her bail.

How does that work? Is there a one-eight-hundred hotline to call? Does Vicky have a get-out-of-jail-free card hiding somewhere? Am I supposed to waltz into the police station, slap a stack of cash down, and demand her release? Should I search for the address of her hidden location? How do I come to her rescue?

These questions bump up against me as I grope in the dark for the plug to the twinkle lights that line the ceiling of my room like stars. When they blink on, my only thought is about the boy framed in the doorway, with a bottle of water held lazily in his hand, and a reckless grin on his lips.

## Chapter 12

I QUICKLY FLIP THE CHARCOAL GRAY SHEETS AND BLANKET ON MY BED over the pillows and sit on the edge. Here, I don't have to make my bed. In Newton, Mum does a daily ten-point inspection. If anyone were to come in here, they'd see evidence of what I've been doing for the last handful of years.

"You have a lot of stuff," Julian says.

Understatement. Guilt brings the water to my lips for a sip. I glance around. In all this junk, how can there not be a chair? Note to self, for future entertaining purposes be sure to procure seating options. I'll also have to do some rearranging or get a dumpster. There's hardly a path to walk.

If the rest of our apartment is a curated example of modern meets luxury, my room is a hodgepodge. Scattered everywhere are books, clothes, piano music, accessories, scarves, disguises, embarrassingly Legos—one of the most difficult things to steal because of the noise they make as they shift in the box, some of my prized lifts—and my collection of old iron keys mounted in a frame. Julian touches one and then picks up a notebook with the makings of a playlist.

"Angry, angsty music. Did someone tick you off or break your heart?" He sounds offended on my behalf.

"Neither," I answer quickly.

For that, I would once have had to been in love. Just then, the place in the middle of my chest buoys and sinks. I look at Julian to make sure he's real. I stand up, to get closer, to examine the almost invisible hairs that thread his jawline, to survey his knuckles and cuticles, to have another look at the curve of his lips. But the fact that Vicky may be gone, for a long time, pushes me back onto my bed.

He flips the page. "Ah, here's a good one. 'Hey Jude.' This has always been my favorite Beatles tune." He taps on his phone.

The opening lines by Paul McCartney followed by piano notes sound through the speakers. I jump up, knowing why Vicky can't listen to it. It brings me too deeply into myself. Julian repeating Flavio's message is too much of a reminder.

"No, not that one," I say.

He silences the song.

I don't know where to go. Now that we're both standing, the bed is too obvious.

He scratches his head as if trying to make sense of me. "So you have a lot of stuff. You like good music, hate poetry. What else should I know about you, Penny Goldfeather?" Gaze fixed on me, his eyelids louver a tad like he's sleepy.

The elephant, composed of bras and underwear nearly taken from his mother's store, and hundreds of things and clothes and stuff strewn around my room, lumber between us, trumpeting the absence of friends and experiences that I've tried to replace with the buzz of the boost.

I want away from the size of the shame. "Do you mind if I change?" I ask, gathering up a pair of skinny jeans and a black sweater.

He bites his lip. Does he think I mean in here? Oh, dear. Inhale. Exhale. I'm suddenly flushed from being seventeen in a room with a gorgeous boy.

"Should I—?" He points toward the door.

"No, I'll..." I dash out, leaving him in my room, alone with all the things that scream so loudly at me. Journals, books, music, magazines, thiefy-stuff. I'm quick as I swap out clothes.

When I return, Julian skims through a thick book on renaissance art, dangerously near a collection of books I've made out of other books and found objects, using scissors and glue. When opened, the pages form words, accordion style. *Dream. Love. Laugh.* They're like bucket list items, things to do before I die.

"So you like art and poetry. What would I find in your bedroom?" I ask, startling him.

"I do like poetry. I'm such a dweeb." His eyes crinkle with laughter.

"Maybe I like that you like things I don't," I reply. The coquettishness nearly knocks me to my butt along with a clutch of shoes and boots I stumble over. I mentally imagine Caroline giving me a high five and then shaking her head at my lack of grace despite years of ballet classes Mum insisted I take.

Julian smirks. "You asked about my room? It's pretty sparse. I took off once. When I came back, my room was empty. Like I never existed. Now I only have a mattress, blankets, some books, ink and paper. As for my room at Dartmont, pretty much the same except for a huge poster of Boston."

His words are like an invitation to tell him more about myself, but I'm afraid that if I do, whatever atomic explosion is happening between us will fizzle.

"What do you do when you're not skipping school?" he asks.

"Steal," I say, but my smile suggests I'm joking. "Rob, cheat."

He squints as though he's deciding if I'm kidding and then swallows his laughter.

"You?"

"I'll show you." He unzips his backpack and a tattered copy of Romeo and Juliet falls out. "Have you been reading?" he asks.

"Not on weekends."

He laughs. "Honig just wants us to highlight the poetic passages. It's not an in-depth study or anything."

I grimace.

"As I said, I enjoy poetry." He reads a few lines about the depths of love from the first act before interrupting himself and saying, "My mother's maiden name is Montague like from Romeo and Juliet. Funny, huh."

I stiffen. *Regina Montague.* Conniving and vicious.

"The other day, while she was lecturing me about college applications, she asked me if I knew anyone with the last name Capulet. I think she's over-caffeinated." He trades the book for a notebook from his bag. "I draw sometimes," he says, showing me a sketch of a graffitied city wall. "I dabble in crime too." His reckless smirk suggests he's not joking.

This time I laugh. "Lawbreakers and cheaters."

"That's us."

As much as I like the sound of *us*, the only pair I've ever been a part of is with my twin. I take a deck of cards from the shelf and shuffle them to occupy my shaky hands. "Want to play a game?" I ask. "It's called Liars & Thieves."

"Sure."

I explain the rules. "Lying and cheating are encouraged... Aces win... Twos are wild..." It takes him a couple of rounds to get the gist, but soon we're betting pennies.

I take a long drink from my water, emptying it as one song ends and another begins, and I win the round.

"I should probably go." At that, his cell phone chimes in his pocket. He glances at it.

"Yup, Scout and Russ are wondering where I am."

"Big night?" I ask.

"Maybe. Skate. Probably over at Eggs. Some stuff to do later." He shrugs. "Nothing much."

"Don't fall in the river."

He walks with what I want to believe is reluctance toward my bedroom door and then grabs his jacket from the living room.

Bird whistles.

"Thanks for sparing my eyes," Julian says. At the front door, he stops. "Hey, you want to come with me? I can give you a ride back to Dartmont afterward."

My cheeks puff with a breath because I hadn't thought about

making sure I'm not marked out of the dorm in thirty minutes and type a quick message to Howard.

I begin to shake my head, but the vacuum of the empty apartment pushes against me. "You don't mind?"

"Heck no. You'll probably liven things up." He adjusts his jacket, but I catch the irrepressible grin that lights up his face.

## Chapter 13

BEFORE WE BREAK INTO THE NIGHT, JULIAN SENDS A TEXT AND THEN receives one, almost instantly. "They're at Bradley's place."

"Should I know him?" I ask.

"He's in English with us."

I ought to become more familiar with this newfound land of Friday nights, English classes, and friends—I might like being a resident.

"Brad is about my height. Wears a black and yellow Boston Bruins hat like he's on the team. Without fail, Honig insists he removes it every day when he walks into class. Front tooth chipped." He taps his finger against his own chipped tooth. "He'll tell you it was a puck." He drops his glance toward his knuckles. "I have the scar to prove it wasn't."

"Do you play hockey?" I ask, hungry to know more about him.

"Yep. The only reason my parents can afford to send me to Dartmont is the scholarship. But he's the hockey player super fan with aspirations to go all the way. A decent guy and one of my best friends."

If I had a best friend, I don't think she'd have a chipped tooth because of me, but I worry she might be missing other things because of my habit—a pair of jeans, a book or two, some jewelry. Guilt grips me from within.

The streetlights in the North End bathe us in flickering peaches and cream. It's so utterly extraordinary that I'm out here, right now, not scheming or scouting. Just being with Julian.

"What do you usually do on Friday nights?" he asks.

"You don't want to know."

"If Bird has anything to do with it, you're probably right," he says because there is nothing else to say to my cryptic response. My life has been so shady.

We talk about school—he missed part of sophomore year when he took off, but he doesn't seem like the kind of person that gets left behind.

"I can relate."

"I can help you with homework and catching up if you want," Julian offers. "If you need it, I mean."

"Yeah, thanks." Despite my checkered hobby slash occupation, if I can master three languages, decipher codes, and handle complicated building plans, twelfth-year prep school shouldn't be impossible. But I wouldn't object to sitting next to Julian in a narrow library carrel.

We pass the Clothing Cloud, but he doesn't acknowledge it. "What kept you away sophomore year?" I ask.

"What's kept you away more recently?" After my vacant pause, he answers my original question. "Tragedy. Your turn."

We dodge the stream of cars as we cross to the other side of the street.

"Leniency and a fellow student who knows how to keep me from being flagged in the attendance software," I say, offering a vague explanation for my own absence with Vicky in mind.

We pass the pizza place from earlier and then head up Salem Street. I know the cobblestones, flickering neon signs, and cafes because this is home, but walking beside Julian, I may as well be on another planet.

When we reach a brick building, nearly identical to all the others, he presses a buzzer. On the second floor, a riot of laughter blends with music and blasts us out of the relatively quiet walk we had. There's cheering at Julian's arrival, along with questions about where he was.

He leans toward me and our shoulders touch. "Hey, everyone, you know Penny, right?"

They don't, except Tegan and Jordyn who sit on a couch by the window. The pair acknowledge me with matching glares.

There are boisterous hellos and then the guy who must be Bradley launches out of his seat, sending a geyser of liquid from his cup. He clamps his hand on top of his hat and points with his other hand at the game on the muted TV. "Did you see that goal?" he calls triumphantly as the winning team takes another point.

Mostly everyone ignores this as if it's a common occurrence. Julian nudges me with his shoulder and we go to the kitchen. He pulls open the fridge and hands me a soda.

"Cheers," he says, tapping his can against mine. His eyes twinkle.

The kitchen cabinets are dark laminate wood with gold handles that remind me of polished pyrite. Worn floral wallpaper hosts framed photos of Bradley and two other boys from birth to the present. Hockey gear features prominently along with a mother and father who look like they've aged, in synchronicity, with this apartment.

"Brad's parents?" I ask.

"They're out of town. Wedding or something. His older brother is housesitting. His older-older brother is in college studying theology. The non-clubhouse boy segment of the Dartmont student body, aka the Boston locals, take any opportunity to get away, even if it means hanging out in what may as well be someone's basement."

"I know the feeling. Mostly." In the proximity of normal teenagers, I'm not sure what to say or do. It's been easy to talk with Julian when it's just the two of us or we're at school and there are obvious topics, but my confidence siphons from me in this social situation with my so-called peers. Caroline makes socializing seem effortless. Vicky made it easy for me to blend in.

"Do your parents care where you are?" I instantly wish I hadn't asked because even though Caroline follows the rules to the *T*—until senior year—like myself, I don't think Julian does.

"Do yours?" he asks.

Still dumbstruck by my inability to answer that question, I don't speak so he does. "My dad remembers being a teenager. He has some good stories. Ball and brawls in the streets, peace, love, and anarchy. All that. He tells me Boston was different back then, a concrete jungle. He's lived in our place his whole life—his parents left it to him. I guess after he met my mother, he straightened out." Julian shrugs. "And I'm pretty sure she was never not fifty-something."

I almost snort soda through my nose and he joins me, our laughter leading the way back into easy conversation. After minutes that I've lost track of, we move into the living room. Bradley is in deep debate about a player and penalties with a guy named Russ.

Julian and I slouch onto a couch with wooden armrests. Scout gives me a wave and introduces himself so I don't confuse him with Russ or Bradley, before sweeping Julian into a conversation about tattoos.

From the group of Julian's friends, I expected more homogony—like in movies. However, each of them seems handpicked from the various subsets at Dartmont to be as different as possible: jock, hipster, and nerd. And then there's Julian who's a combination of all of them sprinkled with skater, romantic—as evidenced by the poetry— a music fan, tough, and totally dreamy. I practically throw up fluffy clouds and rainbows in my mouth. I must've woken up the other morning, downed a bottle of hormones, and not realized it.

When I spot Tegan and Jordyn sitting diagonally across from us in a matching pair of worn recliners, the word *friend* becomes subjective. I do my best to ignore how they confer in a whisper, gazes darting in my direction.

If I had hackles, they'd lift. Where is Vicky or Caroline when I need them?

## Chapter 14

I don't spare Tegan and Jordyn eye contact, but can't ignore them when Tegan, twirling a piece of her hair, says, "So, what made you decide you were finally cool enough for school?" Jordyn asks.

Cool? I shrug off the question.

"Why are you here?" Tegan asks, getting to the point.

I reflexively glance toward Julian. He and Scout debate color tattoos versus traditional ones.

Tegan and Jordyn exchange a look. I will my cheeks not to flush. Inhale. Exhale. I may look like I have RBF, but I rarely make the effort to act like one. Their cattiness confounds me. I didn't receive a guidebook for how to communicate with people like them. This is the kind of jungle territory where I need a guide. Caroline knows how to navigate it but she's traveling with George during the gap year she convinced my parents she needed.

This wouldn't bother Vicky. Then again, the same rules don't apply to her. For once, envy creeps in at how she has it easier simply by not caring. She can get away with anything...probably even murder.

"Wait, you're Caroline Goldfeather's little sister, right?" Tegan asks.

Ah, there she is. Well, not literally, but I've always been in her shadow too.

"Yep."

"And you have a twin. Which one are you?" She asks even though it's obvious she knows.

"Vicky is the infamous Goldfeather sister. I'm the lesser-known accomplice." My delivery is flat.

This situation could go one of two ways. I know this because it's happened before. My relationship to THE Caroline Goldfeather could give me clout, social currency, and these girls will suddenly want to be my BFFs. Or they're jealous haters and will use me to get out all the angst that they can't direct at the queen bee.

Before I find out, Julian casts me a life ring as if he sees the ship going down and nudges my boot with his then tips his head toward the kitchen. Scout doesn't break flow with something about glow-in-the-dark ink and pigments as Julian gets to his feet. Scout rambles on.

The couch suddenly feels extra empty and decidedly shabby as I start to get up. Jordyn and Tegan's expressions bear identical degrees of venom. Not that I want to be friends, but even with my limited experience, I know their line of questioning and body language is more *mean girls* and less *let's go to the mall together and swap fashion tips*.

"They're talking tats?" Jordyn says. "Tegan, show her yours."

To Tegan's credit, she looks reluctant. Vicky's back is a giant canvas with a stunning rendition of a golden heart surrounded by fire and roses, guaranteeing nothing on Tegan's body will impress me.

Jordyn practically shoves Tegan off the chair and pulls the waistline of her skirt down a few inches. "See, a heart," she says with a simpering smile.

A heart, the size of a nickel stains her low back, toward her left hip. Tegan's grin matches Jordyn's when she takes her seat again. Her eyes flutter toward the kitchen. Julian is as oblivious to this exchange as I wish I were.

"Get it?" Jordyn says.

The word *insufferable* comes to mind. Yeah, I get that Tegan tries to stake her claim on Julian.

A burlier version of Bradley appears with a jarring laugh. He lands partially on top of Jordyn, absorbing her lips into his. It's sloppy and in my face, but it stops the potential for a catfight or whatever girls do when the hostility is turned up.

Tegan adjourns, leaving me with a full-screen, high-definition nature program. "Teens in the Wild." I finish my soda, so far out of my own habitat that I freeze. What would Caroline do? Never mind. What would Vicky do?

Jordyn surfaces and asks, "What are you looking at?"

Big-Bradley whispers something like, "Jordyn, play nice."

I don't want to play. I finally get up to find Julian. Scout appears and gives me a nod. "Hey."

"Hey," I repeat.

"Cool to see you around. Sorry I bombarded him like that. I'm on Jules duty tonight."

The question about what that means isn't even out of my mouth before he goes on. "Jules is Julian. He's usually pretty good on weeknights especially when he's at school, but on the weekends, when he can sleep in, we have to watch out. He gets pretty rowdy." Scout shrugs like there's nothing to be done about it except be on guard.

When I don't reply, Scout goes on, "Sorry, you have no idea what I'm talking about do you?"

I shake my head.

"It's like you flipped him on."

Finding my voice, I replace my *hey* with a, "Huh?"

"It's like you plugged him in," Scout says, in awe.

"I don't follow."

"Julian is usually kind of reckless. On a typical Friday night, we'd already be on the roof, creating a human barrier around the edge so he doesn't go flying off doing tricks on his board or keeping him from burning the building down with fireworks he bought on his way back from New Hampshire. We try to keep him from himself and from wherever he goes when he's not with us."

I can't entirely match the description with the guy I've gotten to know the last few days. I thought it was only his smile that suggested daring. I'm the reckless one in the pair, or so I thought.

"Seriously, Penny, he's shirty."

I must look like I'm missing a corner piece or don't speak Scout's lingo.

"Irritable, always in a bad mood, a ticked off kind of attitude. But it doesn't stop there. He's legit." He gives me a crooked look, possibly suggesting I should know all of this since we arrived at Bradley's party together. "Things have sucked for him. His sister, then Tegan cheated on him during that, uh, there are a few other things, too. Let's just say Julian Freese enjoys misbehaving."

This comes as a surprise because he's the one who got me on track when his parents found *me* misbehaving.

Scout adds, "But you're like this sudden ray of light. Cheesy, I know. But it's true."

His expression transforms into a boyish smile and he introduces a new arrival—she has cropped, faded blue hair and wears eyeglasses. "Jaqueline, this is Penny. Penny has been hanging out with Julian."

She smiles like she already knows this and the two of them disappear into the kitchen.

Glancing around, nearly everyone is paired off and locking lips. My fairy godmother didn't tell me that when the clock strikes twelve everyone turns into spit swappers. There's Jordyn and Big Bradley still on the chair. Russ and a girl I recognize from math are together in the corner. The hallway wall holds up Scout and Jaqueline as they smooch. Then I spot the back of Julian's head with Tegan's hands clasped around his neck. She tugs on the neckline of his shirt then brushes her painted nail down his arm. With an impish grin over his shoulder, she flicks her tongue and licks from his jawline up the side of his cheek. Staring directly at me, she mouths the words, *I licked him, he's mine.*

First of all, ew. Do people do that? Then something cold and unyielding rises up within me. It's as though waves crash against rocks, sending parts of me scattering into the sea. The can in my hand falls to the floor, but the rushing in my ears drowns out the clatter the aluminum makes on the linoleum.

I don't belong here.

Making a quick exit, I head toward Fleet Street. Outside of bars, crowds gather in clusters. Couples lean in close. Smoke forms broken halos above their heads.

I'm an outsider. Light drizzle moistens my face as I pass a café with a signboard advertising poetry night. The chalk-written words drool toward a puddle below. I don't want to think about Julian. Cabs creep by, their headlights glistening on the pavement. Over the city night noises, I hear my name.

My thoughts cram with being left behind by someone I care about...again. This time, I follow Vicky's lead and run.

Polyurethane wheels roll over the cracks in the sidewalk at my back. Julian calls, catching up to me on a skateboard. "Wait, Penny, please."

I pause in front of a barbershop, shuttered for the night. An old television casts patches of light on the sidewalk between us. The muted news shows a Swedish scientific discovery demonstrating something about light particles and prisms. There's a Ferris wheel-sized kaleidoscope.

I whip around. "Actions speak louder than words. More plainly than waits and pleases and excuses. They're clearer than all the poetry in the world, Julian." We both step back in shock at my ferocity. Maybe my words are meant for someone else's ears or at least a few select phrases. But she's not here to hear me. Embarrassment, liquid and rushing, fills the fjord of my awareness.

"What happened?" he asks, dumbfounded and catching his breath.

"You did," I respond. I can't help myself. "You should have told me you had a girlfriend or whatever Tegan is."

In the glow of the street lamp, his face crumbles. Apparently, I'm not the only one that has weathered a storm or two. "That? With Tegan?"

I cross my arms in front of my chest.

"She—" He closes his eyes. "She's lonely or bored or I don't know. I imagine she saw us together tonight and—she and I were together sophomore year. Junior year she didn't give me the time of day, but now suddenly this year she wants me back—has this needy possession over me, like I belong to her. I don't. It doesn't matter. That was all before, during sophomore year. Before life got messed up and meaningful." He shrugs and gazes from his shoes to me when he speaks that last word.

I don't budge.

Julian tries again. "In the kitchen, Tegan came up to me and was saying stuff about us. Then she put her arms around my neck and asked if I wanted to go to Bradley's room. She licked me." He makes a face of annoyance mixed with disgust. "I removed her arms, politely said, 'No, thank you,' heard the door slam, assumed it was you, and here I am."

His honest eyes lasso me and say more than the play-by-play account of what happened. The rushing in my ears goes quiet and all I hear is the beating of my heart.

He's here, not there.

The words come out before I can stop them. "I'm seventeen. I've never kissed a boy. Having you in my room, then asking me to hang out, all mean something to me. The way you—" I'm about to list the connections sparking between us, but standing on the street, lost amid all this stuff, overwhelms me.

Julian takes my face gently in his hands and looks from my eyes to my mouth and back again. He doesn't need to ask. His lips land on mine. Soft. Smooth. Almost hungry. If flower petals had more substance or if I could eat stars, that's what this would feel like.

He lingers a moment longer, then straightens. The corners of his mouth lift slightly, uncertainly.

"Why did you do that?" I ask.

His face goes slack, but then he looks beyond my shyness and guilt, my loneliness and hopelessness, staring straight into the wild and big-hearted, adventurous, and bold, the beautiful and honest parts of me. With confidence, he says, "I wanted to be your first kiss, Penny."

I close my eyes, his lips imprinted on mine. When I open them an image on the TV behind Julian flashes a mug shot of a familiar face.

*No. No. No.*

## Chapter 15

My heart presses into my throat and the rest of me is jelly. I want to collapse. I want to flee. I want that giant Swedish light machine to shoot me into outer space. There is no sound through the glass. My eyes are wet and blurry making it impossible to read the newscaster's lips. Then it's the weather report. I cover my eyes. A pair of firm hands wrap around me.

I sink into Julian's arms, trusting he's going to keep hold of me. I remain there, in his embrace as the white noise of the city carries on, unperturbed in the background while my inner world crumbles.

My sniffles slow and my breath comes back.

"Was that your twin?" Julian asks.

I nod and then step back, finding my footing again. My thoughts are a rush of more questions.

"Do you want to go home?" he asks gently.

I shake my head. I don't know what I want to do other than fly into my sister's arms and break her out of jail. But I can't.

He looks down the street toward the neon sign of a diner glowing through the nighttime autumnal gloom. "Want to get some pie?" He says *pie* like the idea is ludicrous, but also a worthy solution nonetheless.

He rubs his hands together on this chilly night. Cuts peppering his knuckles suggest he recently made enemies with a brick wall. He sweeps up his skateboard in one hand and takes mine with the other. His grip is warm.

The diner is brightly lit but relatively quiet. A lone slice of lemon meringue rotates on a plate in the case. We split it. I'm not comfortable talking about Vicky here, but glance over my shoulder at the screen behind me mounted on the wall. It's showing a rerun of *Friends*.

"I'll tell you if the news comes on—" Julian says. Maybe I'm irritating him with my timed twitches to see if there's a breaking news report, but I hope his reassurance is so he can see more of my face.

The meringue melts on my tongue, keeping my words locked inside. In my silence, Julian does an online search for Victoria Goldfeather but doesn't come up with anything related to an arrest. I hold onto hope that there was a mistake. That I imagined it. Am dreaming.

After we devour the pie, he asks, "Do you skate?"

"I've never tried," I reply.

"It always helps me clear my head." The ongoing sadness hidden behind the sparkle in his eyes lessens. "You're clever, seem nimble enough…"

"Nimble? I'm not sure that's a word in the flirting-with-girls dictionary." I turn almost as red as the vinyl booth. "I didn't mean to say that aloud."

Julian chuckles warmly. "There's a thesaurus companion to that dictionary. Agile? Sprightly? Swift?"

"Dork," I say despite myself.

"Aw, I'm hurt," he says, gripping his chest. "Did you mean to say that aloud too?"

Thankfully, my cheeks are quick to return to normal.

"C'mon, skating will be fun," he says.

I hedge, but it's the middle of the night. I won't be able to find much out about Vicky right now. Delaying reintegrating with reality seems like a better use of time than returning to the apartment and crying, scheming, or any of the other helpless things I might do until I know more. Tonight, I steal time.

We walk to a nearby park. The telltale clicking of wheels echoes off cement as other skaters cruise smoothly on their boards. Under the bruised night sky, the cables for the Zakim Bridge are like an illuminated spider's web. I glance at Julian, favored by its glow. His smile lights up the night.

As if he simply can't resist, he tosses his board beneath his feet and jettisons himself down the sidewalk. He slides along a rail, glides around, and then launches the board along a low wall, grinding metal against granite. I spin in a circle watching him loop around me.

His breath chases him when he says, "Your turn. C'mon, you'll love it."

"I'm warning you, if I like it, there could be trouble." We're facing each other, as close as when he kissed me.

"I'll take that risk," he says, angling the board toward my feet. He takes my hands. I didn't know human beings carried an electrical current. His touch stuns.

Somehow, I find the coordination to place one foot onto the skateboard's deck. The ground and earth aren't at all stable. We've merely tricked ourselves into believing it is by wearing shoes instead of wheels. I pick up my other foot. Julian lets go of one of my hands and then holds me by the waist. I lean into him, imagining what it would be like to float, to let go of gravity and whatever else holds me to the planet and drift, unburdened, free. Then there's movement. I didn't calculate that part.

"Soft knees. Eyes where you want to go. Are you comfortable?" His voice is soft and gentle.

I nod because now, I instantly want to zip, slide, and grind like him and the carnival of other guys, moving in and out of the shadows. It feels like a dare.

Julian's fingers hold me loosely as I push off with my foot, heading toward the grass. I manage to lean and curve away before the board scoots out from under me. Thankfully, he was right. I am nimble because I don't fall—only flail a little.

Julian grabs the board and I try again. Then again. By the fourth try, he's a few steps behind me and hoots into the night as I glide. I skate past the large cement egg sculptures, lending the park its name. The Charles River glitters to my right, the bridge, spanning the river, at my back.

Julian catches up to me when I decide I don't want to go for a swim and jump off the skateboard, scooping it up before it rolls into the water.

"You've never done that before?" he asks.

"Never."

"You're a natural. Let me impress you with some tricks so I don't feel like the countless hours of my life I've spent practicing are a waste." He laughs with his mouth open like he might also swallow some of the stars that pierce the sky. "Ollie, pretty basic, pop-shove, kick-flip," he says, listing tricks as he demonstrates.

I watch and my instinct is to study the geometry and velocity of his movements, but instead, I catch on the intensity of his brow and the grin on his face. The result is a boundless smile on my lips. He runs into a grind along the low wall and I remind myself to breathe when he clickety-clacks back in my direction.

He reaches for my hands and spins around me. "Want another turn?"

The tension between us is tighter than the cables lit up on the bridge.

"I'll just watch," I say, dizzy.

"You don't mind?"

I don't, not a bit.

Julian rushes into the midst of the skaters and they move as if doing a choreographed dance until sirens break up the outdoor party.

He rolls up to me, his eyes urgent. "No Skateboarding," he says, pointing at a sign before taking my hand. We race away from the park and toward the street. The old, vacant brick jailhouse blurs by me with flashes of Vicky behind bars. We stop at the entrance to the train station. We're both sweating and our breath puffs in cold clouds, reminding us that we are indeed free.

But my twin sister is not.

## Chapter 16

BACK IN THE NORTH END, IT'S NEARLY DAWN. I TAKE JULIAN'S HAND and lead him up the three flights of stairs to the apartment. I don't ask if he wants to come up. I need him to. Alone, there are too many maze-like holes for my mind to wander down. Where is my sister? What happened? What do I do?

When we cross the threshold, the neon glow of the clock reminds me what day it is.

"It's our birthday," I whisper, realizing in that exact moment as if I was born anew.

"Happy Birthday."

Before I can say something like *thanks*, his lips are on mine. We kiss again. This time, it's a full-body experience. I'm kissing him with my toes and elbows, with my eyes and lips, with all of me.

Bird chirps.

Once more, I catch my breath. I slouch out of my jacket, not sure where to look or put my hands, and thunderstruck with one bold question. Why haven't I done this before? I'm late to this kissing, hot-wired, passion thing. I toss my bag on the table and smooth my hair. Vicky's notebook, among other thieve-y things, reminds me exactly why this is a first.

I've been busy trying to rebel, doing the only thing that someone who has been given everything except attention can do. Steal things I could easily buy on my parents' credit cards.

Imagining I should show hospitality with Julian standing there, leaning against the counter like some kind of skater stud, I've got nothing. I've gone moony. I put my hands over my face. I didn't ask for or expect this lit-up, on-fire, hormone infusion. I peer at him through my fingers. Despite whatever this crazy cocktail is, I want more.

His amused smirk tells me he sees what I can't say. The learning curve of love and romance proves steep.

The kettle boils and I pour us both a cup of chamomile tea. Julian peels my fingers from a box of noodles as I fret about cooking.

"Despite what you see here, I grew up with a personal chef, so, uh, I hardly know how to boil water, never mind fix a meal."

"That's okay. I don't have a habit of eating noodles for breakfast."

"Oh, right."

His expression confirms that he did us both a favor and spared a kitchen disaster. He walks me toward the living room. Bird squawks and I deliver him some fruit, then Julian detours us into the quiet of my bedroom.

I'm suddenly hot and it's not only because of the tea. Julian hangs his jacket on the doorknob and kicks off his sneakers. He's wearing green and white striped socks. I'm nearly out of socks, but do have new underwear—the museum and my "Shopping" trip seem like a lifetime ago.

"So," Julian says when the clutter in my room becomes louder than the silence between us.

"So—" I repeat, insisting that my lungs draw a deep breath. "Scout said you're shirty."

Amusement crinkles his face. "Did he?"

"He had to explain what that meant. Do I need to worry about you?"

Julian steps closer. I am not immune to his swagger. A craving pulses through me. I contract and expand with each breath.

"Do you want to worry about me?" His eyes pour into mine. Forget being reckless, he's a master flirt. That's all there is to it. He knows how to find my melting point.

Vicky's ceramic mug from the other day still sits on top of my dresser. I bet I'd find tea leaves dried in the bottom. I wonder if they hold the answer to Julian's question.

His fingers reach for mine. "I worry about you. That news report that we saw..." He trails off, leaving me to fill in the blank.

Explanations and admissions prick my tongue, but there's nothing I can say without spilling secrets. I'm like dusk and dawn at the same time—smitten with this boy, here in my room. I'm also devastated by the whereabouts of my sister and the sudden awareness I have about how little I really know about her. A tender irritation, like a blister, forms between reality and what I thought I knew.

"I get the sense you don't want to talk about it, but if you change your mind, I'm here." His eye contact tells me he doesn't want to pry but wouldn't be averse to hearing more.

All I know is there is no protocol for getting her back. I'm stuck. Helpless but not alone.

I untie my sneakers and toss them on the floor. I lay on my bed, abandoning my tea, hoping the mattress can absorb the weight of tension and confusion making it so I can no longer hold up my head.

Julian plops down next to me on his back. We both face the ceiling. If the twinkle lights were stars, we'd be gazing up at them, and I'd make a wish.

## Chapter 17

WE'RE BOTH QUIET FOR SO LONG THAT I THINK HE FELL ASLEEP UNTIL he says, "I know that something just happened in your life. I make it a rule not to be judgy. It's an unattractive trait."

"Are you in the market of being attractive?" I ask, unable to help myself.

"Naturally." He tilts his head toward me and winks. He goes on as if testing whether a girl, once sedimentary and now igneous, possibly returning to magma—I've full-on melted—can carry on a conversation, never mind create a clear thought. I wonder if geology can work backward. Time reversed. Maybe then I'd know more about my twin and by extension, myself. Because the big question I'm afraid to let myself think is if she and I are on this road together and the result is jail...

I'm afraid of what the strata will reveal.

"I don't know if you need my help or not, but if you do..." Julian offers gently, turning to me.

My expression must halt him. I don't know what I need. But I hang onto his offer. Forget science, this is something else entirely. Give. Take. I reach for his hand. Our fingers lace easily.

"Vicky would kill me right now." Again, I've spoken my thoughts aloud.

"For holding hands?" He lets go and a pillow mashes into my chest. "Would she disapprove of this?"

"Hey!" I whack him back and we playfully fight over the pillow.

He calls to no one in particular, "Nothing to see here. Just two people innocently having a pillow fight."

We both laugh as we wrestle until he gives up, landing me partially on him, the pillow a cushion between us.

"I'm slowly realizing that instead of parents who cared, I turned to my twin. Follow her rules which are," I clear my throat, "interesting, now that I think about it."

"Should I run? Between Vicky and the bird, now you like a ninja with these pillows..." Julian's laughter is light like feathers.

I am a ninja, black belt, but I don't answer. I'm kneeling on my bed, and he's looking up at me. The tips of my long hair create a secret garden as I lean down. His forehead is smooth, except for fine scars long since healed. He'll need to shave in the morning. Flecks of gold rim his hazel eyes.

"Should you run? Vicky can't do anything because she's in jail." I'm not going to lie, I feel a little freer than usual.

Julian is silent. I lean back onto his bent knees, using them to support me, while he wriggles out of his sweatshirt. His T-shirt lifts in the process, revealing a hint of his waist and ink, lots of ink. Lining his arms are black and white, and colorful tattoos. There is a sailor and a roiling sea. A horse at a gallop, a heart, and a sun. The sleeves of tattoos almost reach his wrists. It's like he's tried to erase or redraw himself.

He smirks as I stare.

I run my finger along a cresting wave emblazoned on his arm.

"How old are you?" I blurt, pretty sure you have to be eighteen to get a tattoo and pretty sure Regina would frown upon so many of them. She seems like the chronically frowning type.

He folds his hands under his head. His shirt hikes up again, exposing the hem of tattoos on his belly. "I turned eighteen last month."

"You've been busy."

"My rebellion started early."

A question pogos in my mind. Is he hanging out with me to rebel against his mother? I cringe at the thought of him overhearing Regina and Phil discussing my actions.

"My mother doesn't tolerate much of anything: swears, untucked shirts, forgetting to say please, video games, skateboarding, girlfriends, ink. There's no margin for impunity with her."

"And your father?"

"He's a very patient and forgiving man."

"So are you, like, a living dare? Because it seems like you're succeeding at breaking her rules." My eyelids do a batting, flirting thing of their own accord.

Caroline would be proud.

"No, you're...an adventure." At that, our eyes lock. Neither one of us looks away.

I whisper, "I don't want to be a novelty, something for you to brag about to your friends or an answer to one-up your tattooed teen rebellion."

His laughter bounces right into me, practically knocking me over with a feeling I've never felt before. I don't know what to call it other than splendid. But my life just got too serious for me to flirt with disaster. Tucked right behind my teeth is my confession. I could tell him everything, right now, starting with how I steal, a lot. How his parents caught me. How entangled I am in Vicky's world. But the risk of him running or shunning me is too great. This time, I steal the truth.

Julian takes my hand, rubbing the back of it with his thumb. "I promise you'll never be a novelty, a passing fancy—or an act of civil disobedience."

I already am. Everything that came before and after Vicky instructing me to walk into the supermarket, pick my favorite kind of candy, and walk out with it lands in my mind.

I curl up next to Julian, tucking my knees between us. "Promises are dangerous."

His lips pucker like those weren't the words he wanted to hear. He rolls onto his side to face me. One long, bare arm, adorned with a wild mustang spans the space between us, resting on my waist. He pulls me closer. "Let's be honest with each other. You can tell me anything."

I want him to be able to trust me, but I don't trust myself. Not with the truth and not with keeping my hands off things that don't belong to me. Not underwear, not shaving cream, and not him. I examine the horse on Julian's arm. It's wild and unfettered. Right now feels too much like freedom for me to ruin it with honesty.

Sadness creases the place between Julian's eyes as he looks at the tattoo. "I had a sister. She was disabled. I mean, abled in so many ways, but she had a problem with her heart. I guess it was related to the extra chromosome she was born with—a genetic condition." He clears his throat. "I was eight when she came along. I remember being so excited when my parents brought the baby home. I thought I was going to feed her and play with her, give her rides on my bike. Well, she wasn't what I expected, what any of us expected. But as I got older, I realized she was so much more. They gave her a few years to live. Then she gave us a few more. Horseback riding was part of her therapy. She loved it. I loved her. She was the best. When she was seven, she started to regress. Then it all happened fast. Lost her during sophomore year."

I rest my head on Julian's chest as hooves gallop across his heart. "I'm sorry," I whisper.

His eyes water.

"It was hard. It sucked. Wicked bad. I miss her every day. But I'm able to look at how lucky I was to have the time with her I did. She had this sense of humor. She was hilarious." He smiles. "She observed everything and had this unique way of turning it on its head to show what really matters in life." For a moment, his face brightens as if turning toward sunlight. Then a shadow crosses his features. "But not everyone in my family sees it that way. My mother thinks she was robbed."

My stomach knots. I don't know what to say. I can't imagine forcing my way through each day carrying that kind of grief. I don't think I'd ever get out of bed.

"The doctors had a line of treatment for her heart condition, still in the experimental phase, but it could have worked. I wasn't ready to give up hope. Our mother was," he says as if he wants to disassociate from her.

I wait for him to go on.

"She made the final decision. She gave Rowena life and ended it."

I squeeze his hand. If I weren't a liar, it would be a promise never to let go.

Julian falls quiet and glances at the clock. "Time helps, but it still hurts. I could hardly bring myself to go to school." He closes his eyes for a moment. "I was so mad. It was so final. Sometimes I hate my mother for not signing the paperwork."

Julian's expression flits from hurt to a hardened refuge of resignation. His eyes flutter to mine. I reach for him.

"She took one person away from me. I'm not letting her interfere again, ever."

Julian's words rush at me like a wave. He wants me. Yet I'm afraid there isn't enough of me to give. I'm spread thin, between Vicky's world—this strange reality where I feel helpless, at a loss, but desperate to take whatever steps necessary to bring her back—and of possibility with Julian.

"Your twin, whatever happened, she'll be out soon," he says, changing the subject, trying to be reassuring. "It can't be that bad."

It can. Likely it is. But I have these early hours to play pretend, to experience a normal life. Then I will steal myself away.

We lay there, hands linked, lost in our respective thoughts. I doubt Vicky was arrested for stealing a pair of panties or even ten. I mentally leaf through all the plans and blueprints, the way she studied security breaches like I now have to study math. What she did was a dozen floors north of shoplifting and maybe a building and block or two away.

"It'll all get straightened out..." Julian trails off as I shake my head.

He rolls over behind me, pressing himself close, enveloping me in his arms, and holding me close.

Tears want to escape. I sniff them back. I'm not sure what to do so I study Julian's arm, clutching me tight, the way the gray shades of his tattoos blend and the lines intersect. "Tell me about another tattoo," I say because that's safer than planning a jailbreak.

## Chapter 18

When I wake up, it's still my birthday. Eighteen. Maybe when Vicky asked what I wanted, I should have said for her not to be arrested. There's still the entire day and hours to go, I assure myself. We've never been apart for our birthday. It's too simple to say it feels like something is missing.

Vicky told me not to ask questions. Information was given on a need-to-know basis. But why didn't I break that rule? Why didn't I ask what I do if she's arrested? Because this wasn't supposed to happen.

I lay there and listen, but I don't hear the sound of her key in the lock. I wipe my eyes and roll over. The night before tumbles back to me.

Julian must've left. Rain patters outside. I slept through the day and blink in the dark. I want to linger, twirl my hair around my finger, and take a long sip of last night, even with its ups and downs, but I can't enjoy it because I'm so afraid of what's happened to my twin. Sure, she's been gone before, but this is different. This time I feel an emptiness that could swallow me whole.

Maybe Vicky pushed too hard against what everyone else in the world seems to observe about limits, regulations, and lawfulness, landing me in this strange limbo of fear and worry. What would she do if she were in my position? Make meatballs and stage a revolt.

I'm hungry, upset, have a heavy heart—and I'm a thief. The perfect recipe for rebellion.

Bird squawks a few times. The heat clicks on. It must be chilly out. My bag is exactly where I left it, the strap hanging over the chair. Papers and books from school jam together in a mess. I pull everything out, completely uninterested in the notion of homework. I check my phone. No calls or messages from my parents.

At least Caroline texts. **Happy Birthday!!! I love you, Sis!** She includes a few emojis. **I keep telling Vicky to come visit. Both of you. It's beautiful here. Sister trip!**

Caroline is traveling with George who is from Greece. But a more interesting question hitchhikes into my mind. Have she and Vicky been talking? That's unusual for a host of reasons, not limited to when we were younger, they'd routinely fight then not speak for days, using me as a carrier pigeon. They also have zero in common. Caroline is a unicorn to Vicky's dark horse.

A twinge of jealousy creeps through me because why would Vicky talk to her and not me? I reply anyway.

**Thanks! Have you heard from Vicky recently?**

**We talked on the phone not too long ago. I text her, but you know Victoria. She never replies.** More emojis. **Love you! Enjoy your day.**

That's it.

The sky chips and scratches amethyst with a storm. Rain now pours down in soaking sheets, streaking the glass on the three floor-to-ceiling windows lining the eastern wall. Through the water, in the center window is an enormous sketch of a girl, drawn in smudgy, waxy charcoal. I can't pull myself away. I imagine Julian's long arms stretching across dawn to brush in the lines of the hair, dusting his hands off, and whispering *Happy birthday, Penny.*

Early on in my life, I did everything I could to stand out. To get attention. When that didn't work, I faded, purposely becoming invisible, to blend in, and to go unnoticed. Julian sees me with a ruffle of velvety hair, eyes that behold the world, and my lips... I bring my fingers there, where his were so recently, and my eyes flutter shut.

I want this. I want him. But I can't have it. I can't drag him into my drama or tell him my secrets. It would ruin everything. To the general populace what I do is wrong especially because my parents are stupid rich. I'm the heiress to a popcorn fortune.

So was Vicky.

Bird and I watch the rain through the outline of the girl Julian sketched as if we're waiting for a rainbow or some other miracle to break through our blemished lives. To give me answers.

I sift through the various conversations Julian and I had the night before and his body pressing into mine with quiet certainty as he spooned me. I wish the rain were enough to wash away all the doubt I've woken up to. Then my mind spirals in on itself and I go through countless discussions Vicky and I had about stealing. Like what to do and when and how and stealth. But nothing turns up for how to get her *un*arrested.

I bring Bird some fruit and eat a mushy apple that's past being ripe.

"Vicky," Bird screeches desperately. I don't blame him. With our world, as small as it is, her presence and approval are the gold stars.

I flash to a vision of what I imagine Vicky did: running from the authorities then fighting and resisting until the last moment. The feeling in my stomach is thick. My eyes are moist. I simply can't imagine her being caught or giving up. She's invincible. Shadowy thoughts batter me. Without any substantial information to latch onto, my mind spins possibilities and paralyzes me with ifs and thens.

What do I do? Who do I call? Will it be weeks or months before she's released? Years? My face is as wet as the windows and tears spill from my eyes.

The dreary weather, being overtired, and the fact that it's my birthday and my parents don't care tells me the web that connects us is as delicate as candy floss in the rain. The light changes outside and the outline of me, the one Julian drew, comes back into focus.

I can't deny that something has landed in my chest. Attraction, affection, desire. I close my eyes, and it's like I can feel the soft yet firm touch of Julian's fingers on my skin, our lips together, deep and raw yearning. He fixed himself there in that tender place. Yet guilt has taken up residence as well.

I'm part of a two-person show. I can't let Vicky go so easily. I can't replace her with Julian. Shame pinches and churns my insides, dense and gloopy. There isn't room for both of them in my life. Not if she has anything to say about it. She has her rules, and she as my twin has the first right of refusal. I can't keep going back and forth. I have to make a choice. Let myself fall for Julian or save Vicky. I have to decide between what's desirable and what is honorable.

I shower, letting myself cry for Julian. We were a flash, a confection, a super-saturated few days of bliss. The truth, tied up in fear of him being taken away if I fall for him, disappears into the winding plumbing, along with my tears. If I get too close and everything falls apart, I won't have Vicky or him. The sudden possibility in my life with Julian brings with it too much risk for disappointment.

I put on a pair of leggings, one of Vicky's black T-shirts, and look at myself in the mirror. My hair hangs around my cheeks. There's no smile on my lips, only the shadowed look of defeat in my eyes, even before I've waged my battle. I don't want to recognize myself right now.

There is nothing to do and nothing to eat. My room still smells like Julian—a little minty, rainy, and all boy. I have to get out of here.

## Chapter 19

Fall is solid in the air. Before, it was just the idea of autumn with pumpkins, cider, and turning leaves. The wind and rain have driven out notions, leaving nothing but turning inward and toward the melancholy of winter. I feel myself aging and not only because it's my birthday, but a kind of maturation I'm not sure my body is ready to fit into. I bet Ms. Honig has a dozen poems on the subject.

Generally, rain isn't ideal for theft because wet feet and clothes leave a soggy trail of evidence, but it's easier to disappear into the gloom. My bag knocks gently against my hip. I shake off the phantom presence of Julian's hand there. I take the train all the way to Newbury. The long ride gives me too much time to get lost in a labyrinth of thoughts that go nowhere.

On the street, the rain has turned into a drizzle, and then thick drops fall, and then it sprinkles again. It's as pensive and indecisive as I am.

I search for the bakery where Vicky acquired cupcakes last year, but the peeling sign on the window says *Sorry, we're closed*. The interior is empty, devoid of anything resembling a bakery. They've moved.

I drift, landing at the epicenter of pop culture, hipster shops. It's three levels of clothes, furniture, accessories, books, and nooks. I've nicked stuff from here countless times. It's my birthday. I don't need to decide. I'll get myself a gift or five. That's what Vicky would do.

Then another thought creeps into my mind. One that has a beginning but no end. One that I'll have to sort out because I've never stolen a person before. How will I break her out of jail?

In the store, the layout is fashionable clutter, with nearly every surface, vertical and horizontal, accounted for. A thief's playhouse. I scout to make sure the cameras and blind spots are exactly where I remember them. While I casually browse a display of trendy plaid, I keep the salespeople in my periphery. A girl restocks a rack of socks. The salesperson with an eyebrow piercing is on the phone at the register, and another one roams the floor asking customers if they need help. As if.

I disappear into the home goods section for a few minutes to give the salespeople a chance to forget my face before I double back, double-check, and do what I do. I test settees and sofas, ottomans and poufs. I consider the seating in my room. The bed. Oh, Julian. If I lived in Victorian times, I'd swoon and collapse onto the zebra-striped divan with a nine hundred dollar price tag.

I've become a stereotype.

I return to the clothing department. I eye a hoodie I'd like to hibernate in, a pair of leggings with a geometric design, and I could use a few more pairs of underwear. Also, socks.

Forget the fitting room. That didn't work last time. No, I'll be discrete, taking off the security tags. I'll work with my hands, keeping things concealed while looking completely normal from the waist up.

The salespeople are in their own worlds. Plus, they probably don't care if a few items go missing. This'll be a cinch. After I've made sure that everyone is preoccupied, I go to the area where I'll be able to remove the tags discretely. A posh chic without a blonde hair out of place, pearl earrings, and clothes that are more elegant than trendy sails into one of the blind spots. She moves purposefully, hyper-focused as her body shifts slightly and she ducks behind a rack.

*Oh. Oh my.*

She's doing my thing. I'm mesmerized. I've never witnessed someone shoplifting before, except Vicky, of course. And this girl doesn't look the type—at all.

She has a light pink Tori Birch bag on her forearm worth much more than whatever she's taking. She's quick and discrete as she slides some accessories inside. Nail polish, cheap jewelry—little impulse grabs, the easy targets. I catch her profile and the hint of a smile when the salesgirl nears. Blondie holds a floral dress in front of her like she's seeing if it looks good. If the employee is watching for shoplifters, Blondie does not fit the profile. If this was a critique session for the young and thieving, I'd say, she's a top student.

I want her to know that I know. We could create a clandestine shoplifting corporation. Vicky would be proud. Actually, probably not.

*Penny, we keep this secret, just you and me. We're a team. We're two people strong.*

The girl flashes me her pearly white smile. My jaw drops. I recognize her. "Cute dress, but I don't seem to see my size."

My thoughts scramble. Do I acknowledge her? She didn't seem to recognize me. What's the protocol?

I nonchalantly glance at her out of the corner of my eye. There's a blind spot by a mirror and a display of pajamas. I wonder if she'll use it, what she'll take.

My bag remains empty. I sift through a tub of underwear.

Blondie appears at my side, her floral scent tickling my nose. I startle and fight a sneeze. I can't risk drawing attention to myself. Incognito and invisible.

She passes me a bottle of red nail polish. "I think this suits you. Oh, and you dropped this," she says and holds out a cell phone.

I shake my head. "That's not—"

She puts the phone in my hand, winks, and says, "Yes, it's yours. Consider it a birthday present."

As I gape at the device, she clicks away. Maybe she's relaying a message from Vicky. Stranger things have happened. I grip the phone. "Yeah. Thanks," I say, leaving off her name. Unless I'm dreaming, that was Queenie Clemmons, former Dartmont student, and my sister Caroline's nemesis.

As I weave toward the exit, I glance over my shoulder. She vanished in a cloud of perfume.

## Chapter 20

As I pick my way back to Fleet Street in a kind of disoriented stupor of fascination, I scroll through the phone. It's clean except for one number labeled *Call Me*. I rack my brain for anyone Vicky mentioned befitting the image of a tall, socialite type with blond hair who also happened to attend my school. Nothing comes to mind.

There was Flavio, but that's it. Whoever else she conspired with was a ghost. Who was Vicky pleading with that night on the phone? Could they help me? Did they double-cross her?

There was her rival, her nemesis, Sandro. I never saw him in person. Only heard exhaustive accounts of how much she hated him. She never told me the full story, but one thing was clear, as much as she hated authority and police, she despised him more. Maybe he tipped off the cops, landed my sister inside, and sent Queenie after me. I left the red nail polish on the table next to the underwear, but was that a message? Was she saying she caught me red-handed?

There's also the possibility Vicky sent her. My finger hovers over the *call* button.

My mind spins and my eyes blur as I stare at the phone, but indecision keeps me from doing anything.

I wake early on Sunday morning in a tangle of gray sheets as buttery sunlight streams across my bare legs. My attention lands back on Vicky, questions coiling in my mind. Where was she caught? She couldn't have taken the golden heart—she was saving that for me, for us. All the shoplifting and scouting was child's play, preparation.

The knot in my stomach pulls taut as I try to free myself from the bedding. I have to figure out how to get my twin home.

I paw around for my phone, but it's not on my night table or the floor. Fascinated by the phone from the stranger, I didn't use it at all last night. It must still be in my bag.

But it's not. My pocket? No. I tear through the apartment, searching for it before I realize Blondie or Queenie or whatever that was must've taken it.

Bird squawks loudly. My thoughts are louder. They land on Vicky, testing me. Then I remember the mug shot. No, she wouldn't go to jail on purpose as part of a master thief training program.

It's still too early to make calls and do research, but even if it weren't, where do I start? Vicky didn't prepare me for this. I want to find her but don't know how. Even if I did, does she want me to?

Is there a rule number four? *If I'm arrested, break me out. Or if I'm arrested, don't do anything to draw attention to yourself and our history.*

What do I do?

I gather my things for the day, including the phone. I linger at the window, emblazoned with my image and Julian's fingerprints. I follow the traces of our footsteps from the weekend, trying to stamp them out from my memory because Vicky's voice would tell me I shouldn't take too many risks. Stealing is enough.

I step briskly onto the quiet street. I'm disinterested in returning to Dartmont but less inclined to stay alone at the apartment. I should distance myself from Julian. Make him forget me. Then his parents can erase that late morning at the Clothing Cloud from the books.

Wandering until I reach the abandoned jail by Zakim Bridge, I wonder what it would take to break her out. I have some research to do.

THE NEXT DAY, at Dartmont, I dismiss Tegan and Jordyn scowling at me on the front steps of Beckwith, the science building. I reject the long, lonely hallways, determined to put me on the same path as a tall boy with tattoos. I crumple the lovely oil pastel portrait that I find under my dorm room door when I hide out there during morning break. It's a sketch in a rainbow of colors, framed in a rainy window, signed *JFreese*. Then I smooth it out and slide it between one of my textbooks.

The periods click by and my mind sticks to Vicky, trying to find a point of entry, a way to get her home.

In English, Julian folds himself into the seat next to me. A bruise blotches the space around his eye and a thin piece of medical tape holds a cut closed on his cheek. I worry his mother found out we were hanging out, took a page from Bird's book, and tried to peck his eyes out. Nevertheless, it's as if he emits an electromagnetic current, charging the air with *us*.

I can't resist.

I must. I must. I must.

It'll be too messy otherwise. There's enough heartache already in my life as I labor over when and how my twin will return. I don't meet his eyes. But I feel as though we drift into the same orbit.

Ms. Honig lectures on rules, syntax, and grammar in various poetic forms and genres. She uses the whiteboard, overhead projector, and has a PowerPoint presentation. She's devoted to this lesson, like a liturgy, like she gets off on rubrics. I resist the order. Rebellion is in my nature...or Vicky's nurture. I rest my head in my hand and let my eyes dip to the floor.

Vicky said that I could learn everything worth knowing on the streets or in real life. She called school prison. I can't imagine Victoria sitting in a classroom, although she very likely sat in this very one.

She's the one behind bars now. She said things like, *Penny, me and you are the same. We break the rules. Stealing? That's us doing things our own way.*

But as I wake to the world, I fear that maybe it was just her way. I worry I was merely her shill.

Ms. Honig drones on about vocabulary. I'm so bored I land back in the stratosphere of my thoughts. But maybe assonance, iambic pentameter, couplets, and syllables will create order and peace in my illogical and jumbled mind. Perhaps life would be easier if it was measured and methodical and had clearly organized stanzas.

Then would everything start to make sense?

Julian nudges my boot with his. Ms. Honig hovers over me. Her lips tighten like she might sting. I didn't realize how deep into the cave of my thoughts I'd traveled. I blink, disoriented, and lend what remains of my fissured attention to Honig.

"As I was saying, Penny." There is a stern emphasis on my name. "The guidelines are there for Haikus and sonnets, odes and villanelles. There are rules, delineated and concise, which you must know before they can be broken." At least that's where I hear the italics in her voice. "Maybe that will appeal to some of you rebels." She side-eyes me. "Don't get me wrong, each form has its through line and if you choose one don't stray, but there's also free verse, free form, free-thinking. I encourage this in you. There is beauty in borders. Order can be useful, but once you learn, you can toss everything I've taught you out the window. It can be bent, remolded, and reformed into something new in favor of the words spoken by your heart."

She paces to the front of the room, erases the whiteboard, and clicks the projector off. The computer goes dark. The lights flick on. She says, "All I ask is that you get honest with yourself. Make a choice. Whatever you do, be true and be consistent."

Julian shifts beside me. I wince when I catch sight of his black eye. There's a pulsation of longing between us. I want him. But I also want to help my sister. It's almost like the bee who calls herself an English teacher is channeling my thoughts toward one or the other and arching her stinger, a threat if I don't choose. I sense the direction of my lean. He's so close, but it's selfish. No, I've already made my choice.

The bell rings. "Your first poems are due Friday. Be ready to pour your heart out to your partner." Her laugh is a thickety buzz. I rush out of the classroom knowing that if I linger, I'll be anything but consistent.

## Chapter 21

I SPEND LUNCH IN THE LIBRARY, SCANNING THE INTERNET FOR anything related to Vicky. Into the search engine, I type *Boston*. Then *arrest* and Friday's date. I add *theft* and *steal* and every other synonym I can think of. Nothing. I can't locate the news feed I saw in the window of the barbershop. Perhaps I imagined it. I'm lost in reports and police logs for the surrounding area before deciding to move on to other nearby cities. I start with New York, reasoning if Vicky were on a job, she'd likely be in a major metropolitan area. I've missed half of math before I find a lead that seems like it could be a match.

The name given at the time of arrest was *Perdida Ochoa*. I lean closer to the monitor, my breath shallow. My stomach grumbles uneasily.

The arrest time was Friday at 10:16 a.m. I was probably in English drooling over Julian. The guilt drills itself deeper. I should be doing something, but I still don't know what. I can't steal her out of jail. Can I? This incident will only serve to confirm our parents' choice to disown her.

The address is somewhere in Manhattan. I copy and paste it into the search bar. It's an industrial-type area with warehouses and identical neutral-colored buildings. I follow up with the police log, reading it carefully, and hoping these meaningless details might help me locate her.

I sigh. Howard plops into a seat next to me. "Hey, Caroline's sister," he says, logging onto the computer.

During sophomore year, we became acquainted over a hacking incident on the Dartmont Dart, our school's online newspaper and messaging system aka gossip channel. I swore myself to secrecy in exchange for him padding my attendance record. "Señora Henderson is going to kick my butt if I don't hand in this assignment on time. On top of that, I have the Cold War thing for Sharpe. That one I can't fudge. You have her, right? And Honig for English?"

I nod.

"I don't envy you. Even though Honig is only a few years out of college, she's so grouchy you'd think Professor Groff personally chose her as his replacement from the beyond.."

My thoughts filter to Caroline's story about the professor's untimely death.

"But that won't help me with the Spanish assignment. Do you know what *por supuesto* means?" he asks.

"Of course."

"What does it mean?"

"Of course," I repeat.

Howard's beady eyes capture mine and then I explain that the expression means *of course*. He laughs, but I don't when I remember what *perdida* means. Loss.

Which is odd since our game is about gain.

I look up the word *ochoa* and find a soccer player, looking sweaty and sultry on the field in his uniform. I instantly think of Julian and his skateboard, the way he moved fluidly, almost gracefully, as if he were an extension of its energy and moved in defiance of the laws of gravity. For a split second, I feel weightless and bulletproof again.

I scroll down and land on Ochoa as a surname, it's of Spanish and Basque origin, meaning *wolf*.

Perdida Ochoa. Lost wolf...or did she mean lone wolf?

I go still. Howard glances at me, fingers racing across the keyboard, no doubt doing something forbidden to the internal servers.

"Thanks for helping me out with stuff," I say vaguely.

"Anything for Caroline's sister." Then tugging on his collar, he whispers, "But I need to cool off at the moment so maybe try to go to class sometimes."

My eyes widen. "Oh, sure. Sorry. Did I—?"

He makes a lip-zipping gesture.

Everything that happened during Caroline's senior year comes to mind. Perhaps I'm not that much different than some of the students here.

"Want to get out of here, grab something to eat?" Howard asks.

I shift from foot to foot, eager to find out more about Perdida Ochoa and that probably won't happen over burgers and fries. "Maybe another time?"

He shrugs and turns back to the screen. "Sure."

I wonder if his computer hacking life is just as lonely as mine is as a thief and if there are a few of us here, quietly rebelling alone instead of together.

## Chapter 22

I bolt from my last class, intent on pinpointing Vicky's whereabouts and getting answers. Yesterday, I struggled with the shock of her arrest and lived in the blink of a fantasy with Julian, but I'm stratifying my life: school, distance from Julian, getting Vicky home. Focused, straightforward, actionable.

If I leave campus now, I'll beat traffic and get there in less than an hour. I refuse to let myself think about how I routinely use my parents' credit cards for long Uber rides, but they didn't even bother with my birthday.

Forget disappearing myself. I've been forgotten.

I burst through the door to the building on Fleet Street and almost collide with the mailman. The mail. I edge around him, pulling envelopes and sales circulars out of the slim box. He passes me a couple more items with a thin smile. I've never gotten the mail before. That was Vicky's job. But there's no time to come up with a dozen conflicting reasons why that might be. I have research to do.

I rush up the stairs and toss everything on the table, spread some peanut butter on stale bread, and flip open her computer. First, I check the history, but before it even comes up, I know she would have wiped it clean. I click on bookmarks, but all she has are the local weather and some food blogs. Mmm, making the perfect alfredo sauce, perfecting risotto, and a lasagna tutorial. Otherwise, she erased as she went. I close my eyes, envisioning her at the kitchen counter, working feverishly.

I glance toward the bay of windows and see my outline, practically etched on the glass. Unbidden, Julian's form appears in my mind. He's radiant and bold, but his hands are in his pockets and I whisper, "Go. It's easier this way." I want to will him from my mind. Maybe I can become as skillful as Vicky at wiping away where I've been and whom I've been with.

I type in the info from the arrest record. Like in the school library, I branch out with the details, but nothing helpful comes up except 4,940,000 irrelevant articles. I search *Perdida Ochoa*. Nothing. I scan the archives on all the local news channels and then do the same for the ones in New York City using the time of the newscast from Saturday night. Bingo. The barbershop must have its TV tuned to an out-of-state station.

Before I press play on the clip, I skim the transcript. For a full minute, I gaze at the mug shot. Vicky's identity is reduced to a string of numbers. Her hair is messy, but her eyes are clear, defiant even. I turn on the computer's sound and start the video.

The perky blonde from the report Saturday night straightens, smiles primly, and this time words accompany the mug shot that appears in the upper corner of the screen.

"Early today, police arrested several professional thieves in a sting that started late last month. Details are being withheld, but suspects include a young Boston woman going by the name of Perdida Ochoa, two males, twins apparently, and a third male by the name of Steve McQueen." She tries to retain her composure at the mention of the last name on the list. "The arrest occurred outside a theatrical warehouse where it is believed several valuable movie artifacts are housed including James Bond's Aston Martin from Goldfinger." She raises her eyebrows.

The camera pans to the male newscaster at her side. Through my shock and the dense tears as I fell apart and into Julian's arms, I'd missed this portion of the report. "Perhaps McQueen needed a Getaway car." He elbows the lady newscaster. They both laugh as she says, "Oh, John. Lucky for us, this Steve didn't make a Great Escape. Well done, boys in blue."

I assume these are references to movies. I don't care. I just want Vicky or Perdida or whatever her name is back, and I want answers. I want to ask her if jail was worth the rush and the high of the heist. I want to know why she constructed this obscure and, what I now realize is a lonely life. But I can't, not until she gets out. Anger nudges me and I nudge it back. I'm still too sad and lost in how fresh this is to be mad, but I sense it there, bubbling beneath the surface.

With little to go on, I continue to scan the internet, hoping for information now that I have a few sparse details to work with. All I come up with is a report on the attempted theft of movie memorabilia and assurances that the items are in good hands. "What about us? Waiting on the other side? Are we in good hands?" I ask.

Bird hoots.

I rest my head on my folded arms. The corner of an envelope jabs my skin. The mail. Vicky always takes it and does whatever Vicky does with it. I cannot fathom the fog I've lived in. Delusional? Naïve? Sheltered? No, no, and no, but in so many ways I am all of those things. She lives in a very specific way, and I just followed her lead.

Tension edges into my brow, my jaw, and my shoulders.

I tear into an envelope addressed to me. Me? It's a water and sewer bill. I riffle through the pile. All four items have *Penelope Goldfeather* printed on the address label. One is a coupon for an oil change, another an offer for a line of credit. The fourth piece of mail is for health insurance. I guess Vicky didn't steal everything, just the money she uses to pay for all of this, and my name. She uses my identity...because our parents cut her off.

I let a fraction of the anger in. It shuttles me to her bedroom where I tear into her drawers. Undergarments, socks, pajamas. Sweaters, blouses, and dresses hang in her closet. There's nothing hidden within her clothes except for the person I believed her to be. I slump onto the bed and drop back. Thousands of paper cranes fly above my head. I want them to swoop down, lift me up, and carry me away. This room smells too much like her and mine still contains a blaze of Julian. I want out of this mess.

I consider opening the ornately carved box on top of her bureau, the lone item labeled with an invisible tag that says *Hands Off*.

She kept parts of herself so private I can't bring myself to breach the unspoken understanding we had. However, I don't stop myself from the small filing cabinet in the corner.

It doesn't open. I get my lock picking set and make quick work of releasing the pins and turning the cylinder. Inside, pre-labeled files hang in alphabetical order: automotive, bank records, income taxes, and so forth. As far as I know, none of these pertains to us even though they each contain a few papers. I find a lease agreement for this address. The name listed is Penelope Goldfeather. There's a certificate of renter's insurance, also paid in full, but see that the expiration date is in March of next year. My name is there too.

I shouldn't be surprised that this isn't a squat or that she used my name instead of her own, but I can't get over the fact that she filed all these documents and made payments like a civilized human being.

She always said that we exist outside, above, and behind the law.

Knowing Vicky was, at least in part, a law-abiding citizen gives me hope that she'll be able to return home soon, carry on with her secret bill-paying life, and explain why she used my name. I leaf through other files and see my name over and over. The grit of her dishonesty abrades me.

I stare at the phone Blondie gave me, tempted to press call. I'd like to reverse engineer last week. Instead, I manage to make myself scarce for the next week, avoiding Julian. As Honig repeatedly reminds us, I have to be consistent. I can't bear the weight of him knowing who I am and what Vicky and I did. I need answers.

Instead, slipped between the pages of my history book that I leave on my desk during a bathroom break, I find a graphite image of me, gazing through a window toward a non-existent sun. It's lines and shadows, negative space and highlights. It's raw and revealing. I look gorgeously glum.

Hovering over me, Tegan hisses, "It's too bad."

I don't want to dignify her with a response, but apparently, I like to antagonize myself. "Do you want me to ask what's too bad?"

"Penny, you tried. I'll give you an A for your effort. The sad, edgy wild child thing you've got going on." She swivels her clawed hand through the air from my face down, noting my appearance, which is dull today. "But you're no one, Penny. Why don't you go back to wherever you came from?"

I must wear an epic version of what my sister calls I-despise-you face because she flinches. The bell rings. Jordyn appears.

"Go on, shoo." Tegan dismisses me with a flick of the wrist.

My jaw actually hangs open. Howard, Neda, and her friend Kristina stand a few feet away, both with their arms across their chests, their heads cocked at the oh-no-she-didn't angle.

Tegan woke up the dragon within. Grabbing her arm, I pull her close.

"Get off me," she hisses.

I don't. "Have I given any indication that I care, even in the slightest, that anything you say to me has any relevance in my life? In my world, you don't exist. I see little more than a vitamin-deficient clown with too much lipstick in an empty circus tent. I hope you step on a Lego."

She huffs, sniffs, and then before she storms off, she says, "You just declared war, Penny."

Howard chuckles. "She had that coming. I loved Legos when I was a kid. My parents, not so much."

"Thanks," I reply but am not sure this is over.

## Chapter 23

When the bell rings for English, I want to run. Pushing myself through classes at Dartmont has become an exercise in robbing myself of pleasure and cheer—not that I have much in supply.

Ms. Honig sits imperiously behind her desk as we file in. She looks like she has a mouthful of honey.

I slide into my seat next to Julian, feeling ragged and like a failure, not that I wanted to do the assignment in the first place.

Honig makes a big to-do about introducing today's activity. "The day has come at last. It's time to read aloud with your partner. It's not only practice in public speaking, but speaking meaningfully, from the heart with passion and gusto. I want to see you shine, hear you emote, and watch you wow." She's impassioned and irritating as she goes on, "Like in real life, I'm throwing you guys a curve ball. Today you will experience intimacy, human connection, and let the power of the spoken word cast its net around you. I ask each of you to rise to your feet and find your partner."

I turn slowly in Julian's direction. Last week, I left behind the effort it would take to fake a fainting spell and escape somewhere. If anyone is looking, it might be in the back of Regina's shop, in the admin building, or maybe the skate park.

Julian's eyebrows crowd together in question when our eyes meet. We get crowded into the corner, mere inches apart. I'm close enough that I can smell the faint scent of cinnamon, clean cotton, and him. It's divine.

*Oh, Penny, come on. I close my eyes. Focus.*

"Class, I ask you now to access your hearts and harness your voices. You'll swap poems and then read aloud. Remember the sound, experience the way the words feel on your tongue, and feel the pulse of poetic truth."

Um, no. I eye the exit.

A murmur spreads like an echo as everyone lemmings the assignment, following Honig off the edge of sanity without thinking.

I clear my throat. Today Julian's eyes are more amber than hazel. I could dive in, without thinking. Excuses along with coherence land somewhere on the ground below. "I um, didn't exactly, uh—"

He interrupts as if he wants to spare me the embarrassment. "I can go first." A smile hints at replacing the slight quiver on his lip. I wonder if he's afraid Tegan is going to knock him down a flight of stairs after she gets the report from one of her minions that Julian and I swapped ostentatious representations of love or whatever it is the heart produces in the form of poetry. Maybe she's the one who gives him the cuts and bruises. She's always lurking around campus, popping up wherever I am, especially when Julian and I are together.

He passes me a folded paper. I don't read it before the poem Julian selected trip out of my mouth. It's about falling in love with a brave girl, someone worthy of being believed in, and someone worth fighting for. Someone not like me. It's an enduring love story told by F. Scott Fitzgerald in under fifty words.

Julian doesn't leave me time to think about what else it might mean. "My turn," he says, reciting the one he made up.

"Opal skies lost to a year of foggy nights.

Within and without the toughest fights.

Cut with flame.

Bruised by blame.

Dense with emotions.

Drowned in potions.
A window opens and my heart appears.
Love is the greatest of all my fears."

And in his purposeful pauses, the curl of the words he emphasizes, the way his lips seem to make love to language, a haiku of my own is born on my tongue.

"I want to say yes.
No is easier I guess.
My heart breaks open again and again and again."

The solar glow of our mutual longing catches flame and burns between us.

"Penny, do you have a poem for Julian to read?" Ms. Honig must have overheard the exchange.

"Oh, um, yeah. I riffle through my bag and find one she gave us earlier in the week. It isn't my first choice, but it says enough. The pinching around her eyes and mouth suggests she doesn't buy it entirely, but the sheet of paper trembles slightly in Julian's ink-stained and scabbed hands as he unfolds it, suggesting the potency of our exchange, just maybe not exactly in the way she expects.

He reads "As I Lay Sleeping" by Antonio Machado. Honig looks on, pleased at the part about golden bees. She nods and moves on to the next group.

I may as well be in a hive because honey coats my cracked open heart. There's a stickiness between Julian and me, one I can't wash off. As lovely as it is, I know I shouldn't do this. I wheel around, spinning out of the classroom and down the hall. I need a minute, or a year in the bathroom, a splash of cold water, and space to breathe.

Before I get to the girls' room, Julian catches up to me.

I press myself against the wall, feeling the cool plaster. He braces his arms on either side of me. He's as out of breath as I am.

He says, "Thinking about you keeps me up at night."

Delightful waves undulate in my chest, knots unravel, and a ship prepares to leave port.

"Kiss me," he says, leaning in until we're a split second apart. "Please."

I lean in a fraction.

We stay there, our lips not quite touching, breathing each other's air.

"I know you feel it too. Just tell me, did I do something wrong? I can—" He stops when I shake my head.

I know better than to pull out the *It's not you it's me* line, but it's true. I have to do this now, ripping off the bandage style. "Julian, I can't do this—us. You're great, but you deserve to be with someone—" Better than me. He waits for me to finish, but I can't. The question in his eyes is too personal.

I start to slip back down the hall, but his courage gallops faster and stops me.

"This, whatever it is we have, it's radical. It's something. It's magical, Penny. I can't stop thinking about you. Day and night. It's more than poetry or chance. Please." His eyes pour into mine.

I lift to my toes and our noses brush. He's warm, but before my lips land on his, someone clears their throat sharply.

"Mr. Freese, Ms. Goldfeather, back to class." Mrs. Sharpe coughs out our names like she was chewing on sandpaper.

Back in English, Ms. Honig still buzzes with enthusiasm as the bell rings. "Well done, everyone. I'll see you here next week, ready to move into part two of this unit where we'll have the renowned and prolific Dickinson, Whitman, and at last, the great Shakespeare joining us in our exploration of poetry. Plus, we'll do a deep dive into Romeo and Juliet. Prepare yourselves for the Capulets and Montagues, kids! Also, I hope you're all looking forward to our excursion next Friday."

As if stung by a bee, I flinch at the word Montague.

## Chapter 24

I SPEND SATURDAY IN BOSTON. IT SLOUCHES BY WHILE BIRD AND I alternately sulk and I try to find out more about Vicky's arrest. I loiter around the police station. I dial the non-emergency number for the cops but don't press call. Does she have a lawyer? Our parents do, but they're not available. I am at a loss. Maybe Vicky was right. Perhaps I'm not ready for whatever is next because I can't even steal her from jail.

It's past midnight on Saturday so technically Sunday morning. Outside, a few cabs slosh by in the rain. The buzzer startles me from my circuitous thoughts. Could it be Vicky?

I say a rusty, "Hello," into the intercom.

"It's me," crackles Julian's voice.

I envision broken hearts by dawn, but my body betrays me with vibration every time I think about him. I buzz him in.

When I open the door, he shyly scratches at the doormat with his sneaker. He clutches his skateboard behind him as if he's in handcuffs. A few cuts mark the side of his face. He seems to have nearly as many scars as he does tattoos. Maybe what Scout said about him being reckless is true.

He limps slightly. The knee of his jeans is torn. He smiles when he sees his sketch of me still on the window. He leans the board against the wall by the door.

I step cautiously toward him like I'm afraid of what lies or truths might spill out if I open my mouth. Instead, I unzip his damp jacket and press my cheek against his chest. He inhales sharply as if he's breathing in an elixir.

"Your knee? Your face?" He smells like crisp rain.

He grips my upper arms, tense with anticipation. Our eyes meet. Despite what Honig would say, sometimes words aren't necessary.

If only to take the edge off, I lean in, planting a leisurely and luxurious kiss on his lips.

"You're bleeding," I say before I let myself get to the point where I completely lose my mind.

"It's fine."

"Take your pants off." I never expected to utter those words to a boy. My blushing cheeks usher me to the bathroom medicine cabinet.

Bird chirrups.

I call Julian to my room and clean his face and knee. His boxers are plaid. If his bare legs were a map, little pricks of light would blink every time I touch him, frantically waving flags emblazoned with *Penny was here, and here, and here*. A gash severs an inked spider's web. On his other leg run the words *She lights up the sky where my heart lives*. It looks fresh, the tattoo still slightly puffy.

"What happened?" I ask after I seal his wound with a bandage.

"Living dangerously." He smirks like it's a joke.

Scout's words ring again. At least shoplifting doesn't result in injury or death.

"You'd know something about that, right?" he asks. "Living dangerously," he repeats.

I don't answer, suddenly afraid Regina told him. "Are you hungry?"

"Starved." He reaches for me, but I slip from his grasp. He falls onto my bed. I want to fall next to him. Instead, I warm up a can of soup and crackers.

He eats quietly while I study him, still on the edge of rain and pain.

## Two Truths and One Thief

When he's done, he takes a long drink of water, and his eyes climb back into focus. I put the bowl and glass on the floor and sit next to him.

"I've been wanting to tell you something. But not at school," he says hoarsely.

Here it comes. I brace myself.

"The other night I overheard my mother talking to my dad. She said your name. She, uh, overheard me talking about you to my dad then I overheard her talking to him." His cheeks tint pink and he smiles. "She insisted that you look exactly like *her*. I don't know who *her* is. Then my dad said, 'Maybe she has a cousin or sister, but that it was in the past and to let it go.'"

I dodge the idea that our worlds are on a crash course. No, Regina doesn't like me for legitimate reasons—I stole from her store.

"She said something about how she'll never forgive *her* for taking the bracelet."

"Underwear," I blurt.

"I guess it was from some guy," Julian goes on, not paying attention to what I said. "My dad said it shouldn't matter because that was from high school. I couldn't really follow what they were talking about. It turned into an argument as usual. They had one tonight too. That's why I left." He sighs. "But on my way out, I heard her tell a story about how she had a girl working at Clothing Cloud when we were going through the thick of things with Rowena. My mother had a bracelet from her high school sweetheart and was using it as a prop on a mannequin. It went missing. She thinks the person in question is you."

A stone tumbles from my throat to my stomach. "Oh." My pause is brief because the next words spit themselves out. "I've never worked at Clothing Cloud, but my twin might have. Do you know the person's name? The *her*?"

"Jude Capulet." He snorts a laugh. "And my mother's maiden name is Regina Montague. What are the odds? It's probably nothing, but I thought you should know because she's trying to make my life stupid-difficult. The thing about my mother is she never forgives.

Not anyone, including herself. I guess I understand that," he murmurs.

My cheeks blister with heat. "She has every reason not to like me. Not to trust me." I meet his eyes. "It was me. She caught me stealing. Not the bracelet, but some other stuff from the store."

Julian leans back on my bed and drums his hands on his taut belly. "My dad told me." He doesn't move.

Relieved, I lay down alongside him. "I'm sorry," I whisper.

"We all do things we're not proud of."

I keep to myself the part about how my sister would disagree. His pulse throbs against me, and then we're kissing like it's us against the world. I drown and surface. I lose myself and come up for air. His hands explore my modest hills and valleys, the curve of my spine, and the squeeze of my thighs.

I've entered uncharted terrain, but the message that I'm a liar and that I'm betraying Vicky blows like wind in my ears. I want to keep exploring. First, I need to course correct. I stop.

Julian looks at me for a long moment then leans on his elbow. "Since we promised honesty to each other, there's something else I've wanted to tell you." He shifts again, sitting up this time and rubs his hand on the back of his neck. "What I said about doing stuff we're not proud of—I fight."

"What?" I blink, unclear as to what he means.

"I fight," he repeats.

Worry about Vicky gets lost in the wrinkles of my brow as I turn my concern to the beautiful and bruised boy before me.

"You've seen that movie, right? Tyler Durden, the soap, the rules..."

I recall the film as something of a cult classic. Flavio, Vicky, and I watched it once.

"I know some guys who're big fans of the movie. The book. Both. We formed an underground fighting ring."

"Like boxing?"

"More subversive, unregulated, unbridled."

I study the results of the blows on his face and hands.

"After Rowena, my sister—I was so angry. It made sense to let it out. When it started, it was for our own amusement. Boys. Sticks. Stones. That whole thing. Then one of the guys figured out a way to monetize it with an app disguised as a sports betting thing. It took off. Now, it's just a game."

There I thought I was the dangerous one. I balk. "So you're not angry anymore and it's just a game, but you still do it?"

"Part of me is still angry. And I'm good at it. Grew up taking martial arts. Also, I figured out an algorithm, how to play the odds and win. I bet and never lose, even when I do, which is rare." He smirks.

"You beat people up and cheat?" I forget about my own secret life.

"The whole thing is stupid and it isn't huge amounts of money. A little here and a little there. Enough for someday. Anyway, no one cares."

"I care." My shock takes the form of more questions. "Why don't you play poker or invest in the stock market?"

His eyes soften and go dreamy. "Or you. I could go in for you."

I pretend not to understand what he means. "You could get hurt. Do your parents know?"

"I'm only brave when I'm rebelling."

"Have you tried being brave without rebelling?" I ask.

He leans in and places his lips on mine. If I were glass, I'd be in pieces. His mouth tells me a story different than the one I've believed —that I'm small, insignificant, an afterthought. If Julian has anything to say about it, I'm the center of his world.

I didn't know kissing could stitch up lies.

## Chapter 25

Picking up on our conversation before Julian blew apart my world with his lips on mine, he asks, "Have I tried being brave without rebelling?"

My shoulder hitches on a shrug. Facing him is like seeing my reflection in a mirror, but not like when I look at Vicky. It's as if Julian shows me who I could be.

His lips quirk. "We're quite the pair."

"Liars & thieves," I answer, holding up the deck of cards. "Want to play?"

"If I win you have to promise me something."

I nod because I'm not only a thief.

"You won't steal from me, and I won't lie to you."

"Okay, but I always win."

"Then if you win I won't steal from you, and you won't lie to me."

I nod then shuffle.

"And if it's a draw we won't lie to each other. We won't steal from each other."

"Then what will we do?" I ask, keeping up the pretense.

"We'll be honest. True. Do things together. Cuddle. Kiss. Break rules. We'll laugh. Eat. Study. We'll live life."

"Those sound like things a girl would do with her boyfriend."

Julian's hazel eyes don't waver from mine, intoxicating me. "Will you be my girlfriend, Penny?"

"Only if you win."

He tips his head back with delighted laughter.

Seated on the bed, we play cards until he wins. He lowers me down beside him, curls himself around me, and just before he falls asleep, he says, "As I said, I rarely lose." He winks at me.

I'm his girlfriend. He's my boyfriend. My eyes are heavy, but I lay awake thinking about what this means until he slips out when the morning sky is on the edge of gray.

As the door closes, Bird cries, "Vicky," reminding me of what I've done.

WITH THE WHEEL of the year spinning us ever closer to winter weather, everyone at Dartmont becomes increasingly restless. I tease myself by catching morsels of Julian—our arms pressing together in the Refectory at a crowded lunch table, our fingers brushing in English, a quick kiss here and there. If nothing else, I'm unfailingly consistent at being inconsistent. Yet, I'm afraid of losing myself, what it means to have betrayed Vicky, and having to endure the devastating outcome of Julian's twisted extracurricular activity. Life, as I know it, will be over. Maybe it already is.

I gather my bag and the mysterious cell phone, still unsure about whether to call Queenie—if that was her.

Outside, bottlecap-sized rain prompts me to run through the quad. I stand opposite the coach bus hired to ferry Ms. Honig's students to Emily Dickinson's birthplace in Massachusetts. The taillights beam through the weepy morning. The inside of the bus is illuminated and cozy. My breath puffs little clouds while I deliberate. Do I stay here and hope for Vicky's return? Do I case the jails? Do I try to live a normal life? If the last few weeks have taught me nothing else, it's that even the smallest of choices, subtlest movements, and single words can have rippling, seismic impacts. My heart wants to be with Julian and rescue my sister. But this is an *or* situation, not an *and* situation. I can't have both.

Julian appears on the sidewalk, half visible in the bus's headlights. I cross the parking lot. Students gather around Ms. Honig who buzzes like she's had three cups of espresso. "Our chaperone, Mr. Honig, my brother who's visiting from Germany, will take roll before you get on the coach." Her voice chips with resignation when she introduces him. "Be sure to sit with your partner."

A burly guy with a square jaw and shaved head stands bored and thug-like by the second bus. He has the same flitting eyes as Ms. Honig. Maybe a few years younger—closer to his teens than his thirties, but they're definitely related. I imagine she uses her powers for good—ensuring that all seniors are well versed in, well, verse. And he, well, he looks like he uses his powers for something else altogether.

She glances in his direction and sighs like she desperately wants him to see the beauty in poetry before continuing, "Once underway, we're going to watch the first part of the Walt Wittman video. On the way back, we'll watch the second half. I want you to take notes because you will have a quiz." She adds the underscore, "Poetry is the marriage of words and souls."

The sentimentality makes me want to barf. If only the school-wide theme at Dartmont this year wasn't cooperation.

I'm vibrantly aware of Julian leaning on the armrest between us as the movie clicks on and I disappear into its glow. I must doze off because about an hour later, I wake to the scratch of a pencil on paper. In the seconds before I open my eyes, I drift along the smooth strokes and the staccato rubbings of Julian's hand in motion. My head rests on his right arm and a notebook balances on his thighs with his long legs pressing against the back of the seat in front of us.

Instead, I watch him sketch the image of a sleeping girl. Her face is peaceful, almost vulnerable, and intimate. It's as if the viewer is looking at her through an open window. He sees so many versions of me that I didn't know existed.

Something vibrates between us, but it's not emotion or longing. It's a phone. My phone. Rather, the one Queenie gave me.

It's a message from the *Call Me* number. **The clock is ticking**.

My pulse does the same but skips the seconds altogether because I don't know what this means.

Leaning back in the seat so Julian can't read it, I reply. **Who is this?**

But I don't get an answer.

## Chapter 26

Time with Julian is like the veil of sleep, that foggy, yet lucid place where inanimate objects might surprise me by sparkling or telling me that I'm pretty. Words rise and float, sink and shuffle like logical and sentient beings. Yet, like so many other moments in my life lately, it's stolen time. In the stillness of the bus, chasing latitudes far away from the scene of my crimes, a familiar celebrity voice weaves Walt Whitman's yarns. With it in the background, I can pretend I'm someone else—because right now, the push to be someone else is stronger than the pull to be me.

I imagine forgiving myself and breathing sweet words into Julian's ear. Then we'll embrace and a kiss will stretch into so much more.

My life will resume a normal tenor, my misdeeds will disappear, and my family will be whole and loving.

The fantasy dissolves when Tegan whips around and yaps at someone in her high-pitched voice. I return to the comfort of Julian's pencil on paper.

Before I'm ready to leave this little bubble, the bus sighs and we've arrived. The roar of the students' impatience jolts me back to reality. The strange reality where I have a rogue cellphone on my person with a mysterious message.

"Check your seats, make sure you have your things, and we'll gather in the atrium," Ms. Honig instructs.

The second coach bus pulls up and out pop the rest of the students. Jordyn, Scout, and Russ appear, swarming Julian.

Ms. Honig calls for our attention and outlines a scavenger hunt, entrusting us to meet at one pm for the Shakespeare performance. Mr. Honig's attention darts as if he'd like to drag race or do something that involves dangerously high speeds. Either that or the buzzing energy is a family trait.

"Remember, this is the main component of your grade this semester. No goofing off. You're nearly adults. I expect you to act like it." Her instruction tempts the opposite. She hands out the sheets listing the various items related to Emily Dickinson that we need to find, explains that her cellphone number is printed on the top, and we're off.

I check the one in my bag again. Nothing.

She assigns Howard, Neda, and a girl dressed in black with pale makeup named Astrid Fox, Julian, and me into one group. Swept into their midst, we meander farther into the museum. Unfortunately for Tegan, she's partners with Brooke Bishop, a devoutly rule-abiding student. I only know this because of the rumor that she turned in six kids last year for plagiarism. I don't judge. The bonus is Tegan won't be tagging along with Julian and, by default, me. She scowls at Astrid and me as Brooke trails Ms. Honig like the suck-up she is. After Tegan mutters something about Halloween not being for a few more weeks, I have the feeling Astrid and I unite under the witch face banner. I proffer a sisterly smile. Astrid scowls and vanishes to brood somewhere in a moldering corner of the museum to write down her daisy-in-the-dark thoughts. Neda looks like she might breathe fire, barbecuing Tegan, on principle alone. I force back a smile.

All the same, Tegan trails behind when we enter the main house. The walls echo with claustrophobic poetic themes—life, death, and love. And now. This bittersweet moment. Julian takes my hand while reciting lyrical inspiration from a placard.

The smell of nearly two-hundred-year-old wood and wallpaper and the delightfully musty scent of books knock me into reconnaissance

## Two Truths and One Thief

mode. I check items off the list, including Dickinson's desk and the statuette on the mantel in the parlor. I could the simple motion detectors at the entrances to rooms and sensors on the windows. A few strategically placed cameras. Security is minimal. This would be a breeze. But a question I've never asked comes to mind. Why take? Why not give?

I let out a breath as Julian answers a poetry riddle for the scavenger hunt: a snowy scene on an oil canvas, a hummingbird, and a portrait of the artist's sister, found in the Homestead and in the Evergreens.

I wander away from thoughts of theft and toward a sloping green lawn leading to a playhouse where we'll see a traveling Shakespeare company perform Romeo and Juliet this afternoon. A couple of birds sing to each other. Somewhere far off a truck crankily changes gears and a plane flies invisibly overhead. Yet, for me, time suddenly stands still. If nothing else, Julian and I have now. I freeze-frame this moment.

His lids get heavy like he's shy but owns it. He leans his forehead against mine. We linger. I open my eyes and close them and then open them again. Then his arms are around me and mine are around him and our lips meet. Our lips say so much without words, writing a kind of physical poetry.

The little hands on my watch don't matter until the voices of students natter close. We draw apart.

Julian and I walk into the mostly-quiet midday town. College students pop onto the scene, grabbing lunch, or shouting to their friends from across the road. A kid on a skateboard clinks by and Julian winces. "My mother took mine away."

I think I'm the reason why. I don't ask. He won't say.

Then I blurt. "I'm sorry I'm not a normal girl your mother would approve of." The very confusion I've been feeling claims his features. "Normal? What does that mean?"

I shrug.

He points to a car with polka dot paint and dinosaur figurines glued to the trunk. "Do you think the person who drives that car is normal?" He drops a dollar in the case of a street performer playing a rock song on the violin. "Him? Or what about the art at the IFA, do you think any of those people are normal? Emily Dickinson, after reading some of her poems, was she normal?" He shakes his head, emphatically. "To take a daring step further, do you think any of those people care? I don't. Painting your car? Playing rock and roll on a violin? Writing about despair and Bobolinks? Me? Fighting, drawing, tattooing? I say forget normal. Do whatever gets you closer—"

"You haven't met my family."

"What about mine? My sister is dead. My mother is a—puckered up prune who—" He squeaks out a laugh at the description. "Sorry, but it's true."

Awkwardness averted.

"Think about it, she's dried and shrivel-y, gives me an upset stomach, and she's bitter. Also, she won't give up on the college pressure. I don't want to have loan debt for the next fifteen years. It's not the only way path to success. My father is awesome and he didn't go to college, but he's irresolute, wishy-washy or something." Julian stops me on the sidewalk. "Penny, by trying so hard to be normal, we end up missing out on who we really are. When we skip out on life in favor of some stupid illusion, we miss the point. It's a relief not to be hung up on normal. You're smart and interesting, clever and mysterious. I like who you are."

The words hover between us. Tears hide behind my eyes. No one has ever said anything like that to me. That they like me. Not Mum, Dad, Caroline. Not even my twin.

## Chapter 27

JULIAN LIFTS THE SLEEVE OF MY SHIRT AND PEEKS AT MY WATCH. We missed the first act. He rests his head against mine. "Come on, let's go be not-normal together." He pulls me by the hand, back through the cemetery, and along a narrow alleyway by a parking garage leading to the center of the town. He unzips his bag and shakes up a can. I watch as he tags the brick in letters with sharp edges. I think it says Rowena, his sister's name. He tosses me the paint.

In pink splotchy, drips, I ink the word *Thief*. The air around us is silent except for the hiss of the can. Then we both turn toward the smooth glide of a skateboard. Julian's smile is irrepressible. We follow the telltale sound to a courtyard adjacent to the parking garage. The wispy bushes and rust-colored mums are a feeble attempt to make the concrete monstrosity eco-friendly. A few guys wheel along the cement doing tricks.

A guy with a shaved head hollers, "I recognize you."

Chins jut and fists form.

Julian smirks. "What? This million-dollar face?" He chuckles at his self-deprecating humor. "Can't say we've met before."

"No, the tattoos. You fought a couple of weeks ago against Billy. Billy the Bullseye. A fight night. I'm Maverick."

"Maverick, huh? Did I win?" Julian asks with a smirk on his lips that doesn't match the sudden darkness in his eyes.

The heat pumping off these guys suggests they wouldn't be opposed to brawling right now.

"Yeah. You were rough," says a guy wearing a flannel shirt.

Their tough exteriors and clenched jaws break into twisted smiles.

I exhale with relief.

A kid wearing a black T-shirt says to Julian, "I thought you were going to kill him. Had it coming though. Billy the Bullseye thinks he's the boss."

"Not what I do or why I do it, but good to know I entertained you," Julian replies, barely concealing the hardening of his features as if irritated by the mention of his activities serving another, more violent, purpose.

Someone's cell phone beeps repeatedly, breaking the tension while Julian and Maverick have a staring contest.

The phone continues to beep. The guy in the flannel lifts his chin in my direction and says, "I think that's you."

I reach into my bag. Could it be Vicky? Queenie?

The messages are from the *Call Me* contact.

**Where**
**Are**
**You**
**?**

It must be my sister. I run blindly toward the parking lot. In the distance, Ms. Honig hovers by a lamppost, conferring with her brother. I have to get back. Now. The pair shift slightly and the angle of her hip and the crook of her finger suggest she's scolding him in guttural German. Before I reach them, she turns and buzzes down the sidewalk toward the playhouse. Perhaps she noticed our absence, but detention doesn't matter right now.

The guy paces as if he'd like to get out of here too. Footfalls sound on the pavement from behind. I'm afraid it's Honig and her hive, but it's Julian.

Catching my breath I say, "I need a ride back to Boston. Now."

"What happened?" he asks.

I shake my head because I don't know, but I think Vicky must be trying to find me.

Honig's brother looks on, barring the entrance to the bus, but it's ridiculous to think the driver would take me back to Boston without the others. "She said to look for two students who went missing," he says in a thick German accent. "She said if I found them to make sure they stay put."

I glance around the lot, regretting not knowing how to drive as uncertainty bashes against urgency.

"She should know I've never been very good at following directions." He winks. "You said you need to go back to Boston? I can give you a ride."

I light up. "To Boston? Really?"

"Do you have a car?" Julian asks.

He surveys the parking lot, lands on a vehicle in the eastern corner, nods, and strides away. In less than three minutes, he returns in the driver's seat of an Audi. The need to get back to Boston overrides reason. Julian and I get in. The man smiles and revs the engine.

It isn't until we reach the highway that I realize there isn't a key in the ignition.

I glance at Julian in the backseat, wondering if he noticed, but his attention is on a field with a pair of horses nibbling grass by the fence.

"You're Ms. Honig's brother?" I ask as the speedometer passes ninety.

"She thought it would be good if I visit." He changes lanes. "I like your country roads very much."

From the back, Julian says, "Are you familiar with our laws, Mr. Honig—?"

"You can call me Dresden."

He laughs. "Just get us there safely," Julian says.

I repeatedly reply to the message on the phone but don't get one in response. The rest of the ride passes in accelerated silence as my mind chatters with fears and possibilities.

Dresden weaves through the traffic as we near the city. I direct him to Vicky's apartment.

He brakes in front of a fire hydrant, leaving the car running.

He looks at his watch. "Under three-quarters of an hour. Is that good timing?"

Julian laughs. "It took the bus two hours."

"Thanks," I say, thankful we weren't pulled over and arrested.

Julian asks, "Do you need the bathroom? Some water? A coffee?"

"I better get back to the museum," he says with a sly smile. He takes my phone and enters his digits. "If you ever need another ride, give me a call."

## Chapter 28

WITHOUT ANOTHER TEXT, HOURS PASS AS I LAY ON VICKY'S BED WITH Julian beside me and the phone between us. The paper cranes wing the air. I think of the story she told me, about how if you make a thousand cranes in one year, you'll be granted a wish upon opening them. I wonder how many wishes sail overhead. It's hard to tell. I wonder what Vicky wished for. I consider unfolding a string of them and asking for her back, but I'm already disappointed, there's no need to prove it won't work.

Julian taps his number into the phone, gets up, and kisses me on the forehead. "Call me as soon as you hear anything."

I want to explain, but my lips only cooperate when they land on his with a kiss.

After he leaves, the suffocating curtain of reality drops, leaving me groping for anything to steady me since I got those messages.

After hours of restlessness merging with disappointment and worry, and no follow-up text, I hire an Uber back to campus.

Instead of going to my dorm, I loiter by a construction site on campus—probably something my dad paid for—watching a couple of skaters do tricks, defying gravity and campus rules. A kid with a red hat ollies down a set of stairs. Then another, with the hood of his sweatshirt up, follows him but slides down the handrail. The snap of wheels off cement purr insistently, crowding out all the clatter in my head.

A kid with neon stripes in his hair that must be reserved for weekend warrior status, floats in the air as he does a three-sixty. Then another skater approaches and launches himself up the stairs. I recognize the squared shoulders and planes of his face as he moves in and out of the shadows. It's Julian. He spots me and almost careens with the guy in the red hat. He wheels around and stops next to me, panting.

"Did you hear anything?"

I shake my head and remind him he said his mother took away his skateboard.

"She went out of town to visit my grandmother. I decided to be a good boy and return to campus." A wicked grin spreads on his lips as he spreads his arms wide, calling into the night, "Give me freedom or give me—" His laughter echoes in the night, but it also calls to mind my twin. Maybe she broke out of jail and is in hiding. The phone feels hot in my pocket as I wait for word from whoever sent those messages. Freedom or death. Right now, all I want is to feel free from this waiting and worry.

Julian leans the board against the bench. We sit under the jack-o-lantern glow of the lantern light above. "Almost forgot, I got you something." He reaches into his bag, pulls out a brown parcel, and hands it to me. My stomach hopes it's a bagel.

I trace my finger around the cartoon sketches of me he doodled on the wrapping. There's one of me writing poetry, but instead of a pen, I'm holding a carrot. There's one of me standing on my head. There's one of me as a bird. It's goofy and perfect.

"A sort of belated birthday present." He shyly shoves his hands in his pockets and the corners of his mouth hitch into a smile. "Open it. You'll hate it."

I remove the paper without tearing it and slide out a slim blue book. In script, on the cover, it says *Romeo and Juliet*.

Julian explains, "Everyone should have a favorite poet."

"Even if they don't like poetry?" I ask.

"Especially if they don't like poetry."

"Who's yours?"

"The Bard, of course," he says as if I might argue the point. I don't.

I hug the book close. Even though Vicky told me not to have favorites, the words, "Thank you," tumble gratefully from my lips.

The guy with the hoodie, who I watched cruise around before I spotted Julian, approaches. "Hey, haven't seen you skating all week. This your girl?" They bump fists.

Julian's smile isn't reckless. "Yeah. Penny."

I'm his girl. If I were like Vicky, I'd sling my arm around his neck, plant a big, wet kiss on his cheek, and say something like, *And he's my guy*. But I'm the shy sister. The wallflower...and I've never been someone's girl.

## Chapter 29

JULIAN FINISHES MAKING INTRODUCTIONS TO HIS CREW. "PENNY, THIS is Luigi, Luigi, Penny."

"Nice to meet you."

"You're bleeding," Julian says, pointing out the gash on Luigi's neck. He angles into the light pouring from the streetlamp and dabs his wound with his hand.

"They have napkins at the student center," he answers as if it's no big thing. "We're going to get some tacos, want to come with? *Mangia*?" he asks in an imitation-Italian accent as a few other guys appear.

"Hash nasty," one of them says, pointing to the gash. "You need to wash the gravel out of that scrape."

Julian looks to me. I shrug, my attention lagging about thirty seconds behind, stuck on the first question Luigi asked and how Julian answered it.

We follow the guys toward the student center. Without Required Attire uniforms, I don't recognize any of them. Doubly so when a cluster of students dressed up like zombies passes us, likely on their way to an early Halloween party. Julian reaches for my hand as if to protect me from the walking dead.

Luigi howls as they pass. One of the guys pretends to be a vampire and mimes biting Luigi on the neck where blood streaks toward his collar. For a moment, I think he might bite back, but then they're laughing.

Julian shares his chips and salsa with me. We avoid talking about the strange call earlier but touch on digital versus paperbacks, strings versus electric, and oil versus watercolor. Luigi and the two other guys, Jose and Johnny, contribute except for that last one.

I forget I'm the only girl in a crew of skaters or what my name, Penny Goldfeather, might mean in certain circles, and that worry twists and snakes in my veins threatening to split me wide open. A notice on the well-worn student center cork board catches my attention—it's a flyer about the grand opening of Dartmont's Institute of Fine Arts secondary location. The skating location will soon be off-limits. Then I snort. Last I heard they were using the endowment to revamp the student center. Guess whoever controls the purse strings wants to impress parents and alum more than the current student body. Figures.

Back outside, our breath puffs into clouds and then disappears.

"So, you brawlin' later?" Johnny asks Julian.

"Yeah. I told them I'd be there at eleven." Julian answers as if consulting his schedule.

"My bets are on you, bro," Luigi says.

I glance at my watch. It's ten-thirty. I check the phone. No missed calls. Not another text. I could go back to my dorm and wait, alone, or snatch this bit of freedom, stalling the inevitable crash back into reality.

Julian reaches for my hand and whispers into my hair, "You don't have to come."

I worry there's meaning between these lines.

"I don't want it to freak you out. Remember our conversation about normal?" He smirks. "I told you, I'm not on that list either, and I don't want my not-normal to upset you."

I don't want to helplessly circle possibilities as I wait for another text. I don't want hopelessness to seize me in the still hours. I take his hand and don't let go.

## Two Truths and One Thief

We skulk past familiar buildings until we're on the edge of campus by a massive drainpipe.

One of the guys calls it the "Covert Culvert."

We enter, seemingly moving back in the direction we came. The corrugated metal turns to a dirt floor and stone walls.

"Where are we?" My voice echoes.

"Dartmont's secret tunnels. Remember Toshi Solomon? He was in your older sister's class. He uncovered this passage and others."

We reach a purple wooden door. A hulking figure—a guy from the football team?—nods and lets us all in.

"You may very well be the first female to show up at one of these," Julian says as the roar of men and boys shouting gets louder. In the clamor, I hear music but can't determine the song. The space opens to a room with a massive domed ceiling. It's dim, but I vaguely make out letters painted on it that spell the words *Old Guard*. My Caroline's run-in with them comes to mind, but I didn't pay much attention to the details.

A line forms behind a kid from math who stands behind a table taking cash. In the center, two others beat the crap out of each other. Spit and sweat shower the nearest bystanders, cheering them on. It's blood and gore and machismo. I have the urge to pull Julian away, but he's smiling like he already won.

"You can bet on me if you want," he says into my ear.

"I already have," I answer.

He smiles and kisses my forehead before a junior wearing a bowler hat pulls him away. I search the crowd for Luigi, Johnny, and Jose, but there are so many figures, sweating and shouting, that it's hard to make out anyone distinctly until my eyes land on Julian, across the room. With his shirt off and his back to the center ring, the tattoo of a compass and birds flying east cover his skin. The guy in the hat wraps his knuckles with tape. Something tells me that isn't enough. He'll have fresh cuts in a little while.

Of the guys still in the ring, one of them is on his hands and knees and the other kicks him swiftly in the gut. He crumbles into something other than ego. The winner raises his hands over his head. There's cheering. Others spit on the loser. I don't want to be amidst the violence that crosses into a twisted form of abuse. Tonight, I steal logic.

I should be anywhere but here and Julian should be with me. It could be an animal shelter or a frozen yogurt shop or a furniture store. I'd even rather be in Ms. Honig's classroom.

Instead, Julian enters the ring. He's raw muscle and tattoos. Someone calls his name over the clatter. Maverick, the guy with the shaved head from the park, appears opposite Julian. They flash with recognition. The two shake hands. I can't imagine they'll go through with it. I can't begin to understand this cruel brotherhood. But now I know where the chipped tooth came from.

The crowd hushes when a guy announces, "Last call for bets."

A husky figure wearing the Dartmont button-down dress shirt and tie pulled loose—like he just stepped out of an office—confers with Julian and Maverick. It's Howard Waddleston. He's the one who made the app. My jaw drops then fastens shut when the guys leave their corners as the bell rings. They match in size, but the skater outweighs Julian in arrogance.

A bell rings. The room is stale breath, sweat, and guttural shouting as the two circle each other like predator and prey. I'm not sure which is which. I don't want to watch. I close my eyes.

Skin slaps skin. There's a storm of shouting and cockeyed encouragement. I peek. Julian lands a punch. A trickle of blood streams out of the corner of Maverick's mouth. He wipes it, staining the white wrapping on his hand.

There's another punch and Julian doesn't pause, he tackles the guy, pummeling him. The crowd surges forward, jostling me out of my spot. I stare at the backs of sweaty necks and shoulders. Arms lifted as if the triumph is their own, someone send a shower of golden liquid down on me. I battle with myself against rushing to the front of the crowd, pulling Julian off the mat, and away to somewhere safe. I lose to self-preservation as I avoid being trampled.

The guys in the room chanting Julian's name remind me of thunder. Electricity pulses in the air, thrilling everyone with the buzz of

## Two Truths and One Thief

violence. I drown in worry as I reluctantly try to find a vantage point. I catch edges and snatches of punching and kicking, grunting and shuffling. I find my way to an opening in the crowd and there's Luigi, cheering Julian on. The blood from his scrape stains his neck the color of wine. I've already seen enough blood. I let the room go fuzzy and concentrate on wishing that no one gets seriously hurt.

After forever, the bell rings again. The crowd cheers. I focus my eyes and land on Julian in the center, his arms lifted with the win. There's blood on his hands and sweat glistens from his brow to his chest. More coagulates under his nose. He's smirking, but not smiling. I can't see, but imagine Maverick in a puddle at his feet.

I wind through the crowd and resist the urge to alternately punch him for being such an idiot and hug him for not being dead. Guys clap him on the shoulder and shake his hand, congratulating him. They palm wads of cash. Their snake-like lips peel into something akin to satisfaction.

"You didn't like that, did you?" Julian asks when I finally reach him. He takes a long sip of water and wipes his forehead with a cloth.

"No," I answer, meeting his eyes with a combination of fear and worry and disgust.

He pulls on his shirt and jacket and guides me toward the door.

I welcome the cold air slapping my face and the hush of the campus after hours.

"I'm sorry," Julian says. "That was a bad idea, bringing you there. I know you're not delicate, but that was stupid."

"Why do you still do it?" I ask because there isn't a question less obvious.

He shrugs. "Because teasing mortality alleviates boredom. Because I'm deficient and incapable of using my own creative resources to solve my problems. Because I'm angry that my sister is gone. Because it's a way to make money. I have a lot of money, Penny. And because I want to punish myself for not being a better person." He stops on the sidewalk. My dorm is at his back. The windows are dark. My phone is silent.

Julian gently grips my shoulders. "Penny, I'm messed up."

"You aren't. You don't have to fight. It isn't worth it."

His eyes search the vacant space behind me, but the answer is closer than that. I wipe a smudge of blood from his lip with the hem of my sleeve. He closes his eyes, leans in close, and then he whispers, "You're probably the most dangerous and hardest fight I've ever been in. But you're worth it, every ache when we're not together, every bruise when I think about losing you."

"Will you stop fighting if I say yes?"

"Yes to us?" he asks. "Always?"

I nod.

He smiles.

I say nothing more and then we're in front of Prince Dorm.

"Want to come up?" he asks shyly.

"That's against the rules, isn't it?" I'm either drunk on anxiety or potential.

"That word isn't part of my vocabulary."

"Clearly."

He nudges me with his shoulder toward the door.

"Isn't this a sneak-in operation?"

"Nah. I'm more of a walk-through-the-front-door kind of guy."

Everything Vicky taught me about being covert rushes toward me. But just like that, we waltz inside.

I glance over my shoulder, expecting someone to try to stop us, but all I see is a shadow cross the foot of the steps leading away from the building.

## Chapter 30

Whereas I consider tiptoeing or performing a complicated parkour move to sneak past authority figures or nosy students, Julian and I simply walk upstairs to the third floor as if this doesn't break any rules.

"What about your roommate?" I whisper.

"I took the top floor, so I don't have one."

When we enter, he tosses his backpack in the corner. "Mind if I shower?" he asks, taking off his sweaty shirt. My heart ticks up a few notches.

When I hear the water running from the bathroom down the hall, I distract myself with a stack of skate and tattoo magazines, along with a few art school brochures next to a fat stack of traditional college prospectuses.

The dim, ivory light spilling from a single lamp illuminates Julian's sparse room. There's a dresser with clothes hanging out of the drawers, a stack of books and notebooks, an empty laundry basket with socks and boxers scattered around it, and hockey gear. I pull the blinds up on his windows, letting the stars in and then sit on the edge of his bed. I spot a binder open to a page with photographs of tattoos and leaf through, discovering loads of color and black and white images.

Julian appears at the door, a white towel wrapped around his waist. Teen girl hormones stampede. "I was apprenticing for a while," he explains.

It takes me a moment to add up what he means and find my voice. I flip to the cover of the binder and read the silver label *Julian Freese, Artist*. "You have tattoos, but you do them too?"

He nods while taking out a T-shirt. The roots of a tree wrap around the length of skin under his arm and the branches stretch toward the compass on his back. "Yeah," he answers with modest pride.

Knowing this secret emboldens me.

He sits on the floor next to me, leaning against the mattress. He flips through the pages as if remembering each tattoo.

I spot a few that are on his skin. "You give them to yourself?"

"Just on my left half." He laughs. "It's hard to get them right on the other side. Most of mine I've collected from other artists, partly so I can study their methods. But I'm running out of room."

"I have plenty of room," I say.

"Do you have any tattoos?" he asks, searching me as if pops of ink will reveal themselves through my clothes.

"Nope." There's so much terrain we haven't explored. Here again, just the two of us, in a bedroom at night, lends to suggestion. I slink by the idea. "Vicky did. A huge heart." I trail off, realizing I'm already pushing her into the past tense.

"What would you get?"

I already know. "Plum blossoms with a few petals blowing in the wind."

He bounces from the floor and retrieves a bag from a drawer. "Sterile. Promise." He jiggles a sealed pouch.

"Wait, what?"

"Where do you want them?"

My smile reaches my ears. "Really? Seriously? Right now? You aren't too tired?" That feeling, when I'm about to walk out of a store with my bag loaded full of stuff, times ten. No, a thousand. The forerunner of adrenaline pulses through me.

Julian bends over and puts his hands on my thighs. Our faces are inches apart. His eyes sparkle. "Anything to keep you here a little longer."

"How about a lot longer?"

If someone were to take a photograph right now, they wouldn't have to say, *Smile!*

I lean closer, waiting for the explosion of his lips meeting mine. My eyes flutter to his. He's looking at me like he doesn't want this moment to end.

"You and me," he says. I don't need to decode his meaning or read between the lines.

I don't waver from his eyes and then we melt together.

After a long kiss, Julian takes his tattoo tools out of his bag and arranges them on a milk crate covered in a sterile towel that he removed from another sealed pouch. He gropes in the corner for the electrical socket and then puts on music.

I take my jacket off and then my sweater, revealing a thin camisole. "Here." I point to my arm. "Scattered blossoms."

He sketches a few on the clean page of a notebook, perfectly capturing the soft curves of the delicate petals and the winding yet sturdy branch.

He fusses with the tattoo gun and it whirs and buzzes. He snaps on a pair of black gloves, cleans my arm, and tells me to take a deep breath. "Ready?"

"Ready."

I look away as the needle pierces, as Julian Freese permanently inks his visual poetry onto my skin. I'm chilled and warmed at the same time. My heart thuds in my ears as the image of a cherry blossom branch evolves beautifully, but then I have an awful thought. I want to see if he has a heart that matches Tegan's. I have to ask the foolish question even if I won't like the answer. "Did you, um, give Tegan the heart on her hip?"

He grimaces and then swallows. The gun goes quiet. He nods.

"Oh. Do you have a matching...?"

His lips tremor in the dim light. Our eyes meet. "No, there's no matching heart."

When an album's worth of songs ends and another begins, he asks, "How're you doing?"

I snap to, adrift in thoughts of...nothing. I'm right here, with Julian, exactly where I want to be. My comfort is unnerving.

We talk about tattoos, which he seems to like more than skateboarding, and definitely more than fighting, or maybe it's just art in general that he loves. When he's halfway done and my watch tells me it's well into the next day, I consider getting an entire sleeve. "I could lay here for hours, letting you draw on me." A fuzzy, sleepy smile blankets my face.

"Yeah? I wouldn't object." He looks up from my arm as he wipes the fresh ink with a clean cloth.

His words run into my thoughts about more ink on my skin. "A beehive, a bird, distant shores..." I mutter, realizing I'm tired, very tired, almost too tired to run anymore. Landing here and nesting with Julian wouldn't be so bad.

I glimpse the sky as it lightens, drifting in and out of dreams. As he cleans his tools and I admire my arm, the sun blushes morning. He pulls me close as we recline on the soft bed. My eyes flutter and shutter, sending me, once more, into the quiet space of contentment. It's lovely here.

What if I really did let the past go?

## Chapter 31

I WAKE TO A DISTINCT BUZZING. HANDS CLUTCH ME CLOSE. MY ARM IS slightly stiff and it takes a beat to remember why.

Blinking my eyes open, Julian's phone rings incessantly. He groggily answers it.

A voice squawks, but it doesn't belong to Bird.

"Julian, explain yourself. No. Don't. I don't want to hear any more of your nonsense. I don't know who you think you are or what you think you're doing. I told you to stay away from girls, especially *her*."

I flinch. I'm eighteen, but nothing prepared me to know how to react to waking up in a boys' dorm room with his mother shouting through a phone. I want to tell her nothing happened. At least, not what she imagines.

"Julian? Are you there? Wake up this second."

His expression goes from sleepy to stony.

"Julian! You weren't worth the hemorrhoids. Do you hear me? Are you listening to me? Have you ever listened? No, you haven't. You're a real pain just like your father."

If I were standing up my knees would buckle. I'm not sure which is worse. A mother who ignores you or one who is straight-up mean.

"Mom, what are you talking about?" he asks.

"I know she's there." The malice in her words paralyzes me.

"Who? What?"

"Don't play dumb. I have it on good authority that you had an overnight guest. Not only is that against Dartmont rules, but it's also against our rules. I pay for you to attend that school. I'm going to report this incident to the dean. You have no business bringing girls like her into your dorm. Young man, I told you, grounded. What wasn't clear about that? Do I need to spell it out? G-R-O—"

"I'm sorry," he says to me, his eyes landing on the tattoo.

Regina carries on. "Grounded meant no girls, especially not her." Her words drip with disgust.

He gets to his feet and starts pacing as she goes on.

"I said no skateboard," she adds.

All I can hear is the word no, no, no. So many *no*s. I imagine Regina can't say the word *yes*.

"You're supposed to be reviewing your options for college. You've amounted to nothing so far, Julian. I expect you to at least be making an effort. You have until the end of the weekend and if you don't get your act together, I'm going to be making your choices for you. And trust me, you'll be walking a fine line. In the meantime, I want you to stay away from her." Not only is Regina incapable of saying yes, it's like she can't seem to say my name either. Like it would burn her tongue.

Julian explodes in a string of expletives and explanations. I've managed to get my shoes on and reach the door. He interrupts himself and says, "Penny, wait."

I hurry through the dorm. Julian reaches for my hand.

"I'm sorry," he says again.

"No, I am. She's wretched." I want to scream at her for him.

"Can I—?"

I grip his jaw in my hands and kiss him. "Whatever it is, yes."

Leaving his phone behind, he grabs his bag and board.

Regina's shouts through the device's speaker fade as we race into the cool October air and across campus. I want to rewind and redo this morning. I realize we're at the culvert that leads to the secret room from last night. That's not something I want to reexperience.

"Come on," Julian says.

"Why are we back here?"

"I have something to show you." He winks.

We walk silently through the pipe as water drips, filling the silence. The room from the night before stands empty and without so much as a scrap of paper or puddle of sweat to be seen.

"Did I imagine—?"

"Last night or this morning?" Julian asks, sounding tired and wishing you could answer yes to both.

"How do you think she knew?" I ask.

He shrugs. "Intuition? An insider? She said she had it on good authority. I don't know and I don't care." His voice echoes off the stone wall of the domed space but instead of an answer, I'm probably smart to put it out of my mind because worry about a visit to the dean's office in Ambrose for breaking the rules is the last thing I need right now.

As my eyes adjust to the dim light, I take in the hidden space. Julian explains about the Old Guard, the campus secret society.

"They were super powerful. Had this creepy annual competition where the loser had to take their own life."

I shiver. "In here?"

He shrugs. "Those are the rumors."

My mind flashes with images of the fight night.

"Word is they got in a lot of trouble recently with the heiress to the school. Were you here for the Jane Swift saga?"

"I know a bit."

"Anyway, they disbanded. But I don't know if I believe that. My gut says they scattered to the shadows and are still working in secret. But who knows."

"What did you want to show me?"

"Ah. When we started fight night, we needed somewhere discrete. Howard knew about this hidden room, among others." His eyebrows ripple. "Anyway, I came to check it out and found this." Julian pulls on the spine of a book on a low shelf in the corner. Where I expect him to recite poetry, the shelf disappears into the wall.

"What? Whoa. Where does it go?"

Julian smirks. "Let's find out."

Just as we're about to crawl through the opening, the phone in my pocket buzzes with a text, startling me so much I actually recoil. Pressing my hand to my chest because my heart pounds, I read the message.

**The Dirty**

Julian's eyebrows lift. "I thought you lost your phone."

I explain the phone but don't give the exact identity of who gave it to me.

"What does that mean?" he asks.

"I'm not sure."

"Whatever it is seems sketchy." He rubs his chin, growing in with a small amount of stubble. "The Dirty."

After he says it out loud, the nighttime glow of a sign, with the words *The Dirty* flickers to life in my mind. I once overheard Flavio mention he'd come from there one night. Then not even a week later, I walked by it while scouting a bank with Vicky, strictly for educational purposes.

"I think it's a sports bar. Soccer mostly. Maybe I can find Flavio there."

The secret passage will have to wait. As twilight descends, we return to Boston. If my parents don't start to question my Uber expenses, then I feel like I ought to bring it to their attention, if only to reprimand them for not keeping better track of me.

I wear a knit cap, a leather jacket, and jeans. I look so much like Vicky, it'll be easier for Flavio to recognize me if I don't see him first.

I muster my moxie as I walk in. Julian follows, an imposing figure like he haunts places like this regularly. A tiled bar runs in an L shape along the length of a brick wall covered in mirrors. Half a dozen barstools are empty, the rest peppered with what looks like a mixture of regulars and hipsters. Groups gather at tables dotting the room, drinking the various craft beers displayed on the immense chalkboard.

# Two Truths and One Thief

A soccer game plays on a TV across the room. I spot Flavio instantly. He clutches an empty glass and stares into its depths.

"When will she get out?" I ask.

Flavio, unshakable in the year I've known him, flinches.

Is guilt eating him alive? Did he turn her in?

"Penny," he chokes out, glancing around. "You shouldn't be here." He staggers to his feet and takes me by the arm. Julian tenses, ready to throw down.

"Then you shouldn't have texted me."

"I didn't. Wasn't sure how to get ahold of you."

I shake my arm loose and nod, telling Julian it's okay.

Flavio drives in silence, biting his knuckle, his eyes blurry. I should probably have taken his keys. He stops in front of the apartment building. I expect him to speed off but instead, he gets out.

When we enter, Bird frantically flaps his wings.

Flavio steadies himself on the table and then in a single exhalation, collapses into a chair. "Birdy," he says and pauses as if short of breath. "It's okay."

I'm not sure if he's speaking to Bird, himself, or me, but it's plain that right now, he is many things except okay. I've never seen him undone. I stand opposite him, afraid if I sit down, he'll tell me something I don't want to hear. I'm not quick enough to stop the dread that lands in my stomach.

He draws a breath and rubs his hands on his pants, studying the fibers or his fingers or something in an alternate universe. "Penny," he says again.

"Do you need something to drink?" I think about opening a window as I try not to consider the very real possibility my sister's sentence is much more serious and much longer than either one of us expected. But if that's the case, I don't care, I'll break the rules, that's what I'm good at. I'll do whatever it takes to get her back.

Flavio's eyes are vacant, but his lips part. "Vicky went missing."

The words scramble. They don't make sense. Is this what Brazilian sounds like?

"She's gone."

"From jail?"

He nods gravely.

"Did she escape? Did someone break her out?"

"No. She is just gone."

"So they lost her?"

Even though the passage of time in this small apartment is virtually invisible, like air or breath, it wheezes to a standstill. I feel suspended, tugged between reality and improbability.

I shake my head. "No, there must be a mistake. What do you mean?"

Flavio's eyes are pewter. I never noticed. Agony replaces the amusement he usually wears. He must have aged at least three hundred years in the last three minutes.

And that's exactly how I feel like I've just aged way beyond reasonable or conceivable. I heard something I never, in a million immortal years ever, thought I'd hear. She's invincible.

"All I can come up with is that she got into some hot water. Had to make a deal or something," he whispers like a prayer for the opposite.

"What kind of deal?"

"I don't know."

"With Sandro," I breathe so softly it sounds like a sigh.

Flavio sits with his head in his hands.

"What do we do?" I ask.

"I don't know. I've contacted everyone. No one has seen her. Whoever busted her out has deep pockets and widespread connections...someone she owed or wanted to use her expertise."

I take this to mean that whoever broke her out with out a trace isn't someone he wants to confront.

Flavio exhales heavily. "I don't know anything other than that she's not safe. She can't be. I failed," he mutters like it was his personal assignment to keep track of Vicky.

Bird screeches like a game show buzzer. Like that was the wrong answer.

"There's nothing we can do," he says as if all is lost.

"We can find her. Free her."

Flavio shakes his head. "I have to go. Do you mind if Birdy comes with me? It would mean a lot, and I'll take good care of him."

This practical detail brings me to my senses, moderately. I get up and stroke Bird's feathers, no longer afraid he'll peck my eyes out. "That's a good idea." My voice is barely above a whisper.

Flavio goes about gathering Bird's things. Julian and I help Flavio carry everything downstairs. The familiar street seems remote, the three of us on the sidewalk, an unreality.

"Along with the phone call, she said if anything ever happened, she wanted you to have this." He passes me a thin envelope. "Take care of yourself, Penny."

The red taillights of his car blur and my trembling hands barely hold onto the proof that my twin existed.

But the truth is even if Flavio won't help me find Vicky, I will.

## Chapter 32

An indistinct amount of time passes. The required student assembly tells me it's Tuesday, but I'm lost and adrift in a sea of confusion and worry knowing my sister potentially traded her freedom for something else... Sandro is the only person I can come up with that would be a risk to her given the things she'd said about him. Did she make a deal with him? Will she have to work for him? The guy she allegedly hates? Where is she?

Movement catches my attention as a woman with long white hair and turquoise jewelry steps onto the stage at the front of the auditorium. I vaguely recognize some of the guys seated nearby from the fight at the Old Guard headquarters.

I'm by no means one of the goodie-goodies at Dartmont. Even though I'm Caroline's sister, I'm also Vicky's twin, which makes me guilty by association. But to know there's a bigger underbelly here than I believed is...interesting. It appeals to the rebel in me. What else don't I know?

Part of me doesn't want to believe Vicky opted to make a deal with Sandro to get out of jail, essentially indenturing herself to him. I'd like to convince myself Flavio's sources had the wrong woman, but I have never seen a person so broken as I had when he told me what happened except when I look in the mirror.

Who are we without her?

I vaguely hear the woman onstage excitedly blustering about the new Institute of Fine Art branch. "It'll be a smaller version of the main museum in Boston, but there won't be anything modest about it." I drift in and out of her boasting about the prestige of the art until she says the name *Brando Muscarello*.

That name grabs my attention.

Something in my mind clicks as I think about the contents of the envelope Flavio gave me. All that was inside was a key—silver and slightly tarnished. Not a golden key encased in gems like Brando Muscarello made as an artful ode to the Cuore d'Oro and a competitor to a certain famous series of bejeweled Imperial Eggs.

My mind races as I try to connect the dots and figure out how to get Vicky back. How to pay off her debt or entice Sandro to change his mind. If I were to somehow obtain the Golden Key, could I use it to buy her freedom? It's almost as valuable as the Cuore d'Oro. Almost.

"I'll take it," I whisper.

Julian glances over at me as a smile rises to my lips. What Vicky would call a scheming smile.

I give my head a little shake to indicate I'll explain later because I don't know how I'll pull this off but only know that Dartmont just offered me an opportunity that I cannot refuse. An opportunity to save my sister.

The rest of the day is a blur except for the moments Julian and I are together, plugged in with technicolor clarity—the curve of his lips, the hazel-brown of his eyes, the grit of his calloused-hand touch. And the research I do online into Brando Muscarello and his *Chiave d'Oro*. The Golden Key.

"That doesn't look like Sharpe's assignment," Julian says, gripping my shoulders from behind when he finds me in the library.

I startle. "No, but it is history." My voice sounds cryptic.

"Care to clue me in?"

"Then I'd have to kill you." I wink.

"Harsh. I'll take my chances." He slides into the swivel chair next to mine.

The corner of my lip lifts in a grin. "This is the Chiave d'Oro, the golden key made by late nineteenth-century Italian artist Brando Muscarello."

"Never heard of him."

"He married into the Faberge family and—"

"Of Faberge Egg fame?"

I flash a pair of finger guns to indicate he got it right. "Muscarello wanted to compete with the tsar by creating something beautiful for his wife. Having studied with the son of the original Faberge, he knew the fine art of gold smithery. Instead of an egg, he made a key." Some say the key opens the Cuore d'Oro, but I don't see how that would work since they're both the same size."

Julian peers over my shoulder to look at the image on the computer screen. I breathe in his fresh scent.

He reads, "Chiave d'Oro. The golden key. The key to my heart. May I ask why the sudden and keen interest?" He eyes me like he knows I'm scheming.

I put the envelope into his hand and say, "In for a penny, in for a pound." Though I won't tell him that the golden heart was Vicky's dream score.

Julian opens the envelope and slides the silver key into his hand. "Not a golden key."

"Not a key I recognize." I shrug. "I have no idea what it goes to."

He looks at the other item in the envelope. It's a photograph, torn in half, of a young man with his arms crossed in front of his chest, gazing away from the camera. He wears a confident if not arrogant smirk. Julian flips it over. In faded pen, it says *Alessandro Roccio*.

"Vicky loved art, history, all of it. During sophomore year, she spent the summer in Florence Italy. Came back a changed person. In a good way. She was brighter if that makes sense. Then junior year everything changed."

"And she got kicked out of Dartmont."

Of course, he's heard the rumors. "Quietly removed, dismissed, and disowned."

"Your parents disowned her?"

"And by de facto, me. I took her side. But they'd cut me off long before in every way except financial."

"That sucks. Why'd she get kicked out?"

"She didn't officially. Our parents took her out. But worse was Vicky went from loving Sandro to hating him, but wouldn't talk about it or that Mum and Dad kicked her out of our family."

"Not even to you?"

"Not even to me," I repeat. "I never met or saw Sandro, but I assume this is him given the similarity with the names. Sandro, Alessandro."

"He can't be much older than us."

"What does Vicky want me to do with this stuff?" I ask even though I know I won't get an answer.

"Looks like someone else was originally in the photo." Julian points to the edge where an arm and shoulder are visible. I blink a few times. "I wonder if it was Vicky. Considering we were twins, she led such a secret life."

"Looks like Sandro was married." Julian points to his ring finger.

"No way. This picture is only a couple of years old."

"My guess is she loved him, but he was with someone else."

My jaw drops as a thought slices into my mind. "Trust me, that would not stop Vicky. Remember? She's the bad twin."

I study the photo again. Sandro has tousled brown hair that looks like it would stand on end if you ran his fingers through it. He's definitely in need of a shave. The rogue look in his gaze tells me everything I need to know. My sister loved him. Of course, she did. Then she hated him. Which also makes perfect sense because she's Vicky. But why?

Now, she's in his debt. Which confuses me. It's like I'm staring at a puzzle and missing a few key pieces.

"If you found yourself with a golden key covered in gems, what would you do with it?" Julian asks, referring to the image on the screen.

I point to the picture. "I'd make a trade. Something valuable for someone valuable."

"You think Sandro has her? Know where to find him?" Julian asks.

"I'm resourceful."

"So you're saying you'll use the key to unlock your sister's freedom?"

Feeling awash with excitement and energy, I smile and give one sharp nod.

"This sounds like as good an idea as me fighting in a secret underground headquarters."

"But no one will get hurt."

"What about getting caught?"

"You've never seen me in action."

"A brand new state-of-the-art building on campus with high-powered security is a lot different than the Clothing Cloud. I promise."

"Are you trying to talk me out of this?"

"Yep," Julian says matter of fact.

"I have to help my sister."

"What about hiring a lawyer?"

"Julian, she was in jail. Sandro somehow broke her out without a trace. I think we're past leveraging a legal team."

His expression flickers as if he doesn't want to hear the truth. "Is there a Plan B?"

"Not yet." I'm still working on Plan A.

Julian rocks back and then scrubs his hand down his face. "Why do I feel like I'm going to regret this?"

"You don't have to be a part of it."

"Where you go, I go," he says as if there's no question or argument to be had.

I've never been part of a pair with anyone other than Vicky. With her, the dynamic was different. She was the boss. I was the underling. Things with Julian are different, equal, yet we each have our own strengths and things we offer.

Tapping my cheek, I say, "I bet the plans for the new campus museum are in Ambrose."

"If I knew a secret way to get in there and didn't tell you to save you from yourself would you hate me?" Julian bites his lip.

I gasp and then make a guess, "The secret passages."

He nods and exhales as I clobber him with a hug. "You're brilliant," I practically shriek with way less cool than Vicky would ever display.

"I'm dumb." He mutters something else that sounds a lot like, And *chin glove,* but I can't be sure.

After dusk, Julian and I return to the covert culvert. The water is a few inches higher than last time and I try to tip-toe along the edge so my shoes don't get soggy.

When the tunnel turns from metal to stone, Julian stops to listen. "It's quiet. That's good."

"Is there another fight?"

"Usually just Friday nights, but you can never be too sure." His voice is disturbingly casual.

"I'm still wondering what you wanted to show me behind the bookcase."

"A library of sorts."

"I thought you were going to say it leads to treasure."

"Depends on what you think is valuable."

My boot scuffs on the uneven ground as if his comment tripped me up.

"It's the private library in the Walbus Mansion up on Snow Hill," he whispers. "We'll go some other time."

We're quiet until we pass the purple door. The shadows cast on the wall from Julian's phone light give me shivers. I reach for his hand. We reach a crossroads.

"Eenie, meenie..."

"Seriously?"

"Kidding. It's this way." We go right.

"I'm surprised Vicky didn't know—" I stop myself, realizing she probably did know all about these passages. I try to ignore how small I feel at how much she kept from me.

We get to what appears to be a dead end. Julian passes me his phone and then smooths his palms along the wall, looking for an opening. It's a flat panel without a handle, indent, or hinge. He pushes on it, but it doesn't budge. He throws his shoulder into it with a grunt. Nothing. He tries the other way, drawing it toward us, but there's nothing to hold onto.

"I could've sworn..."

"Maybe admin found out and blocked it. We could enter Ambrose through a window or pick a lock."

"You'll have to get their security specs first. That building has eyes on it, is locked down tight, and they now have a security guard. Some guys I know wanted to break in and alter their student records."

"And how did you plan to get past them?"

He shrugs. "My dashing charm? Mesmerizing poetry? A knock on the head with my skateboard?"

I snap my fingers "Wait. Howard Waddleston. I didn't think to ask him if he could obtain the building plans and security specs." As soon as the words are out, Vicky's voice is in my head warning me about trust. *The fewer people know, the better.*

Somehow, I shrink even more. Doubt starts to creep in because maybe I'm not cut out for this thief life after all.

## Chapter 33

That night, back in my dorm, I plot. Scheme. Try to figure out how to get the golden key. Vicky would already be on the other side of campus and halfway into the new building.

I guess I'm built differently. Not quite Golden Girl Caroline and not Wild Card Victoria.

But who am I?

I don't know anymore. Vicky would do whatever was necessary to help me. I have to do the same.

The last grains drop into an invisible hourglass as though reminding me that I'm running out of time. The cryptic text message comes to mind.

If the game were two truths and one lie, everything Vicky ever said was a secret or a lie, leaving one truth remaining. I'm a thief. That's all there is to it. I'll steal her freedom no matter what.

Forget the key. That's child's play. To buy my twin's freedom, I need to go bigger. Fortunately, the plan to obtain it is already in place and I know it inside and out, frontward and backward.

The Cuore d'Oro will still be Vicky's big score, but I'll have to be the one to obtain it.

I return to the apartment in Boston. I pull out my phone, request an

Uber, and sneak through the orchard to the road that runs behind the school.

It's after midnight by the time the city lights glitter against the night and I reach the apartment. My focus shifts and sharpens as I study the piece of vellum with the security schematics containing a lot of boxes and symbols.

I trace a path from the entry point, the route to the Empire room, and how to lift the heart from the pedestal without engaging the motion sensors. The whole operation will take less than an hour. I feel reckless with longing. Hunger in my fingertips.

A list on the top of a stack of mail on the table catches my attention. It looks like a shopping list but is titled "Change." The items not checked off include:

- Gloves
- Bird seed
- Hair dye (pink)

For some reason, the word *change* hangs in the air like a suspended flash of heat lightning. All this time, I've been following in my sister's footsteps. Now it's time for me to step into my own shoes.

"Change," I whisper. I breathe in the word and wonder what it might do to my chemistry.

It sounds foreign, not Mandarin, Italian, not even Russian, and definitely not translatable to any language other than the dialect of doing, rather than thinking. Or in my case, not doing: stealing, lying, and cheating.

But I can't do that until after I help my sister, so I change my hair instead. Cotton candy pink like on the list. While I wait to rinse it, I read the note from Vicky. The birdseed. She used to stash money in the bottom of the bag. Flavio took it. Once a con, always a con. Forget him.

A plan forms in my mind and I step into the night. A weeknight drizzle continues to fall from the sky. The streets are hushed except for

## Two Truths and One Thief

piano music filtering out of a restaurant and the occasional car sloshing by.

My reflection streaks by in the window of a vintage shop. I hardly recognize myself other than I look exactly like my twin—she constantly changed her hair color—red, green, blue, black. The plan is to take her place. But first, I need to steal confidence that I can pull off the theft.

Keeping to the shadows, I make my way toward the museum, running through the plans Vicky so diligently plotted and prepared me for.

*Enter through the galvanized hatch on the roof.*
*Scale the old service elevator shaft to the second floor.*
*Right side in.*
*Left side out.*
*Perch on the knee wall and aim for the wooden stud between the watercolor from the Sung Dynasty and the fire extinguisher.*
*Zip over the parquet floor, hovering over the dragon at precisely the right moment and replacing it with a specially fabricated weight the exact size and shape of the golden dragon.*
*Repeat in reverse.*

There are motion sensors. Thermostats. Cameras. And of course, the pedestal itself, which will alert security if it detects a change in pressure or temperature for longer than three seconds.

I wipe my brow as the illuminated white columns of the Institute of Fine Art come into view. My mind races at the sound of skateboard wheels rolling over the street in the distance. I put Julian, as well as right and wrong, out of my mind.

I round to the back of the building and toward a service entrance ramp. Anticipation builds. I scale a damp metal railing. The rolling wheels grow louder. I send Julian's image, the feeling when our lips meet, and the way he held onto me through the most difficult parts of the last weeks, farther away as I climb the ladder on the south side of the building. My breath is loud in my ears as the stars get closer. I vault over the side of the building landing silently on the broad, flat roof.

The familiar layout spreads before me with skylights, hatches, entrances, and vents. I crouch and run to the north side. My feet pad quietly under the blanket of the night sky.

I reach the correct hatch and examine the metal clips securing it shut. One is bent at an odd angle, but I could pry it loose. I'm getting the Cuore d'Oro to use as leverage to pay off Vicky's debt. Get her back. It'll happen in the next ninety minutes. Determination meets opportunity.

A thrill rushes through my veins.

Just as I lift the hinged screen, a strong and determined hand lands on my shoulder. I resist a startle. Holding my breath, I make a split decision on whether to run or defend myself then notice the familiar cuts and scars on the person's knuckles.

## Chapter 34

I lace my fingers in Julian's and turn slowly. Our eyes meet. His sparkle and ask the obvious question. I've told him everything but not this. Not about the golden heart. He wouldn't understand.

"Whatcha doing?" he sing songs.

"Oh, I work for a glass company. Inspecting the windows." I laugh so he knows I'm joking, not intending to lie because he needn't bother to have asked the question. No doubt, he knows what I'm doing.

"Hmm. Considering I have my skateboard, I should see if I can ollie that rail over there." Julian points to a long tube of metal slick with rain.

"The one on the edge? It's a six-story drop."

"I've done higher."

"No."

"No?" His eyebrows waggle like my caution makes him all the more daring.

"That's dangerous."

"And what you're doing isn't?" he counters.

I scratch the nape of my neck. "Fair point."

"So what are you really doing here? Going to steal a painting? Some crown jewels?"

I told myself it's time to change. Here goes. "Have you ever heard of the Cuore d'Oro?"

"No. Sounds fancy."

"Very. During the height of the Renaissance, a member of the Medici family in Italy commissioned a Florentine artist to create a work of art that would demonstrate the true love he felt in his heart for his mistress."

"Sounds like a slimeball."

I tip my head from side to side. "Very. The story goes the original heart was carved from onyx and studded with what we'd now consider blood diamonds."

"Sounds dark."

"His wife found out and had it destroyed. Threatened to have him beheaded."

"Can't say he didn't deserve it."

"He tried to make it right by commissioning another artist to create something magnificent for her. They crafted a golden heart adorned with a mosaic of gems, pearls, and other precious materials that opened to reveal an interior made entirely of rubies and diamonds with the words 'Your heart is mine.' But no one has ever been able to open it."

"Romantic. But don't you mean 'My heart is yours?'"

"No. You heard me right. But the wife loved it. Mercurio Medici went on to have nine more just like it commissioned."

"Let me guess, one for his other mistresses."

I give one sharp nod in affirmation. "Then, some years later, they were all destroyed or went missing. Legend has it the original is the only one that remains. I hear the golden hearts also inspired the Fabergé eggs which later inspired the Chiave d'Oro."

"Fascinating. But we should head back to Dartmont. Like a cat with nine lives, I'm afraid if we don't make more frequent appearances, we'll find ourselves in the dean's office."

"Julian, I have to do this," I whisper and release his hand.

An airplane cruises overhead and a car splashes through a puddle below.

He clasps his hands on top of his head, winging his elbows, and then lets out a long breath. "There's no other way?"

I shrug. Vicky was the planner of missions and misdeeds. "Not that I can come up with."

Julian laces his arms around my waist and then draws me close. "You don't have to do it alone." His voice is a promise in my ear.

"Don't I?" I ask. The risk is too big. "One wrong move and the sirens will blare. The police will come and arrest us both."

After his father's kindness and his mother's hostility, I don't want to put Julian in a more difficult or dangerous situation. Plus, he's never done something like this before. Then again, as far as I know, it's a two-person job. But that wouldn't stop Vicky.

I start to lower into the hatch, "I'll meet you later."

"If you go. I go," Julian says simply. "Whatever happens, we're in it together."

"You don't have to."

"Penny, I want to," he says as if it's the most obvious thing in the world. "You've spent enough of your life alone or in Vicky's shadow."

The corners of my eyes suddenly burn because that's almost the same thing.

He pinches my chin between his fingers, planting a kiss on my lips. A reckless grin grows on his face. "Are we chasing dragons or what?" he asks.

"Hearts. Well, one heart. The golden heart."

"What's it look like?"

"You'll know it when you see it."

The last thing I see as I descend into darkness is Julian's smile. The shaft is claustrophobic. Wires catch on my clothing and a pipe scalds my arm through my long-sleeved shirt. I try to make myself more compact.

Julian grumbles. "It's a tight fit."

"You can still turn around and go back," I offer.

He doesn't shrink from the challenge, as evidenced by the periodic sounds of him wincing on a snag or a hot pipe.

When I reach an L-bend, I open a ceiling tile. The mechanical room with boilers, HVAC equipment, and the central elevator machinery glows with controls and dials. An older elevator hulks in the corner. I lower down, landing lightly on my feet.

Julian's head appears in the hole, his grin wild as he passes me his skateboard.

"Couldn't you have left it on the roof?" I whisper.

He shrugs.

I resist an eye roll. "Put it in your backpack. Clearly, you haven't been schooled in the proper way to thieve."

"Will you be my teacher?" he asks as he lands with a rush beside me. "I'm a quick study. A good student."

I orient myself to the location of the ancient elevator motor. It's a hulking machine, but I want to be doubly sure it's not operational. I don't expect anyone to accidentally hit the service button at this time of night, but it's better to be safe than sorry. According to Vicky, this is the only dangerous part. Then again, she hated elevators and confined spaces for that matter.

Dust covers the belts and pulley system. Satisfied, I enter the carriage, and hoist myself through the ceiling. Julian follows me. I click on a small flashlight and beckon him over with my finger pressed to my lips, demanding he be quieter.

He holds his hand over his mouth, stifling a sneeze.

"There is a night watch and spaces like this echo."

He nods apologetically.

I beam the light upward, just barely illuminating our exit. The rest is lost in eerie shadow until I start to climb with the light between my teeth.

When I reach the second floor, I brace my legs around the ladder and grip either side of the elevator door. Vicky said old elevators didn't have the kind of safeguards they're made with today and it should easily open.

Not so. I grip a jutting piece of metal and it doesn't so much as budge. I press my fingers into the gap with the rubber seal, grit my teeth, and pull. Nothing.

"The doors are stuck," I whisper.

"Do you have a key?" Julian asks from below.

"Ha. Partners in crime are supposed to aid and abet, not tease."

"I wasn't joking," he says, shimmying next to me.

The ladder on the interior wall is barely big enough for one person, leaving us both hanging off either side of it. For the untrained, their hands would be sweaty and their grip unsteady, but I'm confident and centered as I study the door. I'm not sure what Julian is except here...with me. Although, the guy can take and throw a punch without so much as a second thought so he has enough mojo for ten men.

"Don't make 'em like they used to," Julian says, shining the light on the lower left door panel. "Elevator mechanics and building supers used to have a master key used in emergencies to open the doors from the outside. But from the inside..." He turns a bolt, unscrews a nut, and reveals the backside of a small lockset. "Work your magic."

I dig in my bag, producing my lock-picking set, and get started. "How'd you know that about old elevators?"

"Rowena and my mother were trapped in the elevator in our building once. It's been upgraded since because it was face a lawsuit or decommission the thing. I thought it was fascinating—the mechanics, not the being trapped part so I sat behind the elevator guy the entire afternoon he worked on the thing. Asked a million questions. Probably drove him crazy."

Just when I hear the pin release, my fingers falter and I drop my tension wrench. I hold my breath, waiting for a crash, an alarm, anything, but all I hear is the soft swoosh of Julian's breath reminding me to inhale.

Julian parts the doors easily now. We're at eye level with the marble hallway. In my moment of pause, Julian asks, "You sure you want to do this?"

I nod. "Are you?"

"Whatever happens, I have no regrets."

"No regrets," I repeat.

Julian turns to me, his face a sketch in the dim light like the ones he draws. "Have you ever heard the story about the warrior that arrived on enemy shores to wage war? He told them to burn the boats. They were horrified, but then he said there's no going back. No retreat. Their only choice was to succeed if they were going to survive."

"So they burned the boats, giving them no choice?"

The outline of his lips lift in affirmation.

We're doing this. Together. Not Vicky and me, which brings with it disappointment and fear I'll deal with later. Right now, I have a museum to rob and a sister to save...and a guy to try not to fall in love with.

## Chapter 35

I GET MY BEARINGS AND WHISPER, MOSTLY TO MYSELF EVEN THOUGH Julian is at my side, "Right side in. There's a blind spot the camera doesn't reach over here unless the overhead lights are on. Keep to the shadows."

We skulk along the hall, masks and metal ornaments staring ghoulishly from the walls. I channel Vicky's fixation on the golden and bejeweled heart. I'm doing this for her. Laser focus. Julian's sneakers squeak on the floor. We can do this if he'd be quieter. I stop. I wait. I listen.

According to Vicky's plans, the night watch's rounds cycle from the first to the third floor then second to fourth at half-hour intervals. The museum closed at seven. Security shift changed at eleven, meaning they'll be on floors one and two for another half hour. I exhale and continue.

Golden letters spelling *Empire Room* hang on a sign above an entryway. "Concentration. Dexterity. Confidence," I whisper, remembering the points Vicky often reminded me of when reviewing the plans. For Julian, I say, "In other words, this is where it gets tricky. Follow me. Don't falter. There's a laser motion detector at the foot of that wall," I say, pointing to the entryway.

"Do we jump it?"

"No. There's another one about thigh-high. And another about head high and so on."

"Do we disengage it?"

"We squeeze through it."

Julian looks less than thrilled.

We cross to the side of the entryway, pressing against the wall. "No loose clothing, laces, or skateboards." I point to several tiny sensors on the opposite side of the entry so he gets a sense of the amount of space we're dealing with.

Julian swallows thickly as I pass him the board. We'll have to leave it here for now. He sets it down, but the floor is so polished that it slides, landing on all four wheels with a soft *thunk*.

My pulse thuds.

Before he can grab it, the skateboard rolls across the floor to the other side. I close my eyes, unable to watch, but it's so low to the ground that it must avoid the lasers.

We both let out matching exhales of relief. Without another word, I grip the wall beside me, dive between the lasers, tuck myself in, and flip onto the other side of the wall. I quickly move aside, again holding my breath. If he screws this up…

I count to ten, but he hasn't moved. "Are you there?"

"I'm visualizing."

"What?"

"I'm picturing where I am in space and how I want to land."

"But you can't see over here."

"Describe what you see," he says.

"Parquet floor, open space, an urn of some sort, but that's to my right. Just don't come in hard because you don't want to risk knocking into it."

"I was hoping for dark eyes, a beautiful pout, an adorable nose, strong cheekbones, and dark blonde hair."

I can't resist a grin. "Pink. I dyed my hair pink."

"I didn't know since it's tucked under that hat. Let me see." Then in one swift motion, he's standing beside me. "My mother was wrong. All those years spent skateboarding wasn't a waste. I'm quite agile."

I cannot resist grinning. "And funny, hot, dreamy..."

He chuckles privately. "Now what?"

"See that wall? We have to jump from here to there, landing perfectly on the eight-inch space. No room for error because this room is wired."

He stares at the wall, about six feet away. "I failed the long jump during the fitness test freshman year," he whispers.

"You can't fail now," I say and leap because there's no time for debate or second thoughts. The clock is ticking, and I doubt the museum guards will buy the story that we were locked in here when they closed.

I land like a gymnast but resist lifting my hands into the air. I turn, facing Julian, ushering him forward. He motions with his hand for me to turn around and whispers, "Too much pressure with you watching."

With a huff, I turn around. I hear the rustle of Julian's clothing and then he's careening forward. I reach for his jacket, pulling him back. We both drop to sitting and before either one of us can comment, we stare in silence at the golden heart centered on a wooden pedestal and sparkling, bathed in light from above.

A short flight of stairs leads up to the Cuore d'Oro, but each tread contains a sensor that would trip the alarm if we stepped on it or so much as drop a crumb. The other three sides mirror the setup with steps and rails, like a traffic intersection, presumably so museum patrons don't have to wait in line to view the golden heart on display but can surround it.

"Now for the fun toy," I say, pulling out the spool gun, anchor, and zip line. "Vicky always loved this thing. She said it felt like flying."

"Have you used it before?"

"No. Are you afraid of heights?" I ask.

"No. I'm afraid of falling. Will it hold me?"

"I'll hold you."

He secures his skateboard in the backpack as I ready my aim. "See the wooden stud between the watercolor from Caravaggio and the fire extinguisher?"

"How do you conceal the hole in the wall?" Julian asks.

I show him the thin anchor that would leave little more than a pinprick in the plaster.

"And you trust that to hold us?" he asks.

"Vicky tested it when they were building those high-rise condos in Allston." I inhale, lining up the sight. I exhale and release the trigger. Nothing happens. The cable doesn't unspool. There isn't a whooshing sound and then a slight tap when the anchor penetrates the wall. I examine and fiddle with the canister and the valve. I try again. Nothing. My hands sweat. I tell myself not to panic. There isn't time to take it apart.

As I struggle with the zipline gun, Julian stares at the heart, perhaps as entranced by it as Vicky.

The floor creaks above and the building settles. Time is ticking. My hands are sweating. There is no Plan B though at this point I'm working on Plan F—for fail.

"If you were able to use the spool gun, what would come next?" Julian asks.

"Use it to slide across the room, hover over the heart, and replace it with the weight in my bag. It's a gradual process, requiring a steady hand as I dovetail the two and—three seconds. I have three seconds to make the switch." I take out the stone carved to match the shape of the heart in the pedestal, weighted to match the heart.

"Could you reach it from the handrail?" he asks, pointing. "Does it have sensors?" Before I can answer, he says, "There's only one way to find out."

"Wait. By wired, I meant that the rail is flesh sensitive. Like the screen on your phone. If you touch it..."

He pulls out his skateboard. "I just mastered the rail slide. I got this."

I shake my head. "You can't touch it."

"I won't. Not with my hand. As you said, time is running out. Are we doing this or not?"

"We?" I ask.

"We're in this together, Penny."

"I trusted you to hold me if we used the zip line. You trust me to hold you when we skate."

I nod because we only have ten minutes to disappear. Fortunately, the bench is long and we go to the end where we get ready to push off. "You'll only have a moment as we sail over the pedestal and onto the opposite rail and down to the bench."

"Then repeat?"

"It's a trick shot and I've never done it with someone in my arms, but what did you say about me being your lucky charm when we first met?"

I prepare myself to make a quick exchange instead of the precise redistribution of weight when I lift the statue, hoping velocity allows me nothing more than that split second. I also prepare myself to fall flat on my face in the middle of the polished floor, set off all the alarms, and wind up in jail.

I kiss Julian on the cheek. He wraps his arms around me and then we're flying, building speed. We land on the rail, defying gravity as the heart gets closer and closer. I prepare to trade the weight for it, but it slides from my hand. I catch it with the other one, with no choice but to go lefty—a skill Vicky insisted I learn but didn't.

I reach for the heart anyway, but we're going too fast and I know I won't be able to make the trade. As my stomach plummets with failure, my fingers vanish into the heart and then reappear on the other side. Moments later, Julian and I land on the rail, slide down this time, and are on the bench opposite. My legs shake and my hands tremble. With the rush of the movement, Julian smiles his chipped-tooth smile.

"Do you have it?"

I shake my head. "No. It's not there."

He turns around. The heart remains, visible, solid looking, polished and gleaming with gems in the light. He thumbs it in question.

"It's a hologram or something," I explain.

He squints as though his eyes or my words are playing tricks on him. "Are you sure?"

I take a deep breath and nod, demonstrating how my hand went through it. "It was just air. Like a ghost."

We take off and once more, my hand splits the golden statue, only it's no denser than the air we breeze through.

I barely pause on the bench on the other side, but continue to the wall, launch myself through the entryway and laser grid, and scurry down the left side of the hall to the elevator. Without looking back, but with Julian at my heels, I drop down the shaft, back to the machine room, and up the narrow passage to the roof. Only when I see the sky do I catch my breath.

Julian appears half a minute later, takes my hand, and we disappear into the night. This time I steal tears, streaming down my cheeks, and trailing lines as vivid and real-seeming as the precious stones and pearls on Cuore d'Oro.

If it's missing, how will I save Vicky now?

## Chapter 36

When I wake up the next day, it's as though nothing happened. On the other side of the job, I expect a high. Elation. Anything. Instead, there's a void. Did I think Vicky would materialize? Appear and we'd do it together as planned? That she'd pat me on the back, and say, *Well done*? Did I think a golden heart could fill the hole she left?

Maybe. Okay, fine. Yes.

I also thought I could use it as leverage to buy her freedom from Sandro. Turns out, it's not there. The heart we thought was saw was...nothing. A mirage. A figment of my imagination.

It's time to lie low. Blend in. Assuage the guilt. Julian and I erase the night. I pretend the heart doesn't exist. But it does and so does mine, feeling a little fragile at the moment.

How can I live when my other half is somewhere else?

The knots inside me tighten, threatening to strangle me.

During my free period, I get word to go to the dean's office. I can't even imagine what it'll be this time. I consider bolting.

Today, the secretary, Mrs. Dugas, gives me an apologetic smile. "Penny Goldfeather?"

I nod and clutch my bag.

"The absences last week?"

Mildly relieved but worried about Howard, I say, "There was probably a mistake. Sometimes teachers get my sister and me mixed up. She was the class skipper." I mentally apologize for throwing Vicky under the bus. Then again, she'd own up to it with pride.

Mrs. Dugas smiles as though sympathetic and says, "Candy corn? Caroline would always pluck a pumpkin from the bowl when I'd get the autumnal mix during the week of Halloween." She smiles warmly, as if remembering the Golden Girl fondly.

I take a handful and tip my palm into my mouth. "Thanks." Something must've gone wrong with Howard's digital recipe to make absences vanish.

"We'll have to fix this matter." She opens a drawer and pulls out a piece of paper, then adds two more. "Bring each of these to your teachers and have them excuse you." She clicks something on the computer and then prints out my absence record.

I swallow thickly. It accounts for the entire month. Something must've gone wrong with Howard's program.

"We don't want to see you go on disciplinary probation. So be sure to get this cleared up as soon as possible. Understood?" She seems like she regrets having to tell me this like she'd prefer to announce, *You've won a pony!*

"I also see a note here that your academic advisor wants to discuss college options with you. At this time of year, we begin preparing for your future here at Dartmont. She'll call you in momentarily."

My future looks...it doesn't look like anything which is concerning. Caroline was destined for great things, but I was always just Victoria's accomplice. That was my future.

I should be relieved that my parents probably won't bother to scold me when they find out about my truancy. This is further proof that they don't care. It's like they disowned me by proxy. Then again, I sided with my twin.

The secretary turns to her phone as Tegan stalks out from behind a door marked with a white enamel sign that says *Molly Logan*.

"You're here. How disappointing." Tegan's face pinches in a way

## Two Truths and One Thief

that makes it look like she was sucking on a lemon and some of the juice got in her eye.

I have no patience for her attitude. I bite back her sour with my fake-sweet. I infuse my voice with saccharine and strychnine. "Disappointment? Seems like something you're well acquainted with."

From a nearby doorway, Molly Logan calls, "Penelope Goldfeather? It's a pleasure to meet you."

Tegan leans in so close her fruity body wash threatens to give me a headache. That's probably why she's so unpleasant. "I know you've been sneaking around campus at night. It's only a matter of time until you're caught."

It would be a pleasure to steal that stupid smile from her face. "Do you intend to catch me? I'd like to see you try." I hope she doesn't accept dares like Julian does.

I consider how my sister would handle the situation. There would be stamping, yelling, a harsh word or two. Maybe some shoving. If only I were more like her. Then again, is she happy?

"Penny Goldfeather?" Molly Logan repeats, breaking into my thoughts and breaking up the potential catfight.

"Julian and I will see you in history. And in case you forgot the assignment, it's on the evolution of war tactics," Tegan replies, imitating my snark-tastically sweet-not-sweet, voice.

I recall her declaring war on me and prickle, feeling like a target is on my back.

Molly Logan is a delight after my encounter with Tegan, even though I'm not sure I'm interested in college. In theory, based on what my father would call the family pedigree, it's the expectation. Based on my recent exploits, it's one hundred-eighty degrees away from the plan, in that there wasn't one.

I don't even know what I'd study. Art history? That could give me a career advantage.

"We should get you to sit the SATs, at least. Here, fill out this application and we'll get everything started," Molly says helpfully as she passes me a tablet.

It's like a conveyor belt for higher education, the way she moves me from digital form to form. I mechanically fill out my name and address. My gaze travels to Molly's desk—no candy or family photos. Disorganized papers, folders, and books cover every inch of the wooden surface. Nothing to steal except chaos. My eyes catch sight of the name Julian Freese. Below it are three colleges with one of them highlighted and the *100%* symbol next to it.

My pulse throttles. That's news to me.

But it doesn't matter, right? Couples usually go their separate ways after high school. I have to focus. Forget SATs, ACTs, and exams. I have to pull off this final caper—rescue my sister.

I spend all of history on a test that I'm unprepared for and don't care about. It's almost like the longer Vicky is gone the more I become like her. I doodle in the margin until I notice Julian staring at me. He slips out to the boys' bathroom. I follow, hoping Tegan doesn't notice and sends Sharpe to harass us.

## Chapter 37

THE LIGHT IN THE HALL SHOULD SUGGEST THE POETRY OF DUST MOTES glinting. Instead, it's still, like the air after a storm. Julian leans on the wall, his face halfway in a shaft of light, the other half in the dark.

"Hi." I'm unsure where to start as if we find ourselves at a silent matinee.

He puts his hands on my waist and pulls me close as he draws what sounds like a relieved breath. "I didn't see you all morning. Got worried."

"There was a little absence snafu and an academic advisor meeting. Very boring."

"Any future plans?"

I lift my shoulder and lower it. "Like college?" Like him. "I'd like to go far, far from here. How about you?" I ask, wondering what he'll tell me about the yellow highlighted 100% school.

"I want to kiss you," he says as if that'll keep him from losing me to wherever far, far from here is.

"I want you to hold me," I say because I want him to come wherever far, far from here is, rather than *100% College*. But he has his own future mapped out. I rest my cheek on his chest. His heart beats in a steady thrum, and I'd do anything to curl up in there and have a long nap, maybe for a year or twenty or at least until all my uncertainty goes away.

Squeaky footsteps approach.

He kisses my forehead and continues down the hall to the boys' washroom.

Thirty minutes later, when the bell rings, I load my bag. Ms. Honig dips her head into the history classroom and gestures toward me, likely a stab at my absence situation and to make sure I don't disappear during the passing period.

While we walk through the hall, she reminds me she asked to see me after class last week. My mind has been elsewhere.

All through English class, I expect her to swarm and sting, multiple times. Instead, she says nothing to me. She doesn't even acknowledge me beyond a curt, "After class," reminder before launching into the lesson. I lose her lines about Shakespeare to thoughts about Vicky, Sandro, and the golden heart that isn't.

Instead of the golden rule, ours is *Don't get caught.*

Not by Enni Honig, Tegan, the administration, or the police.

As everyone files out of the classroom, I give Julian a little wave. He takes his time like he's waiting for me. Then I motion behind Ms. Honig who's in conversation with Mrs. Sharpe and give him a discreet *She's going to chop off my head* gesture.

Julian reluctantly departs and I don't spare my inner commentary about how his jacket lifts slightly as he adjusts his backpack, revealing his trim waist and tattoos. Then it's just an empty doorway. I suddenly wonder what would have happened, how things could have been different if Vicky wasn't the bad twin. If our parents loved us as much as they do Caroline. Maybe I wouldn't be perpetually watching people leave.

With a glance in my direction, Sharpe exits. Honig closes the door. She says, "Penny, you've missed a lot of class. Not just mine, apparently. Can you explain yourself?"

"No, I don't think I can." For once, it's the truth.

## Two Truths and One Thief

She buzzes to her desk. I've decided she's a bee-spider hybrid with the way she lures me into her sticky web.

"Try me."

I glance over my shoulder as if checking if anyone else is here and then lean in conspiratorially. "Aliens came and took me away for the week. I woke up this morning and I was back in my room. It was the weirdest thing. Also, I might have leaked the secrets of poetry and time. Watch for space invaders with a penchant for rhyme."

"I don't think so," she says, but I detect the faintest hint of amusement. "Try again."

"I was arrested for trying to steal the moon. The rebel legion calls me the Great Liberator. I just want to do it a favor and knock it into some other orbit. Let it be its own planet." This is closer to the truth.

"You're creative, Penny, I'll give you that. Last chance. I'm all ears if you want to talk."

My expression must tell her that I don't.

"There's a fine line to walk in this life, Penny, and you've been stomping all over it. Trust me, if I told you about all the trouble my brother has gotten into over the years—"

"I'm acquainted...with trouble."

She lifts an eyebrow. "I thought that superlative belonged to Vicky."

"We look the same. Makes sense we'd act the same."

"That's not what I've heard about you. At least not during freshman and sophomore years."

"Things change."

"If you want my understanding and it's about a boy, tough luck. If it's something else, your home life perhaps, I'll give you a break."

"It's about everything."

Her gaze softens. "I won't pretend that I can understand, but I will try."

I take a deep breath and gather in the distance between us, wondering if it's worth the risk. "My world has always been really small. Just Vicky and me. Recently, it got smaller, by half." Tears trace their way across my eyelashes, but I won't let them drop.

I think about Julian, by my side and now, Honig reaching out when not even my parents care that Vicky was wrenched from my life. I feel sudden warmth, not quite fuzzy, but not the chill of isolation I'm accustomed to either. "Then, by some miracle, the universe expanded and worlds collided, and here I am, still alone, but not quite so much." I'm not sure what I'm saying makes sense, but I guess part of me is thankful someone cares even if she has a weird hairstyle.

"I'm sorry for whatever you're not comfortable talking about. Really. I can tell you're struggling. Still, you have a responsibility here. Can you find some poetry in what you told me, for the final? If you can manage that, I'll excuse the rest of the assignments you missed."

"You know I don't like poetry." There I go, bucking up against the so-called establishment. She just gave me an out and I stomped over it like she'd just warned.

Her level gaze reminds me she's adept at reading through the lines. "I think the opposite is true. Actually, your life is one long epic. The sooner you acknowledge that the more companionable it'll be. You'll find harmony instead of struggling with dissidence and rejection. Try to be your own friend and ally first. Before you try to step into someone else's shoes."

"How?" All I've ever been is Vicky's Twin and Caroline's Little Sister.

"You do that by finding a way to express yourself, a healthy way. Writing works for some, art for others. Running, climbing, painting, and creating something unique. Show yourself what you want. When I was your age, it was the bees, and still is." She leans in. "Have you ever seen a glistening honeycomb? It's like gold. Like gems."

She has no idea how dangerous, how tempting, my hobby is.

I get to my feet and reach for my bag, ready to be done, and then somehow my world stretches a little wider. It's like I've been asleep with open eyes. This woman with outrageous hair and an obsession with anthophilia is trying to help me.

"Thank you." Vicky is suspicious and untrusting, but who am I? I sit back down in the chair.

At the abrupt change, Honig goggles me and for the first time, a smile plays on her lips. "Is there anything else you'd like to share?"

"I don't know."

"Well, think about it. Ask yourself questions. Be curious. Follow that. I'll see you tomorrow."

I nod slowly, collecting her words like treasure, like rare coins that are all mine. They're ones I'm not sure I'll share with my sister until I know what they mean.

The hall is quiet with just the hum of a vacuum somewhere in the depths of Arundel. The smell is floor cleaner mixed with the crisp autumn air sneaking in from outside...and potential. I inhale deeply. I don't imagine I'll ever like it at Dartmont. Not like I once did, but the constancy of high school is something of a comfort. There's the mean girl, the inspiring teacher, the smells...

If I spend too much time looking back, I might trip. I suppose it doesn't matter where I came from and if I focus too much on where I'm going, I'll miss where I am.

When I step into the afternoon, Julian waits for me on the front steps. The relief and sense of renewal I felt after my conversation with Ms. Honig doesn't follow me outside. I don't know what to say to him. My words wash to some distant shore. The only thing I can imagine doing, after the exhaustion that's been today—these last weeks—is to lie on his bed and let him draw on me with dark inky lines that tie me to him, to this life.

"I only have four minutes until I have to meet my mother and academic advisor. She wants to discuss my future. Lots of college pressure lately." His jaw ticks like he wants to punch something.

After my meeting with Molly and my chat with Honig, I don't want to think about that.

"If I'm late...I don't know what else she can take from me, but whatever it is, she'll try."

I want to force him into defiance, to push him out from in front of the speeding car that is Regina, but we only have a minute and thirty seconds left.

He glances over his shoulder at the stately administration building where I spent the morning. "I have to run, literally." He grasps my hand and kisses me softly.

I slump onto the steps. My head hangs low as I think about Vicky and my future. A short time later, someone sits down next to me.

"I'm starving. Let's go to Neda's," Howard says.

## Chapter 38

"I'm starving." Howard starts walking, pauses, and gestures over his shoulder for me to follow. "We're going to Neda's. You owe me a meal—she owes me an hour on her laptop. I can't risk using the one in the library." He shakes his head dismissively. "I overstayed my welcome in the computer lab and melted down several hard drives. Also, my computer is compromised and I'm waiting on a new one."

My eyebrows lift sharply. "Is that why I have sixteen absences?"

"I'd apologize, but I didn't do anything wrong." He glances around. "I think we're being watched."

"You sound paranoid."

"For good reason."

He goes on to tell me he found his dorm room trashed two days ago.

"Howard, I hate to be the one to tell you this, but you have enemies."

"I also have a barometric sensor on my door, making a key or lock-picking set useless. The door wasn't smashed in but everything on the other side was. No, it was a professional."

"I'm not sure I want to know what kinds of enemies you have beyond campus."

Instead of going to Ellicott dorm or even the Refectory, we stand in the student parking lot. "Which one of these cars is Julian's?"

"His mom is here."

"Good, we'll take hers."

"I don't think she'll like that."

"She already doesn't like you, so..."

My eyebrows can't climb higher. "How do you know that?"

Howard winks one beady eye which looks more like he got a bug in it. "Penelope, I know everything."

My insides swim. "What's at Neda's?"

"Burritos."

Possibly, for the first time in my life, I'm willing to entertain the idea that a burrito might very well solve my problems because I have no clue what else could. Chocolate, maybe? And I need Howard's help with my absences.

"Nice hair, by the way. It reminds me of something." He taps his finger on his lower lip.

"Cotton candy?" I suggest.

"No," he says. "Like Tegan's matching lip gloss and nail polish? When you finally reappear at school, you're practically coordinated, like you called each other last night to plan it." He laughs, deep and throaty. "Sorry. She's nasty and no matter how much she tries to hide it with that fake, sweet innocence, it's obvious. You, on the other hand, wear the hair well."

We reach a small, silver car with the letters *EV* on the side. Howard wears a massive smile as he sets something on the hood, plugs it into his phone then spends a solid minute typing.

"What are you doing?"

"Did the makers of electric vehicles ever consider how easy it is to break into the internal computer and instruct the thing to turn on? Apparently not."

"I'm not sure this is a good idea."

"Burritos are always a good idea and just think, Caroline and George borrowed a vehicle once. We both know the girls in your family aren't known for borrowing." He throws air quotes around the *word borrow*.

He taps his phone and the doors unlock. I glance around then get in.

Howard offers a complicated explanation of what he just did. It's like he wants to avoid thinking about what happened to his dorm room and why our absence status changed.

We go south for almost three hours. I start to worry Howard is abducting me, especially when we finally get off the highway and pass beneath a mega underpass with *the ca-chunk, ca-chunk* of the cars going by overhead. It reminds me of skateboard wheels. Then, a neighborhood opens to tidy homes with picket fences. A little farther on and we turn onto Julian Street. Seriously. The hearts in my eyes must betray me.

"Penny, you're hopeless. Anyway, we're here."

"Where is here?"

"Neda's family's house. Her dad owns Dos Amigos. Best food ever."

After our doors slam discordantly, tinkling music comes from inside the house. The spicy, peppery smell of delicious meals cooked three times a day perfumes the air with what I can only imagine is the scent of home.

Howard throws open the door to a symphony of clattering pots and pans. Rhythmic pop music switches between Spanish and English. The marigold-colored wall and a tapestry of a multi-generational family shelling beans pop vibrantly. I recognize the art from a poster in a store on Newbury Street. A stooped woman with wrinkled skin hustles over and pulls Howard in for a hug. Rapid Spanish follows. Neda appears with her bangle bracelets jangling. Conversation volleys between her and her grandmother. A pair of boys streaks in, one hardly reaches the doorknob. The other is slightly taller and more slender. They hop up and down. Howard beams in greeting.

Industrial-sized bags of rice and beans, baskets of laundry, neatly folded, and a studio's worth of ceramic pottery fill the space. I run my finger along the smooth edge of a glazed bowl. I hear my name. Neda doesn't seem the slightest bit surprised to see me.

"Abuelita, Penny, Penny, Abuelita," Neda says as if that is all the introduction we need—and that's all I understand.

Abuelita gives me a warm hug and then takes my hand, apparently, not interested in letting go. Possibly ever. Her fingers are strong and calloused, but somehow soft at the same time. She has hands that have held the newly born and the dying. She has history written into the wrinkles on the skin opposite her palms. She leads me into the kitchen. Neda and Howard disappear.

Abuelita keeps patting my hand as she stirs a huge pot of stew on the stove. She gestures that I stir using the wooden spoon then she takes a seat at the long wooden table and begins pressing corn tortillas. I keep stirring and stirring. Eventually, I wonder where Howard and Neda went. I glance around for a computer, but it must be in her room. Why am I babysitting this pot of I'm-not-sure-what?

I listen to three songs that make me want to dance. The front door opens and a woman with long silver hair enters and kisses Abuelita, apparently not noticing that a stranger is tending the simmering pot on the stove.

*Neda, Howard, anyone, help me.* I feel awkward and unsure if I should say something. Abuelita consults with the silver-haired woman. I turn back to the stove. Shortly after, Neda returns as though we're sisters or cousins, or proper friends at the very least, just doing our chores.

"Mama, this is Penny. Penny, Mama."

She scrutinizes me, possibly wondering if I poisoned the soup. I must pass muster because she extends a hand and says, "Nice to meet you." Then in a grand sweep of silver hair, she busies herself with the contents of the box she brought in.

In the next few minutes, three men appear, graduating in age and height to about the same stature as Abuelita. Father, brother, uncle?

There's laughter and claps on the back. The person who I assume is Neda's older brother—because they have the same nose and dark eyes —takes the spoon from my hand and takes a bite, burning his tongue.

Neda shouts, "That's what you get." She turns to me. "Every time Abuelita makes *sopita*, Andres has to go and taste it before it's done. No patience, that one."

Andres smirks guiltily.

"Are you going to introduce me to your friend, Neda?" He waggles her eyebrows.

She arches hers. "Andres, this is Penny." She doesn't introduce me to him.

His expression is flirty like he owns the patent on tall, dark, and handsome.

She says something in Spanish and I catch the words *novio* and *amor*. Boyfriend and love. I miss Julian. Andres sighs. She nudges him out of the way and we stand shoulder-to-shoulder in front of the cooktop.

"Brothers," she says by way of explanation. "Do you have any of those?"

"No. Two sisters."

"Right. Duh. I have four. Two younger. Two older."

"The soup smells good," I say, never having a conversation with Neda that lasted more than a few lines.

"Wait until you taste it."

"So no burritos?" Howard asks.

"Better than burritos. This meal is going to blow your mind. Abuelita cooks every day, but Monday, it's like heaven on a plate. Sometimes, I think God even comes down for a taste." She looks me dead in the eyes. "I'm not even kidding."

The two little boys run in and Abuelita hollers playfully at them. Andres clotheslines the pair and lifts them off their feet while he stands, arms outstretched, like a human jungle gym. Their giggles are contagious.

When my wrist and feet begin to ache from stirring, I look out the kitchen window, taking in the normalness of my surroundings. I only saw my grandparents on holidays. My parents were always busy. Caroline too. Mostly, my young life consisted of Vicky, the nanny, and me. I sigh, letting out a breath I may very well have been holding for days. Years?

The door opens again and a giant version of Andres appears, but with a buzz cut, clean-shaven, and in military uniform.

"*Hola, qué tal,*" he calls.

There are shrieks, slamming doors, and a boisterous descent as everyone in the house flocks to the newcomer, everyone except Abuelita.

"Bueno," Abuelita says, tapping me on the hip and shifting me to the side. She nods her head in dismissal. I sit down next to Howard, but I can't pretend the string of nonsensical letters on the computer screen holds any fascination.

Consuela is in tears, kissing every inch of her son's face. Neda's dad cries tears of joy. The little boys hang onto his legs like they'll never let go. There are hugs, lots of chatter in Spanish, and then finally everyone parts ways as Abuelita approaches him with open arms. I think he might swallow her in his embrace. When he releases his grandmother, she quietly leads him over to the stove where he takes up my position.

I thought I'd be relieved, but at least stirring the stew gave me something to do. Now, I don't know where to put my hands. Thankfully, Neda appears out of the fray and gestures that I follow. At last, I think I'll learn the real reason for my being here.

## Chapter 39

I FOLLOW NEDA DOWN A DIM HALLWAY AND SHE OPENS A DOOR TO A bedroom with walls covered in hot, sweaty soccer player posters. She has a carved jewelry box, probably to house her bangle bracelets. Colorful beads, a boa, and snapshots drape the frame of a large mirror. Howard resumes his hunch over a laptop in the corner.

"The good thing about being the only girl is I get my own bedroom. Andres was the only one glad to see Alonso—that's my oldest brother—enlist in the Marines. He finally got his own room. I can't believe it though. He came home a day early. He's been away for too long," she says, jerking her thumb in the direction of the kitchen. "We're relieved."

"I don't want to impose." I glance at Howard, not exactly sure why we're here other than for burritos.

"Of course, you're welcome. My family's policy is the more the merrier." Then she glances at Howard. "Or in this case, three is a crowd."

My skin prickles. "What do you mean?"

"Howard and I have been business partners for four years. I collect the dirt. He's the digital genius."

I suddenly realize she's behind the gossip on the Dartmont Dart. "Oh."

"Yeah. But someone recently hacked in. Posted a threat that only we can see on our side. As I said, three is a crowd."

"I think of it as more of an ultimatum," Howard says.

Neda shrugs. "But like a timer on a bomb, there's a clock, counting down. Despite Howard's impressive skills, he couldn't defuse it, as it were. We have twelve hours until the threat turns public on the dart."

"What's the threat?" I ask.

"It's personal," Howard says.

"Very personal. It exposes all our sources, every last email, text, all of it. If this were thirty years ago, I would've collected everything by word of mouth. Maybe letters that I could conveniently destroy. But now, my methods involve technology so there is a record and despite Howard's safeguards they hacked in."

"They made it so I can't see to get past—" Howard grunts like he's doing strenuous exercise. He slams the computer shut and flops back on the bed.

"Howard. You can do it. You're just missing something. It will come to you."

Something comes to me like a slap upside the head. Something Vicky would scowl at me for. "How do I figure into this?"

Howard sits up and he and Neda exchange a look.

Neda laughs. "The two of you look exactly alike, but you're so different."

Hope lifts in my chest. "Do you know where she is?"

Again, they look at each other as if communicating without words, not surprising since they've been working together, exposing all of Dartmont's gossip since they were freshmen.

"Should we?"

I shrug. "She's been scarce."

"You mean she was arrested," Neda says, pressing her hand to her face as if this is news.

"This makes for an interesting twist," Howard adds.

"The twist is that you guys and my sister..." I trail off, waiting for them to fill in the dots.

"It started with the other sister," Howard says vaguely.

"Do you mean Caroline?"

He nods.

"It's always Caroline. So, what's going on?"

Before they answer, someone hollers, "Neda, dinner."

In the last ten minutes, the kitchen has transformed, the long table set with ceramic plates and cups and overflowing with serving dishes. Each piece is unique, except for the color— the same shade the sky dyes the ocean in washes of blue. There's a lot of chatter, except Alonso is still at the stove, stirring. He gazes out the window as if reorienting himself to calm and peace.

Howard helps himself while Neda piles my plate with items she describes as she serves. "Arepa, a cornmeal cake, empanadas, carnitas, arroz con coco, platanos, ah, and some salsa. There's only *picante*." She doesn't look apologetic.

I wonder who she thinks is going to eat all this food. Maybe she wants to share, but then she leaves me standing there and fills a plate of her own. Abuelita calls Alonso to leave his post at the pot and he gets a plate.

When we've all squeezed in around the table, the room hushes. I put my fork down. Everyone clasps hands and I fumble, gripping Neda's in my left and Howard's in my right. Abuelita says a long prayer.

Then everyone digs in. No one speaks English, and I don't care. I understand this as the language of family, homecoming, and love. I wish Vicky were here. Then I realize, perhaps she has been. I thought I knew everything about my twin. The fact that I don't leaves me with an ache food can't fill.

However, after my first bite, there is a singular focus in my life: how can I make my pants— no, my stomach—bigger so I can taste everything? The flavors meld smoothly with bursts of spice and coriander. It's sweet, salty, and spicy...I don't look up during the chatter. I just chew and savor, until my mind lands on Vicky again. Where is she? Do they know? What don't I know? Feeling left out, left behind, tears prick my eyes, but I tell Neda it's the peppers. Abuelita smiles at me like this is a good thing.

"She's of the mind that if cooking and stirring and chopping doesn't burn the devil out of you, chilies will."

Abuelita gives Neda a stern look.

"Sometimes, I swear, she can understand English and read minds." Neda pushes her plate away.

I don't think it's a good idea to share my shadowy world with Neda. In her kitchen, there is so much joy. Then again, she's the composer behind the Dart. Surely, she's no stranger to the underbelly at Dartmont. Does she know about the fighting ring?

After dessert, that may have permanently changed my molecular makeup—it was that good—everyone goes to the living room and drinks coffee or at least I think it's just coffee. Neda and I follow. I zone in and out as the conversation, first grave as Alonso talks about what I assume is the military to raucous with laughter as Neda's father tells a story. The two little boys go play. The talk breaks off into pairs and threesomes. Neda teases Andres about not just one, but three girls he's dating. I buzz from the caffeine like I could run ten miles into Julian's arms.

Julian's arms—his lips, his smile, and the stories his tattoos tell. I pull out the phone Queenie presumably gave me and move to text him when Neda rips it from my hand.

Eyes wide, she marches to her room. Howard and I follow. If there's a no cell phones at the table policy, I'm ready to apologize.

With her bedroom door closed, she holds it up. "Do you think?"

"There's only one way to find out." Howard plugs it in much like he did to start the car earlier.

"Wait." I wave my hands. "Hold on. Before you go reading my messages, explain. First of all, Neda, why aren't you at Dartmont?"

"Suspended because of my absences." She eyes Howard.

"I did the best I could, but she, uh, had a lot."

"More than me?"

He nods.

"How do I fit in? And Vicky?"

"Remember how I said three is a crowd?"

This time I nod.

"Remember the scandal?" Howard asks.

"Which one?" I ask.

"The one involving your sister." Neda sighs.

"Those were rumors," I say.

"One of them was true," she says carefully, adjusting her hair with a jingle of her bangle bracelets.

Before I can ask what she might mean, Howard barks, "I need another computer. STAT."

I imagine us in a surgical theater. Thing is, there are lives on the line.

Neda scowls. "Howard, do not tell me you broke my laptop. I worked double shifts for a month at Dos Amigos to save up for it. I wanted it to last through college."

"It's not broken. But what I need to do requires more memory."

"I, um, know where there are several."

"Can't use the school's. They're now being monitored." He gives my phone a shake. "I'm afraid, so is this."

My eyes bulge. "I shouldn't be surprised. I came across it in a pretty shady way. I was in a clothing store. Someone gave it to me. Said I lost it. I did lose my phone, but it's not the same one. I thought maybe it would connect me to Vicky." However, I don't tell them about my encounter with Queenie.

A deep crease forms between Neda's eyebrows as if she can't square a circle.

Howard grins. "Now, the plot thickens."

"I'm pretty sure the plot thickens before it twists, but take us to those computers," Neda says.

As for me, I've lost the plot. All I know is that whatever Vicky was involved in, just got bigger. And I'm not sure I can fill her shoes. Then an itty bitty thought creeps in like a sugar ant looking for water.

I'm not sure I want to. But I flick it away. But if the thought is anything like a tiny sugar ant, there will be more.

## Chapter 40

The crisp air carries away the humidity and enchanted spices that clung to me from the moment I stepped into Neda's house. We're mostly quiet as we trace our way to Vicky's apartment.

Outside the building, a figure leans against the doorway. I pause. The possibilities chill me more than the air. I shuffle in front of Howard and Neda, angling myself to distract them from whoever might be there. It could be Flavio, but my imagination generates other, less savory characters—people Vicky might owe money to, for instance.

Radiant Neda, empress of home-cooked meals and the teasing sister with the easy smile, is gone. She wears her usual don't-mess-with-me snarl as her gaze follows mine.

Howard's arms cross in front of his chest in irritation as if he can't be bothered with another shakedown, even though he presumably wasn't in his dorm room for the first.

The person steps out of the shadows.

Howard exhales. "Hey, Julian," he says as though he expected to see him lurking there.

Julian kisses me on the cheek.

"Lurk like that again, and I'll—" Neda starts.

"And there I thought my girlfriend had been abducted."

Howard holds up his hands in surrender. "In the name of burritos."

I quickly explain dinner as we head upstairs.

When I unlock the door, the apartment is like a mausoleum. The minimalist décor, the lack of any discernable smell at all, and the beige walls are the opposite of Neda's house.

"It's peaceful here," she says.

"If by peaceful you mean lonely, then yeah," I mumble.

"I call the couch," Howard says, plopping down, stretching out his legs, and making himself at home before flipping open the computer, balancing on his chest.

I set three more laptops on the table. "There are more where those came from."

His eyes light up and he gets to work.

Neda gawks at the window. Julian's sketch of me still fills the glass. "Whoa." She stares at it a second longer and glances at Julian as if piecing together her understanding.

Like the sketch, I'm filled in with shadows, but it's as though something burns to get out, literally lighting a fire in my stomach. If Julian had a sketchpad, another window, or some other suitable surface, he'd capture my inner battle with gradients of charcoal and flickering, crackling shades of orange and yellow.

"Tell me about the window," Neda says, pointing to Julian's outrageous donation to the simplistic decor.

"A Julian Freese original," I say, glancing over my shoulder.

"Do you have anything to drink?" Howard asks.

"Water or coffee."

"Both," he answers without looking up.

Julian claps his hands together. "So, what are we all doing here?"

"Let's up the ante. We'll play truth or dare. I go first." Neda narrows her eyes at him suspiciously. "So why exactly do you come to school all beat up? Tough home life?" she asks.

Howard clears his throat awkwardly. I take it Neda doesn't know about the fighting.

Julian scratches his head quizzically. "I didn't pick truth."

Neda's glare is harsh.

Julian wavers. "I'd rather a dare."

She shakes her head as if this isn't up for argument. "Looks like you may have already taken one. I want to know more about why you often have scabs on your knuckles. Does it get rowdy in your dorm?"

So Julian knows what he's getting into, I take a dare and blurt, "Neda supplies the content on the Dart." Then to her, I add, "You can trust him."

Julian's mouth forms a soundless *Oh*. "In that case, I'll give you some good dirt for the dart, but first I want to know what we're here. Every detail, even the ones Penny doesn't know."

Clever.

"What really happened to Vicky when she left school?" Neda asks.

I shake my head to tumble my secrets back down. I swallow, but there aren't enough tears in the world to dampen the embers of what's true. "See all this stuff? It's taken. Stolen. Shoplifted." But the words sound like an echo as if I already spoke them a long time ago. As I go on, the story takes on a lilting quality. It's like I've been in a cage and I notice, for the first time, that the little door is ajar. Is that why Vicky left me the silver key? I peer around to see if it's a trick. But with each word, I get closer and closer to whatever waits for me on the other side.

"So you stole this couch?" Howard asks.

Sitting on the floor and leaning against Julian's legs, I nod.

Neda laughs. "The TV? That's a huge television. No way you walked out with it."

"Yup. We had help, but you'll never find a receipt."

She looks around, presumably trying to stump me. "Kitchen table?"

"Ikea."

"Oh, right, it's not assembled yet. Impressive."

She points at me. "What about Vicky?"

"Was she stolen? In a manner of speaking."

"She means why'd she get kicked out of Dartmont?"

My gaze flicks from Howard to Neda. "I don't know. After she returned from her time in Italy, she was different—not the same angst as before, you know? One day, she didn't show up to class. That wasn't unusual."

"She was my original client," Howard says. "She knew I could find my way into the school's computer program and alter attendance records among other things. Vicky pressured me, but I proved to myself that I'm pretty darn good at what I do. Strangely, her file is now gone."

"And so is she," Neda says.

Returning to my story, I say, "I didn't see her for the rest of the day. Again, not alarming. But when she didn't come back to our dorm room after dinner, I started to get worried. Then I saw Mum and Dad exiting Ambrose. Caroline was away for the weekend so I knew they weren't here to see her. They never came to visit us."

Julian looks at me softly as if he knows that by *us*, I mean Vicky and me.

"Two black town cars left that day. One contained Mum and Dad. The other is my sister. She didn't answer my calls or texts for over six months." I shake my head as emotions held over from that time rush toward me.

"If one of my brothers did that to me—" Neda winds up as if she's about to release a stream of expletives.

"Exactly. Finally, she called. Said she was in Boston. I could come if I wanted. So I did." I shrug because there's not much more to say. "She never explained what happened. Caroline said Mum and Dad disowned her." Of course, I sided with Vicky. How could I not? We're twins."

And we commenced our life of crime. Or more accurately, she continued hers and as always, I'm along for the ride.

"Now, you don't know where she is again, right?" Howard asks.

"Was she stolen?" Neda asks pointedly.

"Maybe you guys can help me figure that out," I reply.

The game of truth or dare suddenly got very real.

## Chapter 41

"What I thought was stolen was this phone," Howard says.

I shake my head. "No, it was given to me."

"I mean stolen before that. Something interfered with my hack and then blocked it."

"Why would you think it had anything to do with me?"

"Remember what we said about the twelve hours? The first piece of information they threatened to expose has to do with your sister—the message said Goldfeather goes first."

Julian shifts closer to me. "Which one?"

"I assumed Victoria because officially, she'd still be a student at Dartmont," Neda says.

"Caroline was already exposed for the most part," Howard says knowingly.

"And apart from skipping class, you're clean. Or so I thought," Neda says.

"What does that have to do with the phone?" Julian asks.

"Cell phone thieves sometimes steal phones and repurpose them to operate as conductors—kind of like a hotspot but for the transfer of data. They'll upload programs that interact with the banking info and personal things like that of the new user. I thought maybe this one was being used in that way and was interfering with our communications about your absences and was what they used to hack into my system."

"But you were wrong," Neda says as if that's disappointing.

"Back to the drawing board. Who messed with my operation? Who wouldn't want absences to be deleted?" Howard asks.

"And break into your room?" Neda asks.

I open Vicky's laptop. "Maybe you can break into Vicky's email." I debate telling them about the museum and the hologram, but first I'd like to know what else Vicky might be hiding first.

"Did you try birthdays, significant names, and places? Most people use their kid's info or a sibling, maybe?" Howard asks.

"You mean their accomplice? We had the same birthday. I already tried everything I can think of."

"Someone hacked my hacking software, but I'll see if I can access something that'll work—" Howard nudges me out of the way, sits down in front of the computer, and gets to work, his fingers flying over the keyboard. "There's a way around everything online. Not so much in life. Then again, the world is becoming more and more digitized." He continues with a monologue about computers and how one day we'll all be pixelated.

Howard's voice fades to a hum and I doze off, dreaming of Romeo and Juliet, running from disapproval, from shattered dreams, and toward love. When my eyes blink open, Julian snoozes next to me. The papasan cocoons Neda, also asleep. The dawning sun plays hide and seek behind the surrounding buildings, as though unsure about greeting the new day.

Still seated at the table in front of the computer, Howard slouches to one side, his head resting heavily on his hand, and his glasses askew. I blink my eyes at the blue-green glow of the sleeping computer screen and jiggle the cursor. Vicky's email sign-in sits open with an error message.

I've tried every combination of words that were meaningful to Vicky except one. A word she never used.

I type *love*.

Howard startles awake.

The screen changes. A cascade of emails appear, the most recent from the day of her disappearance—mere days before I learned of her arrest. The subject says *It wasn't me*. The sender's address is simply *Sandro*. Her nemesis? They emailed each other? She despised him. She'd go on long rants about how she'd longed to see him suffer.

I click the email.

There's no explosion and no further message. Just the subject line.

Then the elements missing from her arrest and the missing golden heart become clear. Sandro must have gotten to it first. Just to drive home the point, tipped off the police—then teased her by claiming innocence. *It wasn't me*. Yeah right.

*Rule number two: never admit to anything.*

Or it could have been the opposite. He tipped off the cops and with Vicky out of the way he went for the heart. He would have known she'd been plotting it for years, waiting for the right time. It was her prize. Victoria once told me that even in her circle, everyone respects each other's marks. Vicky was never one to boast about jobs, but surely she made sure everyone knew the Cuore d'Oro was hers. Like with Howard's skills, news travels in whispers and code. And although I was never privy to those conversations, Vicky would have made sure her name and the golden heart were synonymous.

I search for other messages from Sandro and find several saved. In the earliest one, all it says is *Please*. Then the next *Thank you*. In an earlier one, it says *You're welcome*. The last is simply blank.

When a job didn't go as well as Vicky planned or if a recipe didn't taste quite right, really anything that set her off—the internet was down, the neighbor's dog was barking, we'd run out of toothpaste—she'd rant about how much she hated Sandro. I replay the reel of memories. He was boastful, too flashy, a jerk, and arrogant, I remember these highlights, but then slowly, other details return. *"The slob needed a haircut."* She'd say, *"He ought to spend some time studying the job before jumping in with all the machismo of a good-looking Italian who thinks he knows what he wants."* I dredge memories. Times when I was only half listening. Then comes one I should never have forgotten, *"Sandro is the worst kind of thief."*

Did he steal her heart?

I never asked questions, instead followed her favor and found out the answers for myself or got by without them.

Her biggest irritation seemed to be that he always won. Either he was lucky or brilliant, she'd claim, ranting on, but she bet on the former. She'd warn, "*Someday his luck will run out. Mark my words. Someday the truth will hit him so hard he'll never be the same.*"

This made me wonder, did he win because he avoided the truth? Because he lied? If that was the case, they weren't that much different. Maybe that's where the hatred came from. It never occurred to me, but they must have worked together at some point for her to know him so intimately.

"They met in Italy. They must have worked together. Partners in crime. Maybe he taught her everything she knew," I say breathily.

And what do I know? Nothing, except he has the heart. I'm sure of it. They were rivals, enemies. It makes perfect sense that he'd swoop in when she was out of the picture. Maybe he took her out of it, or perhaps she knew he took the heart and that undid her—knowing her prize was no longer attainable, causing her to slip up and land behind bars. The how and the why don't matter. The Cuore d'Oro does.

"You figured out the password," Howard asks, his voice thick with sleep.

"Love," I answer.

He lets out a soft snort of laughter. "Always is."

"Are you going to tell me what you're looking for?" he asks, leaning over my shoulder and peering at the screen.

My debate is brief. He already knows about my missteps and I know his. All of us in this room have secrets, but I no longer have the energy to keep up my guard. That was Vicky's job. Anyway, she was wrong about keeping people at a distance.

"Have you ever heard of the Cuore d'Oro?"

Howard opens a new tab and types the words into the search bar. "I call this my second brain." He scrolls and then clicks his tongue. "The Cuore d'Oro? Apparently, it's breaking news—discovered missing from the Institute of Fine Art."

I goggle the screen. "What?"

"I will be your alibi. You, me, Neda, and Julian," he says.

"I didn't take the heart," I whisper.

"No, you couldn't have, unless you can alter time, but explain—"

The slow shake of my head reminds me of the message on the cell phone and the timer Howard and Neda face. "I didn't take it, but I tried to."

Howard inhales sharply. "I thought you were a shoplifter—lip gloss, trinkets—TVs."

I hold my head in my hands and my confession slips out. "Vicky coveted the golden heart encrusted with rare gems and diamonds. It was the big take we'd been preparing me for." I fall silent.

"We went the other night," Julian says, his voice rough from sleep.

"I followed her protocol exactly. Well, almost. We got in, everything went as planned, and then we had some trouble with the zip line—"

"You broke into the IFA?" Neda asks from across the room.

"I didn't mean to wake you up," I say.

"I wouldn't miss this." She leans in.

"This is not Dart material." My voice is as sharp as a razor's edge.

"No. Of course not. It's much, much bigger than Tegan hooking up with Blaise Webber and that she's been spotted skulking around campus like she's a private investigator who then reports to their superior."

I roll my eyes, but Tegan's declaration of war and the random times we've run into each other, make me wonder, but I have more important things to focus on right now.

Neda says, "You give Tegan too much credit. She's shallower than a puddle, dumber than a dodo bird, and her morning breath smells distinctly of moldy cheese."

We all break into laughter and for once, I feel like I belong. However, a voice whispers uneasily in my mind that we're all liars and thieves, so this can't possibly be the beginning of true friendship.

## Chapter 42

"You stole or whatever, but the big time, really?" Howard asks.

"Really. That was my first time doing something of scale, except we did try to get the plans for the branch of the IFA on campus."

"Let me guess, the passage to Ambrose was blocked."

Julian nods gravely.

"I came across that a few weeks ago. Comes from the other side. Something is going on at Dartmont. But who...why." Howard bites his thumbnail.

"We didn't take the Cuore d'Oro. Tried to, yes." I hold my hand out, recalling how what looked like a solid gold sculpture was little more than vapor. "I reached for it, but my fingers went right through it. It was a projection of some sort. It looked real. It wasn't cloudy or vague and there wasn't a light shining from some hidden space."

Howard scratches his head.

"I wish we had a recording of us skating. It was epic. It'd be viral in an instant," Julian adds.

I get to my feet and pace the room. "But I want it. I'll trade it for Vicky's release." I fill them in about how she was in jail and then went missing. "The rules in the thieving world are few, but one of the unwritten ones is that you don't take someone else's mark."

"Is that like calling dibs?" Neda asks.

I whip around. "Sandro has it. I'm sure of it."

Neda tilts her head and says, "Well, let's get it back from Sandro."

I shake my head. "It's not that easy."

"Penny, if you can figure out how to break into a museum with high security, I have no doubt you can take it back from Sandro, whoever he is. And we've got your back."

"That hologram was pretty sophisticated stuff. If he replaced the real heart with that I doubt he has it sitting on his mantle," Julian says.

"Actually, I wouldn't be surprised if he does. From what Vicky said, he's an arrogant jerk. Loves to brag. Remember a little while back that Delacroix went missing from the Louvre?"

They all shrug.

"Orphan Girl was the title. No?" I try another I heard Vicky raging about. "Or that diamond necklace worth five million from a private home in Hungary? The gold from the Swiss bank in the spring? The vault, completely empty? Except for a record player playing a Beatles song." Vicky never said which one.

No one answers.

"I guess we need to brush up on our knowledge of major heists in Europe," Howard says.

"I pay attention to these things." Or rather Vicky did. The knots in my stomach remind me they're ever-present and getting tighter by the moment. If it had been up to me, would my life be different? Would I just visit museums and admire art? Simply daydream about one day wearing a diamond necklace worth five million dollars, rather than plotting to steal it?

"If you really think it's Sandro, we can figure it out. We can get it back from him," Julian says with hopeful confidence.

"That's the problem." I pause. "I don't know who he is."

"You said—"

"His name is Alessandro Roccio. Vicky hated him. That's pretty much all I know. And I have a picture."

"Wait, you mean you never met him?" Julian says.

"Never."

"Someone must know where he is," Neda says.

I shake my head. "He's invisible. No one has ever seen or met him. His greatest theft is his identity."

"Except Vicky," Julian says. "She knew him."

I heave a sigh. "Yeah." Once more, I realize how very little I knew about my twin.

Howard leaps to his feet. "You said the heart was like a hologram, but not an actual hologram with a projection source, right?"

I nod.

He rubs his chin as if he's contemplating something. "I need to think. I need caffeine."

"He's an early bird," Neda says. "And a night owl. Basically twenty-four seven with this one." She jerks her thumb toward Howard.

"Ha ha. Late at night, while Neda dreams about hot guys, I make myself useful. There are lots of interesting virtual lanes to travel down in the wee hours. I've come across some digital impressionists, you could say. One was trying to replicate the Eiffel Tower. Not going to happen. Plus, why would you want the original in your backyard? But they're pretty successful at coming up with other things. Smaller things. Maybe golden heart-sized things." He adjusts his glasses.

"You think you might know who made it?" I ask.

"As I said, I need some rocket fuel to get the jets fired up, but I think I can pull up the data."

"What Howard means is that everything he's ever seen, read, and heard is stored inside that brilliant brain of his," Neda explains. "Seriously. He remembers what I wore to school on the first day of freshman year."

"That required a cocktail of coffee, espresso, and Red Bull."

"He also knows my grades, schedule, birthdays, and essay due dates. He's like a photographic, sonic, supercomputer. It's a game we play. See what Howard can remember."

Howard hides a bashful smile, but then mumbles, "There are also things I'd rather forget."

The rest of us creak to standing and stretch before going to the diner where Julian and I got pie on the night I discovered Vicky's arrest.

While Howard works on his second cup of coffee and we wait for our breakfast combinations, the morning news flashes on the screen above our booth. We watch the report on the missing golden heart. A museum representative explains the only evidence of foul play is the scratched railings surrounding the display.

Julian grins privately.

"But it wasn't us," I whisper.

"Took 'em long enough to realize it was missing though," he says.

"Sandro got in first and left a decoy. And I want the real one."

Between bites of a pancake layered between a pair of waffles and topped with enough syrup and whipped cream to float a boat, Howard studies websites on his phone, alternating between nodding and making a soft, "Hmm" sound. By the time we're finished, he's on his fourth cup of coffee, his waffles are cold and his whipped cream melted, when he says, "I've narrowed it down."

"I think we have company," Neda says, nudging her head behind me as she downs the rest of her coffee.

I turn as the back of a blonde-haired person leaves the diner. Her stylish wool knee-length coat swishes as the door closes.

"What did she look like?"

Neda glowers. "She looked like Queenie Clemmons from Dartmont. Oh, the dirt I had on her."

Before I can bite my lip to keep from spilling, I say, "Remember I mentioned someone gave me the phone? That someone, I think, was Queenie Clemmons. Caroline despised her."

"Not without reason," Howard says.

"To her credit, the campus has been quieter with Queenie gone...or so I thought if she's somehow involved."

The four of us walk back to the apartment, bracing against what's become a windy day.

Howard installs himself in front of the laptop. Julian showers and I plop onto my bed. Even though I didn't have any coffee and making it up the three flights of stairs was an exercise in resisting extreme sluggishness, my mind whirs while my hands and feet twitch with restless energy.

I join Howard in the kitchen. His leg jitters under the table. His eyes hardly blink as information scrolls across the reflection of his glasses.

"Bingo," he says at last. "That didn't take long. @CornishWallflower173."

"Cornish what?"

"He made the heart visual. It's similar to 3D printing technology, but gives the illusion of substance, though there's no projector. Like fiber optics with each granule—I think they're called—acting as its own light source. The thing is self-contained. Highly sophisticated and nearly impossible to detect as a fake unless, of course, you touch it. The plus for thieves like you is that generally museum employees aren't allowed to handle the art either so it can take a while before it's spotted."

"The scratches on the rails from my skateboard must've tipped them off," Julian says, appearing in a towel.

My cheeks warm at the sight. Neda whistles.

"That was a last-minute modification to the plan. There wasn't time to go back in and polish them," Julian's lips quirk as if he knows neither Neda nor I can stop staring at him in the towel.

"So how do we find this @CornishWallflower?" I ask.

"Julian, we can't focus. Go put some clothes on," Neda orders.

All tattoo and muscle, my boyfriend smirks.

"Right. CornishWallflower173. Focus. Phase two, search the IP addresses. Someone like him—"

"Or her," Neda interjects.

"He or she probably has the IP scrambled, but I can get around that."

"Of course, you can," she says, affectionately pinching his cheek.

Julian yawns. "I'm going to take another nap. Wake me up when you find out more."

"And put some clothes on," Neda calls after him.

"I have to piggyback some software so this might take a while," Howard says.

On her phone, Neda sits beside Howard while he clickety-clacks on the keyboard. I go to my room with nothing to do but wait. Julian lays sideways, passed out on my bed. I silently bounce from music in my earbuds, to magazines, to abandoned paper projects. I flit from one thing to another, feeling hemmed in by all the clothing, the shelves of stuff, reminders of a strange unreality that Vicky and I inhabited after she returned from Italy and our parents disowned her. I collapse into a nest of clothes lying there, claustrophobia from the past closing in when a buzzing comes from the intercom indicating someone is downstairs.

## Chapter 43

When I open the door, my gaze lands on a pair of blue eyes with thick, feathery lashes. Queenie's blonde hair is impeccably styled and the unmistakable scent of perfume overpowers the aroma of stale coffee in the apartment. It's a wonder she and my sister Caroline weren't besties. They're cut from the same ridiculously expensive and luxurious cloth.

"What are you doing here?" I ask.

"You didn't call. You didn't write. Your time is up."

"My time is up?"

"Enough with the petty thieving, Penny. It's boring. You're Vicky's protégé. The real deal."

As I recall the message about my time being up, my face twists with confusion and concern, but I usher her in. There's no telling what might happen if a neighbor overhears.

"Did you steal my cell phone?" I ask.

"I tried to enhance the probability that you'd reach out to me."

I roll my eyes. "You could've asked. Does this have anything to do with Vicky?"

"It has a lot to do with her."

I usher her inside, letting the door slam.

"I make it a point to know everyone. Flavio is our connection if you were wondering—he held you in the highest esteem. I've kept my eyes on you—" She surveys the room as though memorizing the faces and details of each person present, including Julian who shuffles off sleep and stands beside me. She smirks as if she likes what she sees then her eyes meet mine. "I'm Queenie. I'm afraid we haven't formally met."

"Didn't you go to Dartmont?" Julian asks.

"She didn't officially graduate," Neda mutters.

Queenie gives a nonchalant shrug. "I'm on a sabbatical."

"Isn't that for professors?"

"I consider myself an expert so sure, I have my Ph.D." She winks. "In the family business. I learned from the best. Does the name Stefan McQueen ring a bell?"

"You mean Steve McQueen the actor?" Julian asks.

"No, Stefan, as I said," she says purring over the letter *F* before pursing her lips.

I clap my hand over my mouth. "Wait, when Vicky got caught, the news reporter said something about Steve McQueen."

"Stefan, my uncle. He loves old movies and memorabilia. Says it reminds him of a better, freer time." She laughs.

"So he knew Vicky?"

"Flavio, Stefan, me, and Vicky ran the Great Getaway."

My chest sinks at being left out. "What do you want?"

"I was looking for a partner."

"Was?"

A knowing smile lifts Queenie's lips. She tosses a pair of underwear with a Clothing Cloud label onto the kitchen table. "As I said, you're better than shoplifting, Penny. You could be as good as your twin."

"Were you there?" My hands ball into fists. "Did you give me up to the saleswoman?" I step toward Queenie, towering in her heels and a slim skirt. My vision goes as red as her lipstick at the thought that she turned me in for shoplifting.

## Two Truths and One Thief

Julian jumps between us and grips my shoulders, meeting my eyes. "Hang on. Let's hear what she has to say."

Neda aims and fires her best RBF. Vicky would be proud. I'm glad to have her on my side.

"Oh, hi, Queenie," Howard says as if only now realizing we have a newcomer.

"Howard. I take it you received an unpleasant message."

If he's surprised, he doesn't show it. "Thought maybe it had something to do with Penny's phone."

My nostrils flare and although the real muscle in the room stands at my back, I will take Queenie down if she's the reason Vicky got in trouble...or did something sketchy with the phone she gave me. There's probably a rule about not taking cellular devices from strangers.

"That wasn't me," she purrs.

"Why should we trust you?"

"Trace the number. It's clean."

"But your message and the one Howard got on the Dart server sound suspiciously alike."

She lifts her hands in surrender. "I had nothing to do with it."

"Why should we believe you?" I ask.

"And how did you know about the Dart deadline."

"Because I've been keeping tabs on Miss Penny, here. Make sure she doesn't get into any trouble like her twin. I admit to giving Penny the phone. My uncle needs a new person on the team. I figured Vicky taught her sister a thing or two, all things considered. But the four of you together for the last twenty-four hours suggests something juicy is going on. Oh, and if it's about the Cuore d'Oro, we had nothing to do with that either."

"Do you know who did?" I ask.

"No, but I might be able to help you with the issue at the Dart."

"What do you want in exchange?" Neda asks as if knowing nothing exchanged—verbal or digital is free.

"Someone with sticky fingers." Queenie stares at me, practically fluttering her eyelashes as if to entice me.

Something inside bends toward snapping. "No. Once I get Vicky back, I'm going far, far away."

"To college?" Neda asks.

Queenie tips her head from side to side as if weighing options. "If you get Vicky back, I'm guessing she'll resume working with us after things cool off. So I guess that'll work."

"Does Caroline know?" I ask, feeling betrayed for my older sister.

"That Vicky and I were friends?" Queenie clicks her tongue.

"Co-criminals?" Julian supplies.

"Doubtful. Though they had been talking a lot recently."

My insides feel like wet rags being wrung out.

"So who messed with the Dart? Trashed my dorm room and got us suspended for absences?" Neda asks, getting us back on topic.

"I've come up with exactly nothing about the @CornishWallflower." Howard pipes in without lifting his eyes from the computer as though he hasn't given up.

"Howard," I hiss. "Can we trust her?"

Unfazed by the strange utterance and scene Queenie says, "Listen, I'm not a dabbler. This isn't a hobby."

I eye the underwear and then her. "This isn't very professional."

"I gave you an opportunity to reach out to me."

"You could have been more straightforward about it. A phone with a random name and number?"

"I have dirt on Queenie. If she lies or double crosses us, I'll make sure she never works again." Neda's expression is made of brick.

"Have you been paying attention? I don't have a normal job. I only went to Dartmont because my uncle wanted me to have the opportunity to be normal."

"And you call boarding school normal?" Neda asks.

"Fine. He also thought I might have access to intel."

Neda nods. "Uh huh. Which makes that month you dated William Chadwick a lot more sense."

Queenie rocks back on her heels. "Okay. You have dirt on me and the billionaire investor's son."

While they threatened to shoot each other with verbal darts, a plan comes together in my mind. Operation Victorious commences in three, two, one.

"And I have a job to do. I already have the muscle—Julian. The intelligence, a hacker with a brilliant mind—Howard. The Sweeper—Neda and the decoy—Queenie. If you all agree. But I'm missing a key player." I walk down the hall and dial another number on the mobile phone Queenie gave me.

An accented voice answers.

"I need a driver."

Dresden replies in the affirmative and I text the address.

When I return to my spot on the couch, Queenie tells Howard about a former Dartmont teacher with a chip on his shoulder and revenge in his cold heart. My leg jitters. Julian sits next to me and rests his hand on my thigh. It goes still. He lifts his fingers to scratch his shoulder and my leg starts twitching again. This anxious game repeats until heavy footfalls and then loud rapping on the door breaks the silence that follows.

Neda looks up, concerned. "Expecting anyone else?"

I check the peephole. Dresden nods at me in recognition when I open the door.

"A nice lady with a poodle let me in. I helped her with her bags. And what can I help you with?" he asks." With a keen interest in all things shiny and fast, his eyes land on Queenie.

They stare at each other a beat longer before Queenie looks away with a barely concealed blush.

"What are we here to do?" Dresden asks again as though already knowing the score.

"I'm gathering a crew." I turn to everyone seated in the living room and adjoining kitchen.

## Chapter 44

"Like a race car pit crew, a rowing crew, or a—?" Howard cracks a smile even though I have no doubt he knows exactly what I mean.

"Call it a crime ring. A heist society. A redistribution consortium. Think of it as a Robin Hood type of enterprise. Robbing from the rich and..." Saving my sister. Surviving.

All eyes are on me, waiting. For the first time, a thrill at the power and influence I imagine Vicky thrived off rushes through my veins.

"The first question is do you trust me?" I ask.

Julian nods without hesitation.

Queenie says, "I said I wanted a partner. I'll take five if you come as part of package. Penny, you're meant for better things. Bigger things. Golden heart type things."

"You told her?" I ask, aghast.

There's a scattering of *no*s.

"As I said, I know things. I'm perceptive. I knew you went after it at the IFA. What I didn't know is that it was a fake—a digital replica."

Without taking his eyes off Queenie, Dresden says, "Whatever it is, I'll do it, as long as I get to drive fast."

"I like a guy who drives fast." Queenie licks her lips.

I can see why Caroline took issue with her and am glad she wasn't here when Julian got out of the shower.

"I'll ask again, do you all trust me?" Without letting them answer, I say, "You shouldn't. I'm a liar and a thief. But so are you in your own ways. But we have to trust each other. We have to work as a team to pull this off. And above all, no one outside the six of us can know."

Dresden nods.

"My lips are sealed," Neda says.

"Not a word—aloud or typed," Howard says.

"First rule is we do not talk about this," Julian says. "Second rule, we do not talk about this. Third rule—"

"We get it—" Queenie says. "I know the rules."

"Do you?" I count them off on my fingers. "Number one don't get caught. Number two never admit to anything. Number three never get involved." I glance at Julian. "Those were Vicky's rules. I'm writing my own. Don't hurt anybody. Don't steal from anyone who's not a thief. Play the game like you've got nothing to lose." My heart stutters. "And above all else, we have to trust each other. Do you understand?"

There are various sounds of agreement. The main question is do I trust myself? "So, what do we know so far?"

Howard pushes his glasses up the bridge of his nose. "The @CornishWallflower is neither Cornish nor a wallflower. He's a tech expert who works right here in the city as a party promoter—clubs, private events, and stuff like that. I've positively identified him as having fabricated a visual impression of a golden heart for one Hollis Wolfe—he purchased a chunk of gray market gold recently—a close match to Cuore d'Oro, presumably to get the texture and details right even though he used technology to fabricate it. Which means little to us, except—"

"He made a fake golden heart?" Queenie asks.

We catch her up with Howard giving a technical explanation of the advanced 3D type technology.

Queenie snorts. "Sounds as expensive as the piece of art itself."

"I'm not sure its value is measured in dollars. At least, it seemed to have special meaning to Vicky."

Howard continues, "Hollis Wolfe recently gave his two weeks' notice at the Institute of Fine Art, citing a scheduling conflict."

Queenie clicks her tongue. "Which turns out to be one heck of a Halloween party."

"Wait? Hollis Wolfe?" Dresden asks, interrupting what was going to be my question about the Halloween party. "Aka the Lone Wolf in London and Wolfgang Silver in Berlin?"

I tilt my head in question. "They're all the same person?"

"Three years ago. We were racing. He's the reason I totaled my Porsche." Dresden scowls and shakes his, shaved head as though miserable. "Not a day passes when I don't miss *Hase*."

We all look at him, waiting for an explanation.

"Bunny. My car. My first love."

Howard and Neda glance at each other and then away to keep from laughing.

Queenie surveys him with a raised eyebrow.

"Wait. Silver. Silver…Sandro Silver." My head spins. "That's what Vicky called him once. She called him Sandro Silver. Silver tongue. Silver spoon. Silver heart." It was several months ago, late at night. She was exhausted, mumbling to herself in the kitchen while she cooked.

"See, you needed a crew," Julian says.

Vicky tried to do it alone, save for Flavio and the people she must have hired on for a cut, but they didn't collaborate, not that I ever saw—unless of course, that's yet another thing she kept from me.

"The game of aliases leads us to the exact person you were looking for," Howard says. "Sandro Silver."

"What else do we know?" I ask.

"What else do we know?" Queenie repeats with a laugh. "I know almost everything about you, Penny. Your schedule, your interests, your preference to do things solo, wolf-like, your sneaking around campus." She pauses. "Naturally, I was curious about what this group of unusual suspects was doing holed up here for the last day."

I narrow my eyes and notice Neda doing the same.

"I knew about your little adventure at the IFA last week, but what I didn't realize is that a golden heart isn't sleeping somewhere in this apartment. I thought you walked with it. That must have been disappointing."

"You have no idea."

"When Howard told me he was looking for someone who designs virtual impressions, JoJo came to mind. He's a promoter at a club I sometimes work." Her sly smile lifts. "Alcohol makes people with credit cards very careless. But to the point, I recall JoJo mentioning something about a heart. Then I remember a flyer he gave me. It's for a Halloween party." Coming full circle to the reason Hollis Wolfe quit his job due to a scheduling conflict, she produces a thick piece of square black cardstock.

My jaw lowers slightly because Caroline can say what she will about Queenie, but the woman is sharp.

The front of the invitation shows a silver wolf wearing a black masquerade-type mask over its eyes. I flip it over. The back lists info for a costume party, tonight, hosted by The Big Bad Wolf.

"Now that the museum knows it was stolen, replaced by an impression, the real one is probably hidden well, under lock and key," Neda says.

"The address on the card isn't at a club. At least, none that I know of," Queenie says.

Howard types it into the search bar on Vicky's laptop. "Nope. It's a private residence."

"This feels like a long shot," Neda says.

"But Penny said Sandro liked to brag. If this party has anything to do with the heart and is hosted by the Lone Wolf, aka Hollis Wolf, aka Sandro, there's a chance the party mascot," Howard thumps the drawing of the wolf, "will be in attendance."

"You would know something about a costume party, wouldn't you?" Queenie says in Howard's direction.

"A thing or two," he mutters.

Neda arches her eyebrow at the same time I recall murmurings about the Midnight Masquerade and Caroline's involvement along with everything that unraveled at Dartmont after—The Old Guard secret society, corruption in the administration, Johnny Danger, and my favorite math teacher, Nate Boyd, turning out to be majorly sketchy.

"And thanks to my resourcefulness, I am currently downloading the architectural plans for the penthouse suite at this address." He waves the flyer.

"He's good," Dresden says.

"I never back down from some righteous vengeance, but if we're going in, I have to know what's in it for us?" Neda asks. "What are we going to do with the Cuore d'Oro? It's not like we can divide it six ways."

That's a good question. If I get ahold of it and get Vicky back, perhaps she and I can go on one last heist, take something expensive, sell it, and pay them off. But even as I have the thought, I feel juvenile. Foolish. As determined as I am right now, I'm not sure this is the life I want in the future.

Howard angles the computer to show the outline of a room with high security and few access points. "Have a look here. This room is called the Den. It's basically a vault the size of a game room. I imagine there are treasures galore in there. You can probably take your pick for payment."

"If this is Sandro's den, the necklace I mentioned is probably inside, some paintings, then the long list of things Vicky said he stole, including rare gems, bars of gold, gnome figurines—apparently they're worth a million each. Perhaps even relics from world history, antiques, you name it—my sister and Sandro had quite the rivalry going on. As for payment, once inside, fill your pockets."

"I want the necklace," Queenie says.

"Abuelita wouldn't mind the gold."

"Is there a garage?" Dresden asks gruffly.

Howard studies the computer screen and then nods. "Underground. Private. Loaded with V8 engines and petroleum-based vehicles. Penny, what are you going to do with the heart?" Howard asks.

"I have no doubt Sandro is the reason she was arrested and then went after it for his collection. It's payback. I'll use it as collateral until he lets her go."

While Queenie texts on her phone, the rest of us study the residence, taking in every detail. Then, while the others return to the conversation about the potential items they might walk away with, I sit down on the couch with Julian.

"There's a lot to gain, but what do we have to lose?" I ask absently.

"Nothing. We both already lost everything except each other." Julian squeezes my hand.

"And that's not going to change?" I ask, anxiety causing me to sip the air in slow, uneven breaths.

"Never. Rule number four or six. Eight? I lost track. You never lose the ones you love."

"But we know better than that. People die every day."

"We die every day," he says bluntly.

I pinch him. "I think you're alive."

"No, we do."

"What do you mean? Cellular turnover? Like how the body regenerates?" I'm not in the mood for deep thoughts or biology class.

"I'm talking about beliefs we have. False ones. Time to let them die."

My thoughts catch up to his meaning.

"For a long time, I thought I had nothing left. I was willing to fight every night, take myself to the edge and see what was below, have a peek at the other side." His hazel eyes meet mine and his lips quiver. "But I'm done fighting. I want to live for—"

"We have a problem," Neda calls. "It looks like security is unbreachable."

Dresden watches the clock. "Party at ten. It's almost eight." I can hear the seconds passing. This is all happening too fast, but if I let this opportunity slip through my fingers, I'll regret it.

"Speaking of the clock. Let's not forget about the issue at Dartmont."

"I'm on it," Queenie says.

Howard's eyebrows lift.

"It's the least I can do for my alma mater."

"You mean Howard and me," Neda says.

"And the general Dartmont population. As you know, I was the subject of numerous Dart posts and scandals—"

"And you still want to help us?" Neda's forehead furrows.

"Let's say your work kept things spicy." Her nose twitches. "And let's also say that knowing there's some form of accountability isn't the worst thing. Perhaps some campus crime and misdeeds are reconsidered when the potential wrong-doers know that someone is watching." She winks.

"Thank you," Howard and Neda say at the same time.

"There's still the security issue," Dresden says.

Howard takes off his glasses and rubs his eyes. Julian slings his hands around the back of his neck. Bracelets bangling, Neda fishes in her bag and pulls out a pack of red licorice sticks. Queenie narrows her eyes in thought.

"Let's pick up where we left off on our game of truth or dare," I say, catching the newcomers up. I get the sense Howard needs a little motivation. We all do. "Howard, I dare you to take down Sandro's firewall and break into the Den. Queenie, picking the pockets of your neighbors on the Upper East Side or at posh clubs has probably lost its charm. You wanted a partner, now you have five. Dresden, the cars we love can never be replaced, but I think we can find something just as fast as—what was your Porsche called? Bunny? And Neda, it's time to rattle those bangles around your wrist."

The group murmurs assent.

"Rule number five, no job is impossible. Rule number six, we're in this together."

Howard taps his fingers against his lips. "I said it's unbreachable, but I didn't say it's impossible. There's always a way. I just need more coffee and time."

I put my hands on my hips. "We have very little of both, but if we're doing this are we all in?"

"We're all in," Howard echoes, shifting the mood.

Neda, Queenie, and Dresden nod.

"And now it's up to you to figure out the plan," Julian says, kissing me on the forehead.

"So how are we going do this? The old "Smash and grab?" Neda asks.

Howard looks at her quizzically.

She shrugs. "What? I saw it in a movie."

"Are there dogs? I'm more of a cat person, myself," Dresden says, smirking at Queenie.

Queenie leans into me and says, "Despite his rugged good looks and gruff demeanor I think he's actually a big softie."

"Shut out the security and sneak in after everyone leaves the party?" Howard suggests.

"Pinch and prosper?" Queenie asks, naming a con preferred by thieves the world over.

"No, we're going to the party and we're going to take the heart right from under Sandro's nose," I say.

Queenie smiles. "In that case, I'll RSVP adding plus four to the guest list."

## Chapter 45

I GET TO MY FEET, AND PACE IN FRONT OF THE WINDOW, STILL ETCHED with my image, thinking about how we can get into the penthouse and then get out with the golden heart. I'm still thinking when Dresden turns on a soccer game...and pondering possibilities in my mind when Neda chatters away in Spanish to someone on the phone. Still considering options while Queenie files her nails. And still thinking when Julian laces his fingers in mine and lowers me into the papasan next to him.

We smoosh together and at any other moment, I'd welcome his warm weight pressed against me, but there isn't enough time to plan. A *take* like this requires months of research, scouting, dry runs, and intimate knowledge of every inch of the way in as well as multiple exit strategies. Not to mention a complete picture of the security and the backup. All I have is a matter of hours.

And a crew.

I'm still, deep, deep in thought trying to mastermind when Howard shakes his head and says, "The only way in is through the front door."

"No shimmying through air vents? Scaling ladders in elevators? Slinking through narrow passageways?" Julian asks, looking relieved.

"And then we make the getaway," Dresden adds.

"Loco," Neda says.

Howard nods. "The only way into the Den is through the singular door, which is adjacent to the main living space. The air vents would work if one of us were the size of a guinea pig. There aren't any windows. We could go through the walls, but there are sensors embedded every twelve inches and even if I disengaged them, we'd need special equipment to get through the layer of reinforced metal backing the plaster. It would be a possibility if we had more time...and an empty penthouse."

"But we don't," Queenie says, reinforcing my sentiments.

"When you said take it from under his nose I thought you meant more like distract him at the party, sneak into the room via the roof or something, and swipe the thing," Julian says.

"It's impossible, undetected. A veritable fortress." Howard takes off his glasses and pinches his fingers down his nose. "But yes, those were my original thoughts once we got in. I could've helped by scrambling the security feed and disengaging the motion detectors, vibration sensors, and laser grid. But the question is how do we get into the Den—" He slouches.

Despite that Vicky was mostly a solo player whereas I have a team, I know she wouldn't give up. I get to my feet and start pacing.

"In other words, it's like a taco, fried in a pancake, wrapped in a burrito, and grilled into a pizza," Howard says.

"That sounds wrong," Queenie says, turning up her nose.

"Could be tasty." Dresden licks his lips. "I like the food in America."

"You'd eat that?" she asks.

He eyes her hungrily.

"Listen, I've been to some of JoJo's parties. They're usually pretty clean—socialites, celebrities, and the like, but as I said, I notice things. There will be surveillance on the floor, meaning some party guests will actually be security. But at a party like this, I think other guests will be like you and me, and you and you," she says, pointing to us in turn.

"In other words, thieves and liars," I say.

She nods and clicks her tongue.

"I imagine this Sandro guy has a team of thugs who wouldn't hesitate breaking our necks," Howard says.

Julian cracks his knuckles.

Queenie continues. "You can count on the coat check having an x-ray scan slash pat down like at the airport—no weapons."

"But if what you're saying is correct, there's also a chance some of the guests wouldn't mind taking a peek at Sandro's spoils that he keeps locked in his vault room...and being a boastful sort, he won't mind showing them off." A plan begins to form. Then my pacing comes to a halt. A light goes on. I've got it. "The Enigma." I remember Vicky telling me about one of the most difficult cons of all time.

"The what?" Dresden asks.

Queenie squints and says, "I've heard of it, but I don't know if we're..."

"It's all we've got without more time to strategize and plan properly. And we've got each other. We're not going to take the golden heart. We're going to get Sandro to give it to us." I smirk. "Queenie, you said it's a Halloween party. We need costumes. Dresden, can you help her with that?"

He grins. "Of course."

She lifts her head, airily indifferent. "It's crazy and impossible—my favorite combination."

"Maybe we'll get along after all," Neda says to Queenie.

"Howard, what do you need to work with in order to tap in remotely? We'll still need a safe way out. He may give the golden heart to us, but there's no way he'll intend for us to walk off with it, so we have to be prepared with an exit strategy."

He lists some tech and then adds, "And a van that can be parked outside. The security system he has, well, I need to be as close as possible. I'll need all these computers. It picks up alternate wireless, but I can mask it. The guy has layers. He knows what he's doing. Where did your sister find him?"

"We don't need the nerdy details, Howard. My uncle has a van though," Neda says hastily, eyeing the clock. "He's a plumber in Roxbury."

"Traffic is light at this time. You think you can borrow it for the night?"

"Call it done," she answers.

"That leaves me to do a little more thinking." I rub my temples.

Julian's phone vibrates. "I have to—go deal with some stuff."

"Right now?"

"Family emergency—my mother..." He shakes his head and then turns to the group. "I think she's delusional. She firmly stands by the family feud against Jude Capulet—whatever. It doesn't matter."

I squeeze his hand. "I'm sorry, Julian." I explain to the others, "Regina Montague, Julian's mom, thinks Vicky took something of hers while she was working at her clothing shop. I cannot imagine Vicky working, but she probably did steal the bracelet. Maybe tonight we can find a replacement."

Julian rakes his hand through his close-cropped hair. "She won't let it go. When do you need me back?" Julian asks.

I don't want him to leave. I'm afraid if he goes, his mother won't let him return. I'll have to steal something else to buy his freedom. Vicky might like the heist life, but it's not for me. In fact, shame about all the things I've taken burrows deep inside me.

But Julian's lips land on mine, erasing all my thoughts but one. That unspoken word *love* still floats in the air between us.

"I promise I'll be back," he says, telling me I have to trust that we'll have the chance to speak it.

"Ten o'clock is show time," Queenie says. She dips out the door with Dresden, followed by Julian. Howard gathers the laptop, cables, and various pieces of gear Vicky had on hand, leaving with Neda to get the van.

And once more, I'm alone.

## Chapter 46

I study the flyer with the silver wolf wearing a mask over its eyes. A Halloween party is about a hundred degrees from where I'm at. Anyway, what should I go as? A cat burglar? A convicted felon? A nobody?

Vicky took any sweet licks of this life with her, despite Julian and the others. She left me with nothing more than a stain on my heart and knots in my stomach. I stew for a few minutes, thinking about this mess of emotions.

I flop on my bed, the sheets still rumpled from Julian's nap. My copy of Romeo and Juliet, spine split, lays open on my pillow.

I whisper the passage about the boundless sea. The meaning infuses me with new energy.

Mum and Dad never said they loved me. Vicky never told me she loved me. I hardly ever heard any of them utter the word, not even in passing, like, "Oh, I love the sunrise or I love gelato." I'm not afraid to say I love both. And Julian. I love him. That truth washes a bit of the stain away. It loosens the knots ever so slightly. Although I'm not entirely sure the plan to get the golden heart is foolproof, I know what I need to say to Julian.

I recently learned that it's not about what I take, but what I give.

I lay there a few more minutes, parsing out what could have kept the word love from Vicky's lips. Mum's and Dad's too. My birthday text from Caroline comes to mind. She wrote *I love you, Sis.* That's something.

But what kept Vicky from love? Perhaps love it's too risky. You can't steal it. Maybe she tried to take it once and she couldn't walk away with it. Or maybe that wasn't it at all and it really just came down to fear.

She always said words are meaningless. Action is everything. I don't agree, not entirely. Words are powerful and doubly so when backed with action. But words on their own still carry weight. They still have an impact. But what's worse is their absence.

Vicky was afraid of love, but I don't have to be.

My pack of playing cards sits on a shelf, each suit emblazoned with a heart motif. Vicky taught me all the card tricks, the tells, and the strategies. She said it would keep my mind sharp because even in the best-planned job, you never know what challenge or surprise will come up. Just as you never really know what card will appear next in the deck. Except she did. She knew every time and taught me how to keep track. I pick up the deck and shuffle the cards, remembering how we'd spend hours on her bedroom floor, playing until eventually, I started to win. Then I taught Julian until he eventually won. But life isn't a card game because I never saw her leaving and I never saw him coming—or how the way I feel about him fills me up with so much happiness and hope it overflows.

But theft is a game I have to play one more time. I shuffle the cards and clear a space on the floor, dealing them to invisible players, imagining myself at the table and predicting their every move. I know all of the plays in Liars & Thieves where cheating isn't only allowed, but encouraged.

I flip the first card and toss it to the floor, I flip the second, and then another, eventually discerning a pattern. I may not be aces at math, but I can picture the ace of diamonds before it appears. I run through various scenarios. I get it right every time. I do it repeatedly until the cards are gone and my hands are empty. And I feel the same way, all over again.

I could go to the party as myself. That would be amusing, maybe insightful.

Penny, as Penny.

But who am I?

Thief. Liar.

Daughter. Sister.

Loyal. Friend.

Brave.

In love.

Minutes later, Queenie announces her return with a text. She marches into the kitchen with a garment bag and then *tsks*. "You'd think the costume shops would be open on Halloween night. You know, last-minute shoppers."

I give her a wide-eyed look that says, *Duh, you break in.*

She shakes her head. "We did. But—" She squishes up her nose. "They didn't have everything that I was looking for. Instead, we borrowed some costumes for you and your young lover from a theater company." She produces a silken Elizabethan gown in black, gold, and burgundy with plush velvet details, feathers, and lots of sparkle and embroidery. There's also a corset and a mask.

My expression curdles. "I don't think that's quite my style—"

"You'll look divine. And for our man Romeo—" She jostles a hanger in her other hand. "Thankfully there aren't tights involved."

My expression doesn't waver.

Queenie thrusts the dress into my hands and disappears to the bathroom with a garment bag of her own.

"What are you wearing?" I ask, calling after her.

Queenie chuckles. "I was thinking Dresden and I could go as Bonnie and Clyde."

"I said no. I'll only be at the party for a short time. We shouldn't be closely associated—" he answers for her. I startle, not having seen him by the door.

I need to focus. "Smart."

He grins. "I have to acquire our getaway car."

"A Porsche?"

"If only I could take it with me."

"Where are you going?"

"I've overstayed my welcome with my sister." He bows his head.

"Ms. Honig?"

"She doesn't approve of my habits. She wanted me to come here to get a job like her. It's time to move on. Maybe I'll go home. Maybe not." He looks longingly toward the closed bathroom door. "To Enni, the problem is I am more of a wasp or hornet than a bee." He tilts his head, considering. "She loves bees, you know."

I don't quite get the metaphor but do know about her affection for the insect in question as well as poetry.

"I come, I pollinate, I leave. Maybe she'll come with me." He motions toward the bathroom.

Queenie opens the door, revealing herself in a gauzy white dress with sequins and feathers. A white mask studded with tiny crystals covers the top half of her face. She applied a dusting of glitter to her lips. She twirls to show us a flutter of wings.

"I thought she should go as an angel." Dresden's gaze glazes over. "She looks like one."

She curtsies. "For the record, I'm no angel."

"That's what I like about you," Dresden says in his gruff voice.

If Queenie didn't have so much makeup on, I'm sure her cheeks would be pink.

"Your turn, princess," she says to me. "Get suited up. We'll meet there."

"Wait. Be an angel and help me into this," I say, holding up the gown.

"Ha ha."

We go to my room and Queenie wades through the clutter. "Been busy," she mutters.

I fit myself into the gown, and she assists with the zips and ties. I stumble to the closet to find some shoes, my stockinged feet slipping on the playing cards. I whirl around with the spark of an idea.

"Queenie, have you ever played Liars & Thieves?"

"The card game? Of course. Every swindler worth their weight in gold knows it."

"Can you win?"

She lifts her chin. "Do you want me to?"

I smile. "No. But I want you to set it up. Get a game going. Make it juicy. Make sure Sandro is at the table. Entice him. Get him to gloat. We want him thinking about his reputation, about the cache of goods in the Den, and have an irresistible urge to brag about it."

"And then?"

"I have a role for Neda too. She'll bait him, get us in there, and rile him up."

"I see where you're going with this," she says, fastening the corset. "Well, played, Penny."

"That remains to be seen."

She levels me with her gaze. "If you want this as badly as I think you do, don't let your confidence waver, not for one minute. That's the chink in your armor. Your dragon's soft spot. I'm only telling you this because I meant it when I said I wanted a partner."

"I think you found one," I say, motioning to Dresden, just beyond the door.

She smirks privately. "We'll see. Listen, I'm not out to double-cross you or use your weakness against you. But I don't want anyone else to either. I know you can be assertive when you want to be, trust me, I've been watching you."

"FYI, that's kind of creepy."

She pulls my hair off my shoulders, pinning it up. "I've been watching Dresden too. And Howard. Neda was the only one not on my radar. I make it my job to know all the players. So my request is tonight, be your best. Be brave."

"Got it."

"Anything else I need to know about Sandro?"

"I've told you everything I know. He's an enigma."

Queenie smirks. "Nice. Using the Enigma against an enigma."

I snort a laugh. "All I know is that it's likely he'll have the biggest ego in the room."

"Then we're playing blind. You ready?"

"I'm ready to get my sister back."

"Good. Don't forget to keep the mask on," she says, pointing to it on my bed, "what with being Vicky's twin and all."

"If Sandro sees me...hadn't thought of that important detail."

Queenie winks. "That's why we're a team."

The two of them, with Dresden dressed as a mechanic, leave in a cloud of perfume and auto grease.

I pick at the feather on Romeo's hat, worried that Julian isn't back. My phone vibrates.

It's Neda. "Good news. Got the van and Howard is working his computer magic. I'm in costume and ready to roll when you are."

I tell her that I haven't heard from Julian.

"'Oh, Romeo, wherefore art thou, Romeo?'" she recites.

"Something like that."

"Don't worry. We got this."

I could use a hit or two of her confidence. I go on to give a quick rundown of the rules of the card game and her role. "You're going to be the determined and foul-mouthed loser. Bait Sandro. Challenge him to raise his wagers because he's so confident he'll win."

"Got it. Any other tips?"

"Ordinarily, I'd tell you that you want people to like you but forget about you. To be the gray lady and not to arouse suspicion. However, tonight, you get to be the biggest, loudest, baddest person in the room."

She cackles. "Oh, my pleasure."

I wait for Julian for twenty more minutes before leaving him a text, explaining his costume draped over the chair. I leave the key under the mat, foolish and forbidden when under Vicky's roof, and then set out to the party.

## Chapter 47

It's late. Along the cobbled lane, I don't see groups of parents chaperoning kids dressed as princesses and pirates. They're fast asleep in sugar comas. The only people that haunt the street at this hour are people like me, up to no good.

A couple of years ago, Vicky dressed as Peter Pan and I was her shadow, all in black. We stole electronics while honest children got free candy.

Too soon, I reach the penthouse address. It's a modern building with structural steel supporting a vast amount of glass. Cackling laughter cascades from high above. The party on the upper floor must overflow outside onto a balcony. I wonder if Sandro has lived here all this time, relatively close in proximity, or if this is just a hangout, a place to throw a party—though the latter is not likely with the careful security of the Den.

The elevator opens directly into the living space. Black lights and strobes blink shadows into hyper-illuminated ghouls and fools. Spider's webs coat surfaces and gothic decorations make the scene spooky.

There are devils and vampires, including a very convincing Edward Cullen, along with superheroes and villains, mostly the latter. And of course, the requisite burglars, telling me this is exactly the kind of party Queenie suggested it had the potential to be. Interesting that Sandro would host a party just down the street from Vicky's, but I don't have seconds to spare to wander into thought. I have to stay focused.

I recognize a few characters from different jobs. A bank employee who was generous with details, a librarian not opposed to helping with unusual research, particularly source files that weren't in the library's collection. But most people are completely incognito. I'm glad I hide behind a mask.

My phone buzzes with a message from Queenie. **Game on.**

I pass Dresden, sipping a beer and in close conversation with an FBI agent—a costume, I hope. I catch the words *composite brakes* and *nitrous*. His nod is subtle. However, the lighting is dim, fog machines send drifts of white clouds through the frenetic strobe lights, and orchestral music creeps from invisible speakers. Even if Dresden rushed up to me and shouted, "Let's rob this place," I have a suspicion no one would pay attention. Or, they might ask, "What's for taking?"

I circle the room, keeping an eye out for Julian while taking note of the exits, including windows, never mind that we're several stories up. I hope Howard worked out our departure because the only out I've seen is the elevator and that won't get us far.

With the Halloween décor, I can't be sure where exactly the cameras are, but there's a good chance there is one in the cobwebbed candelabra in the corner and if my calculations are correct, there should also be one by the eastern wall with the hanging skeleton. I'm not sure who the costumed security detail is, but a tattooed football player is a likely candidate with the way he sweeps the room every five minutes or so. I help myself to a glass of something green and oozing, just to blend in, and search for the card game. And Julian.

When I reach the dining room, in the center is a round table. Queenie looks ethereal and mysterious in her angel costume, distracting the men with her generous cleavage spilling from the top of her dress.

Neda sits opposite Queenie, a sexy sugar skull, a decoy.

Also seated at the table are a pirate, a ghoul, a superhero, a cat, Elvis, and a wolf—aka Hollis Wolf. Aka Sandro.

My blood freezes as the fine hairs at the nape of my neck lift.

He takes a long sip from a glass filled with amber liquid and ice, his wolf-like eyes ever watchful. Commanding the attention of everyone gathered, and with all of the cool swagger I expect, he slams the glass down, flips his cards over in triumph, points at the superhero, and in lilting Italian says, "Liar." In addition to the wolf headpiece, he wears a black fitted regency-style suit with brocade detail.

I watch another round of the game, which Queenie has a chance at winning, when Sandro says, "Thief," calling out the loser, this time the pirate. He wins again.

I watch Sandro carefully, recalling Vicky's details. Wild, dark hair? Check. Boastful attitude? Check. And yes, he always wins. At least the last few rounds, considering the number of chips in front of him compared to everyone else's dwindling piles.

What Vicky didn't tell me about was his skill, and how he carefully plays his hand, while making it look effortless with each deep belly laugh at a joke or comment made by another player. It's not easy to hate his sly smile.

Sandro's eyes are sharp, lupine, yet the dark smudges beneath them suggest fatigue. Interestingly, the warm notes hidden in his deep voice make me think there's probably someone in this world with whom he uses a gentle tone. I'd built him up to be a bloodthirsty wolf, which he is, but I see something else, something more. Or maybe that's what I tell myself so I'm not quite so afraid.

Queenie's gaze flits over me, just another player, another thief, and a liar. I don't acknowledge her.

Sandro shuffles and Queenie purrs, "I would expect someone with your reputation to have more delicate hands."

Their eyes lock. Whoa. She's good.

"My reputation?" he asks.

She slides her fingers along his. "You know what they say about men with big hands," she counters.

"Do I?"

"They're clumsy. Oafish. Not good at the fine art of theft." Her grin is the feline to his wolf.

My stomach flip-flops. But is he buying it?

He glances up, and for a moment I forget I wear a mask and am afraid he's seen me, as though my intentions are tattooed on my skin. But my worry settles when I spy his slight grin as he concentrates on dealing the hand.

"I don't believe the rumors about your reputation," Neda shrugs. "I didn't expect you to keep all your treasures locked away. Do you have a secret room?" She shakes her head. "I doubt it. You're probably like the rest of us, picking pockets, scraping by, hoping for a big break. A thief, yes, but mostly a liar." I only notice his subtle flinch because I pick up details.

The play only makes it around once before Sandro wins again.

"It's Halloween, shouldn't we make the game more interesting?" Queenie asks.

There's the murmuring of assent.

"Is there room for one more?" I ask, seizing the opportunity.

No one offers to leave their spot because they know they've hooked a whale. Not all of them want to win, Neda in particular, but rather to be in Sandro's presence. Up until now, in crime circles, he's been invisible, and the fact that he's hosting a party tells me two things. He wants to gloat, showing everyone in America that he's a top thief, and in turn, he wants to size up the competition.

The ones who think they'll win are delusional and the ones who simply want to walk away with bragging rights don't realize he'll probably swindle them and they'll land in jail like Vicky.

The big question is, where is she? He probably has her on a job while he's partying. I try to channel her hatred for him.

Sandro peers in my direction through the rings of smoke machine gloom and once more, I contend with feeling exposed and vulnerable, despite my costume.

"Another player?" He looks around the table, pausing on Neda, but she doesn't relinquish her spot.

"You've got big hands," Neda cuts a convincing glare at Queenie, and then says, "But do you have a bigger room?"

"I have a bigger everything," Sandro replies.

"Including your mouth," Neda says.

I knew I could count on her.

He scowls and punches a text into his phone. In a few moments, the football player, a zombie, and a painter, wearing splattered renaissance era garb, appear—now we know who's on his team. He confers with them in hushed tones before turning back to us.

"Let's move this game somewhere more private," Sandro says. He surveys us each individually. "It's safe to say we're all in the same business. And if we're not and you don't belong here, turn back now." His voice echoes with finality.

It doesn't escape my attention that his security detail surveys us each carefully. I glance up at a camera in the corner. I'm sure this is all on film—each one of us carefully observed by the eye in the sky.

We follow Sandro down a hallway and I take another opportunity to note the doors, windows, exits, and vantage points. According to the plans Howard had, the Den is on the other side of the penthouse. I think. But now I'm not sure. The space is circuitous, like the Roman Pantheon.

I take the opportunity to text Howard. **On the move. Be ready.**

After a maze-like walk away from the party, we stop in a library with bookshelves on three walls and a pair of leather reading chairs in the middle. It's smaller than the room we were in before with no space for a large table. I stash the phone in the folds of my gown. When I look up, one of the bookshelves opens into a dark room, reminding me of the secret passage in the Old Guard headquarters. Is this the Den? The only way in? I hope Howard has it figured out because I wasn't expecting a secret entrance.

Sandro surveys each of us before disappearing into the dark. The others shuffle in behind him. With my heart in my throat, I gather my skirts, glance over my shoulder, and with no sign of Julian, step into the unlit space, hoping it's not a trap.

## Chapter 48

I take a deep breath, inhaling the darkness and so much uncertainty. The door makes a suction noise as it seals behind us. My stomach lurches.

Low lighting along the room's perimeter blinks on. Paintings, most in gilded frames, presumably missing from museums and private collections, line the walls. Beside me are several glass cases containing jewels and antiques. There's a table, lined with velvet and stacked with bars of gold. The guy is ridiculous. Sandro doesn't steal and fence his take like the rest of us. He keeps his spoils like a dragon guarding his hoard.

An overhead light in the center of the room comes on and my eyes land on a large wood table. In the center, on an onyx pedestal, is the Cuore d'Oro. The gold glows. The precious stones gleam. There it is. Vicky's prize. All she ever wanted. My resolve returns and my confidence burns through the doubt and worry about how to pull this off.

"You can look. But you may not touch." Sandro strides across the room toward the golden heart. His movements are protective, yet predatory.

Queenie, Neda, the pirate, ghoul, gorilla, cat, Elvis, and a bank-robbing bandit dressed in black with a knit cap pulled low and a kerchief over his mouth, who wasn't part of our group before, comes into focus. The bandit dips his head in my direction, but my attention locks on the Cuore d'Oro.

Sandro gestures grandly. "Thieves and liars, liars and thieves, welcome to the Den."

There's chatter about the stolen, sparkling contents. Still in character Neda says, "Should I be impressed?"

Sandro ignores her and glances at Queenie. "Is this room big enough?"

Her smile is sultry.

"I had it custom built to my specifications before I returned to the states."

Neda, with her arms across her chest says, "Are you here to claim this territory for your own, because—"

Sandro cuts her off. "Sugar Skull, do you know who I am?"

She snorts. "Enlighten me."

"I am the Lone Wolf. Do you know what wolves do?"

Neda's eyes narrow and she snarls. "They grovel at the feet of the dead."

Sandro matches her snort and then in a low warning, he says, "No, they create the dead. Watch yourself, Sugar Skull."

She doesn't waver. "I suggest you do the same." Then she mutters, "Lobo loco."

I swallow hard at this exchange. Yet, it's all part of the game. The ten of us take our seats at the table—the bank-robbing bandit to one side of me and the pirate to the other.

The renaissance painter passes Sandro a sealed deck of cards before leaving the room. The football player and zombie remain, stationed by the door.

"You all know the rules," he says, his gaze landing on each of us at the table. His sharp pause remains on me for longer than is comfortable. I watch his throat bob as he swallows, blinks, and then glances at the deck, not sparing a glance at the bank-robbing bandit.

## Two Truths and One Thief

I remain a motionless fixture, a player, a thief, my expression emotionless and unmemorable.

"Since this is my game—" He clears his throat.

No, it's Vicky's game. She made it up. She introduced it to him. Then again, Sandro takes what isn't his, including the golden heart, breaking the cardinal rules of our underworld.

"I'm adding a rule. You lose. You leave. Understood?"

There's nodding and murmuring of agreement.

Play begins. The first round is brisk and fraught with animosity—mostly between Sandro and Neda.

With a great flourish, Sandro flips his cards over and to the pirate, whom he calls, "Liar," eliminating him from the game.

The pirate makes an aargh sound and shuffles out of the room, muttering about mutiny and having to walk the plank.

Next to lose is Elvis, who doesn't spare us a terrible version of "All Shook Up" while being carted away. Then the cat yowls as she leaves, followed by the ghoul with a spine-tingling moan.

Six of us remain. Sandro smiles lazily from behind his mountain of chips, having won all but one round, which he lost to Queenie. He tosses the cards across the table as though already bored. "My game, I don't leave."

It's pure luck that Neda is still in, considering she has no idea how to play. Either that or she's a quick student. Then again, lying and cheating aren't that hard. It's time for her to make her final move.

I assess my hand, another deal that I'm sure to win but won't on purpose. I'm playing on Sandro's complacency. On his ego. On his sense of largess. When my turn comes around, I discard my winner, banking on one more loss. With ink-stained fingers, the bandit throws a card on the pile. His black shirt hitches, revealing the edge of a tattoo. My heart races.

Julian has been beside me this entire time.

Sandro lifts an eyebrow in my direction, mistaking the change in my expression for having a winning hand, but I play out the loss, only coming in behind Neda to stay in the game.

"Lobo, before I lose, I have to ask why. Why, if you already have all of these riches, did you come here? Why, if you always win, do you continue to play? Doesn't it get boring? Wouldn't you rather do something else?"

"If this is a ploy to get me to go back to where I came from, then I suggest you not bother trying. If you want an honest answer, you're out of luck. A liar and a thief never tells the truth. You should know that. But I will say this, and perhaps it would benefit you, Sugar Skull. I do it because it amuses me. Because I can. Because it's a game. Because there is something I have been looking for, for a long, long time and cannot seem to find. I came here because I am finally close."

"What are you looking for?" Queenie asks.

Sandro snorts. "I won't tell."

"Not even if we could help?" she asks, as angelic as ever.

He shakes his head.

"I hope you don't find it," Neda says at the same time Sandro flips his cards and says, "Liar."

She throws down her remaining cards and storms from the room.

We play one more round and this time Queenie calls out the gorilla as the thief. The zombie escorts him from the room, leaving Sandro, Queenie, the bandit, and me.

"Four is a good number," Sandro says, dealing. "I plan on winning so this shouldn't take too much longer. I have a party I should return to."

"What if we make this a little more juicy? Up the stakes," Queenie suggests as Sandro deals again.

"Hmm. Considering I have the most chips, I suppose we could—" Sandro stacks his hands on the table.

Queenie leans closer, the overhead light illuminating her cleavage. "What if we wager on a larger scale."

He can't look away. "I like where this is going. What do you have in mind?"

"How about the prize is the item acquired from your most difficult job."

## Two Truths and One Thief

Sandro gestures to the pedestal in the center of the room. "You're looking at it."

"The Cuore d'Oro?" Queenie scoffs. "Tell us about it."

"Yes, the Cuore d'Oro. Some call it the golden heart. I call it the apex of my career."

"Nowhere to go but down from here, eh?" The bandit, Julian, speaks for the first time. His chipped tooth shines in the light. I inhale his words because if nothing else, tonight, Sandro will fall from his mountain of treasure, of gloating, and glory.

Sandro chuckles. "That's debatable. What about you? Your most difficult job?"

"I'm still on it," Julian replies.

Sandro nods with amusement and then lifts his chin in Queenie's direction.

She ponders the question. "It was a pink diamond. Cushion shaped. Five carats. Platinum band. An engagement ring."

Sandro scoffs. "Then it was given to you," Sandro says, eyeing her bare fourth finger.

"Was it? It took me six months—I wouldn't call that love and devotion. I never gave it back. It was never seen again." She winks from beneath her mask.

"Where is it now?" Sandro asks, covetous.

"If I win, I'll tell you."

"If you lose?"

"I'll let you put a bigger one on my finger."

"How do I benefit?"

"Am I not a worthy prize?" The flirtation plays out and then Sandro turns to me.

"Juliet? You are very quiet. How about you? What was the most difficult thing you ever took?"

My voice is rusty. "A heart." My own pounds in proximity to Julian's. "Not a golden one," I add.

"Ah, but this cannot be stolen. Lost, but never taken unwillingly." His gaze shifts downward in a flitting moment of vulnerability and sadness. "I tried once. I failed."

"The Lone Wolf shows a soft side," Queenie says.

"My heart? No. It is as hard as the golden heart," he says, pointing.

"Then that is the prize. Whoever wins gets the Cuore d'Oro," Queenie proclaims.

"But I will win," Sandro says. "What do I get? I have no use for a lovesick heart—already have one of those, an incomplete job—likewise—nor this ring you claim to have, because I will not marry you."

"Your heart belongs to another?" Queen asks coyly.

Sandro grunts.

I force my way past the lump in my throat, ready to play my hand. "We'll work for you," I say.

"Oh, you will?" he asks with laughter. "I don't know you. I don't trust you." He glances at Julian. "I'm not sure I like you."

"Pick a job. We'll do it," Julian adds, glancing at Queenie. "You in?"

She lifts and lowers her shoulder non-comital.

"If your services are all you are prepared to offer, then the game is over."

"What do you want?" Queenie asks.

"I'm looking for a person." He taps the edge of the cards against the table. He shrugs. "I will win. But that's what I want. Find this person for me."

Queenie shakes her head. "If those are the terms, I'm out."

"What a shame. You are so lovely. I was hoping we could work together," Sandro says.

She pushes her chair in. "Perhaps someday."

He watches her departure and shakes his head. "I hope so."

I glance at Julian, hoping he reads a smile between the thin line of my lips.

"And only three remain. You are both prepared to work for me and find this person I seek?"

I force myself not to scoff. Is he collecting a team of thieves he'll force to work for him? He may call himself the lone wolf, but we all are. That's the deal in this business. Occasionally, we'll work as a team like now, but in the end, we're only out for ourselves. At least, that's what Vicky said.

In response to his question, Sandro gets a steely glare. He nods at the zombie and football player by the door and they depart.

Let the game begin.

## Chapter 49

Sandro deals the cards. The round is swift. Uneventful. I could do this in my sleep. Julian makes sure to lose to me, not that he could've won given the way I play my hand.

"My my. Have you been pacing yourself, Juliet? It seems you know this game better than you let on." He deals for the last time.

"It's been a pleasure," Sandro says to the bandit.

"He stays," I order.

Sandro tilts his head in question.

"You don't trust me? I don't trust you either. Best to have a witness."

"Fine." He exhales.

I keep my eyes on the Cuore d'Oro and imagine Vicky sitting beside me, guiding me through each turn. I have two aces. If my assessment of the contents of the discard pile is correct, Sandro holds one of them, I'm sure of it. I need three to win. The draw pile is still stacked. He takes a card and smiles.

Is he bluffing?

There is only one way for me to win. Bluff too. Then I'll buy my way out of the bluff. I take my turn and tilt my head a degree or two.

He goes. I go. His turn. My turn. The Den holds our silence, the tension drawing our breath shallow, soundless. Even our movements carry a hush. The golden glow of the heart, so near, reminds me that I'm playing to win.

I draw.

I discard.

He goes.

Repeat.

"They say never to bet against the house. The house always wins," Sandro says, his low, accented voice strained.

I debate between a queen and a two, which I can use as a wild but doesn't have any point value. "And who's the house, Sandro?" I ask.

"Why me, of course," he answers.

We each take another turn.

"Are you sure about that?" I drop the two.

He takes it. "Liar," he calls, triumphant.

I array my cards, displaying the aces. "Winner." At last, I exhale.

He swallows, his lips pursed in defiance, not used to losing. "Where did you learn to play so well?"

"From the best." I get to my feet, gathering up my skirt.

"I see."

I hold Sandro's gaze, not moving from the spot.

"Ah, yes. You would like your prize. The Cuore d'Oro." He walks over to the wall and opens a hidden panel, punching in some numbers. "Go ahead, take it."

I don't hesitate. But the knots in my stomach constrict as I lift Vicky's coveted golden heart off the pedestal. Something is wrong. Then an alarm pierces the relative quiet. My mask hides my incredulity, but not the fire in my words. "Liar."

"And a thief. Why the air of surprise? You said you didn't trust me, and I never said I'd make it easy. Take it. Go. But I promise I'll get it back." Sandro's voice is a growl.

I step into the open doorway, the golden heart heavy in my hands. I run my fingers along the ridges and the gems, my fingers counting each one.

The Lone Wolf's eyes glint in the low light.

A smile lifts my lips. "No, you won't."

Sandro gestures that we leave, dismissing us. "Go on, take a head start. You can be sure that I won't stop until I get back what's mine."

"Is it yours?" I ask.

"Everything is mine." He grabs my arm, the one holding the heart.

Our eyes meet for one agonizing moment. While mine are blue, Victoria's are gray. That's the only difference. At least that anyone can see.

I yank my arm away. "No, not everything. If I'm not mistaken you stole this."

His grip tightens. "Isn't that what we do?"

In two long strides, Julian reaches Sandro, and in one swift motion punches him in the face. "Hands off her."

There isn't time to think about bruises and consequences as the two of us hurry from the Den. Julian thumbs a text as we press through the crowd, but in the maze-like layout of the penthouse, I'm not sure if we're near the elevator or a door or a fire escape. The alarm blares staccato against the music as unicorns dance with gangsters and masked faces leer and jeer in the flashing light.

I expect the football player or the zombie to intercept us, but the mass of costumed partygoers hides us, for now. The glow of Julian's phone reveals him shaking his head. "Howard wants us to go the other way."

"What other way?"

Julian points back to where we came from. "There's another exit."

I glance over my shoulder, worried we're going to get worse than a punch in the face if Sandro's guys get ahold of us. But we're a team. A crew. We have to trust each other. I'm good at concealment. Julian can handle himself and Howard will get us out.

I clutch the golden heart sculpture in my hands, and a belated sense of triumph replaces the prickling nerves I've felt since arriving. It doesn't matter how I got it, but that I did. I did it for Vicky.

We race down a hall, lined with witches, skeletons, ghosts, and ghouls. My breath quickens. Julian has Howard on the phone and he instructs us to turn right and then right again. I feel like we're moving deeper into the center of the building, spiraling ever inward, but Howard knows the floor plan. He's going to get us out.

After another turn down a bending hallway and then passing through a bathroom with two entrances, Julian stops in front of a black door. "This is it." He jiggles the knob. It's locked. "This isn't it," he relays to Howard now on the phone in our moment of desperation.

My stomach clenches with worry that Howard double-crossed us. Ran us like rabbits through a tunnel to a dead end as the Big Bad Wolf bears down on us.

Pushing aside panic, I don't have my lock-picking set, but take a pin from my hair.

Despite the intensity of the moment, Julian smiles, breathing me in. "You're so beautiful when you're being shifty."

"Why thank you," I hear Howard say through the mobile.

Julian laughs.

Focused, I lower onto my knees, working the hairpin into the lock. I twist, listen, rock back on my heels, and huff. "Of course, this isn't just an old ordinary lock. It's digital."

Julian shakes his head, not understanding.

"Tell Howard we're screwed. Tell him that if he sold us out, betrayed us..."

He must hear me.

Howard says, "Penelope, I wouldn't. And I can prove it. You're not screwed. Try again."

I turn the handle. Nothing. I try picking it. There's no click or release. "Tell him there's something lost in translation because the door won't open and—"

Footsteps approach.

I lean against the door, already feeling cornered. I cradle the golden heart against my chest, determined not to give it back. All at once, I fall backward, catching myself on the doorframe.

I hear Howard whoop and then give quick instructions, guiding us forward. Julian and I enter a dark corridor and close the door. I suddenly feel buoyant despite the heavy footfalls from behind the door like we've been bought a few more moments to escape. Julian takes my hand as we race down a spiral staircase. I clutch the golden heart closer—he's my good luck. A smile blooms on my face. One floor. Two floors. Three. Down. Down. Down. We'll be out in no time.

I'm focused and invincible.

White lightning charges my every step.

I am riding high.

I am a boss.

A giant.

I am out the door.

I am...

Caught. My dress snags on a piece of metal on the stairs. The golden heart flies out of my grasp. "No!"

Julian lunges for it, his muscles tensing as it ricochets off the handrail and lands in his hands in one sprawling dive.

Police sirens wail in the distance. We must be nearing the underground parking garage.

My heart thuds as I tug my dress loose and thrust the torn piece in Julian's hands, urging him to wrap up the golden heart. Sandro doubled down and called my bluff. I never expected him to call the cops.

The word *guilty* flashes in my mind, not only because I'm sure the cops will be able to associate me with Vicky, but also for putting Julian in danger, for dragging him into this.

He looks me in the eyes and says, "I don't want to leave you, but we have to split up. I'll go to the van with Howard and Neda. Sandro won't expect me to have the golden heart."

"I don't want to leave you," I echo.

"Odds are Sandro thought I was protecting your honor and we weren't together at the party."

I point toward the ceiling. "Cameras?"

He shrugs. "What else can we do?"

I take a deep breath. "Hide it well. Meet me later." I kiss him on the lips for one scene-melting moment, and we dash down the remaining stairs.

## Chapter 50

I rush through the parking garage, outside, and toward the glowing red taillights of a Porsche idling on the corner. I knock on the window. "Nice wheels. Too bad there's only room for two."

"You can squeeze in," Dresden says. "Sandro has good taste. I've already taken it for a spin. Doesn't handle as well as Bunny, but it'll get us where we want to go."

"Where's that?" I ask.

Seated in the passenger seat, Queenie says, "We're touring Europe—south of France, perhaps—a honeymoon of sorts."

"You got married? That was fast."

Dresden chuckles.

I raise an eyebrow.

"Not exactly the kind of partner I had in mind, but I think I'll give him a chance."

"Isn't that what dating is for?"

"Dating is for amateurs. No offense. And by lifestyle, I mean of the rich and notorious."

My thoughts kite toward Julian.

She holds up her hand, a cluster of diamonds on her ring finger. "Not as stunning as the pink diamond, but they sure do sparkle."

"Congratulations."

"Save for if we're still together in a month." Queenie's smile is wry.

Dresden doesn't look like he has any doubts. This gives new meaning to love at first sight.

"Did you get what you were looking for?" Queenie asks.

I nod. "No stealing required."

"Was it worth it?"

"I'll let you know. Thank you, by the way. I owe you one."

Blue lights flash off the mirrored sides of the tall buildings a few blocks away. Dresden revs the engine. "We better get going before Sandro realizes he was actually robbed."

"He's a fool if he thought he could invite every thief in the city to a party and not expect something to go missing. Speaking of parties, Neda said we should meet her to celebrate—the founding headmaster's mansion on Snow Hill. Please give her our regrets."

"At Dartmont?" I ask.

There's no time to party. The flashing lights and sirens draw closer. Vicky had many reasons for hating Sandro, but one of them was that he didn't like losing. Panic chokes off my voice. This is just an extension of the game. He let me go, but he'll try to get the golden heart back.

"Disappear, Penny. At least for now," Queenie advises.

What happens after knots become so tight they break loose?

Queenie flashes me a pearly smile. "Don't pout. It was a success. Go have some fun and then ghost." She wiggles her fingers and then laughs as they peel away.

I run from the flashing lights, but the anxiety penetrating my skin, like the falling rain, follows me back to Fleet Street. I keep to the shadows and take alternate routes in case one of Sandro's guys follows me, but there's no pattering of boots on the pavement at my back. Nor is there relief. No release, no placid sense of completion, hole filled, desire met. If I'm not Vicky's partner and protégé, if I'm not a thief, who am I?

I am no one. I am nothing. I'm in trouble. Sandro will be coming for me.

My phone buzzes, startling me with a text when I reach the top of the stairs in my building. It's Julian. **Are you okay?**

**I've been better. You?**

**Waiting for you at party number two. It's safe.** He inserts the yellow heart emoji.

The key is under the mat. The door locked, but when I enter, the Romeo costume isn't draped over the chair. I swallow and listen. No sirens. No rustle of someone hiding in the dark. I flip on the lights. Nothing else seems disturbed.

My phone buzzes again and I jump, letting out a little shriek.

**I modified the Romeo costume, but I'll let you decide whether I look good in period dress.**

I exhale with relief. However, I can't go as Juliet. The dress is torn and damp. I tear it off along with any semblance of calm.

I turn to the linen closet and toss sheets on the floor until I find a white one. A ghost? No, not if I need to make another getaway. I tear it to shreds and then wrap the strips around my ankles and up my legs, tying them as I go. The arms are a challenge, but I manage until only my face is visible.

I study the mummy in my reflection like one might an Egyptian display in a museum. I avoid my eyes. I'll vanish tomorrow. I'd like to unbind the tightening in my stomach and toss the line to Julian, with an invitation to come with me. Wherever. Peru. Pisa. Anywhere. For now, I need space from tonight. An entire universe perhaps, but a few more hours will have to be enough.

I wrap my face. Now, in the reflection, I could be anyone. I could disappear right now. I should. But this night is already filled with wins and losses and ghosts and ghouls. I'll blend in until I figure out a plan. This time I need a plan.

Dressed in rags, my ego shot, I get in the Uber and return to campus. Thankfully, the rain remains suspended in the clouds.

Neda shoots me a text. **You need to get your booty over here. Three of the guys from the football team are singing pop songs. It's lit.**

It's so easy for her to fade back into the normal life of a student, a girl with a family, as if we didn't penetrate a major thief's inner circle—the Den—and walk away with a stolen piece of art. Twice stolen. My mind plays tug of war.

Then like the fog drifting toward the moor, I realize I could hide in plain sight. I could pretend to be normal. I could live as if worry and fear isn't worming its way inside me. I pause on the sidewalk. Is that crazy? Could I deny the whole thing? Write off all the lying and stealing and live a straight life? Go to school with Julian, Neda, and Howard? Do homework and essays? Graduate? Attend college?

I could try.

My phone buzzes again.

**Ok, seriously, if you don't come here, at least text me back telling me you're alive. Otherwise, I'm going to send all the undead after you. (Why did half the school dress as zombies? Did I miss something critical?) Mwah.**

I'm not interested in the undead, but get the sense Neda isn't afraid of them. All the same, her texts made me smile even though I don't feel like smiling. I recently learned that friends know how and when to do that without being asked.

The party overflows from the opulent foyer and onto the sprawling lawn. It's not Castle Cleary, but it's fancy with columns, landscape lighting, and a princess balcony. I missed the fine details saga that resulted in rumors of a secret society, bullet holes, and the true heir to Dartmont. But whoever throws this party is generous. As I pass the Mad Hatter and a pop star making out, zombies reach for me.

"I'm already dead, guys," I deadpan from my mummy wrap.

Tegan and Jordyn wear schoolgirl outfits that don't quite meet the Required Attire length rules. A few of the guys—their egos too bloated to wear anything amusing—have trash bags draped over their shoulders. Ironic or superhero capes? The former, for sure. I spot multiple versions of pop stars dancing and their entourages swarming. Then more zombies.

The fear connected to the veracity of my recklessness forces me to disappear into the party looking for a sugar skull—I need an anchor right now, even a dead/costumed one.

Neda plants a big, painted kiss on my mummy cheek and rapid fires about our success.

"Is Julian here? Have you seen him? Spoken to him?" My mouth is dry, but her answer is lost to Howard rushing over. He hugs me and says, "You were great," but the music is too loud to talk or think or doubt, and everyone's dancing. The vibe is fun and carefree, not like the knife edge I walked at Sandro's party. I look for Julian but don't see him in the crowd.

The music is loud, my head pounds, and I'm spent, exhausted in every way possible.

I lurch through the room, one arm slung around Neda's shoulders and the other around Howard's and theirs holding me up. There may be more people down the line, but turning my head in that direction twists the room like a wet sponge. We bump into furniture, laughter erupting out of our thieving collective. One by one, I let go of the strands of concern, triumph, and fear tethering me to my future, the golden heart, and Sandro.

But where is my Romeo?

At last, I spot him in the far corner of the room, bordered by a bookshelf and a window, chatting with Russ and Scout. He's the hottest, tattooed Romeo the world has ever seen. Those clichés of being breathtaking or making the heart stop or skip a beat or three, of falling madly, deeply, and wildly in love exist because they're true.

I was already crazy about him with his crooked, reckless smile and the way his eyes crinkle when he laughs. His casual lean, his muscled arms... It's an awakening and a quickening and I can't get enough-ening. It's a real experience and yet so is not being able to be with the one you love. Like the namesake Romeo, his heart may split right open because of me.

Being with me comes with a risk.

Do I stay or do I go? Do I spare Julian? What about Sandro? The police? The temporary sleeping potion/poison, are my lies. The dagger, the truth. Romance and tragedy tied together, inseparable. Like love and loss. To experience the first makes it much more likely to feel the blow of the second.

Julian doesn't look at me. He doesn't look for me. He doesn't see me. Same old story. Penny in the shadows. It's where I belong. That's my answer to the question. Cut ties. Go far, far away.

The levers and pulleys in my brain jam as I try to close the gap between now and whatever is next. One thing is for sure, after I get Vicky back, I want nothing to do with tonight or Sandro or theft. Maybe not even love. Perhaps Vicky and I are a lot alike after all.

## Chapter 51

Instead of going to my dorm, I take a detour toward the campus IFA, listening for the *cha-clunk, clunk* of skateboards bumping over the new cement paths surrounding the modern building. Instead, dawn greets me with wind bumping over the moor, bringing with them vulnerability, fear about thugs coming to reclaim the golden heart, and about my memories of stealing haunting me for the rest of my life.

Clouds hang in pockets, blurring the trees and forming halos around the lanterns. I shout, "You've given me your worst. Now what?" because I still don't know what to do. In the silence that follows, footfalls echo on the wet cement. I whirl around, fearing Sandro, but Romeo rushes out of the gloom and gathers me in his arms. He hugs me like he'll never let me go.

Didn't Vicky push everyone away, creating a secret life? And isn't that the exact opposite of what I want? But her voice floats through my thoughts like a ghost.

*But it's better that way. Cut your losses now before it's too late. It's what we do. We have each other.*

But we don't. We haven't had each other for a long time. She and I may be twins, but we're not alike in every way. I want to love. To be loved.

The night spins from despair to hope and back again and again.

When we part, Julian holds me at a distance and says, "You have a problem." His eyebrows lift with concern and his lips drift toward disappointment.

"What problem?" Despite his hug, his accusation and distance kick up my defenses. "Are we being honest here?"

"There should be no question otherwise, ever." I detect a hint of steel or iron or some other ore in his voice as though he won't tolerate my lies, ever.

"It's not like you're perfect. You willingly fight people and place bets on the winner or loser or whatever. That's probably illegal." I let a pause punctuate my words and then say, "So, tell me, what's my problem?"

His eyes soften. "You're afraid, Penny." The words are heavy.

"Of what?" I spit like a cornered animal. "Of being caught. Yeah. I'm terrified. You heard Sandro. This isn't a game. The police are now involved."

In my pause, Julian takes my hands in his. "I meant afraid of what could be." Then he recites,

"Do not depart

Or close your heart.

Do not be undone

For we've just begun.

Let the past be your teacher.

And the present a treasure.

Because, Penny, right now, we have each other."

He kisses the tears from beneath my eyes and then moves to my lips. It's soft at first as though he's testing my heart, but I return it with an intense yes, and our lips move with urgency, hunger, and desire.

When a teacher with a barking dog passes by for an early morning walk, we pull apart.

Julian bites his lower lip as though asking a question.

I swallow and clear my throat. "That was beautiful. And true. I lied when I said I hate poetry. My problem is when someone interprets it or anything really and translates it into irrefutable fact." I watch the variants of gray and charcoal in the billowing sky, drifting across the low fields and across my heart. Gray is everywhere. "There is always another side to the story, a detail that can change a person's perspective."

Julian squeezes my hand, giving me courage, which is different from being brave because it means doing or saying something despite what scares me. I take a deep breath. "For all of my life I thought I was living in that gray space, but all I was doing was swallowing Vicky's words, her poetry, and taking it as truth. I'm a thief and a liar, but I don't have to be." The sky claps once as if for my effort. The clouds on the horizon gather and rumble.

"I fight. You steal. Are we going to let this—what we have—die because of that? Or are we going to carry on?" A smile tugs on one corner of his lips.

I eclipse the sun. I'm on the moon and then rocket back to earth, bringing with it words I never believed were true until now. "Unlike dreams and beliefs love never dies. It doesn't expire. It endures, withstands, redeems, heals…"

"Spoken like a true poet."

The sky splits open with rain, washing away my worries, the lies, and the past.

Julian continues, "Let's rewrite Romeo and Juliet. Let's not let other people's mistakes undo what we have. Let's do us."

"Could it be good?"

"If we let it. Will you try?"

My answer is a kiss, big and wet and soaked by the rain.

When we part I say, "We'll go to school and carry on. I can play by the rules. Be a student. A model citizen."

"Is that what you want to do?"

I want to be with him. "I want to write my own story. Our poetry." In the distance, the toll of a familiar bell marks the start of the school day. The night has passed. It's already a new day. "And I'll have to start with the assignment I owe Honig."

Julian pauses as though finding his way into the gray area and deciding if I'm telling the truth.

"I want you to look into my eyes and tell me one true thing about yourself."

I look into his eyes, but instead of words on my lips, all I can give him right now is a lingering kiss before we each go home, agreeing to meet in class later.

## Chapter 52

I SLEEP IN THE MUMMY COSTUME. THE NEXT DAY, AS UNWIND THE fabric, my cell phone vibrates. Neda. **It's the day of the dead. Do I need to say prayers? You didn't text me to say you made it back. Are you alive? Blink once for yes, twice for no.**

I reply. **Can I blink three times for being somewhere in between?**

She texts back. **Very funny. Did you flee the country or are you coming to class? I have manna.**

I have no idea what that means.

The strange thing after a life-changing experience is that the world carries on whether or not the participants or survivors want to keep up. There's still school, bathing, and tax deficits. But in some ways, life also seems to slow down. There are pauses in the day I wasn't aware there was room for. Moments to catch my breath, to pick out the brown M&Ms from the rest (the chocolate-iest), and get a song stuck in my head. Also, to agonize over a significant lack of sleep the last few days. My body is wobbly like gelatin and my head throbs, but somewhere in that mess, there's a spaciousness I never knew existed. Before it was *Vicky, Vicky, Vicky, go, go, go.* Now it's *Penny. Penny and Julian.*

There are suddenly one-thousand-one-hundred-forty minutes in the day that are unaccounted for, moments that are mine. That I no longer give to my twin. There's time to be me, whoever that is. There's time to think carefully about the truth.

I flutter around my dorm room. Honig instructed me to be honest and consistent. I'll try because if the last weeks have taught me anything, taking deceit with me in the moment of my last breath is the worst kind of thievery.

I style my hair in three different ways before settling on a ponytail. When being me instead of Vicky's twin, turns out, things like this matter. I'm rarely so indecisive. Except when it comes to what I'll risk for love. Today, I'll be exposing every part of myself as I step into the life of a normal high school girl, for real this time. I'm already late, but if I work fast, I'll still be able to get in the poem I owe Honig.

First, I have to write it. The words won't come. I wad up my paper and chuck it hard then slam the door behind me. I need to move.

Outside, fog still clings to the old stone buildings like giant cotton balls. The sun, somewhere overhead, diffuses the light making the students and me sleepy and gray. Ms. Honig would say it's a poet's kind of day. Moody and mysterious. Then out of the haze cloaking familiarity, words emerge, like pieces of a puzzle.

*When a chameleon freezes between spots and stripes.*
*When birds lose their footing and forget to fly.*
*When ships appear, after being lost at sea.*
*...And definitions change.*

*Lit with inspiration, I drop my backpack on the damp ground and pull out a notebook.*

*Loners turn into lovers.*
*Heroes fall from the sky.*
*Empty seats fill.*
*...And possibilities emerge.*

The mist parts and Arundel, the English building, looms ahead. I drip through the hall, each step reminding me of how hard it is to be myself because I'm not sure who I am or what's true about me.

The bells ring. I take the only vacant seat in Honig's class, right in the front.

## Two Truths and One Thief

Hands on hips, her gaze locks on me. Her eyes buzz with what to a guilty mind resembles keen knowing—Dresden wouldn't tell her, would he? "We're done with poetry. You can all exhale now. Those of you who still have to present your piece, see me after class." She looks at me sharply and then at her next victim. "We'll sprinkle them in during the last five or ten minutes of the period for the rest of this week. If you don't get it done during this designated time, a zero goes in the grade book."

I plead with the universe for the final words to my poem.

"Moving on. For the next unit, autobiographies and memoirs. We deal only with what is, the truths that make up who we are without flamboyant words and imagery. So take out your notebooks, get a pen, and welcome your stream of consciousness, no censoring. Write down the first ten things that come to mind when you ask yourself, "Who am I? No erasing. Go!"

Ms. Honig wants ten things that come to mind when I ask myself, who am I?

*Liar, thief, liar, thief, liar, thief, liar, thief, liar, thief, liar, thief.*

I write this until I run out of space.

Her voice interrupts the scratching of the pencils. "Stop. Don't lose this piece of paper. It's part of the final assignment you'll be passing in."

My chest is tight and I realize I've been holding my breath. I let it out, but breathing doesn't become much easier when I see Julian isn't here. Did Sandro get to him? Did he take the golden heart? Was Julian arrested because of me? My leg jitters. I can't sneak a text because Honig hovers over me. I can't make a run for it because surely she'll sting and if nothing else, today I'm trying to be normal and play by the rules.

Honig goes on to lecture about analyzing our lives and I shrink a few inches. There is no way I can account for all eighteen years with honesty. Or even the last month. No way. Then again, I am a liar and a thief. I could steal words. I could, but do I want to?

When the bells ring, Honig claps her hand on my desk and says, "Friday. Last chance."

Howard and Neda wait for me outside the classroom. They lead me down the hall and exhausted, we slouch on a cushion under a massive window. "Here, have some of this."

Neda passes me a thermos and a bun dusted in cinnamon sugar. I taste warm, creamy cinnamon-infused drink.

"Horchata." There's still a smudge of makeup below her ear from the sugar skull costume. "Today we celebrate the dead."

She and Howard talk about how living and dying are two sides of the same coin. Her words follow me like a ghost into math and then history with Mrs. Sharpe.

I've been feeling liquid all day with the fog, anxiety, the horchata, and now the threat of tears. Where is Julian?

I watch the clock, zoning out from Sharpe's sandy voice. Five, four, three, two, one... At the bells, I burst outside, like the sun through the clouds. I lean on the rail and text Julian.

Silence.

I'm at a crossroads, literally...where Snow Hill wishbones with the path that leads to Charter Hall. Stopping short, I fear he got caught and is in the dean's office. Getting kicked out. Or worse, Regina is on her way to pick him up. I try to retrace our steps as worry and a lack of sleep reach for me with starving fingers.

I pass the campus chapel and the small cemetery with gravestones sticking up from the browning grass like crooked teeth. The majestic trees cling to a few of their leaves. Toilet paper flutters in the fence and the guts of pumpkins remind me of the night before. A burst of wind chills me.

Crows perch on the stones, *caw, caw, cawing*. I think of Birdy, Flavio, my parents, and Caroline. Their quest for treasure in the form of jewels, gold, power, and fame. But if we don't live for each other? What's the point?

I pull out the phone and text Caroline. **Hey, Sis. Thanks for the birthday wishes. So far, it's been a year. Where are you?**

She replies a few minutes later: **Did you get a new number?**

**Yeah. It's me. Penny.**

**"I'm in Greece. You should visit. It's beautiful this time of year.**

We go back and forth like two people warming up because they haven't spoken in a while, which is true.

Swallowing thickly, I prepare to sign off. **I miss you. Vicky too.**

Caroline doesn't answer for what feels like a long few minutes until she finally replies. **Likewise. I think there's more for us Goldfeather girls on this side of the pond. Trust me. I'll book you a ticket.**

**I'd love to...soon. But I have a few things to finish up here first.**

Namely, find Victoria.

## Chapter 53

IF I WAS A BOY NAMED JULIAN AND I WEREN'T WITH A GIRL NAMED Penny, I'd be skating, at my dorm, in class, or bashing someone's face in. The last I want nothing to do with, the first requires the rain to stop, and when I don't find him in class, I hurry to the dorm.

I hustle toward Prince and flick on my phone to text him again when I see my last message to him didn't send. I press the icon and wait until it confirms sent. I waffle about going inside, worrying he's in trouble and I'll just make it worse. What if Regina is here? Never mind my heart, she might tear me to shreds.

He still hasn't replied. I imagine him in a jail cell, much like Vicky. I pictureSandro hanging him upside down from the balcony of his penthouse. I push away these dismal thoughts.

I text Neda before I open the door. **Please say a prayer for me. Otherwise, next November on the Day of the Dead, you might be celebrating my untimely demise**.

The dorm is quiet except for the chatter of a television from the lounge on the other side of the first-floor hallway.

I climb the steps slowly, suddenly fearing the dorm parent, another student, or a dean spotting me. I avoided the worst kind of trouble at

Sandro's last night. I don't want to go down for something stupid, like sneaking into a boys' dorm.

I knock softly on his door then listen. To my relief, it opens. Julian stands, framed in the doorway, bare-chested and wearing plaid pajama bottoms. Sleepiness lids his hazel eyes.

*Be still my heart.*

A grin as big and golden as the Cuore d'Oro breaks through his sleepy face. But I don't want to play a game or whatever it is high school boys do to amuse themselves with the fragile hearts of recalcitrant girls.

"Where were you?"

Without hesitating, he pulls me toward him, into the warmth of his body, closing the door on my worrisome thoughts.

The bed is a mass of blankets. His computer flashes with a skateboard video. The soundtrack repeats the lyrics to an old classic over and over with jangly guitar in the background. Julian closes the top and his toned and tatted arms and torso flex and tease. He unzips my jacket.

I don't take it off.

He scrubs his hand through his hair. "I take it I missed class. I was sleeping. Last night caught up with me. Didn't feel great."

"Neda has some horchata." Eying the closet in case Hawk Eye is hiding, I ask, "Are you alone?"

He links his pinky with mine. "Not when I'm with you."

Heat rings my neck, unable to escape because of my collar. I throw the jacket off. He takes this to mean *let's make out* and lunges for me, burying us both in the tangle of blankets.

I want to relish this moment, but I wriggle between confusion and trepidation.

"What's the matter?" he asks.

"Is *it* safe?" I start, meaning the golden heart. "I was worried."

"Oh, *it*. I thought you came to check on me. Don't worry. It's in there." He points to the bottom drawer of his bureau and rubs his eyes. "After our adventure last night, my dad got ahold of me because I've ignored my mother's last ninety-nine calls. No exaggeration. I guess my grandmother was worse off than she thought. Thought last night was it."

"I'm sorry."

He shrugs away how this might make him sad. "She's ninety-five. You know—" More shrugging. "But it wasn't about that. My mother won't stop putting pressure on me about college. She's mad at my dad. He stood up to her. In a big way—she isn't used to hearing no. It'll be fine, but all this time she's been running the show, you know? He finally said, enough. Tried to give me some room to make my own choices." His gaze flicks to mine. "Penny, I choose you."

My mouth is on his in an urgent plea not to move from this spot, ever. We kiss madly, rolling on the bed like this might be the last time, but it almost feels like the first time or maybe I'm so newly me that's just what it seems like.

We're panting and hanging onto our breath as if we'll run out of oxygen before long, and then I roll off the mattress and onto the floor with a bump. Something jostles loose inside.

Julian says a flurry of apologies and asks if I'm alright.

But laughter gallops out of me and I have this feeling that I am okay. Not just that I didn't hurt myself, but I'm alright in the world, wherever I am, lying on the floor, romping in a bed, or taking a ramble to a foreign country. I'm okay, wholly, completely alright. The cage in my heart pops open and with it, my heart is finally free.

When I take off my jacket, Julian is delirious with pride when he looks at the tattoo of the blossoms he gave me last time we were in his room. He runs his fingers softly along the branches and then touches the petals like they're delicate and real.

"So I was thinking..." I outline all the tattoos I want, telling the story of these last years, not with words but with pictures. I'm starting to think this might take a while. A while is what I desire, after all.

"Those all sound awesome. What do you want to start with?"

"I was thinking of a golden heart, but we already have one of those. How about a golden cockatoo? But will you put your own twist on it? I don't want it to look like a photograph or a cartoon. I want it to look like he's taking flight."

Julian sketches a feather in grays and then the bird, in watercolor sunset gradients, flapping free. "See this part, the feather will be like this—" He runs his finger up the soft inside of my arm. "And it'll wrap around and the bird will fly up the outside." His fingers are steady. "You like?"

My heart beats out a word that's a decibel above like, but my mouth says, "Yes."

The tattoo machine buzzes and he draws on me again. I watch carefully this time, but mostly at his fingers, wondering how he translates thought into a visual image.

It's well after midnight by the time he's done. I gaze at the beautiful artwork, astounded at how he brought the feather and bird to life on my arm.

"Breathtaking." I wrap my hands around the back of his neck, pulling him toward me. Our mouths meet. His heart drums against mine, and I quiver as his lips dance poems and art across my skin.

We're lost in how right it is when the door flies open.

A female figure fills the doorway. "I knew it, Julian, This is officially over. You're leaving Dartmont. Coming home. Leaving this lying, stealing, trash."

Julian grows at least five hundred inches as he gets to his feet. "Mom, I'm eighteen now. You don't know Penny and you can't talk to her like that."

"Penny? See? Another lie. This is Victoria. She worked at the Clothing Cloud until I caught her stealing. Went by the name Jude. She had different hair and wore glasses, but I knew I'd recognized her."

My skin bumps with alarm while my blood turns hot. I say quietly. "The girl you're talking about is my twin."

"Lies, out!" Regina shouts. "Don't talk to me like that you—"

But I don't hear her. Thunder rumbles in my ears as I grab my coat and bag and rush out of the room. Regina bars Julian's way.

I'm halfway to the door when Phil reaches the top of the stairs, bewildered. "What's going on?"

Regina storms over. "I told you he was grounded. No phone, no friends, no nothing. And what do I find? He's in his dorm room making out with her." She points wildly at me.

Phil glances in my direction.

I mouth, *I'm sorry.*

"Regina, our boy is a young man now. You can't get the past back. Rowena is gone. You might be afraid you're going to lose Julian, but don't you see? You're pushing him away. Eighteen-year-old boys make out, sneak out, they party, and make mistakes. We raised him well. You have to trust him."

Julian is dressed and has his backpack over his shoulder and his skateboard in hand.

"How did you know?" he asks Regina.

"How'd I know what? That you're throwing your life away and getting mixed up with the likes of her?"

Julian's nostrils flare. He opens his mouth as if to defend me then says, "How did you know we were here together?"

Regina wears a triumphant grin. "I have my ways."

"Who told you?" Julian asks.

Her smile curdles. "Your ex-girlfriend and I have gotten very friendly. See, we have a common interest."

"Tegan?" I whisper.

Julian's eyes flash. "And what, dare I ask, is that common interest?"

"You. We care about you, your wellbeing, and your future." Regina's voice softens slightly.

"I appreciate it, but I'll care about myself, my well-being, and my future without your meddling, college plans, or going behind my back to Tegan. Who, by the way, cheated on me and lied, among other things. I'd hardly say she cares about me."

Brushing past Regina, Julian claps his dad on his shoulder and pulls him into a hug. The last thing I hear Phil say is, "Go with her."

## Chapter 54

I LEAN AGAINST THE BRICK WALL OF THE DORM, CATCHING MY BREATH. Feet pound down the stairs, the door swings open, and Julian wraps me in his arms. I drop my head against his chest.

"Tegan ratted us out." Julian vibrates with anger.

I wrap my arms tightly around him and meet his hazel eyes, dark at the moment. "Who cares?"

"I do. I don't want to ever leave you," he says, his voice strained.

"But your family."

"I think we'll be more of a family when my mom and dad get their problems sorted out. She's been pushing me out the door for the past year, pressuring me with college. As my dad said, she's afraid to let me go, but she also wants to be done with me. I think we all need some space, and I certainly don't need her and Tegan stalking me."

*Penny, don't get involved or too close, boyfriends will only complicate things.*

"I suppose I'm not the kind of girl you should bring home to meet your mother anyway."

"You're my kind of girl."

The campus sounds of students switching classes, a couch shouting at the team, and a dog barking fall away. Regina's shouts, ringing in my ears, go silent. Vicky's voice too. There's just breath in my lungs and the rhythm of my heart pounding against Julian's as a new me emerges, like Bird from the feather.

Layer by layer, one act and scene after another, at last, the curtain falls. The truth finally reveals itself in its full, ugly splendor.

For so long I took Vicky's words and secrets not as presiding truth but as absolute truth. Now I can have my truths and they can be honest and elegant. Her version of the truth is now open to interpretation like poetry. I can't unknow the past, but I can move on. Penny, the girl Vicky was talking to is gone—a version of her sister only she saw. I'm reclaiming myself.

"What are you thinking?" he asks.

"That you're my kind of guy."

---

FOR THE NEXT couple of days, I throw my attention into school instead of harassing myself about all things Vicky-related. Things I'll never know.

However, on the weekend, we go to Boston and stay at Vicky's apartment so I can figure out how to use the Cuore d'Oro to get her back. After that, I'm done. Time to live my life with my guy.

I probably need Howard and Neda for this. But as I unwrap the treasure, I yearn to know why Vicky coveted it, aside from its unique beauty. I carefully run my fingers over the glittering gems. Vicky told me gold is a powerful element, offering protection and healing. The golden heart represents power and love. Maybe the latter was the lesson she most needed. Perhaps it has something to teach me. The jewels sparkle and I wonder about it being a treasure inside a treasure. My fingers count the polished stones and pearls. My mind skips from numbers to words.

*When a chameleon freezes between spots and stripes.*
*When dragons lose their footing and forget to fly.*
*When ships appear, after being lost at sea.*
*...And definitions change.*

*Loners turn into lovers.*
*Superheroes fall from the sky.*
*Empty seats fill.*
*...And possibilities emerge.*

I chew on my pen cap and write a few words. The crows outside my window chatter. I scribble the lines out and start again.

*Wind is a whisper.*
*Night is an escape.*
*Tears form canals.*
*...And autumn trees lose their leaves.*
*The world turns and turns and turns away.*
*Lies become truths and truths become lies.*
*The edges of what was once reason crumbles and dissolves.*
*...And the sun comes up. Again and again and again. A promise fulfilled.*

But the question nags. Who. Am. I?

I leave Julian, drowsing on the couch, and go to Vicky's room and draw a deep breath. Her oleander scent drifts toward the corners, fading. I gaze up at the cranes. They flutter, like the tails of many kites, as if the energy of their wish potential generates its own wind.

I tug a long string of paper cranes down and they collapse into my hand like the folds of an accordion. She never taught me how to fold them, but unfolding them is easy enough. I carefully untuck the wings and open a blue paper, pressing it flat. It's blank and white on the flip side. I gaze up at the ceiling, thousands of cranes in blue, purple, yellow, and red. I open them, undoing her wishes, setting them free. When I uncrease a black crane, flip it over, and printed right in the center are the words *I love you.*

I'd like to say the words are for me, but it's then I realize to whom the message belongs. I pull out the photo of Sandro and realize the other half, the missing one, was Vicky. Her golden heart belonged to him.

The pads of my fingers are warm. At my touch, the Cuore d'Oro feels cool and smooth. I count the gems again, like a prayer until I realize it doesn't hold the answer I seek.

Julian still dozes on the couch. My copy of Romeo and Juliet is folded open on his chest. I tip-toe by, open the laptop, and do some research. Vicky never had a Plan B, but I will. I text Howard and ask questions. I make requests. I fight sleep. I do homework. I struggle to find the words to finish my poem. To know myself.

When I nestle next to Julian, he stirs, and I ask, "What do you want?"

"You," he says, his voice husky.

I smile. "Anything else?"

"Freedom," he adds, wrapping his arm, inked with a wild horse, around me.

Me too.

## Chapter 55

The rest of the week rockets by. Phil talked Regina into letting Julian finish the semester at Dartmont, but she calls him constantly, harassing him, demanding he return home, and saying hateful things about me. He stops answering his phone. Then the texting starts, but he blocks her number. Then his phone stops working—she probably had it shut off.

I expect her to appear any moment.

My pink hair is dull so I go to the Dart Mart with a twenty-dollar bill and browse the shades, trying to find the exact match for my natural color. "Do you need some help?" asks the older woman behind the counter.

I cough, covering the wild laugh, which unintentionally tries to burst through my façade. *Yes, of course, I need help.* I would like this gorgeous boy's mom to get off his case and not hate me. It would be great if I could fast forward or rewind to another year, or decade. And while she's at it, how about she makes me a better person? One whose instinct isn't to lie or steal—I grip the bill in my pocket. Wouldn't that be nice?

"Just browsing, thanks." Those three words win the battle against fleeing out of fear that I'll use the five-finger discount. I replace the rush and release of stealing with the ordinary exchange of money for goods sold.

She holds up a box with a color called *sable wolf*. "I think this shade would suit you."

The shade of dark blonde matches my roots perfectly. "Thanks."

I pay. With money.

When I get back to my dorm, I continue my reinvention and rinse away the past. The reflection of the girl in the mirror hardly resembles the person I was a month ago and no longer looks so much like Vicky. I don't expect to be around to work on that autobiography in Ms. Honig's class, but I'm ready to find myself out of the cast of Vicky's shadow, a thief, and anonymous.

The next day in class, everyone is the Friday kind of restless, even the teachers. Tegan is mysteriously absent, as if she knows Regina sold her out. Now, not only has Julian after her, but Howard, Neda, and me too. I bet they have Dart Dirt galore.

I'm on edge because I have the poem due and haven't come up with the last stanza. I struggle through it during my free period before doing the walk of shame to English. I promised Honig I'd have it done. I don't. Lyrical-less minutes inch by. Guilt creeps in. The new me feels bad about this. Then there are only ten minutes left and I move to the front of the class. I clear my throat.

"Penny, please tell us the name of the poem, your theme, and afterward we'll discuss it in more depth," Honig says.

It's now or never. Who am I? Someone who gives up or someone who goes on?

"I call this Truth or Dare. The theme is screwing up and growing up."

Honig's face sharpens at my choice of words, but then says, "Go on."

"When a chameleon freezes between spots and stripes.

When birds lose their footing and forget to fly.

When ships appear, after being lost at sea.

…And definitions change.

Loners turn into lovers.

Superheroes fall from the sky.
Empty seats fill.
...And possibilities emerge.
Wind is a whisper.
Night is an escape.
Tears form canals.
...And autumn trees lose their leaves.
The world turns and turns and turns away.
Lies become truths and truths become lies.
The edges of what was once reason crumbles and dissolves.
...And the sun comes up. Again and again and again. A promise fulfilled."

I pause, glancing out the window. The sun pushes its way past a cloud and an aperture appears. *Courage to change.* I smile. I turn my attention to Julian, at the back of the room, and the next words in the last section form themselves.

"Rainbows form bridges.
Laughter smashes doors.
Patience opens hearts.
We leap...And we're free."

Applause becomes hooting, whistling, and foot stomping.

"Well done," Ms. Honig says over the clapping. I feel triumphant and hope that Julian reads between the lines because when we jump, we'll do it together.

Then the noise, animate and whole, filling the room, dies abruptly. The dean, flanked by two uniformed police officers, stand in the doorway.

"Penny Goldfeather and Julian Freese, please collect your belongings and come with us."

Julian's face is slate.
My knots tighten.
I know where this is going...and it isn't good.

## Chapter 56

As before, I follow the dean to Ambrose to news I won't want to hear, but this time Julian's hand links with mine.

Regina sits primly in a chair opposite dean Porter's desk. Phil leans against a bookshelf. The cops stand in front of the door, including a plain-clothed officer with his detective badge on his belt loop. Disappointment and antagonism seep through the room like vapor.

The dean sits behind his desk and instructs us to sit across from Regina. She glowers. Julian glares. This time there's no dumping of the bag on the counter or Phil's apologetic smile meeting me with something resembling understanding.

I want to steal myself from this situation.

"Do you know why you're here?" the detective asks.

The dark look of betrayal Julian flashes his mother is like a punch in the face, a motionless act of violence so solid that she winces.

"Let me explain," she says. "My son here got tangled up with this girl and her unlawful activities. I was raised never to get involved with a Capulet. Well, I made that mistake and I wasn't about to let Julian. I saw the resemblance and knew she was here in the city, somewhere. I wouldn't rest until I made sure Jude Capulet was behind bars where she belonged. Now, Julian's poor choices, no doubt under Jude's daughter's spell, despite my warnings, will land him right beside her."

My sharp inhale echoes throughout the room. "It was you? You're the reason Vicky got in trouble?"

"I had my eye on her. Didn't realize there were two of you. My brother owns a storage facility outside Manhattan. Said there was some suspicious activity. When I was visiting my mother, I asked him about it. We watched the security tapes. Recognized her right away."

My snarl sends her words back down her throat.

Julian shakes his head and grips my trembling hand.

"I did what was right," Regina insists.

"You did what's unforgivable," Julian hisses.

The detective speaks up. "Listen, we don't have time to discuss family feuds. We're here because we've been given a strong reason to believe these two were involved in the theft of a golden heart from the Institute of Fine Art." The officer turns to us, "Do either of you possess a piece of art known as Cuore d'Oro?"

Everyone's gaze except Julian's lands on me. The temperature in the room doubles. But I keep calm. I slowly bend over and unzip Julian's backpack. I take out the tattered piece of Juliet's dress, unwrap the piece of art, and place it on the dean's oak desk.

"That's all we need to know at present. Julian Freese. Penny Goldfeather. You are under arrest." He rattles off our rights as the officers cuff us. "We'll follow up with further questions at the station."

The officers and detective escort Julian and me from the school as students and teachers alike gape and whisper in our wake. I keep my chin lifted, not in defiance, as Vicky would have done, but with confidence.

The precinct is dingy with years' worth of crimes and regret. A worn path, from the entrance to an officer seated behind a window, scuffs the linoleum. The bank of fluorescent lights shines a spotlight on the fact that I am assailable, but for once not alone and not scared.

I wait in a room for processing until a female officer startles me from my thoughts, from my regret at not taking measures to protect

Neda and Howard if Sandro or anyone else made a connection. "Penelope Goldfeather," she calls.

Other than my association with Vicky, I hope that I remain anonymous. There's no record of me except the forged documents for the apartment and utilities. Vicky owns the fault in this instance and she's in the wind.

As always, I wear the mask of innocence when I join Phil, Regina, Julian, and the police officers, seated around a table. Much like in the Den, the Cuore d'Oro sits at the center of the table.

The detective paces. "We've been investigating a missing golden heart from the Institute of Fine Art. Mrs. Freese informed us that she saw a stone Cuore d'Oro in her son's backpack resembling the item in question. The one we see here." The detective points. "Mrs. Freese also claims that you were Jude Capulet's accomplice. Guilty by association. Do you know that term?"

I don't respond.

"So the question is did you take the Cuore d'Oro from the museum? We've already heard Julian's response. Penelope Goldfeather, what do you say?"

Again, all eyes are on me.

"No, I did not take anything from the museum."

"She took it from me," an accented voice says from the doorway.

From behind the two uniformed officers, Sandro's face, framed by his dark curls, appears. He steps into the room and goes still for a very long moment as if he's seen a ghost before giving his head a subtle shake.

When Vicky and I were young, we'd often pretend to be the other, confusing our parents, nanny, and teachers. Caroline could always tell us apart, but Sandro must've thought I was Victoria for a moment.

"If I may," he says. "They were at a Halloween party at my apartment. Yes, they took the Cuore d'Oro. No, I am not pressing charges. Some other guests, dressed as cat burglars, played a practical joke—they claimed to have stolen it from a museum. These kids here, they took it before I had a chance to file a report, I presume, intending to turn it into the police." Sandro's gaze holds on me.

"Is this true?" the detective asks.

I study Sandro, his eyes tired and one bruised violet from Julian's fist, wondering what brought him here to our defense. Like at the card table, he reveals neither his motives nor his intentions.

I take a deep breath. This is it. "It doesn't matter who took what from where. The problem with this golden heart—" I get to my feet and pick it up, cupping it in my hands as I meet Julian's eyes, Sandro's, Regina's, and then the detective's. "The problem is this golden heart is a fake."

Regina protests. The detective orders me to put the Cuore d'Oro down. Sandro mutters something in Italian. Julian eyes me with surprise and interest.

Turning to Regina, I say, "I know nothing of what sent Jude Capulet to jail, but I do know she held this particular piece of art in high regard. She was of enamored by all things Italian...and hated them in equal measure." My gaze lands on Sandro.

The corner of his lip twitches.

"But what I do know is this golden heart's core is not pure gold. You can weigh it if you don't believe me. Furthermore, these gems are stone composite, not pure. The pearls are plastic. Lastly, the real golden heart has twelve rows of diamonds This one only has eleven. Whoever fabricated it ran out of space on the stone." I put the fake in the detective's hands and with a smug smile say, "You're welcome."

Maybe Vicky didn't think I was ready for the golden heart job, but I did pay attention to everything she ever said about it.

Julian whistles between his teeth and flashes me a smile.

Sandro clears his throat, nods, and with what appears to be a great effort, says, "I am not pressing charges, so if that's all—"

Outraged, Regina demands that the detective detain us.

"Mrs. Freese, according to the laws in this country, your son and Miss Goldfeather are innocent until proven guilty." He exhales, cupping the golden heart. "Of course, we will follow up as the investigation continues and the golden heart's authenticity is confirmed. However, I believe the two of you can go for now."

When I reach the door, the detective says, "I'll be in touch. In the meantime, I suggest you two stay out of trouble."

"Promise," I say.

My departure from that room runs a jagged knife through the knots in my stomach, cutting me loose from my old life. I was this close to going the way Vicky did. But that's not my stage exit. I no longer feel the need to take things that aren't mine. When I step into the autumn evening, I'm closer to freedom than ever.

## Chapter 57

Julian laces his fingers in mine and we walk toward Fleet, thankful for the ground beneath our feet, the city sky above, and our liberty. "How did you know it was a fake?" he asks.

"It was a bold guess. Everything I said was true, but of course, I had no way to confirm it without bringing it to an expert. When Sandro showed up, there was no way he'd risk everything if he didn't also think it was a fake. Maybe he had someone look at it before and they just got back to him with the news or perhaps he knew it all along and that's why he let us take it."

"All part of the game," Julian says.

I shrug because truly I don't know. "Yeah, one I'm done playing."

"Are you?"

I pause on the sidewalk, turning to him. "Yes. You?"

"He nods. Whatever we do, let's do it together."

"What are your thoughts on Italy?" I ask.

"Pizza."

"Hungry?" I ask.

"No, my friend Luigi goes there every summer to visit his Nonna and he doesn't stop talking about the pizza."

"If you come with me to find my sister, I'll buy you a slice."

"Go to Italy?"

"Yeah. I think that's where she is. Just a lark. A gut feeling."

He chews on this a minute. "Not any crazier than some of the other stuff you've done, but Italy is a pretty big place. Any idea of where to start looking?"

We reach the top of the stairs to the apartment and then I realize. "Not a clue. Not yet."

I rush into Vicky's room and pull the lacquered wooden chest off her dresser. It's always been off limits, not like a treasure chest I've been curious about, more like Pandora's Box containing all of her dark secrets.

I brush my hand along the muted gold leaves stretching from the base to the lid. There's a lock embedded in the wood. I belatedly realize this is what the key she left in the envelope is for. I slide it in, close my eyes, and lift it. It smells like somewhere far, far away.

I blink my eyes open. On the top is a photo of Victoria torn in half —the ragged edge matches perfectly with the photo of Sandro.

There are a few more photos in the stack, but nothing recent, and all of them are just of her alone. Not the two of us. I shake off the idea that she didn't want to be a twin. That she's the original lone wolf.

Under this are bundles of airmail letters, all addressed in Vicky's handwriting but not one of them was sent. The addressee: *Alessandro Rocio.*

I don't want to pry or know more of her secrets, so I don't read them.

However, toward the bottom of the box is an envelope from Alessandro Roccio. It's thick. A sticky note on the back bears an international number.

There's also a necklace with a thin heart-shaped charm with the words *P.S. I love you*. I wonder if Sandro gave this to her. There's also a bracelet engraved with hearts and the initials *RSM*. Regina Montague. The weight of realization smashes down. This must be the bracelet the so-called Jude Capulet took from Julian's mom. Maybe it was the first thing Vicky ever stole. After all, she had a normal job at the time.

Beneath this, at the very bottom is a parcel, wrapped in a baby blanket. I carefully lift it out, already knowing what it contains.

I set it on the bed, amidst the lifeless origami cranes, and unfold the wrapping. Julian pads in and places a hand on my shoulder. I gesture that he kneels beside me. Our eyes grow wide. The genuine Cuore d'Oro is more ornate and beautiful than I imagined. It glows golden as though lit from within.

"She left this for you," Julian whispers.

My eyes brim but tears don't fall. "It was her biggest treasure."

"Maybe you were."

I shrug. "But I no longer belong to her and nor does this."

"Do you mean you're not going to give it to Sandro to get her back?"

"My hunch was wrong. I don't think he got her out of jail as payback. Vicky's freedom is up to her."

And that's it. The box is empty. I don't return the contents, locking my twin's secrets back up. I leave them scattered on the carpet, like leaves on browning grass, like the sparse details they are.

Whatever explanations I expected, these didn't require an interpreter or code-cracking. Vicky was selfish and a liar. She lied to me. She made me a liar. I may have been her biggest treasure, but she kept me from the truth, from being myself and from knowing her.

Sadness gains momentum, morphing into anger, then acceptance.

That night, I dream about a man dreaming of quenching his thirst, creating sweet honey made from old failures, and finding internal sunshine, recited in Julian's voice. It remains in my awareness.

Like Vicky's box of hidden desires and failures, I too possess a box of secrets. It's in my heart, but it's no longer empty. It's full of love and hope and has a golden glow.

The next day, I wrap the golden heart in the blanket. "We'll return it to the museum anonymously," I say. "Where it belongs. Not hidden in a box. It deserves to be seen." I'll live my life and give whatever I have left to my relationship with Julian.

After I gather up all the square black sheets, lined with Vicky's origami notes, I put all of her clothing on the bed, taking a couple of T-shirts and a sweater for myself. I stuff the rest in plastic bags and heft them to the door. I strip the linens from her bed and fold them, putting them in another bag along with a few odds and ends.

I bring the filing cabinet and all the documents to the kitchen followed by the furniture. Lastly, I take the artwork from her bedroom walls—a classic shot of a couple kissing on a New York City street and a few silk tapestries. I leave the contents of the lacquered box on the kitchen counter. The rest goes by the door.

It's nearly midnight when Julian and I roll up to the IFA on his skateboard. We scale the roof, swiftly this time, and drop through the hatch, avoiding the hot pipes.

The old elevator controls are as we left them, only it's slightly less dusty. I imagine security has swept the entire place, searching for access points and clues as to how the golden heart was taken, but when Julian finds the tension wrench I dropped last time we were here, balanced on one of the metal relays in the elevator shaft, I have my doubts about how thorough they were. Only the dishonest know where and how to look for the impossible way in.

We move stealthily, eager to get this over with. When we reach the bench, this time the zipline gun does its job. I ignore the possibilities that take aim like arrows. We could make a mistake. Trip an alarm. The detective and Regina could be closing in on us as seconds pass. But there's no time for analysis because I'm flying. It's a one-in-a-million shot, but I'm quick and I'm nimble. I set the golden heart on the empty pedestal and by the time I inhale, I'm on the other side. And maybe luck is with us too.

We go back the way we came. When we return to the night, our feet on the ground, and freedom all around, we whoop. Julian and I are both too jittery for much of anything. We share a slice of pie at the all-night diner and then go skateboard by the bridge. It's a web of color against the dark backdrop of the sky with its crescent moon hanging aloft.

## Chapter 58

The next morning the battery on my phone is dead so when I plug it in I find a dozen messages. Some from the detective, most from Neda. I press call. "Hi, um, I know this is weird, but can you come over? I need some help moving furniture."

"You want to talk about weird? The police escorted you and Julian from Dartmont yesterday. That was weird. You didn't answer your texts. Also, weird," she adds, exasperated. "Howard and I have been freaking out."

"I'm not used to asking for help."

"Well, in that case, if you promise to tell us the story, I'll help you move that furniture or whatever. I'll bring some tamales if you answer every one of my questions." She hangs up.

A few hours later, we're stuffing our bellies with still-warm tamales while she gives me an appraising look like she's not sure if I've gone right or wrong. I ignore it, hardly having to chew the succulent and tender filling. I think pumpkin, corn, and about fifty spices are involved. Maybe Abuelita will adopt me. When we're done, I explain what happened and what we're doing.

"You're sure the golden heart was fake?" Howard asks.

"Want to see the real one?"

"Are you kidding?"

"You can find it at the IFA."

"Wait, do you have it or—?"

"It's back on display," I say confidently.

"How apropos," Howard says. "We've also been on display all week at Dartmont."

"I take it your suspension ended?"

Neda nods and rubs her hands together. "And the fun began. The Dart has never had more traffic with speculation about who sold us out, why you guys were escorted to Ambrose never to return, and most fascinating, why Tegan Valderstadden got a nose job."

I tuck my chin, surprised.

"Because I broke it." Neda cackles. "I'm kidding, but I finally released all the dirt I had on her in one glorious expose about why she can't be trusted with guys or numbers or student records."

"What do you mean?" I ask.

"Howard had a theory and Queenie confirmed it," Neda says, giving him the floor.

"Do you remember Nate Boyd?"

"Of course. I had him for freshman math."

"And he was intimately involved with everything that went down with, uh, Groff, admin, and that whole thing," Howard says as if the topic is still too hot to touch.

"Not only did Tegan sell you guys out to Julian's mom, but she was also hooking up with him."

"Ew," Julian and I both say at the same time.

"And helping him thwart my attempts to control the flow of information. Turns out that Boyd put his time in and out of court to good use and has learned his way around digital alleys and through backdoors."

"Do you mean he hacked into Dartmont's computer system?"

"He's trying to exact revenge and messing up my active role in keeping things off the administration's radar." Howard scowls. "Messed up my whole operations. But for once, I'm standing by the school. After I figured out what was going on, I passed the info along to the deans. Explained what I thought was happening."

"Did you tell them that you cleared all my absences?"

"No, of course not. I said I saw suspicious activity having to do with the Walrus Weekly and the Dart. Fortunately, the admin know next to nothing about tech and believed me. They hired some professionals."

"But what if they find your fingerprints all over the data?"

"I'm their consultant." Howard winks.

"So Nate Boyd is back."

"And as vengeful as ever. But we're close to having enough evidence to take him to the authorities thanks to a little twist of Tegan's arm," Neda says.

"So you think you're going to play along with the good guys?" Julian asks.

"For now. When it suits me." Howard smirks.

"What about you, Neda? How does it feel to be a source of Dartmont gossip?"

"Speaking of that, I was selected as the Royal Lady for Promenade, so pretty good." She puffs up with pride.

Drawing a breath, I say, "I'm going to miss you guys." Julian and I exchange a glance. "Everything in here except the stuff on this table must go. Curbside takeaway."

"Seriously, you want to leave all this stuff on the street? It's valuable. You know people are just going to take it," Howard says.

"Yes, that's the point." Vicky isn't coming back and everything in here bears the word *stolen*.

Neda claps her hands together. "Alright, let's get on with it."

I empty cabinets then cast my attention on the living room and take things off the walls, piling the couch cushions by the door, and at last tackle my bedroom.

We fill boxes to brimming, taking ten trips, at least, up and down, leaving the contents on the curb. Piece by piece I disassemble my old life.

Neda tosses us each a soda when we're done. We sit on the bare floor in a circle. She lifts the can and says, "To the truth."

"To dares," Julian says before taking a sip.

Howard goes next. "To friends."

"To freedom," I say.

"So you guys are leaving," Neda asks, ever perceptive.

I nod. "Permanently."

"Loco," Neda says.

Howard's smile tilts toward sad.

I pass them each an envelope. "It's not much, but I found some cash Vicky squirreled away. Payment for your services."

"Uh, thank you," Neda says. "But I was hoping for gold."

"You can buy your own. And some tech for you, Howard. You guys are amazing. But it's time for us to disappear ourselves in case the stuff with the Cuore d'Oro becomes an issue. It's best we just—" I make a poof motion with my hands.

Neda gives me another hug. If there were a prize for the best hugger, she would win. It's warm and I feel the love, heck, I'm sure even her dead relatives feel it, even beneath her hammer and nails exterior. I pull Howard and Julian in and the four of us stand there, in an embrace.

EARLY THE NEXT DAY, I pack up the items in my dorm room into a single bag. I count my money—it's not much, but I'll get a job and Julian has cash from fighting to help us get started. I can do this. It's time to go.

I load my backpack with a few changes of clothes, the photos, the necklace, and a few other incidentals, including the copy of Romeo and Juliet from Julian. I already erased the rest of the evidence of Vicky and myself. Pausing on the threshold of Moore, I take a deep breath, nod at Julian waiting on the sidewalk, and close the door behind me.

Mist rolls across the moor as I say goodbye to the familiar paths

## Two Truths and One Thief

and buildings. As the chapel bells ring to indicate the start of first period, we say our final goodbyes before slipping from our lives.

Next, we drive to Boston. First, we stop in front of the Clothing Cloud.

The shop owner opposite rolls up the metal shutter and smiles. "Good morning," he says.

Not for long...

I push open the door. The bell jingles. My hand is hot around the bracelet I found in Vicky's lacquer box.

From behind the counter, Regina does a double take. "What are you doing here?"

I pass her the bracelet. "I am not my sister Vicky. I am Penny Goldfeather. But I think this belongs to you. I'm sorry." Without waiting for a response, I exit, letting Julian say goodbye.

A minute later, the bells on the shop door clang behind him. We go to his apartment so he can gather his things and see his dad. My eyes mist as I watch father and son hug.

Our final stop is for our last meal. The yeasty dough of bagels and the rich scent of freshly roasted coffee reminds me of that first day when Julian and I met before everything changed.

I've finished my bagel by the time we reach the bridge. I kiss Julian on the lips and our fingers knot together until the last moment.

"Goodbye," I say.

"For now," he replies.

I look down into the churning, murky water below.

Julian glances at me.

Then we part ways, disappearing into the fog.

## Chapter 59

I HOP THE ORANGE LINE TO THE BLUE. AS THE TRAIN GAINS momentum, the sun burns away the dense haze clouding my mind. I feel a twinge of regret at not trying to live a normal life longer. I could have given it more of a chance, but I can't let that stop me now. I made a choice. As Honig said, be consistent, be true. And my truth takes me far away from here.

As I put distance between the apartment, Dartmont, my various haunts, and myself, the prospect of leaving the city, steeped in my history, slinking around the corners, beckoning from stores and markets, and tempting me in Vicky's voice, lands me on the outskirts of relief. There are a few good memories too, Howard and Neda—me connecting and building my own tribe of brilliant misfits and witch-faced sweethearts. There's also Queenie and Dresden, but I have a feeling I'll see them again.

As the train trundles away from the familiar, I think about starting over, a new life, taking with me what I learned from the old one. I envision narrow streets draped with flowers and the scent of fresh bread. I picture my sister waiting for me.

Can I forgive her? I think so. That's something she can't steal though.

I list all the things I don't know, and probably never will about my sister and myself. Vicky didn't want to be a twin, yet we were dependent on each other in so many ways. All the pseudonyms, alibis, and lies. I can't erase or forget them, but neither do I know what to do with it all. I need an alchemist.

I glance across the train at an advertisement for yogurt. A man in a button-down and a woman in a yellow dress stand close together while gazing longingly at the container of vanilla. In pink letters are the words *What do you want?*

What do I want? Family? Belonging? Stability? Honesty? I intend to create that wherever life takes me. More importantly, I'll answer the question about who I am apart from Vicky and the past.

The old life shaped who I was, but now, as I cut away what failed and the ropes that held me fast, I reveal the true me. The artist's rendition isn't made of diamonds but is just as tough. The girl who will tell the truth, live an honest life, and give instead of taking.

A crackling speaker buzzes. "Next stop Logan International Airport."

The tram leads me away from the city I've always known and into the frontier of ETAs and boarding passes. I sweep into the flurry of business passengers towing wheelie bags and giddy vacationers wearing smiles. I'm somewhere in between the two and firmly between love and new beginnings.

I glance back, imagining Julian behind me, doing the same. I stare vacantly up at the arrivals and departures boards, searching for the next flight to Rome. We'll find our way from there but don't want to be seen leaving together, considering things with the law haven't entirely cooled off.

The agent at the ticket counter looks at me quizzically when she asks, "Baggage?"

I shrug the backpack on my shoulder. "Carry on only. I'm leaving all my baggage here."

"One way, you sure?" she asks, clicking away on the keyboard.

"Definitely."

The ticket agent gives me the total.

## Two Truths and One Thief

I pay with cash.

One manicured eyebrow angles sharply, but she hands me my boarding pass and says, "Good luck."

While I buy a bottle of water and a granola bar from a kiosk, I think about how nothing I ever took was actually free. It came with the expense of guilt and confusion and overflowing baggage I didn't know I'd carried. There's a price to be paid and it's in reality, gravity, the heft of the heart. It's weighed me down for too long now. I want to create a life I am proud of and eager to live, one that illuminates the shadows, that makes me want to gulp the stars in the sky. I want that, maybe I already have some of it. The tattoos on my skin tingle because although I can't erase the past, I can illustrate the future. I'm ready to take flight and leave the rest behind.

I load my bag into a tray for the security scan and show my passport to the security guard—thankful I'd paid enough attention to Vicky to know who she used for fakes of this sort. I shuffle through the line and step onto the other side where a bank of windows frames airplanes arriving and departing. The eastern sky gives the gift of radiant morning sunshine. I glance around for Julian, hoping he's close behind.

From beyond a security gate, a woman calls, "Lou!" She flaps her arms and jumps up and down.

Just then, a man runs by at a full sprint. "Nancy, I'm here, I'm here," he shouts.

The pair hurl themselves together and there are cries of joy and relief like a thousand-day journey has come to an end and the seekers found water, nourishment, and each other. I unabashedly watch the couple kiss, realizing that the simplest and most important thing in this world is love—and it's transformative.

I close my eyes and see the letters Day-Glo bright. L-O-V-E. I am here, making this huge change because I love myself. I blink my eyes open against the tears. I love someone else, too.

A woman with red hair wearing a pink shirt grins at me. "Moving, huh?"

At first, I think she's noting how I'm leaving the country, essentially moving overseas, but her hand is over her heart and she watches the couple, locked in an embrace. A few people clap and whistle as if they're on Team Love too.

My heart hiccups. I search the sea of people: young and old, tired and excited, confident and bewildered, but no Julian.

"Now boarding flight three forty-four." The loudspeaker announces my gate.

My steps are tentative. Where is he? I want to leave everything except him, but if he decided not to meet me, the best I can do is to carry him in my heart. If I go, someday we'll find each other again. If I stay, I might not find my way back to myself. I present my ticket to the agent at the gate.

I locate my seat as a long line of people backs up in the aisle. A fussy, middle-aged woman attempts to cram an oversized bag into the overhead bin. The line turtle crawls forward. I watch out the window, stuffing my cold hands into the pockets of my jacket. Men and women wearing reflective green scurry around, tending to the aircraft. I close my eyes and say goodbye to Boston, my sister, and deceit.

I'm ready for this, but the echo of goodbyes gives way to pounding in my chest. My heart isn't ready to let everyone go.

Never mind that we staged our disappearance with the help of Howard, erasing all data related to us. Never mind that I said goodbye to my old life. Whatever life I live I want it to be with Julian.

Panic rises in me and I unbuckle my seatbelt. I try to get by the wall of people, but unless I could fly over their heads, I'm stuck in my row. I need a paper crane or a thousand to hoist me up. Love is an action word, a verb. It is doing, returning, and not hesitating. I have to go back.

Then I hear my name, "Penny." And he's there, his brow beaded with sweat. He reaches across the seats that separate us. Tears spring of joy spring to my eyes. Our hands clasp. The passengers jostle as he inches closer.

He's nearly out of breath as if he sprinted here. "The train was stuck. Then I didn't know if I got the right flight because there were delays and an airline added another one and security was nuts—" I've never seen him so out of sorts. He speaks in fits and spurts.

## Two Truths and One Thief

The man next to me offers to trade seats with Julian.

"I was afraid I'd never see you again." He searches my face.

I lean closer, gripping his jaw in my hands. "You wanted to know one true thing about me?"

He nods.

"I love you. I may have loved you since the day we met, and I wish it had been longer. But living with this confused beating heart of mine was scary. If I've learned anything, it's that I won't ever take anything from you again, including the truth, including myself. I love you today, and I'll love you forever."

"I love you." Then we kiss like Lou and Nancy did, or rather, like Penny and Julian. And the surrounding passengers cheer.

## Chapter 60

After we're in the air, Julian and I tilt our bodies so we face each other in the seats.

He rings a strand of my dark blonde hair around his finger. "At least a dozen times I worried I'd missed you or you wouldn't be here."

"I'm glad you didn't give up on me," I whisper.

"There's no one saying you have to be the person you were yesterday or the day before or last month or last year." Then he adds, "As long as whoever you decide to be, you decide to be awesome, risk love, and live from here." He pats my chest.

"Thank you for being patient and persistent, for following me and for reminding me that I am not no one, that I'm worth traveling half the world for."

"The whole world. And the moon, a billion of the stars—at least—and the sun."

I grin.

"Thank you for trusting me even when I didn't trust myself because that is a true gift and I accept it. No more taking."

When we arrive in Rome, we lock hands as we navigate the airport, change some money, and venture to the metro. I don't know where we're going, but wherever it is we'll be together.

A warm, buttery feeling comes over me. I feel so right, so completely me and very, very hungry. "I think I need bread. And chocolate. Also pasta and pizza."

Julian laughs. "Definitely pizza."

"How do you feel about breaking a rule and having dessert first?"

He slings his arm across my shoulder. "Already breaking rules, eh? My kind of girl."

We go inside a bakery and order crespelle, the Italian version of crepes filled with luscious chocolate and topped with whipped cream.

In fluent Italian, I ask the cashier where we should stay the night.

Julian smirks. "That was hot." He feeds me a bite and another and another.

⁕

TWILIGHT FADES TO NIGHT, but Rome isn't asleep. I feel newly born as if I'm seeing the world for the first time. My heart and my mind are both wide awake, taking it all in.

I pause midstride. I'm the alchemist. It's up to me to create change and magic in my life. Taxis whiz by, pedestrians dart across streets, and I smell aromatic basil and garlic, the hint of rain, and so much potential.

After a late dinner, hand-in-hand, Julian and I meander the streets until we hear the boom of fireworks, somewhere nearby, lighting up windows and the white-washed corners of buildings.

We follow a hoard of people toward a park, where the sky opens in a blaze of light with the ancient ruins of the Colosseum silhouetted against the glittering heavens.

"I wonder what the occasion is?" he asks.

"We made it," I answer.

Julian spins me around in his arms. We're both laughing and then kissing under the shower of a million twinkling, star-like explosions. He tastes like mint and chocolate and love.

After the show, I pop into a late-night *supermercato*, grab a few items, and pay with a wad of Euros. Then we drag ourselves to the closest hotel. With the travel and jet lag, we're both in desperate need of a shower and sleep.

As the elevator brings us to the third floor, I say, "I can't believe we're here."

"Let's put off plans until tomorrow. Let's just do this now." Julian pulls me close, planting a kiss on my lips.

The hotel room is modest, but the cityscape with its golden domes and spires winks goodnight. The romance of my life, for how painful it was, is also incredibly beautiful and lucky. That winding road brought me here, and I'm thankful.

Julian emerges from the shower, and I draw him near. "I may never leave," I say.

"You'll have to teach me Italian," he says.

I shower, washing away the grit of the past and the exhaustion from traveling.

Lounging on the bed in boxers, Julian tosses his sketchbook aside when I exit the bathroom. I catch the clean lines of a woman, of me.

"*Odore dolce*," he says.

"It's the soap," I answer his comment about how I smell sweet. "Wait. Where did you learn—?"

"Translation app."

I glance at his sketchpad and think about how some things aren't translatable.

"You look more beautiful in real life than I can draw." On his knees, he walks to the edge of the bed and we're at eye level. He clasps my cheeks between warm hands. Our eyes meet and then he looks at my lips and inches closer. Then we're kissing, desire building and we press close, lips, skin, and limbs twisting in knots I never want to untangle.

## Chapter 61

CHURCH BELLS WAKE ME TO A LAVENDER AND SIENNA SUNRISE. I ROLL over, snuggling next to Julian's tattooed chest, breathing him in. "We're still here," I whisper.

Julian kisses me on the forehead. "We are."

After we've drowsed in that languid place of relaxation, I eventually dress but sit back down on the edge of the bed with a note I found in the apartment printed with numbers in Vicky's handwriting pinched between my fingers. I pick up my phone and dial. Howard, Neda, Julian, and I all agreed it must be Sandro's number. Like us, he fled Boston once the police started sniffing around. If anyone knows where Vicky is, it's him.

I leave a message and then sink into the mattress. I don't know what I was hoping for, but it wasn't more silence.

It's not that I imagined my twin flying back into my life, but I deserve a goodbye if not an explanation. Julian sits down next to me, dropping an arm across my shoulders. At least we have each other.

"Where to first?" he asks.

Now that we're here, I'm not sure.

"Let's get lost a little bit."

"I like that idea."

The phone rings.

"This is Alessandro," says a man in accented English. His voice sounds garbled and far away on the line. The connection is poor. "You called?"

"I'm looking for Vicky."

There's a pause and my hope dips.

"Who is this?" His familiar accented voice is baritone, complemented with bass notes of suspicion. I picture dark hair and the need for a clean shave, espresso, and tailored clothing. Beside him, I imagine my sister.

"Her sister," I answer.

"Which one?"

"The one you've met."

"How did you get this number?"

"I found it."

Our conversation goes back and forth as if we're playing Liars & Thieves.

"I have been waiting for Victoria. She's an exotic bird. Always in flight," Sandro says as if playing his final card.

"So she's not with you?"

"Has she ever been?"

"I believe she loved you."

"I loved her more than life. She took much from me when she stopped returning my calls and letters. I wanted to live a quiet life in the country and have a family. I don't think she knew what she wanted. Then she disappeared. I looked for her in Manhattan. Boston. Los Angeles. She was gone without a trace. I thought I saw her once, in a café, but I was afraid she would reject me all over again and that was almost worse than her sudden goodbye. When I located her, I asked my brother to look after her."

My mind scrambles. "Wait."

"Flavio," Sandro says.

"Flavio?" I repeat.

"Yes, my brother. I wanted to make sure she was taken care of and didn't get into trouble. Keep her safe if she wouldn't let me."

I want to be disturbed or upset, but Flavio was never anything but a gentleman...like a brother because he was.

"I thought maybe you got her out of jail," I say carefully.

He scoffs. "I have stolen many things but never a person."

I don't know whether to believe him. "What if I tell you where the real Cuore d'Oro is? Would you tell me the truth about where she is?"

"I already did. But if you tell me where the golden heart is, then I will know where to find Victoria."

Like so many moments lately, it's as if I'm watching myself speak, outside looking in. The conversation turns complicated with the potential for more pain at the mention of connecting with him.

We make plans, but Sandro sounds vague like he suddenly has reservations about closing the distance between the past and the present. All the same, he gives me an address. I have a vision of the world beyond the hotel window, blazing with sunshine. Then past the city to verdant hills dotted with vineyards and stucco cottages. Maybe there's one I could someday call home.

We arrange to meet in a couple of days.

Then he says, "La vita è il fiore di cui l'amore è il miele."

It takes me a moment to translate the poetry. "Life is a flower of which love is the honey."

"I loved Victoria, always will," he says quietly.

My mind wipes blank. Then I hear honking in the background. "I have to go. Ciao."

Julian and I step into the Roman sun and traverse the Tiber until we find cappuccino at a café where the only thing to do is sit a while. Then we walk some more, going everywhere and nowhere together.

We admire the architecture and the cathedrals, watch the street performers, and race alongside the Catamarans and rowboats as they glide along the glassy water of the river.

We reach the plaza leading to the Sistine Chapel. Julian wants to see some of the famous artwork firsthand. "As an artist, it's a requirement," he jokes.

"As a former thief, it's risky," I joke back.

I think about Dartmont and finishing high school. The doors to reenter are closed, but wherever I end up staying abroad, I'll complete my education. I'll learn in school and from life. I don't know if Julian's ticket was a round trip or one-way. I feel a sudden sense of urgency. "I should tell you this now, so it's out there." I clear my throat. "You know I may never—"

"I know," he says. "You're not going back." But he doesn't look disappointed as he passes me a ticket for the museum. "Only forward."

He takes my hand and doesn't let go as we spend a lazy afternoon in the Chapel, looking up, up, and up. I catch myself casing the space, noting blind spots and the geometry of cameras to windows to escape routes and ask for forgiveness for my wayward habits by lighting a candle and saying a prayer.

Julian pulls me back from the edge with comments about Michelangelo, paintings, sculptures, and Donatello. He sees beauty everywhere, but I feel it most of all when he looks at me.

After another day of being tourists with Julian seeking out the best pizza and taste testing all the gelato flavors—pistachio is my favorite—we take a train north to Florence.

We leave the golden stucco and sunlit city behind and open to a countryside kissed by late autumn. There are castles, lakes, and quaint villages. We pass through tunnels, speed by farms, and coast along the backlots of Florence. It's all so enchanting. I want to plant myself here and simply explore.

As we draw closer, I wonder what made Vicky love Sandro and leave him.

When we arrive, the city bustles and Vespas whizz past. Flowers cascade down stone walls. Cats slink in doorways.

"Are you ready to meet him...again?" Julian asks over a shared plate of gnocchi with garlic, herbs, and creamy tomato sauce.

I fill my mouth with the fluffy potato pillows. Now that we're even closer, I'm torn in two. I chew and think. "Yes, but we ought to be cautious. You think this could be a setup?"

"I hope not. But anything is possible. Anything," Julian says.

"Anything is intimidating."

He feeds me a piece of gnocchi. "Then we'll just take small bites. One at a time."

"You know, all we've been doing here in Italy so far is eating."

"And walking, dreaming, kissing," he says, stretching over the table and meeting my lips.

After dinner, Julian and I sit on a low wall in a piazza next to the address Sandro gave me. Julian's right ankle and my left ankle lace together as we watch the visitors. Tour groups pass by in clusters and a dog sniffs bunches of grass growing triumphantly through the ancient stones. The night air is sweet and the moon is half full.

Anything could happen, but nothing needs to because I'm perfectly content with where I am. I kiss Julian on the cheek and when I look up, I spot a familiar figure striding through the crowd.

Sandro.

## Chapter 62

IN THE LOW LIGHT, THE BLEMISH BENEATH SANDRO'S EYE, WHERE Julian punched him, has faded.

I get to my feet. My muscles tense and my mind explodes with questions. Before I can say anything, he wraps his arms around me.

I sense Julian by my side, ready to give him a black and blue to match the other one, but the hug is tender. It's a relieved embrace.

"When I saw you at the police station, I thought—" He threads his fingers through his brown hair, making it stand on end.

"You thought I was Victoria," I finish for him.

"What gave away that I'm not?"

"She wouldn't have risked being honest."

"But I wasn't."

"She wouldn't have done the right thing."

"Then you know we returned the Cuore d'Oro?" Julian asks.

Sandro's eyebrows lift. "No, and I didn't know she had a twin until that day."

"Of course not," I mutter then my pulse races. "Why did you want to meet us?"

"Your tenacity to get the golden heart made me wonder. Then I saw your eyes at the card table, but I refused to believe it until we were at the police station." He wears a wolf-like grin. "I am many things including a thief, but I am not a liar—not when it matters. I would not dare deceive you about this."

Julian's posture stiffens, reminding Sandro that he's there. Then Julian taps my shoulder and smiles gently, revealing his chipped tooth with the reminder that if I'm at all uncomfortable he'll take Sandro down in a second.

"You're forgiven for the black eye," Sandro says to Julian. With such keen observation skills, he must be very good at what he does. "I know you don't trust me yet, but—" He rubs his hands down his face. "But it turns out that everything with Vicky is a lot more complicated than I expected."

I lift an eyebrow sharply. "You're right. Vicky hated you. She—"

"She was mad because I didn't chase after her. When she came here, we fell in love, but this isn't my story to tell."

"No? Then who is going to tell it?"

"I think I might know where she is. Julian, your mother gave it away. It was drifting around the edges of my mind. Seeing you now, I realize I was right."

"Sandro, if you know where she is then why bring us here? Why not go there?"

"So you could see her too. You're her sister. You loved her first," Sandro says, confirming what I suspected when I saw him at the Halloween party. He's not all wolf.

"You say you're not a liar, but you are a thief. How can we trust you?" Julian asks.

"She didn't want to be found. She disappeared. At first, I wasn't the kind of person who'd have made a good father. I am so sorry."

"Wait. What?"

He scrubs his hand down his face. "You don't know what happened, do you? I didn't until..." he trails off.

Questions form a queue. I fold my arms across my chest. It doesn't make sense. None of it, but neither did Vicky. Neither do I. "What about the golden heart? Did you take it from the museum?"

"Let's get the train to Verona and I will tell you that story on the way."

Even though Sandro is only a few years older than us, he moves with the kind of confidence that parts crowds. The town Verona sounds familiar, but when we sit down on the train, I forget about it as Sandro fills us in on the Cuore d'Oro.

"I was in Boston on a tip from an associate. We'd been emailing and the source address was in the vicinity. They thought they'd sighted Vicky—well, her kind of work. Then I learned the golden heart was temporarily on exhibit at the IFA—it had been in storage and was making its U.S. debut. She would talk about it and said whoever held the key to it would own her heart."

I gasp. "You have the Chiave d'Oro?"

"The golden key by Brando Muscarello?" Julian asks.

Sandro's lips quirk. "After she left Italy, we spoke once. Since then, I've searched for her, leading me to Boston. With little progress, I took the golden key, but only because I thought it would draw her out of hiding. Penny, I've missed her every minute of every day. I thought I'd never find her. In the end, I had my brother connect with her. Test things out. They became good friends. For the first time in my life, I couldn't steal the thing I wanted most." His eyes are the kind of sad that cannot be forged. "Then she was arrested and disappeared. Not even Flavio knew what happened. But I think you've led me back to her."

Relief replaces rage. "You did all of this to find her?"

"She was good at keeping secrets. Too good."

"Did you know the golden heart was a fake?" Julian asks.

Sandro wags his finger at us and chuckles. "No. You got me there"

"But you went to the police station anyway? Risking your own anonymity? You could have been sent to jail." I pause and take a deep breath. "Did you know that I was a fake that night in the Den?"

"You are not a fake, Penny. Your eyes. The way you played cards that night. There is only one other person who would willingly lose and lose until she would get what she wanted with a final win. Vicky made up Liars & Thieves and I am the only other person who knew her

333

strategies." He tilts his head. "And apparently you. It took me a while, but I finally pieced it together."

"I learned from the best." My emotions flee into the corners of the night, replaced by the brightening moon and the whisper of a gentle breeze through the open window as the countryside passes by.

"The worst part was I didn't know what happened to her in jail. It was kept relatively quiet as rumors go."

"I thought that you bought her freedom and made her work for you."

He snorts. "Wish I could say it was so."

"Vicky said a lot of things about you that weren't nice."

"They're probably all true."

"Maybe I can decide for myself," I say.

"I'd like that."

I share a little about life with Vicky and the heists without naming names.

"So you planted the virtual impression of the golden heart?" Julian asks.

"It was a difficult commission, but yes."

I ask about how he got into the museum.

He willingly spills his secrets, including a bit about Halloween. "I hosted the party as an effort to lure her out of hiding. If she knew I had the golden heart, surely she'd come." He chuckles. "I was also curious to know my opposition and thought maybe I'd assemble a team in the States."

"Clever."

He shrugs like it's no big deal.

I tell him everything that led to the party, our costumes, and what came after.

"It's somewhat poetic that Vicky got to the Cuore d'Oro first, I took a fake, and then you went after it only to return the real one."

"And here we are," I say.

"So if Romeo and Juliet do not die," he asks, "What will they do?"

"I haven't figured that out yet," I say, explaining that we want to stay in Italy for a while.

"There's a museum in—"

"My life of thievery is over."

Sandro laughs, tilting back in his chair. "Mine too. I retired when I realized that I can't steal love. As I was saying, I was going to tell you there's a beautiful painting of Romeo and Juliet you may enjoy. Julian, you say you're an artist, yes?"

"Tattoos mostly. Graffiti sometimes."

"Are you good?" Sandro asks.

I show him the blossoms and the bird on my arm.

"I would like a tattoo."

Julian raises his eyebrows.

"A wolf right here," he says, pointing to the right side of his chest. "And on the other side, a golden heart."

"A wolf?" I ask.

"Once a wolf always a wolf, but not alone. Wolves are pack animals. The other side for Victoria."

"The last alias she used was Perdida Ochoa. Lost Wolf. You call yourself the Lone Wolf—"

"When she left, she took whatever was good in me with her."

The train slows and the speaker announces our arrival in Verona.

"Verona, like Romeo and Juliet," Julian says.

I brighten. "I knew I'd recognized the name of this place."

"You know the town? At the jail, when Regina Montegue spoke of Jude Capulet, I knew the name was familiar."

Julian and I exchange a smirk.

Romeo and Juliet's city sprawls along a river with citadels and castles, palaces and piazzas. The sun sets behind Lake Garda, gifting us with liquid jewels.

Arm in arm, Julian and I stroll beside Sandro along the streets until we reach the famed courtyard beneath Juliet's balcony. Soft light frames the climbing vines like theater curtains. Visitors snap photos, and I listen in as a tour guide explains that the city adopted Shakespeare's Romeo and Juliet, but that it's all a fabrication. No such story actually occurred here. Fiction as fiction.

"That's not very romantic," I mutter, gazing up at the warm glow of the stone balcony.

"Do you want romance or reality?" Julian asks.

"Both."

"That I can give you." He clasps the back of my head and draws me in for a kiss.

When we part, I say, "I guess I'd rather some stories and some mysteries, remain preserved. It makes life a little more interesting."

"Says the girl who hates poetry."

"Hated," I correct. "And poetry can be true. Sometimes truer than reality." Plus, I reserve the right to change my mind.

A line forms behind the bronze statue of Juliet for photos and we join it. Girls seek their Romeos and students recite lines from Shakespeare. When the shutter snaps, a subtle movement from the balcony above catches my gaze. I glance up, half expecting to see a woman in a gown like the one I wore on Halloween.

Instead, I see myself on the balcony above. Same dark blonde hair. Same silhouette. Same resting witch face. I blink, and my twin sister is gone.

## Chapter 63

I gasp and both guys turn to me. "She was there. I am sure of it." My voice is harder than I expect.

Sandro's eyes flash and he hurries inside at the same time the docent tells him they're closing soon. Julian and I follow, surveying the exits because if I was right about who I saw then Vicky has a lot of explaining to do. And apologizing. Maybe even groveling.

A startling amount of red-hot anger replaces my surprise. My skin burns. My stomach churns. My blood boils even though the evening is crisp.

Tourists come and go, shuffling past the exhibits. A tall man with dark hair descends the stairs, beaming. All these years, I've gone along with Vicky and her wild plans. Been her accomplice, no questions asked. I did what she told me to do without protest. If she'd ever told me she killed someone, I'd show up with a shovel. I was the ride-or-die sister.

But something shifted during this time we've spent apart. I grew up, grew into myself. I'm no longer just Vicky, or even Caroline's, sister. I'm me. Penny. My jaw is so tight I feel like the bones might snap.

From behind Sandro my replica, my twin, peers in my direction.

"Victoria Ann Goldfeather!" I hiss with the full force of months, no years, of backlogged resentment that channels into fury.

"Hi, Penny." Vicky steps fully out from behind Sandro. She holds a baby on her hip.

This time the gasp sticks in my throat, my jaw softens, and my eyes turn liquid.

"Ta-da. For my final job, I stole a baby," Vicky says.

"He looks a lot like—" Julian looks from the little brown-haired, brown-eyed baby in Vicky's arms to Sandro.

Then realization slaps me upside the head. "Is this why Mum and Dad kicked you out of the family?"

Vicky nods slowly. "It's a long story. Their loss. At the time, I hated Sandro because he didn't follow me home. I was being immature. This little guy grew me up fast. I see things differently. What's important. We come here every night now. But I almost could've been Shakespeare's most tragic heroine. Instead, I did the right thing."

"But you were arrested. How—?" But the answers don't matter. I rush forward and wrap my sister and nephew in a hug.

Sandro takes the baby and his eyes are the softest, gentlest. He's in love. And the way Vicky looks at him, there's no hate.

"Wow," I breathe, watching the family reunite. I expect they'll have a long talk later.

For now, we walk along the river until a sweet yet pungent hit of garlic draws us to a tiny trattoria for dinner.

The four of us dote on the baby while we learn that Vicky and Sandro had gotten married during her first visit. Then when she returned to the states, she learned she was pregnant. She told Mum and Dad, they disowned her, and I know the rest.

"Why did you do the Great Getaway job without me? If I'd been there, maybe you wouldn't have been arrested."

Vicky lets out a long breath. "Because I was going down a path...I didn't want you to follow. Penny, you've always been the good twin. Mum and Dad know that. Caroline too. Yet you stubbornly stuck by my side no matter what. I guess I was trying to protect you and in a way, it's a good thing I got in trouble."

I realize then that by stubbornly sticking to her side I was trying to protect her from herself.

"I was so angry. At our parents. At the world. At myself mostly. When I first looked into Alesso's eyes, something changed. But I resisted it at first—motherhood, love, family. To me, those are bigger risks than being arrested. Penny, we're very different but both stubborn. It took me getting in real trouble to finally decide to grow up. To take responsibility." She glances at Sandro as if gauging what he thinks of her monolog...and that she named the baby after his father.

"You could've just told me," I say.

Her face pinches. "You and I have been together through everything. Almost. I guess it was something I needed to do on my own."

I put the timeline together of Vicky's trip to Italy when she must've been pregnant, to her disappearing for a time before returning, more bent than ever on thievery.

"Where did you have Alesso?" I ask.

"Here, actually. Then I got scared. Left him with a family...Caroline's family."

"Caroline Goldfeather? Our sister?" My jaw lowers.

"Yep. She and George are in Greece. It's not far. He was in good hands until I came to my senses. Had to go and get in trouble to do that, but I learned my lesson."

A broken, late-night conversation spools back. "Wait, were you on the phone with Caroline late one night?"

Vicky studies the woodgrain on the table like it holds the answer. "Yeah. She was trying to get me to do the right thing. To come back. First, I had to go all the way to the ground floor. Hit the bottom before I realized what I was giving up and ruining. I had to get out of my own way...and figure out a way to break out of jail. That was my last big con."

These are words I never expected to hear. Once more, my world turns upside down, inside out, but in a good way.

Vicky is calmer and gentler than I've ever seen her. I almost wouldn't recognize her except we still look the same—back to our natural hair color and coincidentally the same length with it tipping our shoulders.

"Does she know about Flavio?" I ask.

Sandro smirks. "My brother. Keeping an eye on things for me until Victoria, as you said, came to her senses."

"You—" She winds up to swat him.

"I did it because I cared, Victoria," The way Sandro caresses her name brings two words to mind. *True love.* He loves her. Was willing to give her space and time to figure out what she needed without letting her stray too far. Waited patiently. Loved her through her personal battle. She must see it because she nuzzles next to him.

Swallowing thickly, I glance at Julian, hearing in my mind the way he says my name. It's terrifying and true in the best kind of way. I blurt, "I always thought Flavio was Brazilian."

"And I thought I'd find what I was looking for by taking," Vicky says softly.

"But you discovered it by giving," I finish.

Julian and Sandro look between us as if witnessing nothing short of a miracle.

"You two finish each other's sentences?" Julian asks at the same time Sandro says, "There are two of you..."

Vicky and I exchange a look I haven't seen (or felt) in a long time. It's pure. Sisterly. Affectionate. All her angst is gone. She left it overseas. Maybe in a museum. Then we both break into laughter.

"Do Mum and Dad know?"

"About what?"

"All of it? Alesso? You being here?"

"Caroline may have mentioned it. I hope, in time, they'll forgive me, but that also means I have to forgive them. They weren't exactly..."

She doesn't need to say more. The fact that they forgot my birthday says everything. Thankfully, we have each other. Our own family now. And from what it sounds like, Caroline is part of it too.

"So how'd you get out of jail?" I ask.

"My final heist."

"Did you break out?"

Vicky winks. "I'll keep that particular con to myself unless you ever find yourself in my position. But I hope, no, I pray that you don't."

"Those days are behind me."

Julian gives my hand a reassuring squeeze.

Sandro shifts uncomfortably.

"We'll talk later," Vicky says flatly.

I expect they will because as far as I can tell, my sister has also put her days of thievery behind her. Vicky played the long game. Rebelled against motherhood. Sandro. Me. But she found her way back.

We rehash the last months then the conversation shifts as we discuss the baby, who sleeps in his papa's arms. I imagine Vicky will be hard-pressed to have him let the little guy go.

We spend the night at Vicky's small flat. I lay awake for a long time, processing the day, and what I learned. Sandro unexpectedly answering the call. Us finding Vicky. She left the number. He made the Romeo and Juliet connection. Unlike Shakespeare's play, I think our production has a happy ending.

The next day, Julian and I cross one bridge and then another, traversing the city, and making our way to the restaurant. He rushes over to a stooped man at a kiosk with a marquee that reads Luccheti d'Amore.

He returns with a padlock and leads me back onto the bridge.

Then I see them, hundreds, maybe thousands, of padlocks line the fence along the bridge.

Julian roots around in his backpack and pulls out a permanent marker. On both sides of the padlock, the *luccheti*, he writes, J + P and encircles it with a heart. He holds it out on a flat palm. I put my hand on top and squeeze.

"I love you. *Ti amo*," he says.

"*Ti amo*. I love you," I repeat.

Then he attaches the lock to the fence. "Here, now, you have the key to my heart. This is a lock you don't have to pick." He places the key in my hand. "Wherever we go, whatever we do, I'm yours, Penny Goldfeather. Now and always."

My own heart opens wider and wider. There's bright light, glinting, and making everything inside and out sparkle. I toss the key in the river because our hearts are already open. I'll never need the key nor will I have to pick the lock. Our love is secure, here on this bridge and in our hearts forever.

We kiss and kiss under the sky. Clouds may have appeared, rain may have poured, and we wouldn't have noticed. Our kiss is infinite.

Julian holds my hand like a promise never to let go, and I return his grasp. I glance down at the water. Even from this distance, our reflections ripple. I'm no longer in the shadows. I look up at the sky, knowing the moon and stars are up there somewhere, and Vicky is, too.

I start talking, mid-thought. "Vicky's actions punctured me, I deflated. But they also punctuated. It gave me the choice to live a stolen life or chose to change and grow. Then love landed on my chest and found its way into my heart, and sprouted wings. It grew and I grew and I became free. I'm no longer afraid of love or myself. No more stealing. No more lies. For now and forever, I'll allow this curving, at times confusing, but illuminating and outstanding life unfurl."

Julian kisses my lips as if to say yes, yes, and yes. And I do the same.

# High School Murder Mystery Series

Dartmont is a prestigious boarding school where students have secrets, tell lies, and try not to die.

**Two Truths & One Liar:** There are three rules: Never get caught. Never admit to anything. Never make a promise.

**Two Truths & One Killer:** A past secret. A present danger. A future forfeited.

**Two Truths & One Thief:** There are three rules: Never get caught. Never admit to anything. Never make a promise.

# Acknowledgments

Thank you readers for joining me on this adventure of mystery and suspense. I appreciate every page you read, each review you leave, and every time you share with fellow book lovers. I hope you've enjoyed this series.

## About the Author

Deirdre Riordan Hall is the author of the contemporary young adult bestselling novels Sugar and Pearl as well as the High School Murder Mystery series. She's in an ongoing pursuit of words, waves, and wonder. Her love language involves a basket of chips, salsa, and guacamole, preferably when shared with her family.

For an exclusive *Two Truths and One Liar (book 1)* bonus scene, subscribe to Deirdre's monthly Newsletter where you'll also receive book news, access to giveaways and deals, and more! Confetti optional.
https://bit.ly/TSWBonus

facebook.com/deirdreriordanhall
instagram.com/deirdrespark
bookbub.com/authors/deirdre-riordan-hall

Made in the USA
Columbia, SC
10 December 2022